CONVICTION

Also by Jack Jordan

Anything for Her
My Girl
A Woman Scorned
Before Her Eyes
Night by Night
Do No Harm

CONVICTION

JACK JORDAN

SIMON &
SCHUSTER

London · New York · Sydney · Toronto · New Delhi

First published in Great Britain by Simon & Schuster UK Ltd, 2023

Copyright © Jack Jordan, 2023

The right of Jack Jordan to be identified as author
of this work has been asserted in accordance with the
Copyright, Designs and Patents Act, 1988.

1 3 5 7 9 10 8 6 4 2

Simon & Schuster UK Ltd
1st Floor
222 Gray's Inn Road
London WC1X 8HB

Simon & Schuster Australia, Sydney
Simon & Schuster India, New Delhi

www.simonandschuster.co.uk
www.simonandschuster.com.au
www.simonandschuster.co.in

A CIP catalogue record for this book is
available from the British Library

Hardback ISBN: 978-1-3985-0571-1
Trade Paperback ISBN: 978-1-3985-0572-8
eBook ISBN: 978-1-3985-0573-5

Typeset in Sabon by M Rules
Printed and Bound in the UK using
100% Renewable Electricity at CPI Group (UK) Ltd

MIX
Paper | Supporting
responsible forestry
FSC
www.fsc.org   FSC® C171272

Dedicated to:

the Dream Team

PART I

1

Five days until the trial

The thought of a murdered family should make me feel repulsed. Enraged, even. And yet, I feel the same giddiness one might feel before a first date; the fervent flap of butterfly wings in my gut.

I sit before the brief for Wade Darling's case, the blood-red ribbon unspooled on the surface of my desk, eyeing the loose pages, well-thumbed from when they belonged to Adrian Whittaker QC. I think of him leaping from the Northern Line platform before the oncoming tube train and wince. A brilliant legal mind, gone. I met him once, and never would have dreamed he would be the type. But then who is, until pushed to their limits?

Just a couple of days ago, I had been green with envy over this case. Any barrister in their right mind would take it: the media coverage, the career progression, the recognition from peers; Queen's Counsel, if they hadn't been appointed already. It is a dream of a trial, when one looks beyond the tragedy of the case. I look to my calendar and mentally mark the day. Wednesday 2 January, 2019: the defining day of my career.

When I was told just yesterday that I had been chosen to defend, I sat and let the news sink in, knowing this would be the case to change my career trajectory forever. If only I had more time to prepare. If my client had been charged with a petty crime, it would be easy enough; there is a blueprint to those kinds of cases. I could recite my argument for a client like that in my sleep. But to prepare a defence for a client facing three life sentences, in what is said to be the biggest trial of the year, in a matter of days?

I break away from my thoughts and spot my hands white-knuckling the arms of my chair. I unclench them, flexing my fingers until the blood flows back to the tips.

It has been a long time since I had a physical brief to grip onto, with the justice system finally having reached the digital age. However, the older, more experienced barristers like Whittaker are often stuck in the past, plagued by the superstition that changing one's ways will affect their performance. I get it. It feels right like this, in the same way a painter must feel holding their brush.

I trace the cover with my fingers, savouring the moment. I have advocated in murder trials before, but never one of this magnitude, and with my upcoming fifteen-year anniversary as a barrister, the timing couldn't feel more poignant. Winning the Darling trial will be an automatic shoo-in for Queen's Counsel. Better cases. Better pay. Those two simple letters after my name that I have wanted for longer than I care to remember. And despite the little time I have to prepare, thinking of Whittaker's decades of experience and expertise helps calm my nerves. If I had to choose a case to take over at such short notice, it would be one of his.

I glance over today's front pages fanned out on my desk. The Darlings' home is splayed over every cover, flames roaring from the windows of the sprawling country home. The Darling murders have graced the headlines for months, and spread through the public masses like wildfire, with everyone from the Scottish Highlands to Land's End forming their own opinions on the case and my client. The truth has been twisted and mangled by their wagging tongues so many times that I know I will have my work cut out for me in bringing them back to the facts. Lies are always so much more enticing.

I pull my copy of the *Metro* from the pile and take a look at my client: Wade Darling takes up the front page, snapped as he was led out of the hospital in handcuffs after he was arrested for allegedly murdering his family while they slept. He is a handsome man, from what I can see of him: pale eyes, chiselled cheekbones, a head of thick blond hair – no easy feat for a man beyond the forty mark. He will certainly be able to woo some of the jury with such good looks on his side, if they can look past his alleged crimes. In the photo, he towers above the officers flanking either side of him, and even in cuffs he has an air of authority. I wonder how he appeared to his family behind closed doors.

I take a deep breath and open the brief, fingering through the newspaper cuttings that have been sliced out with an unsteady hand, and scan the headlines.

HOUSE OF HORRORS: MOTHER AND CHILDREN SHOT DEAD IN FIERY BLAZE

FATHER OF TWO CHARGED WITH DARLING MASSACRE

The horror of the photographs is almost hypnotic. I eye the once magnificent country mansion burnt to a shell, its innards crumbled and collapsed within the wreck; then the aerial shots that the press helicopters took from above as the firefighters were still battling the blaze well into the late hours of the following day, and the day after that, as the thick trail of smoke continued to rise up into the sky for miles. If looked at closely, you can see the corpses of the Darlings' horses, shot between the eyes and left to burn, their remains charred black where they lay in the burnt rubble of their stables. The bodies of the Darling family were found among the mass of destruction. It took almost a week to get them all out; to distinguish their bones from the debris.

I slip the photos of the victims from the brief. Yolanda Darling, forty-two, wife of the defendant; Phoebe, eighteen, daughter of the defendant; and Danny, the youngest and non-binary, just sixteen years of age. All suspected to be victims of an accidental blaze before the signs of arson came to light and the bullets were found in their skulls. They were a striking family, which isn't surprising, what with Yolanda's modelling past. The children shared the same white-blonde hair as their mother, the same stark blue eyes.

Despite not having read the brief from cover to cover, I know the story. It seems everybody does. A husband, father of two, accused of losing his mind and killing his family before setting their country home ablaze. The teens wouldn't have known what happened to them: they were shot dead in their beds as they slept, the entry wounds at the back of their heads. They wouldn't have smelt the smoke or felt the hot lick of flames, nor would they have heard the shots due to the silencer found on the end of the murder weapon at the scene. Yolanda, however, fared worse. She must have seen or heard something, or been awake at the time of the attack, for she was found under the rubble where the staircase used to be, having sustained gunshots to her right knee, her back, and finally her head. The third and final execution. In my mind, I picture her running for the staircase, her eyes bleared with sleep and her hair tailing behind her. I envisage the first shot to her leg was fired to disable her. The second was to throw her to the ground. The last and final bullet was to take her from this world.

My client was found alive but unconscious from smoke inhalation, lying on the ground floor by the back door in the kitchen where he had crawled to safety. He had suffered second-degree burns to his left hand, and there was gun powder residue on the other, his family's blood on his pyjamas. The rifle was found beside him, covered in his fingerprints and his alone.

It's a good thing I enjoy a challenge.

As I read through the brief, I find it is far messier than I expected. Whittaker was held in high regard on the legal circuit, and to peek into his world and find it in such disarray is disappointing. By the looks of it, there are even some vital documents missing – a copy of the prosecution's psychiatric examination report of my client's medical history by Dr Samantha Heche, and at a glance, the witness statement from Yolanda Darling's mother, Annika Viklund. To have these missing so close to the trial doesn't fit with my picture of Whittaker at all, and to see Wade Darling on the list to give evidence is even more concerning. It usually works in a defendant's favour to remain silent during their trial and to let us do the talking for them, forgoing the chance for the prosecution to question them in cross-examination. Perhaps Whittaker's mental health struggles bled into his work.

I glance at the name of Wade's solicitor. Eddie Chester, from William and Chase. Although it would have been

Adrian's job to chase the missing files, it is the job of the client's solicitor to acquire all the evidence the barrister needs. As the barrister, it was Adrian's role, and now mine, to be the mouthpiece for the case and form the client's defence to bring before the jury, but it is up to Eddie to source the materials; the man who has been with our client since the first day the police suspected him of the crime, and who knows him best. Which means both Adrian and Eddie failed to do their jobs. I jot down the missing statements to mention at today's hearing.

A swift knock at the door breaks me from my thoughts.

Artie stands in the doorway with a smirk, mischief sparkling in his eyes.

'Good morning, Neve Harper. Or should I say, soon-to-be Neve Harper QC.'

'You can wipe that look off your face. You'll have given Niall an aneurysm by passing the job to me.'

I imagine what Niall Richardson's face might look like when he hears the news of my appointment to Mr Darling's defence. It won't be the first time we have stood on opposite sides of the bench in a trial. We had been at the Bar together before going our separate ways to different chambers, but our competitiveness never fails to reappear when our paths cross.

'I don't know what you mean,' he replies, leaning against the doorframe. 'I simply gave the case to my most promising defence barrister. A bit of healthy competition never killed anyone, did it?'

Arthur Mills – Artie for short – senior clerk and head of chambers, the man who makes sure everything runs smoothly, and has been a permanent presence in my career ever since I passed the Bar. He is seven years older than my thirty-eight, but has a young, mischievous air about him, as if he is still at university picking his way through freshers and drinking until dawn, puffing on fags like they aren't more than a tenner a pack these days. It is evidently clear upon meeting him that his family's wealth and privilege has meant he has never had to grow up.

'You'll be the most hated clerk in the city this morning. Who'd you have to kill to get your hands on this?'

He taps the side of his nose as he makes his way over to the desk and perches on the corner.

'You sure you can handle it, then?' he asks.

My collar seems to notch closer to my neck, pressing against the ridge of my throat.

'I'm offended you'd ask.'

'I'd ask the same of anyone. You've got less than a week till the trial; no easy feat.'

'That's if the judge doesn't postpone it at the hearing this afternoon.'

'He won't. This case has been delayed too many times, and the public are getting arsey. The CPS won't want people knowing what a complete shambles their judicial system is, will they?'

'We'll see.'

He exhales sharply, his breath laced with the harsh scent of cigarettes, and taps his finger on Adrian Whittaker's case notes.

'Write down anything good before he jumped?'

I flash him a look, and he raises his hands in mock surrender.

'You know me,' he says as he heads for the door. 'I have a knack for crossing the line.'

'Well,' I say pointedly. 'if that's all . . .'

He remains in the doorway with that familiar spark in his

eyes; the sort of smarmy stare a man gives a woman from the other end of a bar, mentally undressing her.

'What do you want, Artie?'

'Nothing,' he replies. 'Just rattling the cage.'

'And why would you want to do that?'

'I've learnt over the years that it pays to piss you off. You're best at your job when you're angry.'

'You're a sociopath.'

He laughs heartily, flashing the dark fillings in his molars. When he recovers himself and sets his eyes on me again, his smile slowly fades.

'All jokes aside – you good?'

He gives me *the look*. The one I always get around this time of year. An offensive amalgamation of curiosity and pity. I feel my guard lock into place.

'I'm fine.'

'You doing the vigil again this year?'

'Like every year,' I reply coolly. I stare down at the brief and pretend to read. 'Will that be all?'

He laughs behind closed lips. 'Yes, miss – I'll be on my way.'

The words swim on the page before me. I try my hardest to concentrate, but I can still sense him standing there, watching me. I know he is smirking without even needing to look at him.

'What is it, Artie?'

I shoot him a look; he is smiling wider now. Forever enjoying a good back and forth. He has always been able to find a person's weak spot, the dagger in a person's side, and twist it. He'd have made a good barrister, if he had ever wanted out of chambers.

'Niall better have his wits about him,' he says. 'All it'll take is one of those glares from you and he'll be shaking like a pissin' dog.'

I listen to him snigger to himself as he heads off down the corridor towards the clerk's office, whistling a playful tune.

When the silence finally returns, I place my attention back to the brief, trying to shake the vigil tonight from my mind. But I can't focus on the words; they become meaningless black blobs, taunting me.

I open my desk drawer, take out my wedding ring from inside, and slip it on. The gold band is cool against my skin after being left in the depths of my desk for days, hidden away along with my thoughts of him. I can barely bring myself to look down at it glinting on my finger and quickly slip it off again, placing it inside the drawer once more. I will put it on before I leave, but for now, all I want to do is forget.

I hunch myself over the brief and begin to read.

2

I sit in the back of the coffee shop at the table furthest from the window, reading over the life of a dead woman as I wait for the man charged with killing her to arrive, when an email pops up in the corner of my laptop screen beside me.

Don't read *The Times*.

It's from Sam, a clerk from chambers. I don't need to ask what the email is referring to. If it had been sent by anyone else or for any other reason, this would have riled me, but I know he means well. They need me to be focused on the trial with no distractions. But of course, I will. I usually avoid all press coverage of my husband, but I feel myself drawn to the story, to him. I type his name into Google followed by *The Times*. The article appears beneath the search bar.

Three years on: the strange disappearance of Matthew Harper

I click on the hyperlink for the article and hold my breath. There is a photo of him beneath the headline, a professional shot he had taken for work as managing director of a charity for domestic violence survivors, the year before he went missing: his hair had started to grey at his sideburns, with fine lines tracing his olive skin, accentuating his eyes as he smiled for the camera. My husband was handsome. Painfully so.

I haven't looked at a photo of him in the longest time. The sight of him brings up too many emotions that I actively keep down. But looking at him now – at the eyes I would stare into endlessly, at the lips I used to kiss – I feel them slowly crawling to the surface.

Edited into the right-hand corner of the photo is a smaller one: the last known photo of my husband, a freeze-frame shot from a neighbour's security camera capturing him during his final run, his white trainers stark in the darkness of the night.

I cast an eye over the byline of the article.

> Delving into the infamous missing person's case that inspired the hit true crime podcast series, crime correspondent Melanie Eccleston returns to the mystery on the three-year anniversary of Matthew Harper's disappearance, and follows up on what became of his Darling.

My stomach pitches at the sight of a single word. *Darling.* Capitalised. A prelude to the link that Eccleston will evidently draw to my life after Matthew's disappearance, and my upcoming case. Sam was right to warn me off it, but I can't keep myself from reading on. I hover my shaking hand over the trackpad and scroll.

> ... Can a man really vanish into thin air? The disappearance of Matthew Harper enraptured the

> nation in 2016, with all our questions unanswered. But of
> all those questions, one dominates: if Matthew Harper
> is dead, whatever happened to his body?

A man goes for his usual evening run at 8 p.m. on Christmas Eve and never comes home, the last sighting of him caught by grainy CCTV footage captured from a property along Western Road. No witnesses. No trace. All it took for the disappearance to hit the mainstream was a popular podcast to feature it as part of their true crime series; the press picked up on it within days, and soon enough the nation was feverishly gripped, dissecting my life and grief with gleeful entitlement. Why would the managing director of a charity, known for his kind temperament and thoughtfulness, suddenly go missing? Online forums appeared overnight to untangle the mystery, cult-like in their devotion to the case and the missing man they had never met, relaying the story so sensationally that the ins and outs of my own life soon became foreign to me. Newspaper articles chased the public's interest, and in turn, the journalists chased me: the woman known for winning criminal trials who had found herself trapped within an unsolvable case.

I always do this – describe it like I would the breakdown of a case. Factual, devoid of emotion. It's easier this way. But something is different this time; perhaps it was the photo of him, looking into his eyes lined with his smile, staring back into my soul from the page, or perhaps it is due to the vigil this evening.

I reach the clincher of the article and wince.

> Neve Harper, a staple figure in the capital's courtrooms,
> failed to slow down. While avoiding all press enquiries

and media interest surrounding her husband's disappearance, she has never shied away from making sure her clients take centre stage, with her stoic face featured just a step behind, seemingly conscious of her better angles so to appear in the best, yet supposedly coincidental, light. One might argue that Ms Harper made a name for herself off the back of her husband's demise, while conveniently refusing to play the victim so not to affect her fierce reputation in the courts. One could even go so far to say that her quiet fame led to her success in acquiring the infamous Darling trial, scheduled to appear before the jury on—'

I slam my laptop shut.

Eccleston has never held back, but to cut this deep is a new low. She chased me for months after Matthew's disappearance, desperate to be the journalist to crack me open. But once the gleam on the story waned, she seemed to as well, but not without making it her mission to smear my character instead. The anniversary never fails to reignite her grudge.

I look down at my hand, shaking violently where it rests on the laptop.

Now is not the time. I can think of him later, at the vigil. Not before.

I drum my fingers against the surface of the table. It has been six months since I had my last cigarette, but at times like these, I long for my filthy habit.

The bell above the door chimes. The café is a favourite of mine, small and inconspicuous, hidden down a back street near to the courthouse. No one would expect to find Wade Darling here. It is practically empty but for an elderly woman sat alone

at a table by the window, and two solicitors from Murrell and
Bergmann sat in a bay to themselves, whom I've known and
worked with for almost a decade. When Wade and his solicitor
walk through the door, it is impossible to miss them.

Wade enters with his head down and his hands hidden deep
within his jacket pockets, his eyes shielded by sunglasses and
his shoulders hunched inwards, giving him a sheepish, almost
hostile front. His once dashing good looks that have been
splashed over the front pages have given way to a man who
seems hell-bent on making himself appear invisible. But even
with his head down, he towers over everyone in the room.

His solicitor, however, is exactly how I pictured him. Eddie
Chester is short, bald, and stocky of build; I can practically
see the arrogance rippling off him. The sort of bravado a man
adopts to make up for a few inches, either in height or else-
where. He barks a coffee order at the barista behind the counter
and boulders over, grabbing the back of the chair opposite mine
and dragging it out with a harsh squeak against the hardwood
floor. Wade slips silently into the chair beside him.

'Good morning,' I say.

'Mrs Harper,' Chester says. 'I've heard a lot about you.'

I notice he doesn't mention if what he has heard has been
good or bad. He reaches out to shake my hand, and crushes it.

'It's Ms,' I reply, as I take my hand back. My pulse throbs at
the tips of my fingers. I turn my attention to my client.

'Mr Darling, it's good to meet you. I'm Neve Harper, and
I have been asked to represent you in your upcoming trial, in
the wake of Mr Whittaker's passing.'

I hold out my hand. His own is cold and quivering, and his
nails have been bitten to the quick. His other hand was burnt
in the fire; the skin warped, healed in odd, fleshy waves. He

slips it under the table when he catches me looking, and takes off his sunglasses. We meet each other's gaze for only a second. The whites of his eyes are bloodshot, looking almost gruesome against the stark blue of his irises.

'I'm sure Mr Whittaker's passing came as a shock, but please rest assured that you are in very capable hands.'

He nods silently. I clear my throat.

'Thank you both for meeting me here. With the press interest around you, Wade, I thought it best we met somewhere discreet.'

He turns to his solicitor, barely registering my words.

'Do we really have to go through all this again? I went through it all with the last guy.'

'I'm afraid so,' I interject, conscious that Chester has seemingly got Wade's confidence firmly in his grasp. Something I need to change, and fast. 'I have all of Mr Whittaker's notes and have caught up on the hearings you've had to date, but it is important that I hear your version of events from you directly, so I can represent you in court to the best of my ability. I understand you've been waiting a long time.'

'A long time?' he scoffs. 'I've practically been on house arrest for a year. I finally get a court date that isn't pushed back and then my barrister jumps in front of the bloody eleven o'clock train.'

Despite his tactless delivery, I understand his annoyance. These days, trying to get a case to court is almost as likely as winning the lottery. Decades of underfunding. An impossible backlog of cases waiting to be tried; not to mention the barrister shortages due to inhuman hours and insufficient pay, and the legal aid sector virtually at breaking point. If a case is lucky enough to get a date, a defendant and their advocate may arrive in court only to find that delays in the cases before them have knocked them from the schedule. From looking at the brief, Wade's case has been postponed twice.

His face is flushed crimson from the frustration of it all, but when he meets my eyes, his complexion quickly fades to white.

'I'm sorry. I just realised you might have known him.'

'Not very well,' I reply with a polite smile, and check my watch. 'Now, before the hearing later today, we have a few things to go through. First and foremost: do you agree to me representing you?'

Darling looks to his solicitor again. It concerns me how much he relies on him.

'Well, you can't be represented by a dead bloke, can you?' Chester replies with a chortle. 'She's good, lad. One of the best. I wouldn't let you get stuck with the runt of the judicial litter.'

Wade returns his eyes to mine and looks me up and down, assessing me for himself. After a tense few seconds, he nods with a sigh.

'All right.'

'Great,' I reply, with a tight smile. 'So today is a quick meeting before the session with the judge to make sure we are ready to go ahead with the trial as planned, but as discussed on the phone with Mr Chester, we will have a more in-depth conference at your home address tomorrow morning to hear your account of the murders. Do you have any questions for me, before we begin?'

Wade is picking at the hangnail on his thumb, plucking at it between his scarred fingertips until he draws blood. He unfurls another a sigh.

'When is this going to end? I can't have the trial postponed again, I just can't.'

I notice his hands shaking on the surface of the table.

'I can't leave the house because of the press; they've staked out on my bloody doorstep. I can't even open my own curtains anymore unless I want to end up on the front page. This has gone on long enough.'

I notice he has centred the ordeal around himself. No mention of his slain family, no mention of grief or justice. Just the inconvenience of being charged. I mentally make a note that this is something we will have to work on, if he wants to win over the jury.

'In an ideal world, we would have more time to prepare for this. I won't lie to you and say that I don't have concerns about taking your case to trial so soon after a change of representation. However, I can only imagine how tough this has been for you, which I plan to make clear to the judge today. If you work with me until the trial, we can be ready. But I must stress, it is only five days away – if you want it to go ahead as planned, I will need your full trust and co-operation.'

We stare at each other across the table, weighing each other up in silence.

'You'll have it,' he replies.

'I'm glad.' I turn to Chester. 'Now I have some questions for you.'

'Me?' he asks, with another of those irritating chortles.

'Yes. Have you worked many murder trials?'

He sits up, puffs out his chest defensively.

'Several,' Chester replies.

'I see. And is it your standard approach to go into trial with vital pieces of evidence missing?'

Wade's eyes widen as he glances towards his solicitor, who is stammering and huffing in his seat.

'What on earth . . . what are you implying?'

'I'm not implying anything,' I reply shortly. 'The brief speaks for itself. We have less than a week until the trial and we are still missing the psychiatric evaluation by Dr Samantha Heche, and a copy of the witness statement from Yolanda's mother, Annika. It's your responsibility to chase the CPS for these documents, correct?'

'It's quite common to have a delay in these sorts of—'

'Not this close to trial, Mr Chester, and certainly not on any case of mine.'

He stares at me blankly over the table, his cheeks growing a deeper shade of pink with each passing second.

'We're not in the courtroom yet, Ms Harper. You're grilling me like I'm in the box—'

'Wade,' I interject. 'What was Yolanda's maiden name?'

'Viklund,' he replies.

'Thank you. And Mr Chester . . .' I turn to him and take in the sight of his gaping mouth. 'Isn't one of your biggest clients the Viklund family?'

The Viklund name isn't one that a lawyer simply glosses over without taking pause; the family probably has the dirtiest money north of the Thames.

A thread of veins throb in the centre of Chester's forehead.

'I don't like what you're insinuating.'

'Again, I'm not insinuating anything.' I slip the document from beneath the brief and place it before the two men. Wade leans in the furthest. 'In the last five years, the Viklund family have paid you almost two point five million pounds for your services. The majority of your company's annual turnover, in fact. That's quite the conflict of interest, wouldn't you say?'

Chester is finally speechless, his mouth ready to catch flies. His whole face has turned beet-red.

'Wade, who recommended you work with Mr Chester?'

'They . . . they came to me. Eddie said—'

'I approached him because I was right for the job,' Chester practically shouts.

'Is that so? I know you mentioned you've worked several murder trials just now, but according to public records you've represented just three clients on such a charge in the last twenty-five years. That hardly makes you the best fit, does it? Which made me wonder what your intentions were.'

Wade is looking at me intently. The sheepish man who entered the café has gone; his eyes have come alive, his shoulders are set straight again. I know I have him.

'Wade, if you look over your shoulder, you will see two men in navy suits. They are Antony Murrell and Robert Bergmann from Murrell and Bergmann Associates. They have represented dozens of clients with charges similar to yours, and are the best fit for your case. As your counsel, I recommend you hire them.'

From the corner of my eye, I can feel Chester's gaze on me, mouth agape.

'You can't do this,' he stutters. 'If you think we will ever work with your chambers again . . .'

'I don't believe we work much with you as it is, Mr Chester,' I reply coldly. 'And you know full well that it is my duty to inform my client of any concerns I have about his representation, under the Bar's code of conduct.' I stare at him, straight-faced, before turning to our client. 'Wade, this is your decision.'

Chester turns to him, staring incredulously as Wade's eyes remain on mine. I see the faint trace of a smile pulling at the corners of his lips.

'Eddie,' he says. 'You're fired.'

'*What?*'

I nod to Antony and Robert, who stand on my signal and approach.

'Mr Chester, Mr Bergmann here is going to escort you to your office where he will collect everything we need.'

Chester is close to combusting. His cheeks puff and deflate with air as words form and disintegrate in his mouth. He stutters manically, looking between Wade and me, before staring up at the solicitors replacing him. His face is so red that he looks fit to burst.

'You fucking snake,' he spits, pointing a thick, quivering finger in my face.

'One of the best, I recall you saying,' I reply, as the barista comes towards the table with their drinks. 'Eddie here will have his order to go, please.'

Chester stands, huffing and cursing in a nonsensical stream as Wade sits with his eyes on mine, grinning silently.

'No wonder your fella ran for the fucking hills,' Chester shouts over his shoulder, before bustling out of the café.

My cheeks flush from the low blow, deepening further as my client eyes me closely, no doubt wondering about the context of Chester's jab. I clear my throat and fix a thin smile.

'Shall we begin?'

3

I sit at the advocates' bench, lining up my armoury: the brief, my notebook filled with thoughts on the case, and next to it, a fresh yellow legal pad for any notes I need to make during the hearing. Niall Richardson occupies the other end of the bench.

This is the first time I have seen Niall in a year or so. The last time we crossed paths was at Hove Crown Court, working opposite sides of the bench on the Bateman fraud trial. I took home the win, and I can tell by his demeanour in court this afternoon that his ego is still bruised. We have won two cases against each other; the Darling trial will prove who will come out on top. Since entering the courtroom, we have exchanged nothing more than a cordial nod.

I assess him from the corner of my eye, checking to see if his wig appears more worn than mine, a sign of experience and maturity rather than unkemptness. I take in every wisp of horsehair that has come away from the fray, the staining around the hairline.

Wade Darling is sat silently in the dock, his wide, nervous eyes wandering about the room as he takes in the panelled walls, the white wigs and black robes. Although he would have entered into the dock before, during the hearings preceding this one – the plea hearing, administrative hearings – stand-ing in the dock never fails to remind a defendant of the fate they may face.

The judge's clerk enters, a short young woman with thick-rimmed glasses, and nods to both Niall and me in turn.

'All rise.'

Before we can fully rise from our seats, the judge enters, seeming to glide from the ripple of his robes, and takes to his seat with a sharp exhalation.

Judge Douglas McConnell, although big in presence, is small in stature. His wig of grey curls seems too big for him, and his robes, usually making a judge appear authoritative and grand, seem to drown his thin, almost petite frame. But what he lacks in size, his sour expression makes up for. His brow is thick and permanently creased, giving him a menacing glare, even when he smiles.

'Good morning,' he says sharply, waking his laptop with a tap of a key, after arranging his files before him. 'Ms Harper, welcome to the case.'

'Thank you, Your Honour.'

The judge greets Niall and then removes his spectacles, the courtroom falling into silence as he does so. His face grows noticeably sombre.

'I would like to start by acknowledging Mr Whittaker, and what a loss it is to our profession that he is no longer with us.'

Niall and I nod in agreement. Judge McConnell leans for-ward, lacing his fingers together.

'But despite the very unfortunate circumstances, I must confess my frustration at the thought of a further delay in this case. Everyone in this room will be aware of the level of press interest surrounding the defendant and the upcoming trial, and frankly, it has become rather embarrassing that we keep failing to commit to a fixed date.'

He peers down at us from his perch. Almost fifteen years of standing before judges in the courtroom, and I still have to stop myself from peering up at them like a child being scolded.

'Any further delays to this case and we will fail to find a single juror in England and Wales who hasn't heard of the defendant or the tragedy at hand. So, I would like to make myself clear: this hearing is being held today to make sure there is nothing more that will stand in our way of getting this matter to trial. I sincerely hope this is the case.'

He checks something on his laptop screen.

'Mr Richardson,' he says. 'Is the CPS ready to proceed?'

'Yes, Your Honour,' Niall says coolly.

'I'm pleased to hear it,' the judge replies, almost admonishingly, as he peers at him through his half-moon spectacles. 'Ms Harper. You've been recently appointed to represent the defendant. Have you been given instructions?'

'Yes, Your Honour,' I reply, my voice confident and without waver. 'The defendant has agreed to my representing him, with another conference tomorrow. Unfortunately, Your Honour, I do have some concerns about the timeline of proceedings.'

Judge McConnell's heavy brow lifts swiftly, raising his sagging eyelids to show the whites of his eyes.

'I do hope you're joking, Ms Harper.'

'I'm afraid not, Your Honour. We are less than a week away from the trial, and yet I regret to inform you that we are still waiting for some key documents from the prosecution.'

I sense Niall shooting me a look from the other end of the bench. Judge McConnell's eyes widen.

'Although I'm sure my learned friend has a good explanation for the delay,' I say, giving Niall a quick, dismissive glance, 'without all of the necessary documentation, Your Honour cannot expect my client to receive a fair trial.'

'Indeed,' Judge McConnell snaps, and glares at my opponent. 'What is it that you're waiting for, Ms Harper?'

'A copy of the examination report conducted by Dr Samantha Heche, and Mrs Annika Viklund's witness statement, Your Honour.'

I catch Niall flicking quickly through the brief to the document breaking down the evidence he and Whittaker will have agreed upon prior to my appointment.

It may be the solicitor's job to source the material, but it's our job as advocates to make sure we have all the relevant evidence to bring before the court. It pays for the judge to see my opposition squirm.

'What is the reason for this delay, Mr Richardson?' Judge McConnell asks.

Niall flushes, shame emblazoned on his cheeks.

'I will have to look into this, Your Honour. But I am sure there is a reasonable explana—'

'*Reasonable*? We are set to begin trial on Monday, Mr Richardson – a trial which has been in the making for close to a year, and of which you have had the most time to prepare. Are you honestly telling me that any delays at this point in proceedings can be considered *reasonable*?'

It takes a lot to rattle Niall. He is usually a strong, unwavering figure, propped up by an almost unbearable ego, but looking at him now, he almost looks like a child. The fear has knocked decades from his face.

'No, Your Honour. I can only apologise on behalf of—'

'I want every necessary document sent to Ms Harper by five p.m. this evening, is that understood?'

'Yes, Your Honour.'

He turns his attention to me.

'Ms Harper, you will call my office and leave word to confirm this.'

'Yes, Your Honour.'

He nods swiftly, and looks between the pair of us.

'Is there anything more?' he asks, in a tone that suggests we daren't.

'No, Your Honour,' we reply in unison.

He stands without another word, and we all rise.

I turn towards the dock and give Mr Darling a nod of confidence, who gives me a hopeful smile in return before he is led out. I turn back to my station and pack away my things.

'Off to a great start, aren't we, Niall?' I say once the judge has left the room.

'You could have called me and chased those files,' he replies with a biting tone.

'Yes, I could have.' I finally meet his eye and give him a forced, closed smile. 'See you on Monday.'

I take my case and head towards the doors.

'If you want to play dirty, Neve,' Niall calls. 'We'll play dirty.'

I walk on without stopping, knowing that my indifference will only anger him more.

Glad to hear it.

4

I stare down at the candle shaking in my grip, wondering to myself how it would feel for my lungs to fill with smoke, like the Darlings' had. My flesh turning to gristle from the flames.

I think of Yolanda Darling's soot-coated teeth, her black smile one of the few parts of her that survived the fire. I think of the roof beams that lay atop her rubbled tomb, and the hours it took to free her. The sparks from the industrial saw cutting through steel and charred cinderblocks. The whine of the crane peeling away the layers of destruction.

It could have been me. It could have been any of us. All it takes is to fall in love with the wrong man, like a game of Russian roulette: passing the gun between us and slipping the barrel in our mouths, pulling the trigger one by one until someone gets the bullet.

'*Neve,*' the voice says urgently, breaking me from my thoughts. 'Did you hear me? I said your candle has blown out.'

I stare at my mother-in-law's face, lit aglow by the candle cupped before her. Even in the low light, I can see her eyes, sharp and questioning, as they take in my dazed expression. Her name is Margaret, which she hates, and insists everyone call her Maggie. Her hair is too short for her face, which has tight, pointed features.

I look down at my candle and the smell of the smoke fills my nostrils. I silently scold myself for letting my mind wander and allowing my impartiality to slip. My client is innocent until proven guilty.

I should be thinking about Matthew. I am so used to blocking him out, a coping mechanism I've sworn by these past three years, but sometimes I fear I am too good at it. Burying down the guilt, the grief, the pain. Hiding my wedding ring in the depths of my desk.

'I said we should have bought those electric ones,' Maggie says. 'Yours has gone out too, Hannah.'

My stepdaughter, who is stood so close beside me that our arms graze one another with the slightest movement. I wonder if I can still call her that with her father being dead. Or presumed dead, I should say.

'It's too cold out here, anyway,' Hannah replies.

'It's not cold,' Maggie replies with a huff. 'It's mild for January.'

'Well, it feels cold to me.'

'That's because you don't eat enough.'

Maggie looks down at her candle and sighs sharply, extinguishing her flame into a curling pillar of smoke.

'We're not leaving until we've said something,' she says matter-of-factly, and takes the lighter from her pocket.

This is the third year we have done this, more for Maggie's sake than ours. There used to be others; people wanted to feel part of something that first year, spawning a congregation of strangers in the park closest to where Matthew went missing, a mass of candles spread out as far as the eye could see. We'd chosen to hold the vigil on the second of January to avoid his memory getting lost in the celebrations. We needn't have bothered. I think of our deathly quiet Christmas dinner last month, with the three of us around the table, the only sound being the murmuring of the TV in the background and the rustling of the paper hats from the crackers rested dutifully upon our heads, while Matthew's chair sat empty. As for the vigil, the public attention around his whereabouts soon waned, and the numbers inevitably dwindled. With no body to lay to rest, and no grave to visit each year, we stand in Maggie's back garden, cloaked in the evening's shadows.

Hannah and I watch as Maggie clicks the button repeatedly and fails to ignite a flame until she is close to tears.

'Maggie.'

I hold out my hand to take it from her. She meets my eyes, hers shining as the warm glow of her home at our backs is reflected in their watery surface.

I light my candle and cup my hand around it.

'Use it to light yours, Han.'

Hannah looks up at me, and I admire her face in the orange glow of the flame: oval in shape, with plump, soft cheeks; large green pools for eyes that betray her every thought, but sharp as a tack despite her young sixteen years. She has the same eyes as her father; they are such a light green that they almost look grey against her auburn hair, the hair she got from her late mother.

Hannah has lived with her grandmother since her mother's death, which happened when she was only a little girl. Maggie browbeat my husband into the arrangement. *A young girl needs a woman to raise her, not a single father who works all hours,* or so she insisted before Matthew and I met. Those closest to Maggie know how better off life is when one agrees to her demands.

Hannah holds her candle to mine, her brow creasing as she concentrates, warmth spreading through my chest as I watch the spark of satisfaction in her eyes when the flame catches. She is the same age now as Danny Darling had been when they were shot in the head. I feel the urge for a cigarette again.

Matthew and I met when Hannah was just six years old, in the park where I walked my dog. Hannah had led her father over to me, wanting to pet Sam. He was an old thing, on his last legs and shook when he had to stand for too long, but his will for life was still strong. As Hannah had petted Sam, giggling as he licked her palm, I looked into the eyes of the man who would become my husband, and smiled.

Maggie holds her candle to Hannah's, the white stick shaking in her grip. We stand in silence with our hands cupped protectively around the wicks.

'I'll start then,' Maggie says, when neither Hannah nor I say a word. She clears her throat behind her fist, shaking with equal vigour.

'Matthew was a good man,' she says, before remembering. '*Is* a good man.'

The embarrassment is contagious. We have all made the same mistake over the years. Is a man really dead without a body to lay to rest, or ashes to spread? But Hannah and I are more forgiving than Maggie would have been, had it been one of us.

'It has been three years since you've been gone,' she continues. 'Three years of calling myself a mother without a son. Three years of wondering where you are. Wondering if you are safe, or if you're . . .'

Her lip trembles. I hate it when Maggie cries; she becomes defensive and callous. I learnt very quickly to stay quiet until the waterworks stop.

'You are missed,' she says finally, gripping tightly to her composure. 'And I love you.'

She nods, like an explanation mark punching the end of her speech; her stiff upper lip returns.

I look down at Hannah, staring into the darkness deep in thought. She meets my eyes and flushes crimson.

'Love you, Dad,' she utters.

'You have to say more than that,' Maggie says.

'I don't know what to say.'

'Try,' she replies sternly.

Hannah's cheeks grow a deeper shade of pink, and her eyes search the slabs of patio, as if she will find the words at our feet. A lock of hair flits across the bridge of her nose. I tuck it behind her ear and give her a friendly wink when she catches my eye.

'I'll go,' I say.

But as I take a deep breath to begin, I fail to conjure more than Hannah did. The words crowd at the base of my throat, and my thoughts jumble. I can feel their sights on me: Maggie, indignant and unrelenting; Hannah, with those hauntingly familiar eyes.

'We miss you,' I say, forcing the words past my teeth. 'Wherever you are, we miss you.'

My throat is on fire. I swallow hard, and glance down at my candle. It has blown out again. The smoke curls up and stings my eyes.

'I don't know why I bother,' Maggie snaps. 'We won't do it again next year. Clearly it's not what either of you want.'

'People mourn in different ways, Nanny,' Hannah says, quietly.

'Well, a few words for your father wouldn't go amiss. It's the respectful thing to do. The *right* thing to do.'

The tears have formed again, chasing the malice of her words. She snatches the candles from the pair of us, blowing out Hannah's and her own in one swoop, before heading back inside.

Hannah has lost both of her parents: her mother to cancer when she was only young, and her father in her early teens. This should be her moment, done her way, but Maggie has a way of making situations only about herself. Although a small part of me wonders if she is right. Might Hannah be following my lead, burying her emotions when it comes to her father?

I look down at her, her eyes busy with thoughts and feelings that don't reach her stoic face.

'She doesn't mean to be nasty,' I say. 'She loves you very much.'

'I wish we didn't have to do this,' she mutters.

'Then we won't.'

As we return inside, Maggie is tidying up the kitchen, working herself into a familiar state. I try not to invite her to mine if I can help it. She treats it as if it is still her son's home rather than mine, entering with a furrowed brow and eyes busy with criticisms. *Matthew wouldn't live like this. Matthew liked a tidy home. Matthew—*

'Thank you for this evening, Maggie,' I force. The confines of the small, galleyed kitchen makes me want to breathe in the cold night air again. Their company is both craved and unwelcome; the double-edged sword of loneliness that cuts into me whichever way I turn. The thought of home fills me with longing and dread in equal measure.

'Can I stay with you tonight?' Hannah asks me.

'It's a school night,' Maggie says.

'I only have to leave fifteen minutes earlier—'

'You struggle to get out of bed at the best of times,' Maggie quips under her breath.

Hannah looks up at me, those large green eyes enveloping me in guilt.

'Maybe another time,' I say, and stroke her hair. 'I've got some more work to do tonight. I won't be much fun.'

'And I'm sure you have homework to be doing,' Maggie says to Hannah.

She nods and slinks out of the room without another word, leaving just Maggie and me. It is as if Hannah has taken all of the air in the room with her.

'Have a good night, Neve.'

I have outstayed my welcome. She heads through to the living room, small and formal, where Matthew and I visited for many obligatory Christmases. I think of my own sitting room that awaits me: a tight box of a room in my two-up-two-down terrace, with only enough space for the tatty burgundy sofa, which Matthew chose, and an armchair by the sash window, which was mine. Bookshelves frame the chimney breast, home to copious volumes of law books. My home's modest size is both a gift and a prison, depending on the day.

'Can I stay at the weekend?' Hannah asks from the hallway.

'Neve has a big case,' Maggie says before I can open my mouth. 'She won't have time to run around after you.'

I want to tell her not to speak for me, but she's right. All of my time will be taken up by the Darling case until the trial is over.

'As soon as it's done with, you can stay for a week. How's that?'

Maggie opens her mouth to protest.

'Deal,' Hannah replies, and gives me a long, tight hug, as

if to seal the offer before Maggie can pick it apart. I wrap my arms around her and inhale the sweet scent of her hair, a delicious concoction of coconut and youth.

'Come on then,' Maggie says impatiently. 'Your homework won't complete itself.'

I reluctantly peel myself away from Hannah's warmth, and feel the familiar ache return in my chest as I watch her head for the stairs.

Maggie goes to the door, wringing her hands as she goes, visibly uncomfortable at our being left alone. One might think we'd have grown close over the years, but that's not Maggie's style. Her world was her child, and then her grandchild; anyone else is merely someone to compete with for their affection. I follow behind her and slip into my jacket.

'You should get some friends your own age, Neve,' she says as she opens the door. 'Hannah needs to make more of an effort with her peers, but she doesn't seem to see the need when she has you.'

I flinch at the jab.

'I'm not just her friend though, am I? I'm her stepmother.'

'I'm not sure what this situation makes any of us,' she replies. 'But I don't want Hannah sacrificing opportunities to have a healthy sense of normality because she's stuck in the past.'

'No one is asking her to sacrifice anything except you, Maggie.'

Her lips purse together, an exhausted sigh huffing from her nostrils.

'Her father is gone, Neve. And with your connection to us being through him, I wonder if it is healthy to carry this on. Whether we should consider putting some distance between us, for Hannah's sake.'

For Hannah's sake.

I swallow down the hurt. I can almost taste it, a bitter tang lingering on my tongue.

'I will be in Hannah's life for as long as she wants me to be. Goodnight, Margaret.'

I raise the handle on my carry-along case of files and law-books with a sharp snap and slip my bag over my shoulder. Something catches Maggie's eye, and her features sharpen.

'You're not wearing your wedding ring.'

I look down at my left hand, still poised on my bag straps at my shoulder. I'd forgotten to put it on before I left chambers. I shuffle out the door and step out onto to the street with my head down.

'I'm glad to see you are moving on so quickly,' Maggie says from the doorway. Her face is even harder than before, looking down her long, sharp nose at me.

'It isn't like that, Maggie—'

'This will make it easier for Hannah to move on too. She can be led by your example. Goodnight, Neve, and good luck with the case.'

She shuts the door before I can reply. I stand on the quiet street listening as the key turns in the lock on the other side, and glance down at where my wedding ring should be.

That's the thing with being a widow. No one lets you forget it.

⚖

I turn the corner for my street, lined with terraced houses that are all of the same design, with large sash windows that stick in the heat of summer, and chatter like teeth in winter, as the laborious chug of a train calls from the tracks that lie just beyond our gardens. There are cars parked bumper to bumper from the top of the street to the bottom, where St John's Church sits tucked between the rows of houses. It looks strange and out of place, like most churches do in the city nowadays, with housing and skyscrapers built around them. Its bell tower reaches far up into the dark night sky, not a star in sight from the pollution of the city lights. I check my watch: it's close to the hour. The bells will ring out soon. I like to prepare myself, to stop from jumping out of my skin; the bells always seem louder at night.

I fish my keys from my bag as I reach my front door and heft my carry case over the threshold. The house is cold and unwelcoming, and the air clings to the smell of neglect. I need to change the bins, dust the place. But it is so easy to leave these things, living on my own. Matthew hated disorder; it often felt like he was following behind me, clearing mess in my wake. I walk through the ground floor, turning on lamps and shutting the blinds as I go.

I wheel my carry case to the sofa and sink into it with a sigh. Silence rings through the house. I should eat something, but I can't bring myself to cook. I'd meant to grab something before the vigil, but I had returned to chambers after the hearing to work on my opening speech. I wonder if I'm depressed, or if I'm simply set in my unconventional ways. I thrive on order and control in my work, but at home, it is somewhat satisfying to throw organisation to the wind.

I pour a large glass of wine, and play one of my favourite albums to work to: violinist Daniel Hope's *Belle Époque*, and take a sip as the strings begin to play. Matthew and I would listen to it together, drink the same wine, the scent on our breath as we laughed, kissed.

I think back to the vigil. How detached and on guard I had been. Maggie's words from the first anniversary of Matthew's

death echo in my mind, when I had been just as emotionally absent.

You're a cold, cold woman, Neve.

The next song plays, delicately plucking me from my
thoughts. I pick up the brief and have just begun to read when
the power cuts out and I am thrust into darkness. I sit in the
silence with nothing but my heartbeat for company and the
anxious flutter of my breaths. I get up with a sigh and shift
a slat in the blinds: the whole street has gone out. That's the
third time in as many months; it often happens around here in
winter. The cold temperatures damage the underground cables.

Gong.

I jump at the sound of the bells. Ten to mark the hour. It's
the sort of sound that carries through a person, strumming
every muscle and nerve.

To hell with this, I think, and down my wine before heading
up the stairs for bed. *All will be right in the morning.*

But as I reach the landing, listening to the bells ring out
along the street, I know the reason for the knot of unease in my
gut: a grown woman shouldn't be afraid of the dark.

I brush my teeth and crawl into bed, the faint scent of Merlot
still tainting my breath, and listen to the now silent street. But
the bells continue to echo in my mind. I wasn't even afraid of
the dark as a child; it was a fear that grew on me as an adult.
When I learnt of all of the terrible things that we humans do
to one another, once the lights go out.

5

I wake to the smell of bleach and the undeniable sense that something is wrong.

I am not in my bed, but hunched over, naked in the dark. I can feel the cold air nipping at my bare flesh. My hands are burning as if they are on fire, but there are no flames, just darkness and the racing patter of my heart. There's something else, too. A creaking sound piercing the gloom, turning my skin to goose flesh.

Creak. Creak.

I breathe deeply and the ammonia hits the back of my throat. I cough and gag it back up, a string of drool webbing from my bottom lip to the floor. I wipe my eyes and mouth and stare aimlessly about me.

The darkness is so thick that I can barely make anything out. But the more I rouse from my slumber, the more I begin to spot small, indistinct details creeping through, shadows darker than the rest.

My knees are burning against the carpet, the flesh hot and sore from friction burns as if I've been dragged. The smell of bleach is unbearable; I blink back watery tears and sniff to keep my nose from dripping. I can just make out enough of my surroundings now to know that I'm at home: the banisters running along the stairwell, the pictures hanging on the walls. The door to my bedroom sways on its hinges with a breeze, and beyond it, the curtains billow at the open window.

Creak. Creak.

I reach for the banister, my palm on fire and wet with slime, and get to my feet. I must have been hunched over for a while, for my back seizes as I attempt to straighten it, and I release a brief whimper as it threatens to give. Through the dark, I reach for the light switch where I know it to be, my fingers dancing clumsily along the wall, until light bursts above my head. I clench my eyes shut, before slowly opening them again, peering at the scene.

My hands are red raw. The flesh has cracked between my fingers and around my nails, and there are raised, red patches where the bleach has burnt through the skin.

The carpet is completely ruined. A yellow pool lies before me where the bleach has sucked the life out of the once grey fibres, glittering with bubbles where I must have been scrubbing with the sponge that is hidden beneath a mass of white foam. A bottle of toilet bleach lies on its side in the mess. I pick it up to find it practically empty but for a few last dregs swishing at the bottom of the bottle, before dropping it to my feet.

I head to the bathroom at the other end of the hall, quickening my pace as my whole body begins to sting unbearably, trying not to cough up the ammonia that has followed me and lodged at the back of the throat. I turn on the shower and thrust myself beneath the ice-cold spray with a gasp, until the shock subsides and the burning slowly begins to cool. I stand there and let the water run in sheets before my eyes, the bleach bubbling around my feet before swirling down the drain, as it finally washes away the daze of sleep, and everything becomes clear.

I am sleepwalking again.

6

Four days until the trial

I sit swaying from side to side with the motion of the tube, convinced that I can still smell the bleach on me. I had stayed in the cold shower for almost an hour so I wouldn't have to face the mess I'd made in my sleep. There is nothing more I can do but pull the carpet up and replace it, but there is an odd sense of shame attached to the act: rolling up the ruined carpet and bagging up the bottle with the same embarrassment as a bed-wetter might feel bundling up their soiled sheets.

I haven't sleepwalked in a while. Months, in fact. A childhood habit rediscovered in my adult life, which became unbearably familiar after Matthew went missing. I would wander night after night, waking up in the strangest of places, wondering where I was or how I'd ended up there. A therapist I was encouraged to see after Matthew's disappearance suggested I was looking for him in my sleep. I stopped seeing her after that.

I try to think of the case, but my mind inevitably returns to last night, my mind wandering as my legs had the night before. I look down at my red, angry hands, irritated from the bleach and the cold. There is no doubt that Matthew's vigil spurred my sleepwalking; it has always been exacerbated by stress.

There is something debilitating about my nighttime habit. It takes me straight back to childhood where I would wander the hallways and rooms of each of my foster homes, waking up in varying degrees of distress, depending on how those I lived with chose to deal with it. Some shouted at me, shook me awake. Others would try to guide me back to bed, whispering encouragement as we went. But no matter how they reacted, they all got sick of me in the end. It wasn't long before I was shipped off to the next home, and the home after that, forever becoming another fosterer's problem. They say sleepwalking can be hereditary, but I wouldn't know anything about that.

All of that was so long ago now; I have moved on, made something of myself, and have found family in Hannah and Maggie, as dysfunctional as we are. And yet, my habit never fails to draw up that empty twang in my chest, the same sensation I'd felt as a child as I wandered the halls of strangers' homes.

I drag myself back from the past, and focus on the task ahead. Today is the day that I will hear the story of the Darling murders straight from the horse's mouth. I wince at my choice of words, remembering the photographic evidence of the fried remains of the Darlings' horses. Yesterday's conference had been administrative in nature; now it is Wade's chance to explain his version of events, and my opportunity to think of how I will defend his case in court. I must think of how the prosecution might spin things in their favour, create retorts to each in an endless back and forth until one of us finally misses; a fucked-up game of judicial tennis.

The tube begins to slow and my stop appears on the digital screen. I reach for the nearest rail and get up as the stop approaches. The entire time, I feel that strange sensation one feels when one is being watched: skin prickling, hairs standing on end. I glance down the carriage and lock eyes with a man staring at me behind his reflective sunglasses. He doesn't look away in embarrassment or falter under my gaze. His eyes remain locked on mine; I can't see them behind the lenses, but I know they are upon me. I feel their hot, almost unbearable intensity.

Looks like someone read Eccleston's article.

The tube comes to a stop, and I depart with my head held high, refusing to look back at the man as I pass the window. Not that I need to look at him to know. I can feel his eyes, watching me as I go.

⚖

'Can I get either of you a drink?'

Mr Darling's mother, Marianne, stands in the doorway to the modest dining room. She is unusually chirpy for the mother of a man charged with killing his wife and children. I suspect it's denial, and wonder to myself if she believes her son's plea of innocence, or if late at night her mind drifts to the possibility of his guilt. It wouldn't surprise me if she secretly suspected him; I have watched mothers stand by their children despite all kinds of monstrous acts.

Antony Murrell is sat beside me, dressed in an impeccably pressed suit and smelling of expensive aftershave, his dark hair perfectly coiffed. We will combine our expertise to construct Wade's defence: Antony will be the one to find the evidence we need, and I will be the one to deliver it in court. I have worked with him on other cases over the years, and it feels good to have a shorthand with someone on a case like this.

'Tea for me, thanks,' he says. 'Milk, no sugar.'

'Me too, thank you.'

She nods with a faint smile, wringing her hands in a slow, methodical rhythm, and turns to her son.

'Tea, darling?'

From the other side of the dining table, Wade shakes his head without a word. Marianne nods and drifts silently towards the hall.

Wade appears to be a broken man. His hair is unwashed and kinked from sleep. His eyes are puffy and bloodshot. I watch as he runs a hand across his mouth, stubble bristling audibly against his palm. He is still wearing his wedding ring. I wonder if he will still be wearing it three years on, or if like me, he will hide it away.

'Thank you for seeing us today, Wade,' I say. 'I know it has been a long process for you, but we should be on the straight and narrow very soon.'

He nods glumly, and the room descends into silence. This isn't a good sign. I need as much information as I can get in anticipation of the trial, but by the looks of him he is in the tight grip of a depression. The glimmer of hope I saw in his eyes at our meeting yesterday morning has long gone.

Wade's mother enters with a tray of tea.

'Thank you, Marianne. Could we perhaps get a coffee for Wade?'

She places the tray down on the table, each cup jittering against their saucers in her shaky grip.

'That's a good idea,' she replies, and glances down at her son. 'Wakey, wakey, Wade!'

She laughs nervously and waits for him to respond, with an eagerness in her eyes that catches my heart. Another reason for her chirpiness, I realise: she is trying to make up for her son's silence; keeping up appearances while he crumbles. When he doesn't lift his sights from the table, her smile slowly fades, and she slinks out of the room again.

'I know you went through your version of events with Mr Whittaker, but it would be really useful for us to hear of the night in question first hand.'

'Like you said,' he says gruffly, 'I've already gone over it.'

Antony and I share a glance, the silence of the room ticking on. By the look in his eyes, he has the same concerns as I do. Our client appears to have given up.

'We need to make sure your version of events is the same as before,' I say. 'And I need to be familiar with the details to defend you to the best of my ability. Reading back over Mr Whittaker's notes won't be the same as hearing them from you directly. It's important we have every bit of information in our arsenal. Like I said yesterday, it wouldn't be wise to go into this unprepared, particularly with only four days ahead of us before the trial. I will feel confident in going forward if you can assure me you'll co-operate.'

Still he sits, shoulders slumped, eyes down. His lack of fight not only concerns me, it infuriates me. I control the urge to reach over the table and shake some sense into him.

'Thirty years,' I say, abruptly.

He looks up at me with those sad, bloodshot eyes.

'I'm sorry?'

'Thirty years – that's the sentence you're likely to serve before you can appeal, if you're found guilty. If you don't want that to happen, I urge you to co-operate. It is in your best interest to do so. Let us fight for you.'

We stare intently at each other over the table. His eyes slowly come alive again with flickers of anger. I don't care if his motivation to help himself is spurred by his disdain for me; whether he likes me or not is irrelevant. Pussyfooting around him like his mother won't keep a guilty verdict at bay.

Marianne returns with a mug of coffee and the same inappropriate smile chiselled onto her face.

'Thanks,' he says to his mother, slowly tearing his eyes from mine. 'Give me five minutes.'

He takes the mug of coffee and heads out the room and up the stairs. We all listen to the floorboards creaking under his weight from the floor above. Pipes gurgle from somewhere in the house.

'It's been very tough for him,' Marianne says. 'What with losing Yolanda and the children, and then being accused of doing something so heinous . . .' Tears spring to her eyes. Her sadness seems to be forever present, veiled just beneath the surface. 'It's been difficult for him.'

'I'm sure it has been tough on you all.'

Her smile is polite and tense, her jaw locked to keep the tears at bay.

'He won't be long,' she says. 'I'll be in the kitchen if you need anything.'

When she turns the corner for the kitchen, I notice the smile has fallen, and in its place is the saddest expression I have ever seen.

'I thought we agreed to go in slowly on the walk over,' Antony says when we find ourselves alone. We had planned our approach as we headed for Wade's address: a rented three-bed house, tucked away in a new-build cul-de-sac. Photographers sculked outside the property for a glimpse of him, snapping shots of Antony and me as we headed up the drive.

'We weren't going to get anything out of him in that state.'

The floorboards creak again above our heads, as a clatter comes from the kitchen.

'So, he's looking at thirty years?'

'Perhaps more. Three counts of murder with a firearm, and arson to boot. I wouldn't be surprised if the judge felt pressured to make an example of him, what with all the public interest.'

We fall into a comfortable silence, listening to Wade move about upstairs, the scent of Antony's aftershave lingering in the air. I look about the room. There are quite a few personal touches, despite the short time they have been at the property, having moved to the city to be close to the Bailey for the trial.

On the wall is a family photograph of Wade and the victims. The children were young; it must have been taken five or so years before their deaths. They have that innocence to them, where life has yet to taint them, and have puppy fat at their cheeks, both with the trademark white-blonde hair they inherited from their mother. Yolanda was beautiful. She doesn't seem to be wearing make-up in the photo, exposing her spotless skin, exquisite bone structure, perfectly straight teeth. But despite her striking features, they bring a sense of melancholy and revulsion, for the bones and teeth were the only things they found of her.

I had been so transfixed by the photograph that I hadn't heard Wade make his descent. He stands in the doorway, having combed his hair and pulled on a white shirt, and his face looks fresher, tinged pink as if splashed with cold water. He follows my line of sight to where I had been looking as he entered, and his face falls. His eyes drop to the floor.

'Mum,' he calls.

We hear the hurried patter of her footsteps.

'Yes dear?'

'Take that down please.' He nods to the picture frame on the wall. 'I can't . . . I can't talk about it with them looking over me.'

Marianne's expression falls as his had. Silence thrums through the air.

'Yes, of course. I didn't think.'

She slips the frame from the wall and takes it with her into the other room, the glass of the frame coveted closely to her chest. I wonder if Wade will let her hang it up again once we're gone, or if the reminder is too much to bear.

Wade sits down with a curt nod.

'Ready.'

'Great,' I reply. 'Let's get started.'

7

'I woke up, choking. That's the first thing I remember.'

His face grew ashen the moment he thought back; his eyes glassy and distant. Antony and I are silent, conscious of allowing him the room to speak. When he fails to continue, I clear my throat.

'What else do you remember?'

'It was the physical reaction that I remember taking in first. The smoke had filled my chest, my throat. My eyes were streaming and I was covered in sweat from the heat. And the room ... Everything in the room was bathed orange from the fire outside the windows. The stables had been completely engulfed, which had spread to the neighbouring trees. I thought ...'

He shakes his head.

'What did you think?'

His throat bobs as he swallows.

'I thought I had woken in Hell.'

Wade appears to be back there, eyeing the blaze outside the windows in a trance. His right lid twitches every time he mentions fire, and when I look closely at his face, I see that he's sweating, as if he is back in the inferno.

'What do you remember next?'

'I tried to call out for them, but my voice was too hoarse; I couldn't get the words out. I made my way to the hall from the living room.'

'Why were you sleeping in the living room?' Antony asks.

Wade flashes Antony a look, irritation etched between his brows as he is pulled from a memory.

'Yolanda and I had had a deep conversation before bed, and I wanted space.'

That will be a point to the prosecution. Having an argument just before the murders will be firm grounds for suspicion. I want to dig deeper around this, but am conscious of going too hard too soon. This is a point I will certainly come back to.

'So you stepped into the hall ...' I say.

'Yes,' he replies. 'That's when I saw the intruder.'

'Can you describe him to me?'

'It was hard to see from the smoke.'

I skim through the brief for the blueprints of the house, and place my finger on the doorway he speaks of. The house is nothing but a burnt-out shell now, set for demolition after the trial. But looking at the blueprint, I imagine how the house used to be: the Darlings running up and down the stairs, sitting down to eat Sunday roast in the dining room facing the grounds. I wonder what Wade sees when he looks at the blueprints. Whether he sees the good memories or the bad. Life or death.

'We have the floorplan here.' I trace my finger from the living-room doorway to the stairs, and back again. 'There is only six, perhaps seven feet between them. You couldn't make out anything at all, from such a close distance?'

'Like I said,' he says pointedly. 'It was almost impossible because of the smoke. Not just the smoke in the air – it had stung my eyes. It felt like pins had been pierced into them. They wouldn't stop streaming. But if you were to put a gun to my head . . .'

I stiffen at his choice of words. It's a strange description to use. Even more strangely, he doesn't seem to notice the connection. I remind myself it's a common figure of speech. But the fact that it didn't register with him rattles me.

'I would say he was about my height, and he appeared to be wearing all black. He was wearing a mask or a scarf across his nose and mouth, and a hood over his head. He was holding my rifle.'

'You knew it was your rifle immediately?'

'No, only later. As I said ... it was difficult to see. He stopped at the bottom of the stairs, and we stared at each other for a few seconds. I asked who he was – shouted it at him – and he dropped the gun and ran for the front door. I had locked it before going to sleep, but it was wide open. He bolted out into the night before I had even grabbed the gun.'

Anthony leans forward.

'He dropped the rifle? Gave you a weapon to potentially injure him with? Why didn't he shoot you too?'

His right eyelid spasms again.

'Clearly it was part of the plan to frame me, because I picked it up, putting my fingerprints all over it. I ran to the door but he was nowhere to be seen.'

I think of the photo of the murder weapon tucked inside the brief, covered in my client's bloody handprints from where he handled the gun after discovering the bodies.

'What did you do next?'

'I turned back for the stairs.' He pauses, holding his breath. 'I knew I was going to find something bad, but I didn't know what. Or maybe I did and I didn't want to believe it. The intruder had come from upstairs, where my family had been sleeping.'

I watch his throat move as he swallows. His eyes sheen over.

'There was blood on the stairs. Not a lot, just droplets. They must have dripped off him as he was heading for the door. But the higher I got, the more I found. The drops turned to streams. The streams to pools.'

He glances at me briefly, before his eyes fall to the table top. I could see the horror in them, the fear. His hands start to shake, and he subconsciously picks at his nails.

'You knew it was blood the moment you saw it?' I ask.

'No, not completely. I failed to make the connection, or maybe I was in denial from the shock. The only thing lighting my way was the fire roaring on the other side of the windows, making the blood appear black. I just remember the cream carpet was completely soaked. It was wet under my feet. Warm.'

He makes a grimace, as if remembering the feeling. This rings true. The first responders found him barefoot, noting the soles of his feet were red with what would turn out to be his wife's blood.

I watch his Adam's apple rise and fall. His face has grown paler.

'There is a curve in the staircase. It was the feature that made Yolanda fall in love with the place. I remember when we went to view it for the first time. She stepped into the foyer, saw the grand, curved staircase, and looked at me. She was in love. We both were.' He looks down at his hands, his jaw clenching as he grits his teeth behind closed lips. 'When I made the turn on the stairs . . . I found her.'

There is a tense silence. From the outside, it would appear that I am giving him time to collect himself, gather his thoughts. But in truth, I am watching him. Analysing every minute reaction that the memories bring up, to decipher if he is telling the truth or spinning a lie: the muscle twitching at his temple, the tears pooling in his eyes. His whole body is shaking now.

'She was lying on her back on the staircase ... looking up at me.'

His voice breaks, and two tears fall simultaneously down his cheeks.

'How was she lying on the stairs, Wade?' I ask softly.

'Head first, her feet closer to the top. Her nightgown had ridden up, and I could see the gunshot to her knee.' He covers his mouth; his jaw clenched tight on either side of his face. 'Blood had soaked through her chest from the shot to her back. And her head ...' A whimper slips out, and he clenches his fist tighter, his teeth harder. 'Her hair was soaked with it. Her face ... her beautiful face ...'

All the colour has drained from his complexion. For a moment I fear he might be sick, but I push on. It was difficult enough to get him to open up. He might not allow us a second time.

'What did you do when you found her?'

'I sobbed, and held her. She wasn't stiff – she was floppy, deadweight. I cradled her. Checked her pulse, although I didn't need to. She was dead, I knew she was – but it was like I couldn't believe what was right in front of me. I kept telling her to wake up.'

She wouldn't have been stiff so soon after death. The rigor mortis would have taken at least an hour to set in. I immediately think of questions the prosecution would ask him, if he were in the witness box. If his wife was shot and fell on the staircase, why didn't he wake from the noise her body would have made? Did he really fail to hear the intruder enter through the front door and pass the open doorway to the living room on his way to the stairs?

He wipes tears from his face with the brutish rub of his fingers. Fresh streams fall in their place.

'I knew then my children were dead too.'

'How did you know that?'

'The house was on fire. Their mother was dead. Had they been alive, they would have called for me. Tried to escape. The only reason for the silence in the house was that they were dead too.'

He takes a deep, heaving breath, and sighs it out of him. He wipes his face again, this time on his shirt sleeve.

'I tried to move her to the landing, but she was so heavy and slippery from the—' he stops. When he speaks again, his voice is hoarse. 'I didn't want to drop her. I got up and went down the hall to the children's bedrooms. I was covered in Yolanda's blood. My hands were black, and my clothes felt wet. Their bedroom doors were open. They always closed them, and had before bed that evening. I was crying.'

His pulse is racing, I can see it beating in his neck and the forked vein at the centre of his forehead. His chest is motionless with a held breath.

'They had both been shot through the head in their beds . . .'

He exhales and instantly doubles over as if from a physical blow, and sobs into his hands.

'Let's take a break for a moment,' Antony says. When I turn to face him, I notice his eyes shimmering with unshed tears.

I nod and clear my throat. I am sat in a room with two men, one sobbing, the other trying to compose himself, while my eyes are bone dry.

Perhaps it's because I'm good at keeping the barriers in place for the sake of professionalism. Or maybe it's because of my own pain, my own guilt. And if I open that door . . .

You're a cold, cold woman, Neve.

I dig my fingernails into the back of my hand to keep the memories at bay. But however hard I try, I can't rid my mind of the thought of him, as if Matthew is sat on the other side of Wade, staring straight back at me.

⚖️

After a fifteen-minute break, we are back at the table ready to proceed. Wade looks wearier than when we started. His eyes are swollen and red again, and I can sense the depression clawing him back into the sorry state we first found him in. I need to get more details out of him before he completely shuts down again.

'Thank you Wade, we are almost done. After you had discovered the children, what did you do?'

I note that I sound cold, almost clinical, but I can't give him room to fall apart again.

He closes his eyes with a sigh. Emotionally preparing himself. When he opens them again, he is back in the past, those bright eyes jaded with pain.

'I don't know how long I was up there, holding each of them in turn. The smoke . . . it had made me drunk, almost. I was dizzy and disorientated, and came round in Danny's bedroom when the windows smashed from the heat and glass showered down on us. I didn't want to leave them behind, and contemplated bringing them all into the master bedroom so we could all . . . be together. The only thing that kept me from closing my eyes again and succumbing to the smoke was the thought of the intruder getting away with their deaths.'

I imagine them all lying on the Darlings' marital bed. Faces frozen and pale like porcelain dolls, with Wade nestled among them, waiting for release.

'When I returned to the hall, the fire had grown. The smoke made it impossible to see. The air was completely black with it, and the floor was scorching hot from the fire burning below. I got down to my hands and knees and crawled for the stairs. I had to pass Yolanda. One small mercy was that I could barely see her through the tears and the sweat from the heat. I made my way down on my hands and knees, slipping on the . . .'

He looks down at his hands with such a pained grimace that I wonder to myself if he sees his wife's blood there, and in what capacity. Literal? Figurative? Perhaps both.

'The fire was ripping through the ground floor. In the living room, the sofa I had woken on was completely ablaze. The walls were blackening where the fire was burning through from the other side. The path to the front door was blocked by fire. I could barely breathe and coughed so hard that I retched. All I could keep thinking was that I shouldn't be alive. I shouldn't be living through this.'

Antony goes to say something, but I stop him with a subtly raised hand, lifting it slightly from the table top. Wade is on a roll, remembering beat by beat. I don't want to pull him out of it until he's done.

'I made my way down the hall towards the kitchen, crawling on my front, completely flat to the floor. The whole time I could smell fuel, and realised I had put my hand in a pool of gasoline. That's when I saw the door to the cellar and my gun room was open.'

I imagine the fire creeping inside and licking each of the unspent bullets. It takes over two hundred degrees Celsius of heat to set off a bullet, according to my research. I imagine how the gunpowder would have exploded over and over, sending metal shrapnel in every direction. According to the records, Wade had around five hundred rounds stored in the gun room. Not surprisingly, that wing of the house all but burnt to the ground.

'In your statement, you said the gun room was key-coded.'

'Yes. I made sure it was secured before going to sleep. Always do. So whoever opened the door knew the access code, and knows me well enough to have chosen my favourite rifle.'

He looks down at the burnt flesh on his hand. His fingernails have grown back in abnormal shapes, small little half-moons hidden deep in the flesh of his gristled fingers.

'I crawled through the open doorway of the kitchen. It was completely ablaze, but I couldn't turn back. There was a clear path to the back door, but I was losing consciousness. I could feel myself drifting. The room was getting dark. I must have passed out and come to again, because suddenly I was screaming.'

He clenches his scarred hand into a fist, the warped fleshed growing taut from the strain.

'Why were you screaming?'

His brow creases as if in pain.

'My hand was on fire.'

He puts his injured hand in the other and massages the scars with his thumb in small rotations.

'I managed to get to the back door and open it before I slipped unconscious. The next thing I remember I was in hospital, where I had been in a coma for two days.'

He finishes his story with a mighty sigh, and the breath seems to drain the life out of him. When he meets my eyes, I see how utterly exhausted he his.

'Thank you, Wade. I know that must have been difficult for you.'

His gaze alters in an instant. He looks at me with such rage that I flinch.

'How could you *possibly* know?'

Antony tenses up beside me, and my cheeks flush.

'How could you possibly know how it feels to hold your family dead in your arms? To wake up in hospital and learn that your entire world has burnt to the ground? Tell me, how on earth could you relate to that?'

His face has grown red with rage, veins snaking from his forehead to his temples. I can feel Antony squirming at my side, eager to jump in should I drop the ball with my response.

'I apologise if I offended you, Wade. That wasn't my intention. I only wished to commend you for going through this again – I can only imagine how hard it was for you.'

His expression softens. I move the brief towards me, eager to change the subject and take back control.

'Firstly, I need to recommend that you don't give evidence during the trial. I noticed you're on the list of witnesses. It might seem counterproductive not to speak in your own defence, but you have us to do that for you. If you give evidence in court, you give the prosecution the chance to cross-examine.'

'The last guy didn't seem to have a problem with it,' he says. 'I'm saying my piece. That's the end of it.'

Why would Adrian have agreed to something like this? It's not just bold, it's reckless.

'This will make things harder for us—'

'I'm giving evidence, Ms Harper. I won't change my mind on this.'

Antony and I share a defeated glance. We'll try and tackle this again later.

'The other issue we have is, the only evidence to suggest that there was an intruder in your house that night is your statement. There were no vehicle sightings we could tie to the area for means of the intruder's transport, no positive identifications of the man you describe. For all intent and purposes, you could be plucking the idea of the intruder from thin air.'

'It doesn't change the fact that I'm telling the truth.'

'No, but it does make it harder for us to convince the jury. As you can imagine, anyone can commit a crime and blame it on a person that no one else can verify. Unless of course, you believe there is someone in your life who meant you and your family harm, who had the motivation to carry out the murders that night. Who might have known the keycode to your gun room, like you said. The Viklund family are known for their illegal activity. Do you think that could have played a part?'

'No. The Viklunds would know who had done it if that were the case; it wouldn't be playing out in court.'

'So you don't know of anyone who might have done this,' I retort.

'I do,' he replies.

Antony and I look to one another. Wade has never named another possible suspect before, unless both Antony and I missed it in the brief, which I doubt.

'Who?' I ask.

The silence echoes through the room again, thrumming like a pulse.

'My former business partner, Alex Finch. He lost everything, just as I had. Money, the business, his wife was leaving him. But I had something he wanted and could never have.'

'And what was that?' Antony asks.

The seconds draw out, the only sound being the tick of a clock behind our heads. Wade sighs again, and meets my eyes.

'My wife.'

8

Antony and I sit in silence at the back of the wine bar where we have claimed a quiet nook as our own. The table between us is covered with law books, witness statements, pathology reports and police interview minutes, and empty cups from our last round of coffees, before finally going for a bottle of red wine to share. When the waitress had brought it over, she caught a glimpse of the photograph exhibiting the blood on Wade's clothes and turned completely white, before I tucked it out of view.

Antony's lips are stained burgundy from the wine, his brow furrowed while he reads over the notes Eddie Chester and Adrian Whittaker had written up on our client's last movements in the days leading up to the murders.

Wade's revelation about his business partner continues to echo in my mind, but the sceptic in me refuses to rest. Why would he wait to share this fact, if it would prove he has been wrongly accused of murdering his family?

Wade was arrested at the hospital six days after the murders, and brought in for questioning, with the police interview detailed in notes included in the brief. Wade refused to speak until he had legal representation, answered no comment thereafter, and was held in custody until he was granted bail the following day. The only public comment he has made since his arrest was his written witness statement issued to the courts when he was represented by Chester and Whittaker. I read over it for the umpteenth time, familiarising myself with his account on the page, which I must follow to the letter in my defence. His account hasn't changed since this original statement: each beat matches up with the details he relayed today during the conference, except for the revelation about Alex Finch. Wade's motive for concealing such information will have to be highly credible if we are to get it past the prosecution and the judge at this point in proceedings; otherwise, it will appear to be nothing more than a desperate attempt to escape the charges.

The prosecution case against my client is strong. The murder weapon is registered in his name and covered in his fingerprints. The blood of the victims was on his clothes and person. They have their suspected motive: Wade had a mental breakdown due to his financial struggles and planned to kill himself as well as his family to escape the situation he had put them all in, with specialist witnesses to back up their claims. I begin to read over the witnesses the prosecution plans to bring before the jury. We can expect to hear accounts from Yolanda's mother, the first responders on the scene, the detective on the case, the ballistics expert. The list goes on. They are going to paint the picture that our client fell into a deep depression after the closure of his business and murdered his family in a case of familicide. The explanation of the word has been printed out and clipped to the page.

Familicide: the murder of one or several members of one's own family, often resulting in murder-suicide.

I am re-reading Wade's medical history and his use of antide-pressants, which the prosecution are bound to use against him to fit their agenda, when Antony breaks me from my thoughts.

'How did his business fall apart again? In a nutshell.'

I take a sip of wine and sigh, my breath tasting of Merlot.

'The company sold a particular pump for swimming pools for which they created the design and owned the patent for. After many years of success, they began to spend more than they made, taking out a string of loans that never got them out of the red. To make things worse, they dipped into the employee pension fund to try and bail themselves out, and by the looks of it there is even potential evidence of insider trading on his business partner's side. That'll be a whole trial of its own once this is over.'

'Right. And this business partner of his, Alex Finch. What was his role again?'

'Finance director and member of the board.'

'So essentially, he was the man to spot these problems both before they began and as they arose?'

'Theoretically, yes, but I suspect they both have a cross to bear.'

'What's the history between Wade and Mr Finch?'

I flick through the paperwork to refresh my memory, as my head spins from the pages of facts.

'They met at university and went into business together in 2006. Wade was the man with the knowhow about the product and would be the man to sell it and build their clientele, while Finch was to grow the business around it and source the funds.'

'So if we want to skewer Finch, we need to find out if he was the one who authorised the money being taken from the employee pension fund, and created the downhill spiral for the success of the business. Paint him as a man set on destroying Mr Darling's life: his business, his financial security, and finally, his family.'

'There will be a paper trail, I'm sure. If it has anything to do with Finch, as Wade suspects, we have our alternative suspect. But we'll need to secure his motive too.'

'We could paint Finch as a lover scorned?' he asks. 'For wanting Yolanda but not being able to have her?'

'That could work, but we'll need more from Wade on what happened between them. The only way we are going to get the suspicion off him is to have someone else to pin it on. If we're going to find the evidence we need to back up this claim, Wade needs to lead us in the right direction.'

'Isn't it too late to admit evidence?'

'Not if it's key to giving the accused a fair trial. I'll threaten to push the trial back to assess the lead should it not be accepted; then the judge will have to accept anything we have if he wants the trial to commence as planned.'

Whittaker did none of this while Wade's case was under his charge. He had had the case for months, but as I read and re-read through the brief, I can't see which direction he planned to take it. No alternative suspects, no alibi or character witnesses to offset the prosecution's suggested motive. I feel that same pit of disappointment twist in my stomach.

What on earth was he thinking?

'So as for our witnesses,' Antony says, picking up a document from the table. 'We have Mr Finch; the nurse who disclosed the news of their deaths when he woke from his coma; the pathologist to analyse the bloodied clothes to prove it was deposited when he discovered the bodies, rather than being evidence that he killed them ... Then there's Wade himself, if we can't persuade him otherwise. But out of all of them, Finch is the one who could be the most damning for the prosecution's case?'

'Yes. Although I must confess, I'm concerned about the timeline we have to nail this. Three full working days to focus on this isn't long at all.'

'You think we should push for more time?'

'The judge would fight it with every breath in his body, but if we prove it will impact Wade's right to a fair trial, we could sway him.'

'But if we can nail Alex Finch to the cross then we have our defence, right? The police didn't interview him, from what either of us can see. They suspected no one else but Wade. If we find out more about Alex Finch and Wade Darling's relationship, and Finch's alleged infatuation with Yolanda, we'll have him as a key suspect the police missed, and rip their investigation from under them. Then we could really win this thing.'

Antony's excitement shimmers in his bloodshot eyes.

'You think we can get what we need in that time?' I ask. 'Because if we turn up on Monday and try to push the trial on the day, the judge will make it impossible. We'll need to do it before nine a.m. Monday morning or not at all.'

Antony thinks it over, chewing on a fingernail until I hear a faint, bone-like crack. He nods once, conviction in his eyes.

'We can do it.' He pauses, taking me in. 'You don't seem convinced.'

I sigh, rubbing the bridge of my nose.

'There's one thing that's troubling me. Wade has had a year to mention Alex Finch's obsession with Yolanda, which had it been investigated, might have rendered his trial obsolete and sent the police scrambling for new suspects. He could have saved himself all of this grief, but has only done so now, right before the trial. Why?'

I watch his eyes moving busily as he tries to think of an answer.

'Wade is essentially suggesting that he's sat on this information for a year,' I continue. 'Unless he had an extremely good reason for doing so, it will look like he's making a last-ditch attempt to lay the blame at someone else's feet.'

Antony returns to biting his nail, and it takes all of my will-power not to intervene, tap his hand away like an adult might do to a child.

'We have the conference with him in the morning,' he says. 'We can apply pressure then, get more out of him. I'll look into his business partner some more too and see what I can find. Wade said Finch's life had fallen apart, just as his had. That'll be just as much motive to suspect him, just as the police suspected Wade.'

'Sorry to disturb you,' the waitress says, breaking us from our thoughts. 'But we close in ten.'

'Christ, have we been here that long?' Antony checks his watch. We have been at it for hours. The glass frontage of the bar is black with the night sky. 'Thanks, I'll take the bill.'

I slug back the last dregs of wine and begin to tidy up my paperwork, slipping it all into my trusty carry case, as the sense of unease continues to gnaw away.

'I've got a gut feeling about this,' Antony says as he tidies his side of the table. 'If we nail Finch, we'll win this. I just know it.'

I smile, but inside, my stomach churns with apprehension. I don't know what it is: it's not a thought, but a feeling. The sense that something isn't quite right.

'Don't worry about why he took so long to tell us,' he says, reading my face. 'We'll get an explanation tomorrow.'

⚖

I rock with the motion of the tube, listening to it grind and clank against the tracks. The dark tunnel passes on the other side of the window, with its soot-covered wires snaking along it like veins.

The carriage is freezing, but riding the Metropolitan Line is a godsend compared to the likes of the Bakerloo Line, which I take to get to courthouses on the south side of the river. The former is fresh and open, where one can walk from one end of the train to the other and watch as it tails around the bends; and the other, its carriages older than I am, covered in black grime with gang tags carved into the plexiglass, and seats that one must peel away from when they reach their stop.

The tube is almost empty. Most of the passengers got off at King's Cross, then Farringdon. Just a few nightly stragglers remain dotted along the train: a woman with plastic bags at her feet that chime with wine bottles, muttering to herself in a way that sets my hackles rising; a young couple huddled close together, laughing at something on one of their phones; and a man at the far end, dressed in black sports gear, a coat and cap, and sunglasses shielding his eyes.

I close my own and let myself move with the train, my head and spine bobbing as if in water, when my carry case knocks into my knee with a sudden kickback of motion, and my eyes spring open, my mind back on the trial.

In tomorrow's conference, I hope to discover the link between Finch and Yolanda. With the trial fast approaching, I won't be afraid to push Wade for the answers we need. I think back to his dishevelled appearance on the other side of the table. When he had spoken of the fire, sweat had broken out along his forehead. When he described finding his family, the pain welled in his eyes, shivered in his bottom lip. And still, he allowed himself to be wrongly accused of their murder, withholding the information on Alex Finch until now.

Why?

I close my eyes again and think of the scene, blow by blow. Fourteen rifle shells were found about the property. All of the horses and show ponies were shot with the silenced rifle before the family were violently laid to rest. I imagine the smell of gunpowder in the air, the nervous shuffle of the horses in their stables as they waited for the end of the rifle to reach them, the thud of their bodies against the hay. Then the gasoline, thick in my nostrils, and the spark of the lighter scratching in my ears, before the dark November night was set ablaze and the full moon was hidden behind the smoke.

I open my eyes with a sigh. Is Wade Darling innocent? Is he guilty? It isn't my job to know; to feel. I am not hired to decide who is right or wrong. That is for the jury to decide. Something I remind myself of every time I take on a case that makes me question my moral compass. I mustn't even allow myself to wonder, in case it impacts my impartiality – I cannot afford to form a grudge against the man whose only chance of a fair trial rests firmly on my shoulders.

The death of the Darlings, and the thought of the empty house that awaits me, makes me think of Matthew. He usually creeps to the forefront of my mind when I find myself alone. I had been emotionally detached during the vigil; I was practically gritting my teeth through it. I wonder if Maggie and Hannah spotted my cold front. Guilt fills my gut, sloshing from the rocking motion of the carriage, as I attempt to bury the thought of him again.

The tube slows and judders to a stop at Liverpool Street. The doors open with a mechanical whine and the young couple depart, followed by the lone woman trailing off behind them, clinking and chatting to herself as she goes. The doors shut behind her and we return to the dark depths of the tunnel.

I start to get myself together as the end of the line approaches. A short walk from Aldgate to Whitechapel and I'll be home. Sometimes I take the District Line to take me straight there, but on nights like this, when my mind is weighted down by work, I crave the fresh air to clear the fog; to feel the night breeze against my pores after so many hours in the stale air of chambers and courtrooms.

A shadow catches my eye: the man dressed in sports gear is heading along the train. It is just the two of us now, and I suspect he will be heading further up the carriage to make a dart for the station exit to avoid the extra walk along the platform. The closer he gets, the more he seems to tower over me; his trainers must be a size thirteen. But instead of passing me by, he sits in the seat directly opposite mine, slipping off his sunglasses and smiling, smelling of cigarettes and Brut.

I stare at the man. Dark-haired and broad-shouldered, with pitted olive skin that's wrinkled around his eyes. I sigh quietly to myself, hardening against the man's presence, my face souring; it wouldn't be the first time I was hit on while on the tube.

'Hello, Neve.'

The use of my name makes me pause. We stare at each other wordlessly, rocking in sync with the carriage, as my heart rate slowly begins to climb. I wonder if he is a former client. By the intense glare of his eyes, I must not have won his case.

'You don't know me, if that's what you're thinking,' he says, as if I spoke aloud. 'But you will.'

I glance up at the rolling train sign towards the ceiling. *The next stop is Aldgate, where this train terminates* moves across the screen. I slowly reach into my jacket pocket for my keys, slipping one between my fingers as my pulse pounds feverishly at the tips.

'That won't be necessary,' he says, nodding towards my pocket, and opening his coat with his free hand. The other is hidden within. Pointing the handgun at my gut.

'We have some things we need to discuss,' he says. 'Where shall we start?'

I pry my eyes away from the end of the gun. My heart is racing so fast that I feel sick; my stomach coils.

'I know . . .' His smile breaks open, flashing jagged, yellow teeth. 'Let's start with how you murdered your husband.'

9

I stare down the dark, endless eye of the gun. One tug of the trigger. One bullet. That's all it would take. He whips his aim until it is pointed directly at my heart, and I brace myself with a jolt, waiting for the bang, the blood. The gunman laughs to himself behind closed lips.

I have met many criminals in my time in the courts. Nine times out of ten, the people I defend are sad, lost souls who never stood a chance at any other way of life, and ignite pity rather than fear. It's the small percentage of criminals I'm afraid of – the remaining one out of the pitiful nine. The type who laugh as they point a gun at a stranger's chest.

We stare at each other in silence and sway with the motion of the carriage, but his aim never strays. My eyes sting, too terrified to blink; to take my eyes off him for even a millisecond.

Let's start with how you murdered your husband.

My heart drums against my ribs. My airways slowly seal shut. I sit before him, practically choking on my own breath, as his words sink in. The man stares at me from the other side of the carriage, watching me with a smile.

He knows.

I think of ways I could try to escape, and imagine myself dashing towards the nearest exit. But I have too many belongings, too many layers, whereas he is free to move at a second's notice. I wouldn't stand a chance. I clench the keys until metal teeth dig into my palm, thinking of all the places I can jab him if I need to: the base of his throat, his eyes, his groin. The entire time, he is smiling at me, the gun unwavering in his grip.

'If it's money you want—'

'It isn't,' he replies.

I try to swallow, but shock has leeched my mouth dry. I lick my coarse lips and glance up to the CCTV camera between the doors on either side of the carriage.

'They won't see the gun, not from here.' He wags it tauntingly from side to side where he hides it at his hip. 'They'd only know what happened when it was over.'

I imagine my chest cracking open with the bullet. Blood exploding against the window at my back; soaking into the fabric of the seats. I wonder who would have to clean up the mess.

'Then do it,' I hear myself say, voice shaking. 'If it's not money you want, if there's nothing I can do or say to stop you, then just do it already.'

He throws his head back and laughs, the sound carrying all the way down the empty train.

'They said you had balls,' he says. 'Suppose you have to, to kill a man like you did. Tell me, did the police ever suspect you?'

'I don't know what you're talking about—'

'Oh, I think you do.'

Adrenaline surges through me. I feel the need to grip onto something, but stop myself. Even through my terror, I know I mustn't look weak. The whole time, I ask myself the same question over and over, the words swirling in my mind in an endless, dizzying loop.

How could he possibly know?

We sit without a word between us, rocking with the carriage to the clanking, grinding sounds of the tunnel.

The transport police will be able to see his face through the CCTV now that he has removed his sunglasses, won't they? If he kills me, they'll find him. My death won't have been in vain. But from the angle of camera, his cap will be covering his features. I glance at the dark tunnel on the other side of the window, praying for the platform to appear; witnesses waiting for us beside the track. But of course, there won't be. Aldgate is the end of the line, and this is the last train of the night.

'Look, if you've got something to say, then say it,' I stammer. 'The train is about to pull up at any minute.'

He grins, seeming to like the fight in me. A man who enjoys the game. Despite the fear clouding my mind, I can't shake the niggling thought that I recognise him from somewhere. It's not so much his face or his height that I remember, but his eyes. He has the sort of stare that peels off one's clothes, one's skin, until it is peering into your soul. I recognise him in a flash: this is the same man who had watched me during my tube journey en route to Wade's address this morning.

He has been following me.

'You're defending Wade Darling in his upcoming trial,' he says.

So that's what this is about. He says this as a statement of fact rather than a question, and I sit waiting for the next blow, failing to see how the case might be connected to what I did. I was so careful; I didn't tell a soul, leave any trace. The only people in the world who know of my husband's murder are this stranger and me.

I look at the man, desperately trying to decipher his possible motive, looking for the slightest tell: the twitch of his mouth, a gleam in his eye. I wonder if he is a distraught family member of the victims, or perhaps a disgruntled shareholder of Mr Darling's bankrupt company. He could even be a crazed follower of the story, with no personal connection at all. The thought of sitting across from a man obsessed causes sweat to break out beneath my blouse.

'Big gig for you this trial, I'm sure . . .'

The tube will be pulling up at the last stop any minute now. I could kick off my shoes, sprint as hard and as fast as I can until—

'. . . It's a shame what happened to his previous counsel, isn't it?'

My thoughts stop dead. His eyes narrow as he smiles knowingly.

'Adrian jumped . . .' I say. 'He took his own life.'

'I can tell you what his last words were before the train hit him, if you like?'

Winding rivulets of sweat slink down my ribs from each pit.

I imagine the scene: Adrian Whittaker innocently standing back from the tracks as he waits for the tube home, when a strange man thrusts him into the oncoming train from behind, feeling nothing but the stranger's hot breath against the nape of his neck and rough palms thrust into his spine. There one minute; gone the next.

Bile spits up my throat. I stare at Whittaker's killer, gripping my hands together in my lap until every drop of blood is squeezed out of them.

'Why on earth would you want to kill Mr Whittaker—'

'For the same reason we're sat here tonight. You have something valuable, something I want, and I have something of yours you want to keep hidden. So, I'm going to offer you a trade.'

I sit in my shock, wondering how the evening has transformed into this. I had been getting the tube home, a journey I have taken so many times. I had been slightly tipsy from the red wine when I sat down in my seat. Now I am stone cold sober.

'And what about Adrian? Why didn't he get to trade?'

'He did,' he replies. 'But he didn't want to play along.'

I stare at the man's unwavering smile, each of his crooked teeth. The ridges between them are stained with dark tar from cigarette smoke.

'W-what . . . what do you want from me?'

'Wade Darling mustn't get off,' he says seriously, the amusement gone from his eyes. 'He is to go to prison for a very long time.'

He tightens his grip on the gun, his palm rasping against the handle. His finger moves slowly towards the trigger. My heart skips so violently that a wave of nausea rips through me.

'I can't throw a trial,' I stutter. 'I have a duty—'

'But you also have a dirty little secret, don't you? One that you're desperate to hide.'

His smirk makes me feel ill. He could be bluffing, waiting for me to assume too much; watching as I dig my own grave. I know from my experience in the courtroom how easy it is to twist a story with just a few facts, spin a narrative until it points in the direction you want.

'The people I work for,' he says. 'They have a way of bringing buried secrets out into the open. They don't take kindly to being told no. Adrian Whittaker thought he could outsmart them. That would be a fatal mistake on your part.'

'Who do you work for?'

'You know full well I won't answer that,' he replies. 'You'll lose the trial, Wade Darling will go to prison, and you can keep your sordid secret to yourself.'

Despite the terror, I almost scoff at his arrogance.

'You make it sound easy.'

'It would have been easier, had you not pulled that trick with Wade's solicitor. Eddie Chester's role was to help you lose the case. You'll have your work cut out for you now, but that's your affair. I'm just the messenger.'

That's why Eddie had approached Wade. He will have purposefully failed to deliver those files to help, rather than hinder.

I nod towards the gun.

'Well, if you're planning on kill me, it won't matter, will it?'

'Who said this bullet is meant for you?' His smile widens. He draws out the silence between us, staring so deeply into my eyes that the sounds of the tunnel fall into the ether. It is just him and me, swaying lightly from side to side, staring into each other's souls. 'Hannah's a pretty girl.'

I had never fully believed one's blood could turn cold until Hannah's name left his lips. His words hit me square in the chest, the utterance of her name lodging a breath in my throat.

Hannah.

I grip the keys tighter, trying to keep myself in my seat while eyeing the soft skin at the base of his throat. I could lunge forwards, end this. But the reality of the situation pins me to my seat in fear.

This man hasn't just been watching me. He's been watching Hannah too.

'If you hurt her—'

'Nothing will happen to either of you if you make the trade. You can be angry with me all you want, but her fate isn't in my hands – it's in yours. The same goes for that little secret of yours . . . you decide what happens now.'

The tube starts to slow. The man clicks the safety on his gun and slips it in his waistband. It's only then that I allow myself to soften; my head is throbbing from contracting every muscle in my body. The Messenger returns his sunglasses to the bridge of his nose, and my reflection stares back at me, hued green from the coloured lenses. I look gaunt with fear, almost as though I have aged a decade between Liverpool Street and the end of the line.

'So,' he says casually. 'Guess you've got a decision to mull over, eh? I'd make sure Wade Darling goes to prison, because it's him or you. His freedom or yours. And then there's sweet little Hannah, of course . . . You'll be of no help to her behind bars. Who knows what could happen to her.' He looks me up and down with those predatory, infringing eyes as he rises to his feet, somehow even taller and broader than before. He could crush the life out of me if he wanted to. I jolt at the sound of a tired voice coming over the tannoy announcing we have reached the end of the line.

'And what if I go to the police, and tell them what happened here tonight?' I stutter. 'What then?'

He stops at the door as the tube pulls up at Aldgate Station with a squeal of the brakes. The doors open with a hiss and whoosh of stale air. He stands at the threshold, watching me. The smirk returns to his lips.

'Then your secret will be out in the open,' he says. 'And I'll pay a visit to sweet, sweet Hannah.'

He pats the gun at his hip and gives me a wink, before slipping away as suddenly as he appeared.

10

I am sitting in the empty train carriage, staring at where the gunman had been. The silence of the station on the other side of the open doors is ringing in my ears.

Guess you've got a decision to mull over, eh? It's him or you. His freedom or yours.

I had been on the train home, a journey I have taken over a hundred times. I am familiar with every jut in the tracks, recognise the faces of frequent passengers and the stops they call home. Now the familiarity of the journey has been ripped from under me and I don't recognise it at all. My blouse has stuck to my back with sweat, and my palm is indented with deep, purple craters from gripping onto the keys.

I hear a man's voice and a bolt of fear rips through me. The conductor is staring in at me from the platform edge.

'I said it's the end of the line, love. Gotta get off.'

'Sorry.'

I take my carry case and step out onto the deserted platform in a daze. All there is to be heard is the cooling thrum of the tube train as it winds down, and the distant whisper of traffic calling down the stairs from street level.

I am the only passenger. The man from the tube is nowhere to be seen.

'You sure you're all right, love?'

I jerk again. The conductor is approaching me, his brow creased with concern.

I catch my reflection in the framed tube map behind him. My face is as white as a sheet and my eyes look empty, as though a piece of me is missing; just like the woman from the tube had appeared as she muttered to herself, bottles clinking at her feet. I manage to force enough composure to reply.

'I'm fine, thanks.'

I drag my case towards the stairs and take it by the handle as I ascend, gripping onto the rail like a lifeline, the conductor's eyes burning into my back as I go. I'm swaying from the shock, rather than the drink I'm sure he suspects.

I reach the top of the stairs and pass in a haze through the barriers. The evening chill seeps in through the open station from the street.

I step out into the night and take a deep breath of fresh air. The panic hits me as soon as it fills my airways.

Let's start with how you murdered your husband.

Tell me, did the police ever suspect you?

Hannah's a pretty girl.

I hide myself away in the nearest doorway; it feels like there is a foot crushing down upon my chest, pressing my ribcage against my organs.

The people I work for, they have a way of bringing buried secrets out into the open.

A single word makes my heart jolt.

Buried.

I raise the handle on my case and break out into a sprint, my case jolting against the uneven pavement and kicking the backs of my heels as I race for home.

They know where I buried him.

I turn the corner for my street and lurch violently as my heel cracks beneath me, snapped in two like a wishbone. I stumble out of my shoe, kick off the other with a huff of breath. I can't remember the last time I ran as fast or as far as this, and stop to catch my breath as the muscles in my legs spasm from the strain. The church sits at the other end of the street. Witnessing my sins.

I'm almost home.

I snatch up my shoes, chuck them in the carry case, and run along the street as I hunt for my keys, stray stones digging into the soles of my feet. My hands are shaking so violently that I can barely hold the key to the lock as I reach the front door.

'Evening, Neve.'

I flinch with the sound. My neighbour, Lucinda, is stood outside her door with a bin bag in her grip. She has wiped off her make-up and slipped into a baggy sweatshirt and jogging bottoms, her hair tied up in a messy bun. Very different from her work attire, selling commercial real estate. Her smile fades as she takes in the state of me.

'What on earth happened to your shoes?'

I look down at my feet and see blood stained between my toes. I must have stepped on glass.

'Long story,' I reply, and fit the key into the lock.

'Your foot is bleeding—'

'I'm fine.'

Leave me alone. Please.

Any other time I would stop to chat, but tonight I can't get free of her quick enough. She isn't my friendly neighbour, but a hurdle. I open the door and take my first step inside.

'Are you sure?' she asks, her voice an octave higher.

'Yes,' I snap curtly, and hike my carry case up the step. I slam the door shut behind me and sink against the door.

I heave for breath, my heart hitting the wood at my back like a jackhammer. Lucinda is a nice, thoughtful woman, and on any other night I'm sure she would say the same for me. Now I will have set off alarm bells. I can't help but think like a barrister: should tonight become pivotal in a case against me, Lucinda will remember it.

Something wasn't right. She was scared and bloodied, and completely barefoot. She looked like she was running from someone, or in a hurry to get somewhere.

I will have to make an excuse and extend my apologies. Cover my tracks. I have spent these last few years trying to appear as the perfect neighbour to avoid any suspicion after Matthew's disappearance. To keep people from noticing the blood on my hands. I can't screw it up now. But the thought of more lies makes my throat tighten. Lies upon lies upon lies. The secret I have kept all these years, the guilt I have kept inside. The Messenger has dragged them out into the open.

Maybe I deserve this.

I should feel safe now I am home, but it is as though Matthew is here, waiting for me. I can smell him, feel him. As the memories draw in, I almost expect him to call out my name.

I peel off my jacket, drag on my nearest pair of shoes, and bolt through the living room for the kitchen. The chicken I left out this morning to defrost is sitting in its saucer in a pool of defrosted ice, tinged pink with blood. It was just another morning, nothing unusual or exemplary, with no notion of what was to come. I scramble at the lock on the back door, throw it open, and sprint.

Stray locks of hair stick to the sweat beading at my temples, and the sky has started to spit, but all I can think about is what lies ahead. The grass is damp with the night, licking at my ankles. I imagine Lucinda watching me run into the darkness from her window.

When I returned back inside, I caught sight of her running down the garden from my window, despite the dark and the rain. I have never seen her like that before. It was as if she had lost her mind.

I clamber over the wire fence separating the lawn from the train tracks, and wince as it claws at my inner thighs. Long, jagged rips run down my inseam.

I stand before the moonlit rails, my thighs smarting. The tracks stretch along the back of the terraced houses and go on for miles. I peer at my watch. The next train is in five minutes or so, passing the back of my house at quarter-hour intervals.

The stones between the tracks move and dislodge beneath my feet, and I stop before the small patch of woodland on the other side. The past comes to me in violent flashes.

Thwack.

I hear Matthew's head crack open.

Thwack.

Blood splatters against my face.

Thwack.

He's near dead, but I keep on hitting.

Thwack. Thwack. Thwack.

I haven't been here since, but the memories are as fresh as if it were yesterday. The smell of blood creeps into my nostrils. Nervous sweat slinks down my sides. Seeing it, hearing it, it's enough to make me sick. The guilt feels solid, swelling in my abdomen; a meaty black mass inside of me. I'd vomit it up if I could; stick my fingers in my mouth and prod the back of my throat until it was steaming on the cold ground.

I head into the darkness, making my way through the small knot of trees, drifting between the past and the present in my mind.

Thwack.

Twigs and undergrowth crack beneath my feet.

Thwack.

I count the trees, following the mental map inside my head.

Thwack. Thwack. Thwack.

I freeze when I reach it, and my knees buckle. I catch myself against the nearest trunk.

Someone has marked the tree with an aerosol paint can, the colour red as blood. X marks the spot.

I drop to my knees before the tree with a crunch from the undergrowth, my husband's body buried directly beneath me. I scratch helplessly at the red paint until my fingertips are bloodied and torn and bark has dug beneath my nails. Rivers of tears snake towards my jaw as the church clock tower strikes the hour, each gong of its bell calling through the darkness.

They know what I did. They know everything.

11

Three days until the trial

I ride the Metropolitan Line, listening to the jarring squeak of people's shoes after getting caught in the rain, the rustle of wet anoraks. The sort of sounds that make one's teeth numb. I grit them together and look down at my shaking hands.

I cut my fingernails right back to the beds after breaking them against the tree. There are still splinters dug deep into my fingertips, littered with small cuts where I managed to tweeze out others. After I had found the mark on the tree, I ran back inside, saddled myself with supplies, and returned to the scene, scrubbing at the trunk until the air reeked of chemicals and I had bleached the life out of the bark; its dark brown shell turned off-white, like bone. As for the cut on my foot, thankfully it only needed a plaster. I close my eyes and try to calm myself.

I spent the night pacing, unable to sit still in case my panic took hold and consumed me entirely. But nothing helped me escape *the fear*. The fear that no matter what I do, the truth will come out in the end, as if I had buried a bomb among the trees rather than a body, and any minute it will blow my life to smithereens. It has been ticking for three long years; the persistent backdrop to my every thought.

Guilt tugs at me. The consequences of one wrong act ripping through those closest to him and changing their lives forever. People often said my husband adored me in ways they had never seen before. And then I took a golf club and ground his skull into the hallway floor.

I am woozy with exhaustion, and my jaw throbs from grinding my teeth through the night. My first instinct was to run. I didn't know where. I didn't know how. It wasn't a logical train of thought, but visceral. I can feel it even now, twitching incessantly in my legs.

His freedom or yours.

Sweet, sweet Hannah.

When I sat in the aftermath of what I had done, dripping with my husband's blood, my first thought was to call the police and confess. Pay the price for my sudden burst of rage. I picked up my mobile phone, the screen bloodied in my grip, and pressed one nine, then the other, my thumb shaking over the third. I paused. If I confessed to what I had done, I wouldn't just lose my job, my freedom. I would lose the only family I have ever known. Hannah and Maggie would never speak to me again, and I would have no one else in the world.

Now, their love is bittersweet. When Hannah looks at me, I shiver with shame. I took away the person she loved more than anyone else in the world, and here I am, taking that affection as my own, to fulfil my desperate need for a family. I thought the toll would only be against me; that if Hannah and Maggie didn't know what I'd done, we could carry on with my secret buried deep within me. But now the price is to be paid in the form of the Messenger, putting Hannah's safety in jeopardy because of me and my lies.

How did they discover what I did? I left no trail of where to look or how to find him. I did the deed alone, in the dead of night. Even the police couldn't find him, with their countless searches and sniffer dogs, which had been fooled by the rabbit carcass that I'd found by the tracks and buried just above his grave to throw off the scent.

Now my secret has finally been dug up.

Wade Darling mustn't get off. He is to go to prison for a very long time.

My stomach pitches at the memory of his low, menacing tone.

The client conference is within the hour. I am expected to sit before my client while quietly planning how I can twist his case and condemn him. I place a hand on my stomach to keep it calm. I can't throw the case for my own gain, however desperate my circumstances may be. The sense of duty is engraved in me. There is right, and there is wrong; black and white. There is no grey area to use to one's own advantage, or the justice system would collapse like a house of cards. Pull one rule away, and the whole thing topples.

I can't call the police either. They pose just as much of a threat as the Messenger. I might as well be handing myself into their charge and leaving Hannah to fend for herself.

The only person I know who could possibly help me is dead. Adrian Whittaker went through this very dilemma: he had the same ultimatum, the same goal thrust upon him. I wonder what secret he had that the Messenger held against him. We all have skeletons in our closets. But not all of us have them buried at the foot of the garden.

If I don't do this, they'll hurt Hannah, and everyone will know.

I think of all the heinous things they might do to her,

imagining all the possible ways she might die in gruesome, heart-skipping detail, all the while wondering why. Dying not for her sins, or her father's, but mine.

I wonder how I would throw the trial, if I had to. When I took the case, the possibility of losing the trial seemed almost inevitable: no other suspects in the police investigation, only his fingerprints on the murder weapon, the severe depression he experienced leading up to the murders. But after working with Antony last night, we have found our path to redeem him: Alex Finch could be the perfect scapegoat to completely undermine the police's investigation and have the case thrown out. So if I were to sabotage the trial to save Hannah and myself, I would have to keep that from happening. I'd have to somehow stop Antony from chasing the lead he is so keen to secure.

The carriage feels hot and tight, and I struggle to catch my breath where I am trapped between the passengers on either side of me. I dig my fingernails into my thighs.

Who does the Messenger work for? Who would go to these lengths for a conviction?

Just like when I work a case, I immediately think of the person's motive. Whoever the Messenger works for, they want Wade Darling to pay for his alleged crimes. By law, my client is innocent until proven guilty. His fate isn't their decision to make, nor is it mine. It is down to the jury and the jury alone. Whoever the Messenger works for clearly isn't willing to take that chance.

The Viklunds. It has to be. Not only are they related to Yolanda and her children by blood, they have the criminal means to master something like this. The family seems to evade the criminal justice system at their own will. Police charges are dropped. Court cases fall through and never appear before a judge. If they have Eddie Chester in their pocket, I am sure they have many others in the profession who can be bought into doing their bidding. Or maybe they have more people like me, forced to trade in secrets.

If we pushed back the trial, I would have more time to try and get out of this situation, try to find another way to protect Hannah and still give my client a fair trial. Keep the world from knowing what I did.

I can't decide what to do now. I need time to think, to breathe, and get through this conference.

I hear my stop announced over the speakers and take hold of the railing to steady me as I get to my feet. As I approach the doors, the hairs on the back of my neck rise to attention, sensing something that stops me dead in my tracks. The heat of someone's gaze prickling on my skin.

The Messenger.

My entire body goes cold. I feel like a doe stood in the cross-hairs of a rifle, waiting to be blown away. He will look like an average tube passenger to everyone else. He had appeared that way to me before he approached. He wears dark jeans and the same large trainers, a black tee and hooded sweatshirt. That black cap covering the grey. He blends into the commuter crush perfectly. No one would suspect he is holstering a gun at his hip. The tension is so thick between us that everyone else inside the carriage fades into nothing but wet, rustling shapes.

The doors whizz open and I force my way onto the platform, pushing through the maze of hot, slick bodies as I yank my carry case behind me. A woman yelps as it jostles over her foot.

I shoot a look over my shoulder and scan for his face among the scrum. I wonder what they would do, if he shot me now. I imagine the crowd parting like the Red Sea as my body slumped to the ground, a brief beat of silence before the screams began echoing through the tunnel. If the shot didn't kill me, their panic would. Crushing me beneath the stampede. Boots breaking my ribs. High heels piercing my face.

'Can you stop pushing me?' the man in front spits, his face scrunched into a snarl.

The stairwell leading to the ground level is hot and airless. Almost as if the walls are creeping inwards and pressing us into one mass of flesh. I stumble on the steps as the crowd moves upwards and scramble for the railing, but I can't reach it. My lungs continue to shrink, and shrink.

We reach the escalators, and I latch onto the black railing, my pulse pounding in my grip. As we pass halfway, I steal a look over my shoulder. He is stood on the escalator too, with just seven people between us, that knowing smirk carved into his face.

I scramble for my phone as I near the end of the escalator and rush towards the barriers, almost slipping on the wet, tiled floor, scanning my e-pass at the nearest gateway. The confirmation beep seems to take a lifetime. I stand, shaking and silently pleading for the barriers to part. When they finally open, I rush through them before being yanked back with such violence that I let out a yelp, and whip around. My case is stuck between the barrier doors. I pull at the handle furiously to try to dislodge it, until hair falls in my face, and my cheeks flush hot.

'*Miss*, don't do that!' the ticketmaster says from the other side of the barrier. The passengers on the other side are all glaring at me, tutting. Two teenage girls are laughing at me. He taps his card against the reader and the doors open. I almost lose my balance as the case gives, and whip around without thanks, looking for the Messenger. Waiting to see his face smirking out at me from the crowd.

I step out into the pouring rain. A shoulder knocks me to the left. A briefcase hits the back of my knee from the right. I walk blindly as the rain falls in my eyes, fighting my umbrella that quickly turns inside out with a gust of wind. Exhaust fumes from the road scratch at my throat and my lips taste of rust from the rain. I am just about to hide in the nearest doorway when I feel a large hand grasp onto my arm. I tear myself free with a cry and spin around.

It's Antony.

'Christ, sorry. I didn't mean to scare you. Are you all right?'

I must look horrendous: panicked and breathless, my shirt and blazer soaked through, hair plastered to my face. He is completely dry under his umbrella, and always looks and smells so clean, but for the cigarette burning between his fingers. There is not a hair out of place in his dark brown quiff. I look about me, but the Messenger is nowhere in sight.

'You all right?' he asks again, holding his umbrella over the both of us. His aftershave fills my nostrils.

'Fine,' I force out, and nod towards the tube. 'It's too hot down there.'

'Tell me about it. It should be illegal, cramming us all together like that. Like cows in a bloody cattle car.'

He catches me looking down at his cigarette.

'Want one?' he asks, before taking a drag.

You have no idea.

'I quit,' I mutter absently.

'Good on you.' He takes one last puff and crushes it underfoot. 'Let's get a cab. We can catch up on the case on the way.'

He stands at the kerb and flags one down to a quick

succession of horns from disgruntled drivers, taking my carry case and opening the door for me in one swoop. I clamber inside and sink back into the seat, before peering out of the window at the bustle of people leaving the tube. A mass of faces, void in the eyes, zombie-like in energy and formation. That's when I see his eyes peering out at me from behind the blur of passers-by. The Messenger is stood in a doorway of a closed-down butcher's shop. Watching me. Smiling.

Antony slams the door behind him, breaking me out of my trance with a jolt.

He gives the driver the address before turning to me with a grin. My heart is still racing, but there is an element of relief, being safely away from the Messenger and ending his pursuit. It takes all of my focus to meet Antony's eyes.

'I was up all night looking into Alex Finch. Wade was telling the truth about Finch's life falling apart. Not only were his personal finances hit hard by the failure of the business, but his marriage broke down, too: Mrs Finch asked for a divorce *three days* before the murders.' His eyes glitter with excitement as dread seeps through me. 'Once we find out how far Finch's obsession went with Wade and Yolanda, we'll have a motive that practically mirrors the prosecution's accusations of Wade Darling, and undermines the police investigation pinned against him.'

This is why I suggested Mr Darling hire him. Antony is ambitious, meticulous. He gravitates towards a challenge, rather than buckling beneath it. It's exactly what I want in an acting solicitor. That is, until now.

I must stop Antony from asking Mr Darling too many key questions about Mr Finch until I come up with a plan. But how can I possibly avoid it, when that is the very purpose of this client conference?

If I can't stop Antony from progressing with the trial, I will have to stop it completely. I need to persuade our client to request more time. I'll have more of a window to find a way out of this.

As the cab pulls away, I peer out the window towards the butcher's shop in search of the Messenger, but he is nowhere to be seen.

12

As we get out of the cab outside the Darling residence, Antony asks again if I'm all right. I tear my attention from the lone photographer stood twenty feet from the drive, snapping photos of us, the camera's lens seemingly blinking with each shot.

'I'm fine,' I reply, forcing a smile. 'Just tired. Late night working on the case.'

He nods, seemingly placated, and we head up the garden path. Every window at the front of the property is shielded by drawn curtains and blinds, keeping out prying eyes and the photographer's zoom lens. It adds a melancholic air to the property, as if the Darlings' sadness pulses behind the glass. Plants in flowerpots that Marianne would have bought to brighten up the place have been left to die in winter, their old stalks slinking down the sides of each pot like brown, withered vines.

I wish my lie to placate Antony had soothed me too. I wish I was merely tired, rather than absolutely terrified.

All I need to do is persuade Wade to delay the trial, so we have more time to prepare. I am not leading him astray.

My heart thumps wildly against my ribs as Antony knocks on the front door.

At least, not yet.

'Don't dive straight in about Mr Finch,' I say. 'It's clearly a touchy subject for him and we don't want him to shut us out.'

Before Antony can reply, Marianne Darling answers the door, which pulls against the security chain as she peers through the gap. As soon as she recognises us, she shuts the door to unfix the chain and opens it wide, making sure to stand near-flat to the wall to avoid the photographer, before shutting it again.

'He's been out there every day for the past two weeks,' she says, as she peers through the peephole. 'He doesn't say a word. He just stands there, staring at the windows in the hope we'll open the blinds and give him a shot. You should see him when he sees a twitch of the curtains or hears the squeaky hinge of the front door. Jumps up like a dog hearing the chime of its dinner bowl. Greedy little—' She clears her throat, seemingly remembering herself and the company she's in, and turns back to us. 'I can't wait until all of this is over.'

Her naivety is almost endearing, if not concerning. Her son is embroiled in one of the biggest criminal trials to have taken place in the last ten years, and yet she speaks of it as if it will all float into the ether the moment the trial ends. She hasn't thought of the stream of articles that will keep the story alive, both online and in print, raking over their story year after year. Photographers will want photos of her and her son for decades to come. *Where is Wade Darling Now?* The headline reads in my mind. There will be documentaries commissioned. Podcasts rehashing old ground. YouTubers relaying the story to creepy music in the background, to a demographic the papers will have otherwise missed. This isn't a blip in their lives they will leave behind them. They are wrapped up in a legend that is set to be told and retold long after they have gone.

'How is Wade today?' I ask, noticing the slight shake to my voice.

I catch a brief flicker of sadness in her eyes at the mention of his name.

'He's doing fine,' she replies, unconvincingly, her eyes falling anywhere but on mine. 'Let's go through.'

Marianne guides us along the hall to the dining room we had occupied the day before. Wade, however, is nowhere to be seen.

'He didn't get much sleep last night,' she says, when Antony and I both turn to her after finding his seat empty. 'I think yesterday drained him. He's been sleeping this morning to catch up. Please,' she signals to the tray on the table. 'Help yourself. I'll go and get him.'

Antony and I take to our seats in silence. The room is stuffy and artificially hot from the central heating, making my skin itch mercilessly beneath my clothes. Sweat begins to break above my lip.

If Antony succeeds in getting the details on Alex Finch from Wade this morning, we've effectively got his route of defence: we'll have a man the police failed to suspect, an investigation that was pinned against our client from the start. With enough details, and evidence to back up Wade's claims, I will have the opportunity to create doubt in the jurors' minds.

You must be sure that the client is guilty, beyond a shadow of a doubt.

Doubt. It's a defence barrister's main weapon in their arsenal. And Antony is set on delivering it.

It's all happening too fast. The trial is just days away. The defence argument is almost formed. Things are aligning at the very moment I need them to stall. My heart races.

Hannah's a pretty girl.

I think of the Messenger's tone, the sly smile curling up from the corner of his lip.

I just need a bit more time.

'You don't look well,' Antony says beside me, breaking me from my thoughts with a jolt. 'You're all sweaty.'

What is he thinking? What does he suspect? Can he sense my guilt, see the fear in my eyes?

Just as Antony opens his mouth to speak again, Marianne returns.

'I'm sorry,' she says. 'Wade says he isn't feeling up to it today. He's too exhausted.'

I have to fight back my sigh of relief. Antony, however, looks fraught.

'I can only imagine how hard this is for him, but with the greatest respect, we don't have much more time. If Wade wants to win this trial, he'll have to push through.'

I can see he is sweating too, but for different reasons to me. I had been panicking at the thought of the trial moving forward, whereas he seems fearful of it stalling. Two people supposedly on the same team, fretting over the loss of deeply opposing objectives.

'I'm sorry,' she replies. 'It's just not possible today. You'll have to come back tomorrow.'

'Tomorrow ...' he stutters. 'We don't have time for this, Mrs Darling. If we don't ensure a strong defence, your son will go to prison for up to three decades or more. It's imperative—'

'Would you excuse us a moment, Mrs Darling?' I ask.

Antony stops, his mouth open. Clearly he had hoped I would echo his thoughts.

'Of course,' she replies. 'There's no rush. Please ...' she signals the tray again. 'Do help yourselves.'

When Marianne leaves the room, the air becomes stifling again. Antony looks at me with his eyes darting up and down, trying to read my expression.

'We can't force the words out of him,' I say. 'We need him to work with us, but pushing too hard could mean he shuts down. We can't afford for that to happen.'

'We don't have time for this,' he spits under his breath. 'He either talks now or he's off to prison. You know that.'

'Or there's another option.'

'What's that?'

'We could delay the trial.'

'*What?* You heard what the judge said. No more delays.'

'McConnell won't be able to refuse, if it's conditional on the client getting a fair trial.'

'I can't believe you're considering this. We practically have the information we need to back his defence. All he needs to do is tell us what we need to know and I can hunt down the necessary evidence—'

'But he's *not* telling us, is he? We can't force this out of him, Antony. That's not how this works. We will give him a day. Visit again tomorrow and try to get him to talk. But if we don't, I'm meeting with the judge to push the trial. If we can't defend him, we have no business trying to represent him in court.'

Antony sighs and wipes his face with his hands, his pale skin flushing with blood. I wonder how late he was up last night.

'Fine. We'll give him one more day. In the meantime, we can

do some further digging to make his defence airtight. We're close to cracking this, Neve. I can feel it.'

That's what I'm afraid of.

Marianne walks back into the room.

'We'll be back tomorrow morning to speak to Wade then,' I say.

'Yes, I'm sure we can make that work.'

'It's important you do,' Antony says, as we get up from our seats and approach the hall. 'If he doesn't talk to us, he's looking at a long time behind bars.'

'I'm well aware of that, Mr Murrell,' Marianne says, prickling at his tone. 'I'll do my very best.'

We walk down the hall and through the front door, back into the cold, grey day.

I have twenty-four hours to figure out what the hell I am going to do.

13

I sit down in the wine bar, nestling in the corner of the room in a high-back leather chair, with a pile of paperwork on the coffee table before me, and reluctantly order a pot of tea rather than something stronger.

I had returned to chambers after Wade failed to appear for the conference, but soon found myself feeling caged, pacing back and forth like a lion before black, cylindrical bars. It's the sort of fear that sucks the air from one's chest, paralyses a person to the spot. After no more than an hour, I'd had to get out of there, and was only able to draw a deep breath when I turned the corner of the street, far enough away from my chambers with its inscription in the stone above the front door: *Lus est ars boni et aequi*. 'The law is the art of goodness and equity.'

I was completely unprepared this morning, going into the client conference; my only saving grace was Wade's inability to speak with us. I won't be granted the same mercy again. Next time, I must be prepared. Which means I have to work out what the hell I'm going to do.

I pick up my legal notepad, the yellow paper shining up at me, but all I can do is stare down at the pristine page as each of my fears runs through my mind.

I need to focus, treat this approach with the same emotional disconnection that I would any other case.

I take a deep breath and begin.

My first goal is to push back the trial and buy myself more time. If I can keep Wade from answering Antony's questions about Alex Finch, so that Antony is unable to paint him as a suspect the police missed, then I will have the grounds to request the delay. We can't go to trial without a sufficient defence. But Antony won't make that easy. In fact, I'm positive that he will make it virtually impossible; I won't be able to keep Antony from chasing his lead indefinitely. If I want to delay the trial, I will need to focus on Wade himself; sow seeds of doubt in his mind about our not having had enough time to prepare. That the risks of going forward as things stand will make a guilty verdict much more likely. Outnumber Antony two to one. I remember how broken Wade had seemed yesterday, unwashed and melancholic, and then this morning, when he refused to appear at all. He's clearly lost the will to fight for himself.

What if he doesn't want to push the trial back and fight for his freedom? What if he has truly given up? That would work in my favour of course, if Antony wasn't by my side, eager to continue with the set date. But if I can't stop Antony from pursuing his lead, and I can't persuade Wade to agree with pushing the trial back, we will be headed towards disaster.

I sit back in the chair, my mind spinning in dizzying circles, and take a deep breath.

If Wade won't fight for himself, his mother will. Perhaps I can get Wade to delay the trial through her. Two routes of attack. I write down Marianne's name on my pad and scribble down my thoughts.

I feel slightly buoyed by my first plan of action, until my thoughts return to the Messenger. I hear his gravelly voice in my ears, remember the smirk pulling at the corner of his lips. Dread slowly fills me up again.

Even if I give myself more time to figure out what to do about my situation, how can I possibly get out from under this stranger's grasp? I don't know for sure who employed him, or what I can possibly do to make it all go away except to go through with the Messenger's demands. And who's to say there won't be something else they want from me, after this? Another reason to hang my crime over my head, keeping Hannah in danger? Who's to say this will ever end?

If I want to escape my predicament for good, I need to find out who the Messenger is, and more importantly who sent him. If I find out who they are, and I'm able to push the trial back, I might be able to find a way to stop this before proceedings commence. But I know I can't possibly do this alone. I need someone removed from the business, yet knowledgeable. Dependable, while asking as few questions as possible. In short, I need a miracle. Stress pulses at my temples. I knead them forcefully, as if the pressure will force out the answers I need. A name springs forward in my mind. Fredrick Hurst, private investigator and former client.

It has been five years since Fredrick and I last spoke, and as I pick up my phone and scroll through my contacts, hoping I still have his number stored, I fear he might have new contact information; maybe even quit the business after he was dragged through the courts. I click on his name and type out the text, the phone quivering in my grip.

Fredrick, it's Neve Harper. Is there any chance we

could meet? Preferably somewhere where we'll be
lost in a crowd.

Having two plans of action makes my furled shoulders ease
slightly. But I know the worst task is yet to come, one I cannot
put off any longer.

I look down at my tea, which I have inadvertently left to cool
without taking more than a sip. I raise my hand to beckon the
waiter and order a medium glass of Merlot, then call him back
to request a large glass instead. For this next task, I'll need it.

My heart begins to drum inside my chest. I flick over a new
page to jot down the next stage of my plan, sick to my stomach
at the thought of what I am about to consider.

I must premeditate how to throw the trial if all else fails.

The thought of even considering it makes me flare with guilt.
My main role in the courtroom is to ensure my clients get a
fair trial; I'm the mouthpiece for the defendant, essentially the
one person in the room who is unilaterally on his side. Then
there are the moral aspects within me: what is right, and what
is wrong. What is good, and what is evil. I don't miss the irony
of this; a killer pondering their morals.

Just when I think I cannot bring myself to plan such a
betrayal, I think of Hannah. Her youth, her innocence; all the
years that lie before her. She mustn't fall to harm because of my
actions. The conflicting goals tug at me from within.

*This is only a last resort. I'm only doing this as part of a
back-up plan.*

But despite my attempts to quell my fears, it's tough to even
fathom such an act.

It's hardly worse than murder.

The waiter returns with the glass of Merlot, and I take it

with a trembling hand. I should have ordered food to go with it. I can't remember the last time I ate; this trial has completely devoured my appetite. I take a large sip and poise the tip of the pen on the page.

If I'm going to sabotage the trial without being detected, I will have to appear to be following our plan to the letter. Which means I have to essentially perform two roles at once. I must be both efficient and inefficient, supportive and deceitful.

I write down a list of the witnesses both for the prosecution and the defence, detailing their purpose while drinking the wine heartily as I go. Names peer up at me from the page, and as I take them all in, it's difficult to escape the lives hidden behind my scrawled words. This job can devour a person's soul if they're not careful. It becomes frighteningly easy to see a list of names like this as mere words on a page; to see witnesses, defendants and victims as nothing but pawns in the game. But as I look at them now, wondering how I can twist their testimonies to my advantage, I realise the magnitude the repercussions of my actions will have upon them. My actions won't just affect Wade Darling. There are multiple necks on the chopping block. I go through the list of the prosecution's witnesses to assess what evidence they will bring.

First, the prosecution will call Yolanda Darling's mother, no doubt to paint a picture of the woman she was before meeting Wade, and the ins and outs of their married life. To show the jury that the victims are more than just photos beneath the headlines: they are children, grandchildren, confidants. Rebutting testimonies like these is tough enough at the best of times: if I go in too intensely, the jury will think me heartless and calculated, but if I approach my questioning too softly, their stories could well win over the jurors. Antony won't suspect any wrongdoing on my part if I tread too lightly here, but he will expect me to go in for the kill with the next witnesses.

The crime scene personnel will be called next: the first responders who attended the scene, followed by the detective on the case, Detective Inspector Markus Hall, the witness I'm most concerned about. If Antony manages to get information on Alex Finch, I will be expected to decimate DI Hall's character and the integrity of his investigation, question repeatedly why he failed to consider other suspects in the case, until there are enough holes in his testimony that the jury will lose confidence in his version of events. This is usually my strongest skill; I've been known to have detectives leave with lumps in their throats after I'm done with them. There is no way I will be able to avoid questioning him like this; my motive would be far too clear. Which means, if I'm going to question him in the way Antony, Wade Darling and the press will expect, I will have to sabotage our case in a different way. I will have to find something else conclusive on my client that helps him fit the crime. I pick up my wine glass to take a sip and find it empty, as my phone vibrates on the surface of the coffee table.

Fredrick
Of course. Blackfriars, platform 1, 4pm?

I stare down at the message. Once I follow this path, there's no going back. I will be putting my plans into action. They won't just be ideas or scribbles on a notepad. I will be preparing to commit an act that is wrong on every ethical, moral and legal level. I lean back into the chair and close my eyes with a sigh.

I don't even know if I have to go through with it yet. I'm just assessing all of my options. I mustn't make myself sick over this, not yet.

But my plans aren't just hypothetical, not when I must actively hunt for evidence to disarm my own client's case, even if I don't use what I find; the act will have been performed. I need Fredrick to discover who the Messenger is and who he is working for, but that's not all. I have another job for him. One I will have to fall back on, should all my other options fail. It is the only way to keep Hannah safe, and keep my secret from getting out.

My phone shakes in my grasp. I look to the empty wine glass, wishing there was enough for one final sip for courage, before typing out my reply.

See you then.

As I collect my things and get ready to leave, I think of the Messenger. It's all well and good employing Fredrick to find out more about this man, but I'll need to take other measures to keep him from using my crimes against me. He knows of the body, but there will be more he has yet to find, more pieces of evidence he could pin against me.

I walk towards the door, trying not to sway, and silently make up my mind.

I need to destroy the murder weapon.

14

I stand on the platform at Blackfriars Station, perched on a bridge across the River Thames, and look out at the city. The sun has almost set, giving everything it touches a burnt, orange hew. Tower Bridge, the Shard, St Paul's Cathedral, they are all set ablaze by the sun's rays, as the darkening waters of the river slip beneath the platform.

The last time I met Fredrick Hurst, he was my client, after he had been charged with stalking by the man he had been paid to investigate. I got him off swiftly, with no case to try. He had been invasive, yes, but all within means of the law. It shouldn't have been taken to trial in the first place; a civil lawsuit maybe, but certainly not criminal. After the win, Hurst had said he would help me if I needed anything in return. I never thought I would have to cash in the favour at the time, but I'm grateful for the opportunity now.

The glass of wine I had has worn off, all but for the hollow, uneasy feeling in my legs. I could have done with another glass to calm my nerves. As I stand waiting for Fredrick to arrive, the request I have to ask of him gnaws away at me. Asking for help with discovering the identity of the Messenger and his employer is one thing, but to ask for information on my own client to potentially use against him is quite another.

From the corner of my eye, I see a figure approaching. Fredrick walks with conviction. A man with a purpose. He has shaved his head since I last saw him, and he looks skinnier than I remember, thin about the face and shoulders. But his height, standing at around six-five, gives him a commanding presence, as his long black coat billows behind him. He doesn't smile when he reaches me; he's not a smiling man.

'Ms Harper,' he says. 'A pleasure.'

'It's good to see you,' I reply, meaning it. 'Managed to stay out of trouble?'

'If I hadn't, you'd have been the first person I called.' He does smile then, or at least his version of one: the slightest rise to the corner of his mouth.

'You said you wanted to see me. This about a case?'

'Sort of.'

A train pulls up at the platform, and I turn back towards the view, staring through the plates of glass giving view to the city. I don't speak until the passengers have departed and dispersed, and the train pulls away from the platform again.

'I'm working the Darling trial.'

He whistles through his teeth.

'He did it then?'

'What makes you say that?'

He arches his brow.

'Only the worst people need the best lawyers.'

'You're not painting yourself in a very good light there, Fredrick.'

He gives me a wink. I release a heavy sigh, and cast my eyes towards the view again.

'I'm not sure how much I can say.'

'Whatever you tell me doesn't leave this platform.'

A rush of warmth flushes through me. It feels so good to be able to lumber this on someone else, even if most of the detail is missing. I won't tell him everything, but I can tell him enough, and for a minute or two I won't be alone. I look about me and find the platform empty.

'I'm being blackmailed. Someone wants me to throw the trial to ensure Wade Darling is found guilty. A man is threatening me on someone else's behalf. The only person I can think of who could be responsible is someone from the Viklund family. My client's deceased wife – the murder victim along with her two children – her maiden name is Viklund.'

Fredrick falls quiet as soon as I utter the name. In the reflection of the glass, I spot his chest deflate with a sigh. A shiver runs through me as a breeze ripples along the platform.

'And this blackmail,' he says. 'I assume the consequences of not following through are—'

'Bad.'

'How bad?'

Whoosh. Thwack.

Hannah's a pretty girl.

I swallow hard and meet his eyes.

'Really bad.'

'And you can't go to the police?'

I shake my head, and feel the sudden surge of panic return. It is as if talking of it aloud has made me finally realise how bad my situation is. I can't turn to the police for help. I can't forgo the Messenger's demands; he killed the barrister before me who tried that. The train tracks at my back feel too close all of sudden.

Fredrick doesn't ask me why, and I know then that I have made the right decision in contacting him. Anyone else would want to know what the Viklunds had against me, why I couldn't call the police. But Fredrick allows me to keep my cards close to my chest.

'And you know they'll go through with it, if you don't comply?'

'Adrian Whittaker, the lawyer who worked the case before me—'

'The chap who jumped in front of a train?'

It had hit the news due to his stature, but still, it surprises me that Fredrick knows of him.

'He didn't jump.'

My voice comes out hoarse, the fear gradually choking me. Hurst nods solemnly.

'What do you need me to do?' he asks.

'I need to know who the Messenger is, and who is employing him. Maybe there is something I can use against them in return – blackmail for blackmail. Anything at all to give me some leverage. You know, I'll keep their secret if they keep mine.'

He shakes his head.

'If it's the Viklunds we're talking about here . . . they don't work that way. The only people who know their secrets are either within their close circle, or they're dead. Adrian Whittaker is proof of that.'

He is being gentler than usual. The hard man who doesn't smile, softening beside me. I wonder if he has a child, a partner. What his life looks like once he hangs up his coat of an evening.

'What does this man look like?'

'He's tall, perhaps six-two, six-three. White, late-forties, acne scars on his cheeks. Deep voice. He was wearing a sports cap, hooded sweatshirt and jeans when I met him.' I pause for thought, realising I've just described tens of thousands of men in London alone. 'I'm sorry, that's probably not much help.'

'I'll do some digging around, and see what I can find. I'll look into the Viklunds first. I'm sure that'll lead me to him.'

'What sort of fee would you take for a job like this?'

He waves me away.

'Pro bono. That's what you guys say, isn't it?'

'You really don't need to do that.'

'I know.'

We fall silent. The lights have flickered on above us, and beyond the glass the sun has set; the Thames is black but for the city lights reflecting in its waves, with only the last few embers of light shining on the glass Shard, the very tip of St Paul's dome.

'What is it they have against you, exactly?'

My mind darkens with memories of the past. My monstrous crimes; the endless list of sins I've committed. I wonder if he would still help me if he knew what I have done.

'They know something about me – something I've done. It was years ago, and no one knows but me; at least, that's what I thought. It isn't something they could have discovered recently; it had to have been when it happened, but that means they would have to have been watching me before they even had a need . . . when the Darlings were alive.'

He nods.

'People like the Viklunds like to have influential people in their pockets to call on should they need them. Most can be bought, but others . . . they need a push.'

'So, there's a possibility they've been watching me?'

'Like I said, you're one of the best. They would want you on side. All they had to do was keep an eye on you and wait for you to trip up; to give them something they could use against you later.'

'But they didn't choose me for the case, not initially.'

'You probably weren't the only person they kept an eye on.'

So they had been watching Adrian too. I wonder how many others they have kept tabs on. Do they sit in the public gallery, watching us at work, picking us out like they are at a cattle auction? They will have enough people on their list in case I don't comply, like Adrian failed to do. Back-up after back-up.

'Let me see what I can do. When do you need to hear back?'

'The trial starts Monday.'

'I better get to work then.'

We stand before each other, unsure what the proper eti-quette is to wishing farewell to the private investigator who is your last hope, and for him, a dead woman walking. He touches my arm and gives it a gentle squeeze.

'You're tough, Neve. Remember that.'

I have one last thing to ask him. The request that, once uttered, cannot be taken back. This will set the wheels of my deception in motion. Even if I find a way to evade the Messenger's conditions without throwing the trial, I will have to live with the fact that I did this.

'There's one more thing.' I slip a file from my carry case. 'I need you to find information on someone.'

I can't bear to look him in the eye in case he sees the shame within them. He takes the file and peeks at the first page. His demeanour changes when he reads Wade Darling's name.

'What kind of information?'

I have to practically force the words from my mouth.

'The damning kind.'

I still can't bear to meet his gaze, to glimpse the disapproval in his eyes.

'If he did something bad in his past, I need to know of it. If he ever raised a hand to a spouse, failed to gain consent in a sexual act, conned anyone in business. Even a speeding ticket. I need to know of every mistake he's ever made.'

'Why would you want to know about something like that? To bury it?'

I don't answer. My silence, it seems, is telling.

'I see,' he says.

I finally look at him then, terrified I've lost his support, taking his confidentiality a step too far.

'So you'll do it?'

He looks deeply into my eyes. Perhaps he is assessing if I am someone he should trust; if I am a good woman in a bad situation, or whether I'm simply bad to the core.

'I will.'

He heads off the way he came without another word, the coat billowing behind him as he goes, as I process what I have just done; the betrayal I have set into motion. It is as though I have taken the first step off a ledge, my foot dangling above an unknown abyss, as I silently pray not to fall.

15

I return to an ice-cold house and reluctantly shrug off my coat, rubbing my arms to get my blood racing as I turn on the heating. The radiators crackle to life, with the familiar sound of the boiler purring from the kitchen. It isn't long before Fredrick's words drift back into my mind.

Families like the Viklunds like to have influential people in their pockets, to call on them should they need them. All they had to do was keep an eye on you and wait for you to trip up; to give them something they could use against you later.

It's likely the Viklunds have been keeping tabs on me, but how? Just the thought of them lurking nearby without my knowledge makes it feel like my home has been violated in some way, like an unwanted touch. Just like when Matthew went missing, and the crime scene investigators searched about the house in their crisp white suits, rifling through every drawer and cupboard, opening every book on the shelves in the hope something incriminating fell out. They pulled the sofa cushions apart, yanked out their innards and stuffed them back haphazardly, peered behind every picture frame on the wall. But they didn't find anything to help discover what had happened to Matthew. Not even a single trace of blood.

Whoosh. Thwack.

I scrunch my eyes shut as the memory comes. The scene in my mind is bathed in red: blood splatters, a pool at my feet, swipes of it sprayed violently up the walls from the swing of the club, all unravelling as the church bells chimed and I stood above my husband's body, wet and dripping with him, club in hand.

I used to think I would be useless in a moment like that. But despite my shock, my legal knowledge and need for damage control crept through. I thought back to cross-examining a forensic crime scene investigator about blood traces, or lack thereof, at a crime scene. She explained that when a suspect used a chlorine-based bleach product to clean up a crime scene to cover their tracks, blood still remained, even after multiple applications. However, when oxygen bleach was used, it eradicated all traces. Environment-conscious homeowners using the more natural counterpart have no idea they are using a product that could help them clean up a murder scene without a trace. It even smells less potent, further disguising when excessive amounts are used. But what I didn't know was that, while I was scrubbing away at the evidence, the Viklunds were somehow watching my every move.

The doorbell rings, ripping through the silence in the house. I slowly make my way towards the door and slide back the cover on the peephole. Hannah stares back at me, fidgeting on the doorstep from the cold.

I turn the latch and shiver as the evening breeze slips into the house. Hannah looks up at me from the street. Tears shimmer in her eyes.

'Han, what's the matter?'

She promptly bursts into tears, covering her face with her spare hand. In the other is a black duffel bag filled to the brim. I usher her inside and shut the door behind her.

The Messenger. He's approached her, like he accosted me. That's my first thought. I think of the places I should have jabbed him with my keys when I had the chance. The soft skin at the base of his throat. Those dark, repulsive eyes.

Hannah sniffs back tears as she dashes the streams from her cheeks with her sleeve.

'Nan and I . . . we . . .'

She can't seem to catch her breath, huffing for air between words.

'Give me all that and sit down.'

I take her bag and coat, placing the duffel at the foot of the stairs and her coat on the banister, and sit beside her on the sofa. Her face is blotchy and red.

'We had an argument,' she says. 'Nan is such a bitch.'

You're telling me.

'What happened?'

She takes a deep, shuddering breath, before sighing it away and looking down at her lap, picking at a loose thread on her sleeve until the fabric bunches.

'She said we shouldn't see you anymore because Dad's gone. That we were holding onto you for all the wrong reasons. That . . . that keeping you in the fold wouldn't keep Dad's memory alive.'

A twang of pain nicks at my chest. I knew Maggie was cold, and knew what she thought of mine and Hannah's relationship, but I didn't foresee her stooping this low. Actively trying to pry us apart.

Maggie knows they are the only family I have.

'She feels threatened, Han, that's all. We're close; it must be hard for her at times.'

'Why are you sticking up for her?' she asks, brow furrowed.

'I'm not. What she said was wrong, and hurtful. But that doesn't mean things have to change between us if you don't want them to. I want you in my life for as long as you want me in yours, and no one can change that. Not even your nan.'

Her expression softens, her shoulders lowering, and I think of her as a six-year-old again, giggling as Sam licked at her. How Matthew and I looked at one another over her head. If only we had known what lay ahead. We'd have bolted in opposite directions.

'Did you run away?' I ask.

'She knew I was coming here, if that's what you mean. I told her I would rather be with you than her.'

I glance towards the home phone and see the flashing red dot of the voicemail inbox. Maggie will have filled it to capacity with her angry ramblings, no doubt. When I look back to Hannah at the other end of the sofa, I see the nerves have returned, that same desperate hope flickering in her eyes again. I know what's coming before she even opens her mouth.

'Can I stay here for a while?'

I look into her eyes, which are the spitting image of her father's. It is almost as if Matthew is staring back at me from the other side of the sofa. A memory resurfaces in a sudden flash: Matthew's death stare, his eyes locked with mine in a lifeless gaze.

'How long were you thinking?'

Tonight, she looks and seems far younger than her sixteen years. Sometimes, she almost appears as a grown woman in the way she holds herself, but as she sits on the sofa with her cheeks flushed from the cold and her eyes as wide as a doe's, she looks more like that little girl again.

'Not forever,' she replies. 'Not yet anyway. I thought maybe we could . . . try it?'

We haven't even set foot in the courtroom, and already the Darling trial has taken over my life. I don't know how I could possibly juggle having Hannah waiting for me at home, what with chambers calling for me to sit at my desk until the early hours working on the case. And if the Viklunds are watching me, having Hannah stay here could put her in danger, couldn't it? Staying here could put her in harm's way. But with Hannah in front of me, the Messenger's threat against her feels all the more real now, like a living, breathing thing, watching us from the corner of the room. I would be able to keep a close eye on her, if she were here.

I can't let anything happen to her.

Her eyes fall to her lap, her throat bobbing with a nervous swallow.

'It's okay, I get it.'

'No,' I reply quickly. 'I want you here, of course I do. I was just thinking how we could make it work with my trial.'

Hannah quickly springs to life. 'You wouldn't even know I was here. I have school, and homework, and a bunch of my friends live nearby. I cook for myself when Nan is out, and I wash up every night. I'll clean up after myself and I promise I won't get in your way.'

My heart breaks at the excited tone of her voice. If only she knew who I truly am. What I am. A monster to fear, rather than a stepmother to love. If she knew of what I did, she would hate me more than anyone else in the world.

'Let me speak to Nan. Why don't you go and run yourself a bath?'

She jumps up eagerly, as if I might suddenly change my mind, and heads for the stairs.

I had decided too quickly. I should have put her off, thought about this more thoroughly. This trial, and the task I've been given to destroy it, will be enough to drive me crazy in the coming days. Having Hannah here, greeting me each morning, sharing the sofa of an evening, the very physical embodiment of my guilt looking me directly in the eye? It will be enough to push me over the edge.

But helping her is the least I can do, after what I've done.

'Erm, Neve?' Hannah calls from upstairs. 'What's that?'

'What's what?' I shout back.

'That.'

I climb the stairs, wondering what she could have found. Living on my own, I could be – or should I say *used* to be, what with Hannah staying here now – careless about where I left things, with no one around to see them. When I reach the top of the stairs and see Hannah standing in the hall, my heart pitches.

She is staring down at the mess I made of the carpet during my sleepwalking episode.

I had cleaned up as much as I could, after I scrubbed the burning bleach from my body, but the carpet could in no way be redeemed. There is a large yellowish-white pattern all over the hall floor.

Hannah looks at me, awaiting my answer.

'Oh, that. I spilt a glass of wine and accidentally used bleach to try and clean it up. Made more of a mess than I'd started with. I've been meaning to pull that up.'

'Oh, well . . . you don't have to do it now,' she says, as I get to my knees and start pulling the carpet from the hem. 'I just wondered what it was, that's all.'

I pull the edge of the carpet free with a grunt, hearing the fibres rip from the tacks keeping it down, and pause when I spot chips and dents in the floorboards beneath. I'd made them with the golf club, whacking the floor on the odd time I missed Matthew's head.

'You're right,' I say, and push it back down with shaking hands until it lies flat. 'I'll do it another day.'

'Are you okay?' she asks, her tone tinged with concern.

I feel dizzy, have done ever since I saw the marks I made with the club, as if all the blood has drained from my head. All the blood had drained from Matthew's too, in this very spot.

I grab the banister to get to my feet.

'I'm fine, you go and run the bath.'

As soon as the bathroom door shuts behind her, I drag the rug from my bedroom and out into the hallway, and place it over the stain. It covers most of it, with only the odd yellow splash creeping out from the sides. Another reminder of everything I've done.

I must be more careful, now that Hannah is staying here. God knows what else she could find.

I am sat up in bed working on the case, pages of the brief fanned out before me and scrunched-up yellow pages from my notepad strewn across the bedspread, while listening to Hannah unpacking her things on the other side of the wall. The more she makes this house her own, the less it feels like home to me. I have grown so accustomed to the silence, my own familiar way of things. Now I feel myself treading carefully when I walk, keeping myself covered in case she steps into the room without knocking.

This was a mistake. I never should have allowed her to stay.

Maggie hadn't taken it well on the phone. I barely said a

word before she began shouting down the line at me. It went this way for most of the call before she finally hung up, cutting me off mid-word.

Sitting across from Hannah this evening has made my situation all the more urgent. The Messenger's threat of harming her had been terrifying but almost otherworldly, as if it were nothing more than a frightening hypothetical. Now she is here, sharing the same rooms, breathing the same air, making the threat dangling above our heads feel overwhelmingly real. I have been going over my plan for the witnesses ever since, looking for ways I can navigate each cross-examination with my main objective in mind. My eyes are burning from lack of sleep, and I occasionally feel the pull of my lids as my brain desperately tries to rest.

I have worked far longer than I should have, and not just because of the approaching conference tomorrow morning, but in fear that when I close my eyes to end the day, I will sleep-walk again. I think of Hannah finding me, how frightening it would be.

A yawn rips from my mouth. I collect up the pages of the brief and tidy them away in defeat, throwing the discarded balls of yellow paper to the floor for the morning. I can't stay awake forever. I pause when I see the details of one of the notes I'd written: *destroy club tomorrow.* I rip it into as many pieces as I can and pile them on the bedside table, before switching off the light. I lie in bed trying not to think of the sounds it made, the mess it left behind. My heart races at the thought of seeing the murder weapon again, feeling its cool metal neck.

Whoosh.

Thwack.

Crack goes his head.

I wince and turn over in bed, lying in the dark as I listen to Hannah go about her unpacking. All the while, she has no idea what danger I have put her in.

She shouldn't be here, it just isn't safe.

Eventually, I hear her head towards the bathroom to get ready for bed, then return to her room with the quiet click of her door, as she too settles down for the night.

I slip out of bed, take the chair from my dressing table, and jam the back of it beneath the door handle. Only then am I able to close my eyes to sleep.

⚖

I wake with a gasp and the call of the church bells.

The cold night air sucks into my chest. My skin is speckled from the elements, the icy breeze billowing the few clothes I have on. I look about me, blinking away the confusion, but all I see is darkness.

Gong.

Gong.

Gong.

I am not in my bed. I am standing, barefoot, my toes almost blue against the dark earth. I am wearing nothing but night shorts and a cotton vest, and a cardigan that is inside out, whipping against me as the wind picks up. My cheeks are wet where I have been crying, tears I have no memory of shedding. My eyes slowly adjust to the dark, and slowly but surely, I realise where I am.

I am stood before Matthew's grave.

My chest heaves up and down as I eye the untouched earth at my feet. The cold air burns my throat. Tears fall as the panic takes hold and I look about me, only to find the dark night's shadows each way I turn, all except for the train tracks gleaming beneath the moon. Beyond the fence, my lawn sparkles with dew. All the lights in the house are off but for the kitchen, where I must have lit the way before leaving the house in the middle of the night. The bell tower peers over the roofs, its last chiming bell echoing through the night.

The hyperventilation doesn't slow. The panic doesn't ease.

Hannah.

I rush towards the fence, the stones among the tracks digging into my naked soles, and straddle over to the other side. My feet slip on the wet grass and leave footprints along the patio as I reach the back door, which I had left ajar, squeaking faintly on its hinges.

The house is freezing, the air damp with the outside chill. I creep inside, clicking the door shut behind me, and look about me for any mess I might have made in my sleep. The number of times I have gone about supposedly tidying, putting files and books in the oven, the washing machine running with an empty drum, pyjamas soiled with urine where I'd gone without properly undressing. That's if I'm lucky. The bad nights are when they are linked to my past: waking up surrounded by bleach, or stood above my husband's grave.

I sway up the stairs, still blinking away sleep, and creep towards the door to Hannah's bedroom by the light of my own, where the chair lies on its side and the door has been left wide open. My grip shakes on the handle, and the internal springs stretch loudly as I push down. The hinges creak with the movement, light from across the hall moving with the motion, until it illuminates her peaceful, sleeping face.

I release a heavy sigh as I shut the door quietly and creep back to my room, picking up the chair and replacing it by my dresser as I go. I know I won't get another wink of sleep. The stress of my wandering will fester within me, and I'll only toss and turn fitfully until dawn. The clock on my bedside table tells me it has gone three in the morning.

I slip into my dressing gown, pick up the work that I'd left beside my bed before sleeping, and take it downstairs with me. As I pour myself into the trial, I try to ignore the relevance of where I had woken up; my subconscious leading me to my worst deed, and the biggest problem I have yet to solve.

Matthew.

16

Two days until the trial

If someone tells you not to think of something, what do you immediately think of? It's the same with sleepwalking. You tell yourself you won't, that you have control over your own autonomy. And then you wake up in the cold, in the dark, far away from your bed, not knowing how you got there or what you've done.

Before this trial, I hadn't sleepwalked in a long time. I'd had a bad relapse after Matthew's death, but as the months passed, the sleepwalking slowly began to ease. The specialists said my sleepwalking could have been triggered by the trauma of my childhood, lacking a stable home, which became a pattern with stressful life events thereafter. I couldn't sit for an exam, or start a new job, or go on a first date without spending the night wandering. Now the trial is bringing it out of me again.

I stand in the garage on the small lot tucked away a few streets from my house, waiting for the beep from the machine charging up the battery of my old trusty Audi. Matthew and I bought it for driving out of the city at weekends, or for when we had business meetings or trials outside of London. The garage is musky and smells of damp, its asbestos-clad structure covered with thick tendrils of spider webs.

I had left the house at six this morning. I couldn't bear the thought of Hannah's face, excited at the thought of us living together, in case she saw my dread staring back at her. Instead, I took the coward's way out, leaving the spare house keys on the breakfast table with a note and twenty pounds in cash, telling her to text me if she needs me. On my way out, I had to step over the morning paper on the doormat, where Wade and I stare up from the roll; another of Eccleston's articles about the case that I can't bring myself to read.

I stand listening to the whir of the battery charger, trying and failing to calm my frantic heart. I'd dressed in casual wear for this morning's deed: a plain grey sweatshirt, old dark jeans that are an inch too loose, and dirty trainers, a navy cap covering my face. My suit hangs in a carrier in the back of the car with my heels in the footwell, ready to change into after the deed is done.

Soon enough, I will be holding the weapon that killed my husband. A Callaway 'Big Bertha' golf iron: clad with black carbon at the tip, its steel spine reaching just below my rib-cage. The last time I felt the cool metal in my hands was the morning I cleaned off the blood, bleaching the club within an inch of its life. Just the thought of it brings the memory of the whistle it made as it cut through the air. The crunch the head made as it met Matthew's. The tuft of his hair that was stuck to the tip.

Whoosh. Thwack. Whoosh. Thwack.

I bolt towards the bucket on the tool shelf and vomit. Dust billows up into my eyes, and my throat and teeth sting with each retch, but all I can focus on is the horrendous sounds the club made. The battery charger beeps three times before falling silent, and I rest against the wall, breathing in the dust, the scent of damp and stomach acid.

After the murder, I knew I had to do three things. Hide the body. Clean up the crime scene. Conceal the murder weapon. The body came first – and what a night I chose to do it.

As the night sky was lit by fireworks ringing in Christmas Day, flashes of colour exploding from a neighbour's garden, I tried to concoct a plan. I couldn't drag the body to the car; the streets were teeming with drunken stragglers, and front doors were forever opening and closing with partygoers. Even if I parked right outside the house, there would have been too many opportunities to be stumbled upon.

I couldn't leave the body and wait for a better opportunity either. I knew it wouldn't be long before it started to smell. Foul gases and rotting flesh attracting bluebottles. We have all heard the horror stories of neighbours complaining of a bad odour seeping through the walls, only to discover a body on the other side.

My best chance was the woodlands just beyond the train tracks. I had to wait for the Midnight Mass service to end, and for the partygoers along the street to finally go to sleep, but it seemed like the safest option, at least in the short term. That's what I thought to myself at the time. But he has lain at the foot of the garden ever since, taunting me whenever I dare to peer through the window.

I grab the bucket and retch again.

When I'm finally done, and my stomach has nothing left, I stand on shaking legs to tidy away the battery charger and climb behind the wheel. It has been a long time since I sat in this seat. The memories Matthew and I shared are pressed into the sagging leather; each scratch and scruff on the dashboard. The markings have completely worn off the gear stick from his strong grip. I turn the key in the ignition and the engine stutters to life.

He is so present in here. I can smell his aftershave as if he were next to me. My hands shake at the wheel, and I grip tightly, until my palms rasp against the leather. I turn on the radio to distract myself, and freeze as soon as I hear it.

Our song.

I'd clicked on the CD player rather than the radio. I smack the butt of my palm against the power button, and kill the song mid lyric.

Love of my life, you've hurt me . . .

My heart is thumping wildly, my palms slick with sweat at the wheel as I am met with a rush of emotion. Tears spring to my eyes and I blink them away.

I need to destroy the club. Chances are, the people who work for the Messenger will be looking for it too, as they did with the body. I can't allow them to hold another thing over me.

I press the button for the garage door and lower the window for a breath of fresh air. The cool morning breeze drifts in, sending a shiver down my spine. *Someone just walked over my grave,* Matthew used to say.

I wonder what he would say to me now.

⚖️

I sit in my car outside the storage unit, forcing myself to take deep, slow breaths.

I had been a mess throughout the drive, convinced I was being followed. My tired eyes would clock the Messenger in every car tailing behind mine, spot him in the men eyeing me from the path as I drove by. I must have seen his face a hundred times, my heart jumping in my chest with each perceived sighting.

The lot is the perfect place to keep something hidden. It is a forty-minute drive from home and set back from the main streets, with only an MOT garage and a vacant building waiting to be let for its neighbours. I chose this place for the self-service access that is available during out-of-office hours: a key fob for the secured entrance, and a keypad for each respective storage unit.

The cold morning breeze sends a shiver right through me. Another person crossing my grave. The storage unit looks small from the outside, but beyond the entrance lobby is an endless corridor, leading to door after door of strangers' belongings, each with their own story: deaths, new beginnings, long-kept secrets. I press the fob key against the reader beside the door and step inside.

To my relief, the security protocols seem to be the same. I sign in at the desk, using an initial for my first name, and my maiden name for my second. *N. Norton.* The door leading towards the storage units squeals on its hinges as it opens, sending a high-pitched echo down the long, cold corridor. It still has the same metallic smell, the unwelcoming chill. A corridor of secrets, hidden away under lock and key.

Each step I take echoes against the metal doors; they're the roller kind, similar to the shutters one might see drawn over shopfronts after hours. I count the units as I go, waiting for number 34 to appear, as my body instinctively tugs at me to turn in the other direction. I pass units 30 and 32, breaking out in a cold sweat as I reach mine.

The first time I came here, the murder was still fresh. It had been hours, rather than years. I could still smell his blood on me despite my scrubbing, hear the screams as though they were happening at that very moment. My hands stung from the bleach, my skin flushed and angry, cracked between my knuckles and around my fingernails. I press the numbers into the keypad beside the door.

2-4-1-2

The keypad beeps and flashes green, and I reach down for the handle, pulling it upwards with a deafening clatter as I rise to my feet, the metal rolling above my head until it reaches the top and the corridor falls silent.

The rolled-up rug lies alone in the centre of the room.

I am shivering from the adrenaline and the cold. My whole body seems to be repelled by the sight, squirming like a strand of hair before a flame. But I can't tear my eyes away.

I step inside the unit, drag the door down behind me, and crouch before the roll, feeling the edge of the rug in my grip. The underside feels as rough as I remember; the same material that gave me friction burns as I lugged it from the car. It had been with us in every one of our homes, a hand-me-down from Maggie. We made love on this rug, spilt drinks during parties, with no notion of what it would be used for in the end.

I place my palms flat on the roll and push, watching it unfurl along the length of the unit in a cloud of dust. I cover my mouth and nose and cough as it hits the back of my throat. When it settles, I turn back.

The golf club lies inside.

I blink back the memories, and despite my better knowledge, I reach for it, my hand quivering before me as I lower it towards the club, but as soon as I graze the cold metal with my fingertips, I flinch as if I've been stung and roll the rug up again.

The rug is heavier than I remember. When I try to lift it, my back almost gives. I had been fuelled by adrenaline when I brought it here; I would have done anything to make the ordeal end. I lumber it up with a groan, and hold it before me in both hands.

After I've sealed the door behind me, I carry the rug back up the corridor and out of the lot to the car, and drop it in the boot with a *thunk*, before hiding away in the safe confines of the car. I close my eyes and listen to the loud, anxious rasp of my breaths, feel my heart pulsating feverishly in my chest. I only meant to store it here for a week or two, to give me time to figure out what the hell I was going to do with it; its presence here has hung over me like a black cloud ever since.

Hindsight, they say, is a wonderful thing. I have regretted using the club ever since that night. You can't burn metal, or hide such a long, awkward thing. But I didn't think of the aftermath. The only thing I can remember knowing in that moment was that I wanted him dead.

I wipe the sweat away from my face, and pinch at my sweatshirt to peel the fabric from my damp ribs. I've done the first part of the task.

Now I just need to destroy it.

⚖

I drive at a crawl towards the car park of the tip, pull up in the nearest spot and cut the engine. There are already a number of cars parked up, but to my relief I can't see any queues, meaning I can quickly slip in and out before crossing paths with too many people. But there will still be witnesses who could recognise me.

I have to look normal, act normal. Just like everyone else here.

I lower my cap, slip on my sunglasses, and get out of the car, retrieving the rug before setting off.

Can I dump the club and rug together, or do I need to rid myself of them separately? As I step through the main gates, I eye the large, towering containers of waste, with steel staircases and platforms to stand upon, each with its own particular contents. I scan each of them as I pass, looking beyond the rows of disused fridge-freezers and washing machines reflecting the morning sun off their white, dented bodies, until I spot the sign for metals.

I lumber the rug under my arm to rest on my hip, and cross the potholed forecourt for the metal disposal. There are other people here, emptying an array of junk from their vehicles; dead, brown Christmas trees added to an already toppling mound.

I approach the staircase and latch onto the railing, trying to stop myself from glimpsing the ground below through the metal grating, getting further and further away the higher I climb. The rug grows heavier, burning the muscles of my thighs, my back threatening to give.

I reach the container and look down at the gleaming, rusting metal within. I hoist the rug onto the lip of the container, and pause. My heart is racing; not just from the exertion, but the fear.

It's the club, it's brought out the worst in me. I can't stop thinking of the night I held it in both hands, past and present bleeding together. I am stood before the container, but in my mind, it's Christmas Eve. I listen to the church's bell tower ringing in Midnight Mass, matching the swing of my club.

Gong. Thwack.

Gong. Thwack.

Gong. Thwack . . .

The cheers of my neighbours brought me round as midnight rang, and I paused with the club above my head, blood splattered on my face, in my mouth. Fireworks burst on the other side of the windows, flashing us in reds, whites and blues. My husband's once beautiful face beaten into pulp beneath me. The wet meat of him reflecting each burst of light.

I snap back to the present at the sound of my name, my stomach plummeting at the familiarity of the voice.

The Messenger is stood tall, looking down at me where he stands on the other end of the platform by the stairs. He wears that same, dark grin on his face.

I blink furiously, half convinced that my paranoia is playing tricks on me. But it's him. It's really him.

'Good morning,' he says, and nods towards the rug. 'I think you have something that belongs to me.'

How did he know I would be here? How did he follow me without me seeing him?

As my heart races and my thoughts jumble, he reaches out for it, grazing the back of my hand with his leather glove; it feels like cold, wet skin, sending a shiver of revulsion through me. As he moves towards me, I see two men stood at the bottom of the steps.

He tugs lightly, but I don't unfurl my grip. His breath is warm, and his closeness is both terrifying and strangely intimate.

'Remember what happened to Adrian Whittaker. I suggest you don't make the same mistake.'

Hannah's a pretty girl.

I close my eyes to bury my reluctance, and let him prise the rug away. I open them again and watch helplessly as he walks down the metal steps with the rug held securely under one arm.

I stand in silence as the Messenger and the men head off into the distance, and I am left empty-handed, with my heart in my mouth.

They knew exactly what I would do. They know every step I plan to make before I even make it.

But how?

17

I sit on the tube, slowly piecing together how I had played right into their hands.

If they had known where I buried the body, they must have been watching me for a long time, but clearly, they hadn't known where I kept the murder weapon until I led them right to it. As far as I'm aware, I haven't been followed since yesterday morning; they must have wanted to lull me into a false sense of security, to feel bold enough to collect the club and lead them directly to it. Perhaps they were following me all day, but they didn't want me to know it; conspicuous when it pays to be, and hot on my heels when they want me to know that I have nowhere to run. I must assume they are following me everywhere I go now. That everything I do, everything I say, will be scrutinised.

I am only a few stops away from my next conference with Wade. Despite my nerves, I am far more prepared than I was yesterday, even if my 3 a.m. start and this morning's events have robbed me of energy. I take a deep breath and close my eyes, and remind myself of my plan. My main goals of the meeting are to keep Antony from asking too much about Alex Finch, and persuading Wade, and his mother if necessary, to push back the trial so I have more time.

The tube stops at the next station, and as we pull away again, my phone buzzes with a text from Antony.

Hey, just saw you on the tube. See you in a sec.

I glance around me for the Messenger among the passengers, suddenly paranoid that I'm being followed again. Then it hits me.

My phone.

I'm furious not to have thought of this before now. The amount of stalking cases I've worked on where the defendant has used their victim's phone as a means to follow them. But it's something so outlandish that I would never have dreamed it would happen in my own life.

I stare down at the phone in my grip and unlock the screen, swiping anxiously through the apps. There are the usual suspects: social media, email and photos, the running app I haven't opened in months. I scroll through the pages of apps scanning for anything that might grab my attention, and pause.

The *Find my Mobile* app.

I didn't even think of it. It's one of those apps that I downloaded with my new phone and then immediately forgot about, only needing it if my handset went missing. It tracks where my phone is at all times in case I lose it. If they were able to hack into it, could they track my every move? Or worse, might they see everything I type, hear everything I say?

I need to talk to Fredrick.

'Neve—'

I jolt in my seat.

It's Antony. The tube has started up again, but I had been so engrossed in my own thoughts that I hadn't even realised.

'Christ, you're rather jumpy at the minute, aren't you?' he

asks, looking down at me with a playful grin on his face. He is dressed in a checked grey suit and a camel overcoat, his polished leather shoes matching the satchel bag at his hip. In his hands are two takeaway coffee cups.

'Latte no sugar, right?' Antony says, passing me a cup as he sits down beside me.

'Thanks.'

Antony looks about us at the near-empty carriage before returning his attention to me.

'I've done some digging on Alex Finch. He is definitely a factor in the Darlings' downfall, but get this: the police never even spoke to him.'

A man sat further down the carriage has taken out his phone from his pocket and is tapping away at the screen.

Is he relaying everything we say?

No. I'm being paranoid.

'Definitely?' I take a sip of coffee. 'You sound confident.'

'I am, and you should be too. Finch was all over the paperwork for Wade's business. Signing off on the big decisions that would come back to bite them; even seemed to be the driving force behind the Ponzi scheme they had going, according to the paper trail. Hell, Finch might even have been leading Wade along too for all we know, and keeping the dirty dealings under wraps. The third-party companies suing them for unpaid fees name both Wade Darling and Alex Finch on the complaints, but it seems Finch was a big part of why the business went under, if not the main catalyst.'

'That doesn't mean he killed the Darlings.'

'Not outright, no, but it certainly plays into the obsessive, jealous angle, doesn't it? From looking at the copy of the company's books we have on file, Finch used to do his job well.

The company wasn't failing when he began his dodgy business tactics, which means he's either a greedy son of a bitch, or—'

'Something happened to make him change tack.'

'Exactly,' he replies. 'It all happened in the year leading up to the murders.'

My heart is racing. He has sunk his teeth into this case and is refusing to let go.

'And you said his ex-wife filed for divorce three days before the murders,' I say, thinking aloud. 'Which suggests they would have had marital problems during that year too. It sounds like Wade was right when he said Finch's life was falling apart.'

I have to give it to Antony, the idea sticks. Wade said Finch wanted everything he had, but the one thing he couldn't have was his wife. If Finch's world was crumbling around him, and he snapped under the pressure, perhaps the murders were his way of exacting revenge.

'But why wouldn't Wade mention it sooner?' I ask. 'What does his ex-business partner have on him?'

'Got to be something bad.'

'But what's worse than your family being murdered, and being framed for it?'

'I'm determined to find out.'

While I have been sleepwalking, taking in teenage runaways and trying to destroy murder weapons, Antony has found a way to spin the prosecution's argument in favour of our client. The very thing that I cannot afford to happen, if I have to go through with what the Messenger demands.

'Good work,' I mutter, and look up at the tube map; the next stop is ours.

'You don't seem too pleased,' he says.

'Only because I know you won't like my plan B.' He stares

back at me, waiting. 'Look, I know you want to run with this trial, but if we don't get what we need from him, I'll be urging him to push it back.'

He goes to speak, but I cut him off.

'I'm not ushering him into the dock if the defence case isn't ready, and nor should you.'

'Of course not. But if we *can* get the information, if it's right there, on the tip of his bloody tongue, we've got to try and push for it, no?'

'Right. Except it's his job to give us instructions, not the other way around. We can give him the best legal advice, but that doesn't mean he has to take it.'

He looks away, and we rock with the carriage in silence as the seconds tick away from us. The tube begins to slow, and our stop appears on the other side of the window.

'You're right,' he says finally. 'I know you are. But let me try and get this out of him. If we know the truth, we can make sure we get the evidence we need to help him win this thing.'

He looks at me, pleading with his eyes like a dog for a scrap, as the tube comes to a stop.

I never should have chosen you for this trial, I think to myself.

'Let's hope he's willing to play ball.'

⚖

'No,' Wade says from the other side of the table.

Antony and I sit in silence, in the same seats as before. I can feel him practically twitching beside me.

'Why not?' I ask, staring him down. He says nothing, crushing Antony's hopes to dust.

'Wade, whatever you're holding back could be the very thing to help you avoid being found guilty,' Antony says.

'There will be another way,' he replies, crossing his arms.

'There isn't,' Antony says. 'If you want to avoid being sentenced for these crimes, this is your chance.'

'Then I'll go to prison,' he snaps. 'I told you, I'm not talking about this any further.'

Why wouldn't he? What could he possibly be hiding?

Poor Antony. He must have been up half the night digging this up.

Wade sits, stoic and defiant. I look down at my notes for ways to lead him off the topic.

'I think what would be good to do today is go over the days leading up to the murders. How you were doing as a family, how your marriage was going ... how you were feeling, in the final days. You were depressed due to the closure of your business, is that right?'

'Do we really have to talk about this?' he snaps.

'The prosecution is going to use your depression as a reason for committing the murders. They will paint you as a man who lost his mind and saw red. I need to know as much as possible to accurately convey the true nature of your experience to counteract their narrative.'

He chews on his bottom lip and looks away, his eyes on the window. He stays like this for some time, seemingly transfixed. Finally, he speaks.

'That last week before the murders was ... dark. I had learnt we were being sued by multiple suppliers for unpaid invoices, and I knew I had nothing to give them; I couldn't even afford my lawyer. Everything I had built for myself and my family was crumbling before my eyes. I knew I would have to file for bankruptcy, and what that would mean for the future. No reputable bank or business contact would lend me the start-up money to build another business off the back of something like this.'

'Did your wife know about the business?'

'No. I was too ashamed.'

'So she had no idea about your financial predicament? Hers too, essentially, what with you being the provider for the family?'

'She knew nothing. I tried to buy myself some time, to fix things without having to worry her. I borrowed money to keep the accounts full so she wasn't any the wiser. But as our situation got worse, I knew I couldn't hide it from her anymore. It was only a matter of time before word spread to our group of friends, and I wanted her to hear it from me. But I didn't get the chance.'

Silence falls upon on the room.

'How were Yolanda and the children during this time?'

'Yolanda was aloof,' he replies. 'My depression was like a dark cloud over us. They were used to me taking care of things, and for the first time I couldn't. I was failing. We all felt lost and disconnected, like a house full of strangers.'

'In what way was Yolanda aloof?'

His face softens as he thinks of her.

'I think she was purposely stepping on eggshells around me. She knew I was in a bad way, and didn't want to tip me over the edge. My mood swings were . . . irrational.'

'Were you ever angry with her?'

'Not in an abusive way, if that's what you mean.'

'I wasn't insinuating that at all. We're on your side, Wade.'

The lie makes me break out in a sudden rush of sweat. I feel the heat prickling the skin of my back, speckles forming above my lip.

He softens slightly, his shoulders lowering from the tensed hunch he had them in.

'Yes, I was angry, but not about anything logical. The depression ... it made every small task impossible. I could barely string a coherent thought together, so if my family so much as spoke to me, I snapped, or became tearful. It was an impossible situation to put them in.'

'But it wasn't your fault, Wade,' Antony says. 'It was the depression, not you.'

Wade's eyes sink to his lap. I wonder if he believes that.

The mood swings, the walking on eggshells – these give the prosecution many opportunities to paint him in a darker light. A man to be feared, rather than helped.

'I barely spoke in the final days leading up to their deaths. I hid away in my office, trying to soften the inevitable blow of the business closure. I would go for walks in the woods, hunt.'

'With the murder weapon?'

His eye twitches. 'Yes.'

Antony sits forward in his seat. I can see by the eagerness in his eyes that he is done with my deflections; he's ready to return the questioning to Alex Finch.

'What about your business partner? What communication did you have with him in those last days?'

Wade straightens in his seat.

'It's important we know of anything the prosecution might bring up in court.'

He crosses his arms and looks to the window.

'Why were you sleeping on the sofa the night of the murders?' Antony asks, his tone more desperate than before. 'Had you and Yolanda argued?'

'No, actually. We had reconciled. We'd gone through a rough patch.'

'What kind of rough patch?' Antony asks.

Wade stares out the window again, shutting himself down. I can practically feel the heat of Antony's anger bubbling away inside of him.

'Had you thought to tell Yolanda about the finances then?' I ask.

'I wanted to, but we had just reached a good place; I couldn't bring myself to tell her and ruin the progress we'd made.' His eyes glaze over. 'It would have killed me to see the look on her face when I told her.'

I look down at my notes. It's time I presented the idea of pushing the trial to him. I take a deep breath and am just about to speak when I'm cut off.

'Wade,' Antony says abruptly. 'I'm going to put it to you straight because we don't have much time. At present, it looks like the jury won't be on your side. If you know something that could help us – could help *you* – you don't have long to tell us. On Monday, the prosecution is going to paint you as a monster. A liar. A killer. A failed husband, father and businessman. It is going to be character assassination. They are going to insinuate that you killed your family to hide the shame of your failed business. They will take every opportunity they can to make you seem like the ghastliest man that has ever stepped into the courtroom, and at present, you're gifting them the chance. If we don't have all the information to counteract their claims, it's highly likely that the jury will believe them and consider you guilty.'

Antony stands.

'It's your life, your freedom. We will do whatever you

instruct. But if you change your mind, and you decide to be open with us – to fight for yourself – then get in touch. Otherwise, we will see you on Monday for the trial.'

Although his speech is similar in sentiment to what mine was to be, I am left feeling a lingering sense of unease. His words run the risk of inspiring Wade into action, rather than delaying him. I assess Wade intently, looking for the slightest flare of provocation in his eyes. He remains in his seat as Anthony heads for the door, strides down the hall and out into the street.

'I'm afraid he's right,' I say. 'It doesn't look good for you, Wade. I think we may need to consider requesting to push back the trial to a later date. I said we could work towards the set trial date during our first meeting, but only if you worked with us. Pushing the trial seems to be the only other way to give us more time to prepare your defence. If there *is* another way to tackle this, we'll need time to prepare.'

Marianne is stood listening in at the kitchen doorway, pale with angst. When Wade doesn't look up at me or register my words, I rise to my feet as Antony had.

'Mrs Darling,' I say softly as I reach her. 'The wisest thing Wade can do at this stage is agree to push the trial. Right now, we don't have enough to defend him – if the trial commences on Monday . . .'

'They'll lock him up,' she replies, her voice thick with dread.

I nod, and give her a sympathetic smile, before taking one last glance at Wade. He is sat at the table in silence, staring down at his burns. I almost will him to make the right decision, wishing my eyes could burrow into the back of his skull and see what he is thinking, what decision he plans to make.

My freedom depends on it.

18

I stand on the dock, waiting for the 18.56 RB2 river bus from Westminster Pier where I am to meet Fredrick.

I pull my coat closer to my body, as the chill of the breeze bites at me through my clothes. The journey from Westminster to Embankment only takes five minutes, so he can't have much to tell me. Perhaps he has found something that he doesn't want to get caught up in, and he has asked me here to withdraw his support. I know I wouldn't want to get caught up in this voluntarily.

I trace my finger along the edge of the cigarette packet hidden in my coat pocket. I had bought them after the conference with Mr Darling before returning to chambers to work on the case, the need for relief clawing at me from within, but still, I can't bring myself to spark one up after abstaining for so long. But the temptation continues to whisper its sweet encouragements in my ears.

'Screw it,' I mutter, and pull the packet free. I peel off the cellophane, pick out the silver foiled paper covering the cigarettes, and breathe in the fresh, familiar scent of them. I prise one free with my teeth and cup my hand around the lighter, inhaling deeply. The first hit goes straight to my head, and for a brief few seconds, I feel nothing but bliss.

The river is black with the night but for the bursts of colour rippling in its waves from the London Eye, illuminated purple and stark against the evening sky. Behind me, Big Ben towers over Westminster, clad in unsightly scaffolding, and beside it, Westminster Bridge carries the bright lights of city traffic from one side of London to the other.

The night is ice-cold. If someone were to fall in the water, they'd have hypothermia in minutes. I have always thought that would be the worst way to die. It's often said that burning is the ghastliest end, but if you're lucky, the smoke gets to you before the flames. Cold water stabs at you, slows your blood, numbs your legs until you can't kick to keep afloat, and slip silently below the surface.

After planting the seed into Wade's and Marianne's minds to push back the trial, and having Fredrick working to free me of the Messenger, I feel I should be experiencing an element of control. But that same adrenaline-fuelled restlessness plagues me, and as soon as I returned to chambers I spent the rest of the day obsessively going over each of the prosecution's witnesses and planning how I could twist their evidence to suit my best interests over those of my client, as I battled the guilt within me with each and every turn. I stand at the dock, shoulders slumped and eyes hooded, exhausted from the endless fight. At least Hannah is at a friend's this evening; her text said she wouldn't be in until after dinner.

The river bus appears slowly from beneath Westminster Bridge. I smoke my cigarette to the filter as the boat drifts towards the pier. Fredrick is already aboard, waiting for me. I had called him from my work phone at chambers and explained my suspicions about the Messenger tracking my phone, warning him not to contact me through my mobile anymore, which is turned off at the bottom of my bag.

There are five or so people waiting to get on the boat. Londoners unsteady on their feet after sinking a few too many drinks. I wonder where they have been, and where they are all off to; it's easy to imagine everyone has it better than you: better jobs, better relationships. But in this case, it must be true. I can't imagine anyone here being in a worse situation than mine.

The boat docks and we head aboard. I cross the gangplank, eyeing the black, chopping water below, and almost feel it tugging at me, beckoning me down, before stepping safely onto the deck.

I walk along the row of seats towards the prow of the boat and recognise Fredrick sat with his head down, halfway along. He doesn't look for me as we board, and I continue to the front as he instructed and take a seat by the window.

The boat grumbles into motion, and we set off along the Thames at what feels like a snail's pace. The city passes us by. There aren't too many people on board, just straggles of passengers riding alone, some suited up, others casual. Everyone is dotted about to give each other space, a luxury rarely permitted on the underground. I hear the crack of a drink can; the man two rows behind me takes a glug of a pre-mixed gin and tonic.

After a minute or so, I feel the rustle of Fredrick's coat against mine as he sits down beside me, the scent of oaky after-shave filling my nostrils.

'Good evening,' he says, his breath visible in the air. 'Couldn't have got yourself into this trouble during the summer?'

His nose and cheeks are red from the cold. He is dressed in the same black overcoat, buttoned up to the navy scarf wrapped tightly at his neck. His shaved head is covered by a black flat cap, his hands hidden in leather gloves.

'Out of my hands, I'm afraid,' I reply, and force a smile.

I hear the man behind us slurp from his can of G&T, and have the sudden urge to reach around and snatch it from him, guzzle it down until there are two bubbling streams of it seeping from either side of my mouth.

'You were right about the source,' he says, speaking low. 'The man who accosted you works for the Viklunds. They've worked together for some time; he seems to be their go-to man for things like this.'

A part of me doesn't want to know who the Messenger is, to put an identity on the man. It makes him seem more real. A man with a history. I don't want to think of him as human; he would have been a baby, a child, an uncorrupted soul until something happened along the way to turn him into the monster he is now. But despite my reservations, my curiosity gets the better of me.

'Who is he? The Messenger?'

'Leon James. A nasty character with a charge sheet as long as your arm.'

'That makes me feel better,' I quip. 'What has he gone down for in the past?'

'Extortion. GBH. And he's rumoured to have committed far worse.'

'It's fitting, at least.'

'I'm sorry not to have better news. But it's good to know who you're dealing with.'

I don't know what I had been expecting. Of course he would be a dangerous man. I think of the gun he pointed at my chest the day we met.

'And the Viklunds? Are they as bad as the rumours suggest?'

He nods solemnly, which tells me they are even worse.

'I'm still looking into them, but they have connections throughout the city. I can't imagine you're the only one being . . . exploited like this. The Viklunds don't have any one means of business – if there's a way to make a living from a crime, they play a part in it.'

Despite the conversation, my thoughts drift to Fredrick himself. I wonder if he has cottoned on to what I've done. I am known for my husband's disappearance just as much as my legal work. Perhaps he looked further into me too, when he was digging into the Messenger. Maybe he can see right through me. See the blood dripping from my hands.

'I don't know what to say. Thank you, I suppose.'

'This is just the first step,' he says. 'I'll dig around, see if I can get wind of anything more that might be able to help you.'

'Thank you.'

I turn my attention to the window and admire the lights of the city. The night suddenly feels colder; my bones ache with it, and my teeth chatter behind my lips. I clamp my gloved hands between my thighs.

The boat begins to drift from its course towards the side of the river as Embankment comes into view.

'And the other thing we discussed?' I ask, my eyes straight ahead. 'Anything there?'

'Yes,' he replies. 'Something I think you'll be able to use.'

He doesn't say what I might use it for, and for what outcome, but in a few simple words, it's clear he knows of my motives: preparing for the last resort, to use Wade as my sacrificial lamb.

He hands me a file. The cover is blank, with no hint of what might be inside.

'I'll get off here, you leave at the next,' he says. 'I'll call you when I have more.'

'Thank you,' I say, meeting his eyes. 'Do you have enough time? The trial begins on Monday.'

'It'll have to be,' he replies. He places his gloved hand over mine, and gives it a comforting squeeze, to the sound of squeaking leather. 'You're not alone in this, all right?'

I hadn't realised how alone I had felt, until I heard those words.

'Thanks.'

He gets up as the boat pulls up at Embankment.

'I'll see you soon,' he says, and gives me a comforting wink.

The night feels colder just a few miles up the river. The wind carries an arctic chill, bringing water to my eyes; the sort of cold that makes one's skin ache. I look for him on the shore over my shoulder as the boat pulls away, and see him standing at the dock, giving me a nod. Behind him, the view of the city glows.

I turn back to the file in my lap. It seems so inconspicuous, and yet it seems to burn into my thighs with all the possibilities it might hold. I lift the cover and begin to read, my face slowly draining of colour as I take in the potential evidence I could use to damn my client, if I choose to put it in the wrong hands.

What Fredrick has given me isn't a mere spanner in the works, it's explosive. If this were sent to the prosecution, they may well have won the case before it has even begun. It is perhaps the best hand I could have been dealt.

I just pray I don't need to use it.

19

I sit in my armchair in the living room with the new evidence on my lap and a glass of wine in hand, wondering how I could possibly bring myself to unearth this against my client.

I was wrong before. It isn't explosive evidence. It's nuclear. No defence barrister would be able to dodge this bullet. This information wouldn't just smear Wade Darling's character. It would implode our entire route of defence.

I drink the last gulp of wine in my glass and assess the prosecution's case laid out before me. This would be the evidence needed for them to win, no questions asked. It would give credibility to every one of their claims, but had been buried so deeply that even they struggled to find it. The question I have now is: do I use this to my advantage, or bury it as far down again as I can?

My guilt rears up, closing about my throat in a chokehold.

It hasn't got to that point yet. I mustn't drive myself mad over something I might never have to do.

But as I open my eyes again and stare down at the evidence laid in my lap, I know the odds of avoiding the Messenger's demands aren't exactly in my favour. I jolt out of my thoughts at the sound of Hannah's voice.

'You okay?' she asks from the sofa, remote in hand. 'You look really pale.'

I force a tight smile.

'I'm fine. A bit stressed. Nothing wine won't help.' I get up with my empty glass. 'Want anything?'

'I'm good.'

I head into the kitchen and brace myself against the counter for a moment, trying to stop my head from spinning with thoughts.

If I sent this to the prosecution, I would be destroying a man's life. Stealing away any chance of a fair trial. It's grossly unjust. It would make me despicable.

But what if it's the only way to protect Hannah, and keep my secret? What then?

I pour myself a generous glass of red wine. I'll need to sleep tonight, and this will help to keep my mind from wandering.

I step back into the living room and pause.

Hannah is up from her seat, peering over my paperwork sprawled across the footstall before my armchair.

'What the hell are you doing?'

Hannah jumps at the cutting sound of my voice and spins around.

'I was just . . . curious.'

She steps aside as I march over to my armchair and snatch up the files. She'd been glancing at the document Fredrick gave me.

'This is confidential information. That's really not on.'

'I was interested what you did in your job. I'm sorry, I didn't know—'

'You did know, Hannah. You wouldn't have waited until my back was turned if you didn't know it was wrong.'

I take the files and the glass of wine with me towards the stairs.

'Lock the doors before you come up. I'll see you in the morning.'

I march up the stairs, the wine glass shaking in my grasp.

I wake standing in the dark.

The room is pitch black. So dark that the air before my eyes appears thick enough to run my hand through. I am naked. I can't see myself, but I feel the nip of the cold room all over my body, gooseflesh running up my thighs and across my buttocks, raising the hairs on the backs of my arms. Through my fear, I feel the whisper of pain: my teeth are ringing, and the skin on my wrist feels like it has been burnt.

The rush of blood pulses in my ears, my thoughts running in a muddled, anxious loop.

It's happening again it's happening again it's happening again.

My eyes slowly acclimatise to the dark, colours peering through the shadows, forms and shapes breaking through the wall of black. There is movement before me. Twisting. Turning. The realisation of where I am hits me suddenly, like a fist in my gut.

I am not in my room. I'm in Hannah's.

My body shakes, my aching teeth chattering together. I am stood above Hannah's bed, watching her. Through the darkness, I can see her milky white skin, her eyes closed with sleep.

I back away, tripping over a piece of clothing that has been left on the floor, and stumble. Hannah stirs, her limbs unfurling beneath the sheets. I watch in terrified silence where I am flat against the door. She sits up, squinting to see through the dark. I don't breathe. I don't think. The only lifelike thing about me is my rampant pulse screaming from beneath my skin.

Seconds pass, feeling like minutes. I listen to her breaths, sleepy and ragged, before she groans and turns, flopping down on the bed again. When her breathing slows, and I know she has returned to sleep, I edge open the door and click it shut behind me.

In my room, my bed is messy and unmade where I threw my covers off in my sleep. The restraint I had tied to my wrist to fix me to the headboard is on the floor: a fabric belt from a jacket in my closet. No wonder my teeth hurt; I had gnawed myself free, the fabric frayed where I'd bitten at the knots.

I get back into bed, shivering beneath the covers, and bind my wrist to the headboard so tightly that my fingertips swell with blood.

I mustn't let this rule my life again. It's just the stress of the trial; things will calm down as they did before.

But as I try to return to sleep, one question niggles through my brain.

Why had I been standing above Hannah's bed?

20

One day until the trial

The trial is so close now that I can practically smell the wood panelling on the courtroom walls, hear the creaks of the juror's chairs. I glance up at the clock on the wall of my office in chambers, the seconds ticking away from me as the hand whirls around the face.

Breathe. Just breathe.

I close my eyes, resting back in my chair before my desk. I'd managed an hour's sleep, perhaps two, interspersed between nightmares that made me wake with a violent jolt each time, tugging at my restraint, in fear I had been walking again. I woke the final time to the sound of my name, and Hannah's pale, frightened face peering through the doorway to my dark room, asking if I was all right.

I was dreaming of murdering your father.

I imagine Hannah in the witness box, relaying my tossing and turning to the court, adding her name to the ever-growing list of prosecution witnesses that could be used against me at trial: the neighbour, the stepdaughter, the solicitor, the client. But there is a way out of this, something I hadn't allowed myself to even think of, until meeting with Fredrick. That's if

I can bring myself to do something so despicable as sacrifice a man's life for my own.

My thoughts return to Hannah. Last night had been too close a call. The memory of waking up beside her bed, staring down at her through the darkness, is enough to bring up the taste of bile.

She can't stay another night. I need her to go home.

I pick up my work phone with a shaking hand and dial Maggie's number. She answers on the fifth ring.

'Maggie, it's Neve. Don't hang up.'

She sighs at the other end of the line. 'What is it? I was about to go out.'

'It's about Hannah.'

'Of course it is,' she says, with an exacerbated huff. 'I expected this.'

'Expected what?'

'It was only a matter of time before the shine of having Hannah all to yourself would wane. It's not as easy as it looks, is it, looking after someone other than yourself?'

'It isn't that, Maggie. The case is taking over, and I'm not able to be around as much as I'd like. Come the trial, I'll barely be at home at all.'

'So you want me to take her off your hands?'

'I wouldn't put it like that.'

'The answer's no. You both made your bed – made me the bad guy, ganged up on me – now you need to lie in it.'

'This isn't a pissing contest, for Christ's sake. This is about her care. My job—'

'Your time is not more precious than anyone else's. You chose to come between Hannah and me, and these are the consequences. When she's had her fun, she'll come home again.

You wait and see. But I'm not going to be made out to be the bad person here by demanding she does.'

I go to respond, but she cuts me off.

'Now if you'll excuse me, I have to go out.'

She ends the call before I am able to utter another word, and I am left listening to the endless tone shrilling in my ear. I replace the phone back on the dock with a sigh and rub my tired face.

'Sleeping on the job?'

I jolt up in my chair. Artie is stood in the doorway leaning against the frame, his smirk slanted across his face.

'No,' I snap. 'I was thinking.'

'Let me take a load off then. Fill me in. What's your argument for Mr Darling's case?'

'I'm not really in the mood, Artie.'

'Oh come on,' he says, and perches on the edge of the desk. 'You know old Artie likes to be kept in the loop.'

He peers down at me in his usual way, before glancing over the open law books on my desk. He wants to know how I'll defend my client. Except, I hadn't been looking for ways to defend him. I had been researching ways to condemn him. The last thing I need is Artie picking my plan apart.

My work phone rings. I briefly hope it's Maggie, calling to change her mind, and fumble for the receiver.

'Yes?'

'Neve. It's Antony.'

'Antony, good morning.' I wave Artie away, who chuckles to himself and gives me a salute, before heading for the door.

'I've heard from Mr Darling,' Antony says. 'He wants to speak to us at midday.'

I hold my breath, willing him not to utter the words I know are coming.

'Oh?'

'He wants to talk about Alex Finch.' I can practically hear him grinning down the phone. 'I think he's going to tell us something important.'

My heart sinks.

'Right,' I say, and cough nervously. 'I'll be there.'

I hang up the phone and sigh into my hands.

This is it. The moment I've been dreading. The point where Wade reveals his hand, and I have to deliver my own in response. Whatever he is about to tell us, I won't be able to keep Antony from asking all the questions he's wanted to about Alex Finch, which will be a direct chance for us to show the police investigation in a suspicious light. That's unless I blow it out of the water with the truth about Mr Darling's past.

I take a deep breath, hold it in my chest, before finally letting it unfurl.

I don't have to do anything yet. All I have to do is listen to what he has to say.

But deep down, I know. I know that whatever he is about to put to us will push me to act; to defend me, defend Hannah.

It will come down to him or us.

⚖

Antony and I sit across from Mr Darling in the same seats as before.

Wade looks more prepared this morning. He has dressed and showered ahead of time, shaved off his stubble, styled his hair, put on a crisp white shirt and dark jeans. He looks ready. Almost as if he has an objective of his own for this meeting.

I try to keep the panic suppressed, smothered behind a

professional smile, silently willing him not to take us down a path from which we can't return.

'Thank you for coming,' he says, in a low, serious tone. 'I'm sorry I haven't been more open with you during the past few meetings. I had my reasons, but now I see it's the only way.'

He glances at his mother, and I wonder what they talked about in our absence. I had hoped Marianne would urge him to push back the trial, but clearly it backfired. Instead, it seems she has talked him into opening up. I sit before him, bracing myself for the inevitable blow.

He takes a deep breath.

'I didn't want to talk about Alex Finch, not because of our business dealings, but because of my family. My wife, in particular.' He looks down at his hands, lacing them together on the table top. 'I told you that Alex Finch wanted my wife. But what I didn't tell you was that, for a time, she wanted him too.' He clears his throat, averting his eyes momentarily before meeting mine and mine alone. 'They had an affair.'

My heart jumps with the blow. If Alex Finch was sexually involved with Yolanda, and their relationship went sour, it takes the heat off Wade as the sole suspect. His defence just grew remarkably stronger.

You stupid fool. You've damned us both.

The silence has ticked on, with neither Anthony nor I saying a word. Anthony is the first to speak.

'Why didn't you tell anyone about this before?'

'I didn't want to give the prosecution a motive for murder,' he replies, matter-of-factly. 'And I didn't want my wife to be disgraced before the nation. She would die all over again if she knew that people knew of her indiscretion. They would judge not only the type of woman and wife she was, but what kind

of mother she was. Our children were her world. I couldn't do
that to her, even after everything she had done to me.'

'You didn't want to give the prosecution a motive,' Antony
repeats. 'As in, if you disclosed that your wife was having an
affair with your business partner, you would have had cause
to kill them?'

'That's one way the prosecution could have spun it, yes.'

I am still sat in silence, unable to bring myself to speak, to
force encouragement from my lips when all I want to do is
beg him to take back the words. To undo the mayhem he has
unknowingly caused. He has hooped his own noose without
even knowing it.

'Can someone else confirm this?' I say, my voice strained.
'I find it odd that the police didn't find evidence of the affair
during their investigation.'

'My former business partner, for a start.'

'And if he denies it?'

'Then the evidence will speak for itself.'

He reaches for the empty chair next to him, and lifts a wad
of pages from the seat and puts them on the table.

'Their phone records.'

Antony and I stare down at the files in disbelief.

'Alex ordered new work phones for our employees and
added two extra plans to the order, so that he and Yolanda
could contact one another without being caught. The police
didn't find Yolanda's, what with it being incinerated in the
fire and the phone plan being on the business account under a
different name. If they looked through Alex's work phone, they
wouldn't have found anything. Although I don't believe they
looked into him much at all. They suspected me from the very
beginning.'

I look to Antony; his eyes are bright with hope.

'May we see them?'

He hands over the documents, a fat wad of pages containing hours and hours of communication. This couldn't have been a mere dalliance. This was a long, committed relationship. I turn the first page and begin to read.

'The affair started three years ago,' Wade says. 'Alex and I would go on group holidays with our families. Their kids, our kids. It worked well for a number of years. Perhaps some of our best memories were on those trips. It was the trip to Alicante that they first slept together. They did it right under our noses. Emily, Alex's wife, was pregnant with their third child at the time. Their full-blown affair began on our return.'

Antony reads out a text message, dating back to 2017.

'Come to the office. W's out. I want to fuck you over his desk until you come all over my—'

He clears his throat and looks up, cheeks flushing, before continuing to read in silence. I watch as Wade tries to compose himself after what he has just heard. He takes a deep breath and sighs it from his nostrils.

'We went on one last holiday after that. They had been together a year by then. They were at it like rabbits, according to the text messages. They were messaging one another while we were all sat around the pool. Feeling each other up beneath the table in restaurants, the same table where our children were sitting.

'It was in 2018 that things got more complicated. Alex wanted more. He said he would leave Emily, his wife, and that Yolanda should do the same to me and the kids, so they could be together openly. He would leave the business, start his own – likely planning to take half our clientele with him, knowing him. But Yolanda didn't want that. This was in August, a few months before the murders.'

I skim towards the month. The texts are noticeably colder. Alex is sending far more, while Yolanda responds with short, sharp replies.

Meet me at the usual place and time.

No. I love my husband

Sure seemed like it when you were fucking me.

What would W think of that? That I had you more times in a year than he had? Doesn't sound like love to me

Stop. I love my husband. My children.

Or what? Usual place. 8pm.

'He became obsessive,' Wade says. 'Alex doesn't like being told no. He was a nightmare to have as a business partner, in that respect. And Yolanda learned the same lesson.'

He relays the story calmly, but beneath the surface, I can see the rage. His jaw flexes whenever he says Alex's name.

'How did you find out?' I ask.

'A member of staff brought these records to me during the annual audit in 2018,' he says. 'She found the phones on the bill but couldn't trace them to any of my employees, so she looked a little deeper and saw the content. Due to their unprofessional nature, she raised her concerns.'

'And you knew it was your wife?' Antony asks.

'Yes.' He clears his throat. 'The initials they used for themselves, and for me and Emily; the way my wife's accent worked into her text messages. Alex's usual pushy tone he uses across the board.'

'And how did you react?'

His eyes fall to the surface of the table.

'I was devastated. Angry initially.'

'When you say you were angry,' Antony says. 'How did you express that?'

'I didn't. I was at work, at my desk, staring through the glass partition to Alex's office across from mine. He smiled at me, and I forced one back.'

Tears fill his eyes. He blinks them away, swipes them from his face with the back of his hand.

'Did you tell Yolanda that you knew of their affair?'

'Not for a long time. I didn't want her to leave me. I hoped she would get tired of the game they were playing, and eventually come back to me.'

A client discovers his wife and business partner have had a three-year affair right under his nose, and instead of expressing anger, he lets them continue. His business partner allegedly ran their business into the ground and stole his wife, and he is only mentioning this now, in the final days before the trial. No matter how well he expresses his story, a jury won't believe it. Not unless Alex's motive for murder eclipses his.

'What do you believe happened the night your family were killed?' Antony asks. 'Who do you think the masked figure was?'

He sits quietly in contemplation, as if he is choosing the right words before he opens his mouth.

'Alex Finch ruined my life. He took Yolanda away from me, he destroyed my business, and then he took what mattered most of all: he killed my family in cold blood, and left me alive. To take the fall, yes. But I know Alex – he would have wanted me to feel this agony. Alex Finch is responsible for this – I would bet my life on it.

'The man I saw in my house. The man who knew the code to the front gates and to my gun room, the man who knew my favourite gun, and the rooms where my family and I slept . . . He is the only person who could have done this.'

Antony and I stare at him from the other side of the table, stunned by the bombshell.

'What would his motive be, to destroy your life like this?' Antony asks.

'He has always wanted what I had. When I got a girlfriend, he got one too. When I proposed to Yolanda, he proposed to Emily the month after. When Yolanda and I had Phoebe, he and Emily began trying. When I decided I wanted to start my own business, he worked his way into it until it was his too. We have been best friends since we were at university; I just thought he was insecure and competitive – I didn't realise how obsessed he was until it was too late. He had stolen my wife, driven my business into the ground after running it like a fuck-ing Ponzi scheme and keeping me away from the books. And before you ask why I didn't insist on seeing them, on keeping a better eye on my business – I didn't because I trusted him. I trusted him with my life.

'Alex grew up in a world where he was never told no. He got what he wanted his whole life. Yolanda was probably the first person to truly reject him.'

'And your children?' I ask. 'Why would he hurt them?'

'He knew that would hurt me the most.'

I take a sip of water, needing a minute to process my thoughts. The glass shakes in my hand. He thinks he is saving himself by telling us this. But in actuality he is digging himself a deeper hole and dragging me down with him. I return the glass to the surface of the table.

'The most important question here is why you waited until now to expose this. You don't owe him or your wife anything, after they betrayed you. I say this because it could appear that you're using Alex as your scapegoat just before the trial starts. So why did you wait so long? Why should the jury believe you?'

His eyes flicker, perhaps with a memory.

'When I discovered the gravity of the situation – the affair, the state of the business – I plunged into a deep depression. My whole life had turned out to be a lie, and there was one sole man responsible. Alex sat at the seat of the fire like a cancer, eating away at everything I loved. I didn't tell anyone this because I knew how it would make me look, if it was brought up in court.

'Three days before the murders, I invited Alex to come hunting with me. We went into the woods and walked a while. He was on edge; he must have sensed that I knew what he and Yolanda had been doing. I had called him out to the woods to tell him everything I knew: the affair, his part in the failure of the business. Everything. I wanted to hear it from him, but before we could get into it, he tracked the buck I had been after for months – the most beautiful thing you've ever seen. I didn't want him taking another prized possession from me.

'He tracked it to the edge of woodland, and as we walked, space grew between us, approaching the buck from both sides, before stopping and raising our guns. I remember it so vividly. I could see his breath in the air each time he exhaled, the rosy tip of his nose from the cold. He raised his gun, aiming between the trees. And I raised mine. Towards him.'

I brace myself, trying not to let my reaction show. His eyes have become razor-focused as he recounts the tale, as if he is peering at his target in the crosshairs of his rifle.

'Alex caught sight of me in the corner of his eye, and we stood like this for what felt like hours. I knew what he had done, and he knew he had reached the end of the road. He had taken everything from me, or so I thought at the time, before the murders happened. And yet I couldn't bring myself to do it. However much I wanted him to pay for what he had done to me, no matter how much I wanted him gone – I couldn't do it. I raised the gun and shot in the air. He practically jumped out of his skin, and the buck scarpered. We walked back to the grounds in silence, and before he left . . . I said something I would regret.'

'What did you say?' Antony asks, engrossed in the tale.

'I said if he ever came near me or my family again, I wouldn't hesitate. I would kill him on sight.'

The room thrums with tension. It is so quiet I can hear the faint nasal breaths from Antony at my side, hear a clock ticking from another room.

'That's why I didn't mention it until now,' he says. 'I threatened to kill him, with the very gun that would be used to kill my family three days later. My lawyers at the time, Eddie and Adrian, advised me to submit no comment. But the longer I went without mentioning it, the more I realised I would look like I was spinning a lie if I were to bring it up so late in the process. But now I know the country will think me a killer either way.'

Of course. Adrian and Eddie Chester would have led Wade down the wrong path, knowing how guilty he would look should he bring up the only thing that could exonerate him later.

A single thought makes me break out in a cold sweat.

Is Wade innocent?

'Alex Finch wanted everything I had,' Wade says, his voice hoarse. 'And when he couldn't take it for himself, he made sure to take it away from me.'

We sit, reeling in the silence. My guilt grows at the thought of his innocence. He trusts me to save him, to do the right thing, and the entire time I have been thinking of ways to save my own neck. But as Antony and I look at one another, I know he has had the same revelation as me.

Adrian missed something crucial when he was appointed to the defence. He had wanted to bury this because he saw it as a way for them to undermine the police investigation, providing a strong defence for Mr Darling. He saw his ultimatum as black and white, but what lies before us now is the most beautiful shade of grey.

To Wade's confusion, I smile.

He doesn't know it, but he might have just saved us both.

21

I stride down the street from Mrs Darling's address, tuning out the sound of Antony's incessant chatter as he matches my stride, jittery with adrenaline. I had thought the evidence proving Wade Darling's innocence would make my objective harder. Now I realise how wrong I was.

'This evidence of the affair with Yolanda,' Antony says. 'It throws everything the police have concluded into question. It shows how little they have searched for other suspects. This isn't just an oversight, it's a failed police investigation, which means—'

'There is a chance I could call for the case to be thrown out.'

'Exactly,' he beams, grinning wildly. 'It's perfect. Fucking perfect.'

I feel so on edge; the excitement is electric. But my anxiety has me doubting this sudden possibility of freedom. Could it really be so simple? The Messenger said I had to lose the trial – but I wouldn't need to if there was no trial at all. Wade and I could *both* walk free.

'Is the evidence admissible at this point?' Antony asks.

'The judge won't throw this out, it's too strong. The fact that the police didn't investigate Alex Finch as a suspect means the prosecution cannot definitively prove the investigation has been thoroughly carried out. They cannot prove, without a shadow of a doubt, that Wade committed the crimes.'

Hearing me say the words aloud makes the opportunity seem all the more tangible. I have the overwhelming need for something sugary and full of carbs, and try to think back to when I last ate.

'But what if the judge does reject it?' he asks. 'There is so much media attention around this. To then have it thrown out right before commencement after so many delays . . . the courts would be made a fool of.'

He's right. Every pair of eyes in the country is on this case. It's mentioned every night on the six o'clock news, featured on every newspaper front page. The growing uproar from protestors and women's rights groups. One can't pass a newspaper stand without having Wade Darling's face stare back at them.

'Then I will have to make my argument completely airtight,' I reply, a nervous rasp to my voice. We stop at the fork in the road. 'I need you to look into this former employee who found the call records – we'll need her as a witness if the case goes to trial. The judge would be hard pushed to not admit a new witness at this stage if he plans to press ahead with the prosecution's case the way it is.'

'Got it,' he replies, nodding excitedly. 'When will you call the judge?'

'I'm going to do it right this second.'

He grins, visually exhilarated by the prospect ahead. I can't help but smile back, and take the pack of cigarettes from my pocket.

'Thought you didn't smoke anymore?' he asks through a smirk.

'This close to trial, all bets are off.'

We part ways as I head east towards the tube station, my pace growing faster and faster, dragging on the cigarette as I go. This is my get-out clause. I won't need to sabotage the trial because there won't be one. I can lay the blame at the judge's feet, telling the Messenger that it was orchestrated without my knowledge, that the Viklund family could appeal, and get the case back to court. Only I would make sure to be long gone by then.

I don't want to lose my life in London and the career I've built, to lose the only family I have ever known in Hannah and Maggie, but I won't be able to stay here waiting for the Messenger to reappear. I'll need to cover my tracks, find a way to keep Hannah safe, and then get the hell out of this city.

But first things first. I slip my phone from my pocket and scroll for the number of Judge McConnell's office.

⚖

'I'm sorry, Your Honour. But I thought it best to bring this to you immediately.'

The judge stares at me from behind his desk. He looks angry, resentful even, but as the information sinks in, his shoulders sag and his eyes close with a heavy-bodied sigh. He slips off his glasses and pinches the bridge of his nose.

Calling a judge into work over the weekend doesn't set up one's chance of success in one's argument well, but with the trial looming, it is the only chance I have to bring the new evidence to light. Despite his frustration at being torn away from his Sunday plans, I can see the necessity of the meeting settling in.

Niall is sat in stunned silence beside me. I can feel him practically vibrating with rage at my pulling the rug from under him. I had sent the damning phone records electronically to his chambers shortly before the meeting, knowing full well he wouldn't have time to read them; his clerk might not have even opened the email yet. But had he done his due diligence, he wouldn't have been caught out. His ego thought he had the win in the bag.

'I'd like to see the phone records,' Judge McConnell says.

I pass the wad of paper over the desk, hole-punched and arranged in a binder.

'I would like to see them too, of course,' Niall adds sharply.

'I sent them to your chambers electronically, but here is a physical copy for you.'

I pass another copy towards him, and watch his cheeks burn red. He isn't a man who reacts well to being duped, and I can see the words he wished he could call me burning in his eyes.

We sit in the silence of the judge's chambers, with nothing but the tick of the clock and the soft, whistling nasal breaths of the judge as he reads.

Sat before the judge, I feel my confidence in my plan begin to waver. Suppose he won't throw the case out to protect his own hide? He'll want to be on this case as much as Niall does – the notoriety, the cemented reputation. Dismissing the case certainly won't carry the same merit. There is right and wrong of course, but in the end, we are all walking, talking egos, wanting our moment in the spotlight.

This has to work. It is the only arsenal I have.

My palms grow damp in my lap, and I fight to wipe them dry in case either of the men see. Sat beside me, Niall is flitting through the pages of the text messages, the paper sounding like a cracking whip with each violent flick. His breathing grows faster and shallower the more he reads.

Judge McConnell drops the binder on the surface of the desk. 'For crying out loud.'

His professionalism slips only briefly, as the credibility of the evidence hits him. He shuts his eyes for a few seconds, emits a sigh, and opens them again.

'Am I to believe you didn't have these tucked away for this precise moment before the trial?'

'Some trick,' Niall adds.

'No trick,' I reply. 'Just a scared client who has finally opened up with the right counsel.'

'What sort of man tries to bury evidence that could get him let off bloody murder charges?' Niall asks with a scoff.

I turn my eyes to the judge, refusing to reply. If Niall wants to know the answer to that, he'll need to discover it when cross-examining my witnesses, if he gets the chance.

'I might ask you what sort of police investigation doesn't uncover a lousily covered-up affair and a clear alternative suspect to boot,' Judge McConnell rebuts.

Niall and I both sit in silence, waiting for the judge to continue.

'This isn't . . . ideal,' he says. 'In fact, it's a bloody nightmare. The CPS will look like a laughing stock. The press and the public will inevitably go mad.'

'And an innocent man will go free,' I add.

'Don't push it,' he snaps, and sighs once more, his eyes falling on the binder of text messages on his desk. 'I will need to think about this.'

'Of course,' I reply, and turn to glance at Niall. He can't even meet my eyes any longer. His hands are curled into fists in his lap.

'We will go ahead as planned tomorrow unless I say otherwise,' Judge McConnell says. 'My office will leave word in the morning.'

'Yes, Your Honour,' Niall and I reply in unison.

The judge glances towards the door and back again – our time is up. As soon as we step out of the judge's office, Niall is on me.

'That was so fucking dirty, Harper. You could have given me a heads-up.'

'If you'd done your job properly, I wouldn't have had to.'

His face boils red, cheeks the colour of pigskin.

'He won't pull it,' he says, stepping so close to me I can smell his breath. 'You really think he'll dismiss the trial, after all this time? Right before it's set to start? He'd look a fool, we all would.'

'Not all of us.'

He is practically shaking now, his livid eyes set firmly upon mine. I can't say it doesn't please me to see him so rattled. He is one of those men who need to be knocked down a peg or two every so often to keep them falling victim to their ever inflating ego.

I watch as he storms off towards the doors, and huff out a relieved sigh.

McConnell has to throw out the trial. He'll look like a crony if he doesn't.

All I have to do now is wait.

'Ms Harper?'

I open my eyes. The judge's clerk is stood in the doorway of the office.

'Sorry, I have a man on the phone for you. He said he's been trying to contact you at your chambers, but keeps missing you.'

'Who is it?' I ask.

'A Mr Hurst.'

Fredrick.

'You can take it in my office.'

'Thanks.'

I follow her inside, my palms tingling by my sides. What could be so urgent for him to call me through the judge? The clerk holds out the phone, and I rest it to my ear.

'Neve Harper.'

'Neve, I'm glad I've tracked you down.' I had expected his usual cool tone, but there is an unusual buzz of excitement to his voice. 'I've found something.'

22

I arrive at the decided meeting spot, a bench looking out at Tower Bridge on the north side of the Thames, and find that I am the first one there.

The air is sharp, and the evening is dark with that unmistakable tang of winter on the breeze, similar to burning cinder. The path along the river is quiet. Only the odd person passes me by. The majority of the time I am alone, watching the bustling city reflect its light in the chopping river. Fredrick, however, is nowhere to be seen.

I wait for ten minutes, then fifteen. The chill of the bench has leached into my thighs until I am shivering beneath my coat, and the sound of my chattering teeth fill my ears.

My phone makes me jump. I had meant to turn it off, to keep from being followed. I silently curse myself as I slip it from my pocket. It's Artie.

'How's my favourite barrister?' he asks when I answer.

'Busy,' I reply.

'I'm sure you've got time to run an update by me, after your not-so-subtle brush-off this morning. I'll get one of the lackeys to go and get you a coffee tomorrow if you're nice to me.'

I warm to his playfulness and lean back in my seat.

'Well, if you must know, I might have just successfully ended the trial before it's even begun.'

There is a beat of silence before he speaks. When he does, the playfulness has gone from his tone. 'What do you mean?'

'I mean, the CPS screwed up. The police investigation ignored a clear alternative suspect in the murders, placing all of their bets on our client, and the CPS failed to spot it. I ran the evidence by the judge and he's contemplating whether to throw the trial as we speak.'

'What evidence?' he asks.

'Text messages between the defendant's business partner, Alex Finch, and the defendant's wife Yolanda, revealing an affair. She ended it – to his dissatisfaction – and then there's the clincher: Finch's wife filed for divorce just before the murders. A motive for his business partner to enact revenge is just as strong as the case of familicide against our client, and the police failed to investigate it. At this point there's no case to try, it shouldn't have even got this far.'

Artie doesn't react like I might expect. I had expected him to laugh, or speak through his usual grin. But the silence rings out on the other side of the phone.

'Don't you lot run anything by me anymore?'

'I thought you'd be pleased.'

'Well, it's hardly a victory, is it? All this momentum, fizzling out at the last second due to what, a technicality? It's a win by default.'

'Well, I'm sorry if the defence of my client's best interests is disappointing to you, Artie, but I have to say I didn't really consider your score card when I was weighing up the thought of striking three life sentences from my client's future. What's the problem? Put a bet on us for the win, did you?'

'I'm not saying it wasn't the right decision, miss – you know best – but these big decisions, surely you'd want to run it by one of us before jumping into action?'

'Who's the advocate for the defendant, Arthur, me or you?'

He clears his throat.

'You are, miss.'

'Would you like the job instead?'

'No, miss.'

'Then I suggest you let me get on with it.'

I hang up the phone and sigh the frustration out of me. Whatever I do, whatever I say, I have a man giving me his two cents. If it isn't Antony, it's Artie. If not the judge, then Niall. There is Wade, and then there is the Messenger. The only man I truly want to hear from is Fredrick, and he is still nowhere to be seen.

I check my watch. Almost twenty minutes late. As long as I've known him, he has always been on time. My imagination runs rampant, thinking of all the things that could have held him up.

Stop panicking. He said he'd be here, so he'll be here.

I turn off my phone and dislodge the battery. There had been nothing from him, but then there wouldn't be, with the risk of the Messenger keeping track of me. What if Fredrick has left me a message at chambers changing the location? What if I got the time wrong? My thoughts continue like this, round and round, my shoulders knotted with nerves.

I wait until thirty-five minutes have passed and my fingers appear almost blue, until I cannot bring myself to wait another minute more.

Maybe he's found something about the Viklunds that scared him off.

I walk back the way I came and towards the main road, my

eyes down and bracing myself from the cold. That's when I see the flash of headlights behind me, and look up.

That must be him.

I sigh with relief, and instantly feel my heart begin to calm, as I pick up the pace and head towards the roadside. I reach the driver's window and watch the glass lower.

The Messenger stares back at me.

'Get in,' he says.

⚖

Thirty minutes have passed by the time we enter the abandoned industrial estate. I am sat in the back of the Messenger's car, with a large burly man squeezed in beside me. In the front sits another man, with the Messenger behind the wheel. No one has said a word since I got inside the car.

The estate sits a stone's throw from the Thames. A landscape of grime and discarded oil drums, bronze with rust, with the teasing gleam of central London in the distance, which is quickly enveloped by the fog creeping in from the water; I can smell it on the breeze from the driver's open window: the faint lingering scent of salt and scum.

The buildings have been graffitied and vandalised, and every pane of glass has been smashed. As the car turns in, the headlights cast over the glint of broken bottles and rusting beer cans, the red beady eyes of pigeons peering through the windows from their perches in the rafters. The car moves at a crawl over the potholes pitted in the tarmac, making my racing heart jolt out of sync with each jutter.

I hear a thud from the boot behind my seat. It isn't the first time I've heard this sound. Every few minutes, I feel the sensation against my back; hear it at each stop light as we squealed to a halt. I think of a cannister of fuel rolling back and forth, sloshing its stink into the fabric. Or maybe it's a gun and a shovel chiming against one another in a morbid death call.

I should have run.

The car passes warehouse after warehouse, driving at a crawl towards the water's edge. As we get closer, two men appear through the mist, stood before a dock that slowly peters out into the fog. They are dressed entirely in black, their faces void and their eyes seemingly on me, piercing through the windscreen to where I sit in the back seat, crammed between the door and the wide-shouldered stranger. The view of the city has been engulfed by the fog.

I feel my bladder clench. My kneecaps are chiming together like teeth and my pulse is so fast that a wave of nausea ripples up my throat. Fear has a scent to it: the salt of sweat, tinged with something sweet and rotten. I taste it in my mouth, smell it on my breath.

The car pulls to a stop and rocks back and forth with the shifting weight as the doors open and close. I am led out roughly, the man's grip pinching at my arm through my sleeve, but I don't make a sound. Despite the terror coursing through me, I have the overwhelming need for them to think me stronger than I am.

The air smells of rotten fish and pollution, and at my feet, oil shimmers in the puddles in the pitted concrete ground. As we near the men, I feel the mist wet my face.

The Messenger stops in his tracks and turns to face me, that familiar smile cutting into his cheeks.

'Do you know why I brought you here?'

I hear another bang from the boot of the car and think of the cannister of fuel, the gun and spade.

I shake my head.

'Let's remind her,' he calls behind us.

I hear the boot door open. The click of the lock and the air-pressured whine of the mechanism as it rises. It is hard to see through the slips of mist drifting in our path, but I hear a bang, a grunt. Shadows move amid the fog. And then they appear.

Fredrick is dragged into view by the two men the Messenger and I made the journey with, his feet trailing beneath him. His hands are zip-tied in front of him and his eyes are wide with shock. I have never seen someone so pale. I know in an instant that I have killed him by bringing him into this. More blood on my hands. Adrenaline courses through me with such ferocity that I feel it tingling all over my skin, in my eyes, my tongue. When Fredrick parts his lips and coughs, blood splutters down his chin. The banging I had heard had been him, locked inside the boot. So close yet out of reach.

'Still not sure?' the Messenger asks with a grin. 'Do you remember what I told you about Adrian Whittaker? About him trying to outsmart us?'

I try to swallow, but my mouth is bone-dry.

'. . . Yes.'

The Messenger thrusts me towards the dock, the shock of it forcing all of the air from my lungs. I find my footing and look out at the mist.

'Walk,' the Messenger says.

So I walk. I head into the fog in a death march; the dock creaks with each step, the cold brown water lapping around its pillars, spitting up through the cracks. I can hear the Messenger behind me; the calm pattern to his breathing. The planks are so rotten that I fear each slab of wood will give beneath my feet, and can feel the dock shifting with our weight. Ahead is nothing but a thick wall of mist, until I approach the end, and shadows appear, black shapes morphing into silhouettes. Two more men stand at the edge, with indecipherable objects at their feet. I slow as I see them, and feel a prod in my spine as the Messenger urges me on. At their feet, I realise, are concrete cinderblocks and chains.

My heart leaps. I instinctively step back, only to turn and meet the Messenger's chest with a thud. I feel the heat of him, the thrum of his heart beneath his clothes. His musk gets stuck in my nostrils. Behind him, Fredrick is being dragged along the dock, his feet strumming against the planks until they pass us and reach the edge, and he is thrust down to his knees. He is eerily silent, as if he too is trying to appear braver than he is. Death chops in waves before him, and still, he doesn't beg. He doesn't ask why. He stares off into the fog as the men jostle about him, looping the chains around his torso, through his bound limbs and over his neck.

'He didn't know . . .' I stutter. Fear has me in a chokehold. The words come out strained. 'This was all my doing. He didn't know what I was getting him into—'

'Neve,' Fredrick warns, urging me into silence. One of the men punches him in the back of the head. I yelp at the sound of the brain-juddering thwack, and bite my lip to stop myself from speaking in case I cause him more pain.

The chains rattle as they criss-cross around Fredrick's body, as the waiting water chops incessantly. The cinderblocks are pushed to the very edge of the dock.

I want to tell them to stop, to allow me a moment to catch my breath and think of ways to reason with them. But as I go to speak, the words lodge in my throat. I'm too terrified to utter a word, even as I beg my lips to part.

The two men drag Fredrick to his feet, and I look up at the

Messenger towering by my side. He meets my eyes with a grin. This is my opportunity to say something, to stop this from happening. But just as I finally part my lips to speak, and as a desperate croak slips up my throat, he turns away and with a nod of his head says, 'Do it.'

The men kick the blocks from the edge.

'*No!*'

Fredrick is yanked from the dock. A quick flash, and then he is gone. The dark water envelopes him whole.

The Messenger grabs the nape of my neck and propels me towards the edge, a splintered scream bursting from my lips. I am led with my head down, hair whipping into my eyes, until my face is held directly over the water where Fredrick fell.

He is going to make me watch.

The water is choppy and wild, bubbles rising from Fredrick's lungs, but I can't see him from the filth in the water, only the tips of his fingers breaking through the surface as he tries to claw himself up and draw breath. But I know that beneath, he will be staring up with those stark blue eyes, kicking and thrashing helplessly against the chains.

'This is what happens when you don't listen,' the Messenger whispers.

The bubbles grow scarcer and scarcer. From the thrashing in the water, I sense Fredrick's movements slow. I wait as life leaves him, and his body falls still, until finally, it's clear he has passed, lolling against the pull of the chains beneath the surface. My tears splash silently into the water.

I am shaking violently from shock, as if in spasm. I can't stop staring at the surface, imagining those lifeless blue eyes staring back at me.

Then they start fitting chains to me.

I am thrust upwards, and the chains looped over me, through me. My hands are yanked behind my back and tied. I always thought I would beg for my life. Kick and scream and bite. Do all I could to live. But I am frozen to the dock, staring out at the shifting mist, as silent tears run down my cheeks and the chains tighten and tighten, pinching me where they meet at my chest, my back, my thighs.

'Did you think we wouldn't find out about your little trick, trying to have the judge throw the trial?'

The metal weighs me down, and the blocks are moved towards the edge of the dock. I hear a sound, like a puppy's yelp, or a distant siren, and realise it came from me.

How could he possibly know that? I was so careful.

The realisation hits me square in the chest, voiding my lungs of air.

It's over. It's really over.

'You still have a choice,' he says from behind my back. 'You can still get yourself out of this. Wade Darling or you and Hannah, remember?'

I stand before death, biting the flesh of my cheeks to keep from crying out.

Him or us.

Whoosh. Thwack. Whoosh. Thwack.

'Do it,' the Messenger says to the men.

I feel their hands on me; a hard snatch of the chains. They are so strong that I am practically lifted off my feet, waiting to be thrown. I gasp in the mist.

'I'll do it!'

The hands yank me back, and my legs give. I slam down onto the planks. My head knocks against the wood without my hands to break my fall.

The Messenger reaches down and snatches the chains at my back, lifting me up so my ear meets his lips.

'Next time,' he whispers. 'It will be your sweet little Hannah.'

He drops me again with a thud, my brain rattling in my skull. As the men begin unfastening the chains from the blocks, I look down through the cracks in the planks at the chopping water below, imagining Hannah staring up at me. Thrashing silently until the life leaves her eyes.

23

The day of the trial

I wake up to the sun beaming through the window. I hadn't drawn the curtains before sinking into bed. At least, that's what I guess happened. Everything is a blur. My last memory was of lying on the dock as the chains were pulled from me. I don't remember the journey home, nor slipping my front door key in the lock. Hannah was there, I know that much. I can remember flashes of her, the smile slipping from her face, her lips moving but her words not reaching my ears. *I don't feel well,* I remember saying. But not before knocking back two straight brandies. For the rest of the night, I dreamt that I was drowning, staring up at the Messenger where he stood on the dock above. But as far as I'm aware, I didn't wander in the night. There's that mercy, at least.

I am fully clothed, with my feet still firmly in their heels. The sun is hot on my face, and I squint to look about for my phone. Three missed calls. Voicemails. All from the judge's office. My heart jumps in my chest as I scramble up to a sitting position. I wasn't in my right mind and didn't set an alarm – it is almost nine. I should be in court preparing to begin trial in an hour.

I rub my eyes furiously to rid them of the yellow orbs from the sun and play the voicemail.

'Ms Harper, this is Nicola Bennett calling from Judge McConnell's office. I'm calling regarding the Darling trial set for commencement this morning. Please give me a call back as soon as you can.'

I hang up and bring up the call log on the screen, noticing how the phone shakes violently in my grip.

Personal reputation or not, McConnell can't go ahead with the trial with such an oversight in the police investigation. If we proceed, he must know I could push for there being no case to try, when it comes to the end of the prosecution's case. I wonder which he would find more humiliating in terms of the press.

The judge postponing the trial is my only chance to get out from under the Messenger's hold on me. To form a plan to protect Hannah and me, before the trial recommences again. Otherwise, I have no other choice but to proceed with his demands. Last night was proof of that. I press the phone to my ear and listen to the dialling tone, my heartbeat echoing in the other.

When Nicola answers the call, I notice immediately that she sounds tired and stressed. Her voice is an octave higher than usual.

'Nicola, it's Neve Harper returning your call.'

I hear her sigh with relief on the other end of the line.

'Ms Harper, I was worried I might have missed you. Thank you for calling me back.'

She clears her throat as I wait with bated breath. Whatever comes out of her mouth will determine my fate. Sweat breaks out all over me. I sit in wait, feeling the warm trickle of it running down my ribs.

'Yes, the Darling trial. Judge McConnell has considered your evidence and—'

There is a muffling at the other end of the line, and a distant, tinny voice muttering in the background. My heart is lodged in my throat.

Come on, come on, come on.

'Ms Bennett?'

The line clears.

'Apologies, Ms Harper, it's a bit manic this morning. The press is calling off the hook about this, we can barely keep our phone lines open.'

I sigh silently and rest my head against the headboard. My heart is beating so violently that I can barely focus on my breathing.

'Neve,' she says, in a tone I can't distinguish. 'The judge has decided to proceed with the trial.'

It hits me like a blow. I close my eyes as the panic rips through my every nerve.

Nicola has continued talking, but I've not registered a word, catching only her last sentence.

'. . . it seems someone leaked the possibility of a mistrial to the press.'

Niall.

It was a genius counter-move. The only thing that could have kept the judge from dropping the trial would be to throw his reputation to the wolves of the press. By having them threaten to slander his character and reputation before he'd made the call on whether to proceed, it would almost definitely affect his judgement and overall decision.

I imagine Niall getting the same news, the inevitable grin sweeping across his face.

'Right,' I reply, trying to compose myself.

'Sorry, Neve – it was a close call.'

'Thanks.'

I hang up and sit in silence.

We are going to trial.

The fear crushes down upon my chest, until I am shaking from head to foot, and tears wet my eyes. I force myself to breathe, taking small sips of air.

It's Wade's freedom or mine.

A knock at my bedroom door jolts me from my thoughts.

'Come in,' I force.

Hannah's face peers through the gap in the door.

'Are you okay?' she asks. 'You looked really bad last night.'

Her complexion is pale, and her eyes are wide with worry. I would feel guilty for troubling her, did my fear not have its hands wrapped about my neck, squeezing the life out of me.

'Fine,' I reply. 'Shouldn't you be at school?'

'I don't feel good either,' she says, her voice turning child-like, almost baby-ish. 'Maybe I have the same bug as you.'

I doubt it.

I don't have the capacity to take this on; I don't have the mental space to call the school and report her sick, nor jump through any other hurdles they might put in my way. If she wants to play truant, I'll let her.

'I'm running late,' I say, and clamber out of bed. 'Do I need to call and let them know? Or will they get the message if you don't show?'

'Don't worry about it,' she says.

So I don't. I grab my towel from where I'd let it dry on the radiator and head towards the bathroom when I hear a knock at the front door. Hannah and I both freeze.

'Are you expecting anyone?' I ask.

She shakes her head.

I pass her for the stairs, my heart hammering as fast as my feet, as the knocking picks up again. I reach the bottom, notice how bad I look in the mirror above the mantle. My hair is wild from sleep, with dark circles framing my eyes. I don't look like myself, but like a creature. Wild. Dangerous.

The knocking starts up again.

I open the door. A man dressed in an orange fluorescent jacket stands before me. My eyes drift from his face to the name of the company he works for above his breast. *Thameslink*. On the other side of the road, another man in the same jacket knocks on the door of number forty-five.

'Yes?' I ask.

'Sorry to disturb you, madam. We're just doing the rounds to confirm the railworks commencing this week.'

I stare at him, a piercing whistle screaming down both ears. *Did he just say . . .*

'Madam? I'm confirming the railworks behind your property.'

'W-what railworks?'

'We sent a notice to each resident last month.'

'No you didn't,' I stutter angrily.

'We delivered them by hand, madam. This is just a courtesy call to confirm—'

'I didn't get a letter,' I repeat, as if that will change anything.

'I'm sorry for that, madam. Perhaps you thought it was a piece of junk mail?'

As if that matters now. The taste of bile is rising up my throat. I raise a shaky hand to it.

'What . . . what works are you doing?'

Whoosh. Thwack. Whoosh. Thwack.

'We will be laying a new track alongside the existing line.'

'But surely there isn't room—'

'We've had permission to remove the trees on the far side,' he says. 'This was quite the hot topic last year. There was a meeting with the local residents. Have you lived here long?'

I have gone completely cold.

'Yes. I ... was distracted. I have a demanding job. When does this work commence?'

'Today, madam—'

'*Stop calling me madam!*'

His eyes widen, and his colleague across the street peers over his shoulder at the commotion.

'When will you be removing the trees from behind my address?'

'This will be the first task, but I'm afraid it would be difficult to estimate when—'

My mind is reeling so fast that I can barely pin a thought down. Only one persists: Matthew, rotting in the ground. I stare at the man in a blind panic.

'Apologies for any inconvenience, mada—' he stops himself with a nervous cough, before trundling off to the house next door. I click the door shut.

The body.

They are going to unearth the body.

PART II

The Prosecution

Day One

24

The weather is ice-cold. The sort of air that feels wet with each breath. Londoners pass me by in a huddle of rustling coats and coiled scarves as I stand before the Old Bailey, looking up at the ray of sunlight breaking through the clouds and beaming upon the Bailey's dome, illuminating Lady Justice where she stands in all her bronze-gilded glory. A sword in one hand, scales in the other. She represents blind justice: fairness, honesty, integrity. Everything I do not.

I don't think I truly realised what I am to face until now. Before hearing the news about the trial this morning from the judge's office, there seemed to be a window of hope where I thought I might still wriggle out of it. A point where a clear route of escape would open up before me. But time has run out, Fredrick is dead, the trial is about to begin, and now of course, there's the matter of the body.

I have always feared this day would come.

When I had buried him there, it was not with the notion that it would be forever. He was too close to home, literally and figuratively, and if he were found, fingers would inevitably point towards me. But once the deed was done, I couldn't find the strength to go through with it again. Now I fear I have left it too late.

The panic is sudden and overwhelming. I clench my fists to ground myself.

I can't think of that now. I must tackle one problem at a time.

My other problem stands before me. I peer up at Lady Justice, gleaming from her perch.

I have never knowingly lost a case before. Never jeopardised a client's fate for my own. Not just because I love my job, but because I'm tied to a strict view of right and wrong. This is my comeuppance for tipping the scales. The consequences of my crime.

The evidence I have against my client is nestled safely in my carry case. It is as if I can feel the weight of it, the pull of my guilt. But whenever it becomes too much, I think of Hannah, and my fear for her safety drowns out everything else. I must find a window in the day to deliver the evidence to the prosecution. I say this to myself factually, devoid of emotion, but as soon as it comes time, I know the fear will grip me, for once I do this, there is no going back. The trial will only end one way.

The press has crowded before the doors. They won't have caught Wade, who was escorted into the building by Antony earlier this morning, but they will expect me to give them something. After Matthew's disappearance, the press and I agreed on an unspoken rule where I would discuss my work but not my personal life. To deny them now would be inviting them to dig deeper into me rather than my client, picking at my life like vultures.

I take a deep breath, my exhalation unfurling in a cloud.

I can do this, I think to myself, in the hope that I'll believe my own lie. *Because I don't have a choice.*

I cross the street towards the doors, bracing myself as the press catch sight of me and begin their onslaught.

There is no going back now.

⚖

The inside of the Bailey is essentially two worlds: the past and the present. On one side, you have the original building. The same doorways the likes of Myra Hindley and the Krays passed through to face their crimes. Decades of bloodshed tried and sentenced; British history that has bled into the walls. The other side is modern and cold, where the juror chairs don't squeak and the panelled walls on the courtrooms still smell fresh. I can't help but see the similarities between my surroundings and my life. The present ever plagued by the past.

I pass through the building for the de-robing room, listening to the echoes of my heels on the cold hard floor, when I hear the hard clap of footsteps growing louder behind me.

'It appears your trick of attempting to throw the trial didn't go according to plan, Harper,' Niall says behind me, stopping me in my tracks. 'Sorry about that.'

I turn to face him and see the victorious grin on his face. Humility is something Niall never quite mastered.

'Your plan worked though, leaking it to the press. I suppose I owe you congratulations.'

'You can save your congratulations for the end of the trial,' he replies. He steps closer, the smell of coffee lingering on his breath. 'Your theory of the second suspect won't stick – you know that, right?'

With so much at stake in my life, Niall's competitiveness seems childish in comparison. I watched a man die last night. Now I stand before another, watching as he strokes his ego, playing a trivial game of back and forth. I long to care about nothing but the win; to have nothing more at stake. To have this burden lifted from my back. I turn to leave and feel a tug on my arm.

'Are you still playing dirty?' he whispers. 'Any more tricks up your sleeve?'

Having a man so close to me, lay his hand on me – it makes my skin crawl. I cannot help but think of the rough, calloused palms of the Messenger thrusting me towards the dock's edge to watch Fredrick die.

I snatch my arm away, and turn without giving him a response, my stomach somersaulting as I quicken my pace towards the ladies' room.

I push my way into the bathroom and stop before the mirror, waiting to discern if I am alone. All the cubicles are free, and the only sounds to be heard are the incessant drip from the furthest tap, and the quick rush of my breath.

I was too distracted to check how I looked this morning, too terrified to care. But as I stare into my reflection, I wince at the sight of the woman staring back at me. I am deathly pale, and my prominent cheekbones almost make me look gaunt in this lighting. The life has been drained from my eyes.

Despite the trial before me, my mind returns to the body. I can see it in my mind, rising from the earth tangled in tree roots as they are clawed from the ground to make way for the new track. It's one thing to bury a body in plain sight when you have to, but to gamble twice, and do so again, seems far too reckless. But now I have no choice. It's not *if* I will move the body, but *when*.

I have no other choice.

But of course, I do. I could pay for my crimes. I killed my husband, and with murder comes the consequences. I of all people should know that. But then having my life and those I love at risk muddies the water. It isn't just about me paying my price, and Wade receiving a fair trial – it has become something so much bigger. I think of Hannah – so innocent, so pure. So much of her life has yet to be lived. I deserve to pay for what I have done, but Hannah deserves to live. I cannot condemn us both. The Messenger's threats seem all the more real after Fredrick's death. I remember the thrashing of the water as he bucked against the chains, the bubbles from his lungs slowly dissipating on the surface of the water until he went still. I look down at my shaking hands. More blood is upon them now. I might not have fixed the chains about him, or thrust him from the dock. But I killed him. I dragged him into this mess, and now his body is floating at the bottom of the Thames. I scrunch my eyes shut at the thought of the wild, chopping water. The memory of the Messenger's grip on my neck burns into my skin. I rub the same spot and sigh heavily.

I am so sorry, Fredrick.

My watch ticks quietly at my wrist, the seconds counting down to the commencement of the trial. To the decision I must inevitably make.

The door to the bathroom opens. I straighten up, reach for the tap, and begin washing my hands.

'Good morning.'

I jolt at the sound of his voice. The Messenger stands by the door, the smirk firmly on his face.

'You shouldn't be in here,' I hear myself say.

He releases that vile, smug laugh I've come to expect of him. The arrogance seeps from him, exuded from every sound and movement.

'That's the least of your worries,' he replies, and steps closer.

He doesn't stop until he is behind me, and we stare at each other through the mirror. I can smell his breath as it cascades down upon me: minty fresh, with a hint of tobacco smoke lingering beneath.

'I just wanted to check in on you, after last night,' he says through a smile. 'My buddies didn't think you'd show. They were sure they'd need to man the airports, but I told them you'd come. I said you had the biggest pair of balls on a woman that I'd ever met. I was right, of course.'

I say nothing and look down to turn off the tap when his hands latch onto my head and snap it upwards, until I am staring back through the mirror. His fingers are laced in my hair, the tips digging into my temples and cheeks.

'You understand what will happen if you fail, don't you?' he whispers. 'I've made myself clear?'

His hands squeeze tighter around my head. I can feel the pressure burning into my eyes, my pulse drumming against his palms. His fingers pull at my hair until tears creep into my vision.

'But I suppose prison is the least of your concerns, isn't it? What with young Hannah. Such a pretty girl.'

'I'd kill you,' I whisper.

He cocks a brow. 'Do your job, and nothing will happen to either of you. You have my word.'

'Your word,' I spit. A single tear snakes from my eye, running off his thick, meaty finger. 'I said I'd do it, didn't I?'

'Just making sure you haven't lost your nerve.' He kisses my crown tauntingly, and a wave of nausea rips through me. 'It doesn't look like you have long, either ... not with those rail workers setting up shop behind your house. How long till they dig up your dirty little secret, do you think?'

I feel my entire body stiffen.

Christ, he really does see everything.

'And hey ... if you ever feel yourself wavering in court, or you find yourself forgetting what's at stake, all you have to do is look towards the gallery – I'll be watching.'

The door opens and he quickly drops his hands.

'Oops,' he says to the woman at the door. 'Wrong room.'

He steps out, giving me a wink over his shoulder as he goes.

The woman gives me a concerned look. I nod that I'm okay, and wait until she has used the bathroom and left again before I bolt to the nearest cubicle and vomit.

I wipe my mouth, check myself over in the mirror, and take a deep breath.

My decision is clear to me now. No hope, jading my objective. No last-minute saves. I am alone in this, with one objective and one alone: protect Hannah. Even if the consequences are monstrous to me.

Then there is the matter of the body.

I can't deal with this all at once. At the Old Bailey, I will concentrate on the task at hand. Only when I have clocked off will I let myself consider what else is in store for me.

It's time to meet Antony and our client before the trial begins, to go over our plan of action and give our reassurance before making our way to courtroom one.

Then, I will destroy our case from within.

25

Wade Darling is waiting for me at the other end of the corridor, in conference room three.

It's simple enough to concoct a plan for oneself; play out scenarios, set goals. But to execute a plan that is detrimental to another person, all while looking them in the eye, is not so simple at all. I am stood at the top of the corridor, willing my legs to move.

Think of Hannah. Think of the body. Think of what happened to Fredrick. This is why you're doing this. It's us or him.

As the pit of worry grinds into my stomach, I pick up my phone and fire a quick text to Hannah, asking about the progress that's been madewith the railworks, before thrusting my phone back in my bag.

I walk down the corridor as if on autopilot, heading towards conference room three, as my heart rate climbs with each step, and pause before the door, frozen by the prospect of the task that awaits me on the other side.

It's us or him.

I raise a shaking fist to the door, my pulse thundering in my ears, and knock.

'Come in,' Antony muffles behind the door.

Inside, it is a tight cubbyhole of a room, with barely enough space for the desk in the centre of it. There are no windows, no art on the walls. Just a tight, airless space. Both of the men are looking up at me expectantly, waiting for me to join them; Wade is sat on one side of the table, Antony on the other. I take the seat beside Antony and bid them both good morning.

'How are you feeling, Wade?' I ask.

'I've been better.'

He has looked better too. He must have been up the whole night, for he is paler than I have ever seen him, with dark rings around his eyes.

I am about to destroy this man beyond repair.

I dig my nails into my thigh to keep the guilt from engulfing me.

'Well, after our conference yesterday, we have good reason to believe we will win this case,' Antony says. 'We have a game plan now, one that we're all determined to see succeed.'

Antony sits tall and composed, speaking with a firm, reassuring tone. I have known him long enough to be aware that, behind his professional façade, he is as excited as a boy. I peer down beside me. His right leg is restless with anticipation, juddering up and down. I sit forward to speak so I appear engaged, rather than downright terrified.

'I will run through how the day is going to go, Wade, and then I will break down how the trial is set to commence. Then you can ask us any questions you may have.'

Wade nods wordlessly, peering down at his cupped hands on the table. He has begun to trust us more, or at least become more comfortable. When my eyes are drawn to his scars, he doesn't hide his hand beneath the desk like he would have in the beginning. Back when I deserved his trust, before I had been dragged into doing the Messenger's bidding.

'So, this morning will start with the empanelling of the jury. There will be a jury panel of about fifteen or sixteen potential jurors, and twelve names will be called. Before they take their oaths, the names of the witnesses will be run by each of them for any juror to declare if they have a connection with any of the people named – if they do, they will be replaced by one of the remaining members of the public from the jury panel. Once the jury is assembled, you will have a chance to object to any particular jurors, should you recognise their name or face for example, to ensure you have a fair trial. They will then be sworn in, and the trial will commence.

'The advocate for the prosecution, Niall Richardson, will deliver an opening speech. He will describe what their argument is for charging you, and explain how they intend to prove your guilt to the jury. They will state their case, list their witnesses, and try to persuade the jury with as many buzzwords as they can cram in. Then it will be my turn to give an opening speech, to counteract their claims and defend your case.

'Once the opening speeches have been made, the prosecution will call each of their witnesses. They will question them to elicit the answers they need to condemn you, but I will then cross-examine each of the witnesses to poke holes in their state-ments and create doubt in the jurors' minds. The prosecution has the harder job here – they must prove to the jury that you caused your family's deaths, beyond a shadow of a doubt. Our sole purpose is to create that doubt.

'At the halfway point of the trial, when the prosecution have delivered their case, the roles will be reversed. I will call the witnesses speaking in your defence, and question each in turn to help deliver their statements. The prosecution will then cross-examine each witness to create doubt, as we will have with theirs.

'Once this is complete, the prosecution and I will each give a closing speech, and the jury will be sent off to deliberate and decide upon their verdict.'

I look at Wade on the other side of the table, and see a glint of trust in his eyes. My heart plummets.

'The prosecution's argument,' Antony says, 'is to push the notion that you murdered your family. They will call witnesses to try to assassinate your character, imply your mental health struggles were your motive. They will do everything they can to create this image of you, but please do keep in mind that we expect this, and that you have Neve on your side, who will cross-examine each of their witnesses to disarm each of their claims.'

I force myself to nod.

You have Neve on your side, he'd said.

'When will you mention the affair?' Wade asks me.

'Once we've reached the middle of the trial, and it is our turn to call witnesses. We want the prosecution to dig their own grave, before we seal it shut behind them.'

I flinch at my poor choice of words, and the thought of Matthew's body being discovered by the rail workers stops me mid-flow. I cough nervously.

'They will have based their entire argument on you as their sole suspect. Then we can deliver the blow to undermine their entire case, with the truth of the affair. Our evidence of a potential second suspect will prove they didn't consider any other option, thereby delivering an incomplete and biased investigation.'

Wade nods slowly, drinking the information in. The

room feels unbearably hot. I can feel my skin prickling with approaching sweat; my chest is incapable of drawing anything but shallow sips of air.

I haven't lied to Wade, not yet. I have explained exactly how the trial will go. What I have failed to tell him is that, before the prosecution has delivered their case, I will have sent the evidence I have against him to their quarters, and as soon as it is admitted into evidence, the countdown to the end of the trial begins. I will look to be on his side, fighting the good fight, but when we least it expect it, the evidence will be revealed, and the defence case as we know it will be blown to smithereens.

I give him a tight smile.

'You have nothing to worry about, Wade,' I say, delivering my first lie.

He nods again with a grateful smile, his throat bobbing with a nervous swallow. Antony checks his watch.

'I say it's about time we go win this thing.' He gives Wade a comforting squeeze on the shoulder. 'Let's do this.'

We all rise from the table and file out. I let Antony lead the way, trying not to let my nerves show as I decide when I will send the damning evidence to the prosecution. I will let the morning play out: the summoning of the jury, the opening speeches, the first witness or two, and as soon as we have our first break, I will send the evidence to the prosecution, and ensure Hannah and I get out of this in one piece.

When we part ways and I am alone, I check my phone for any word from Hannah on the rail works.

I have no new messages.

26

My robe is trembling around my legs where I sit at the advocates' bench. Facts I thought I had embedded in my mind and been able to recite on my walk to the courtroom are gone, lost to the pages of my notes again. It will be my fifteen-year anniversary as a barrister come spring, but as I stand in the courtroom, I feel my throat burn with the same nerves I felt when prosecuting in my first trial. The wig on my head is already starting to itch, and the collarette around my neck has tightened like a noose.

The jury has been selected and the judge has introduced the case. What lies before us now is the trial itself.

The court is deathly quiet but for the odd rustle of pages and scrape of chairs. The chatter from the public gallery has fallen to a whisper, after the buzz of excitement that stalked today's onlookers to their seats. I half expect to hear the rustle of popcorn or spot the the glint of opera glasses pointed in my direction, taking in every thread and fold of my robes.

Niall stands to deliver his opening speech, exuding the sort of confidence that is earned, not faked. His white wig has yellowed over the years, now the colour of a smoker's fingers; years of experience and respect stained into the horsehair.

'Members of the jury, the case we are about to set before you is centred around one family: the Darlings.'

Niall stands with his spine straight and his head high, his eyes set firmly on the jurors' bench. His projected voice echoes off the panelled walls.

'The Darlings, it seemed, had everything. An adoring, close-knit family, with the big beautiful house, the fast cars, millions in the bank, horses' stables, and acres of land with a private woodland. It is an awe-inspiring story of one man working to the bone for everything he ever wanted, and bestowing it on those he held dearest. But this story, members of the jury, is a lie.'

Niall pauses for dramatic effect. He isn't a classically handsome man: his hairline is slowly receding beneath his wig, and his nose is slightly crooked, with his chin too large for the rest of his face. But his eyes have a way of transfixing anyone they settle on.

'In the early hours of Saturday the seventeenth of November 2018, the defendant's wife, Yolanda Darling, and their two children, Phoebe and Danny Darling, died in a fiery blaze at the family home. Initially, it appeared to be a tragic accident. But once the smoke had cleared, a far more sinister story emerged.

'What had once appeared to be an accidental tragedy quickly became a murder inquiry. Phoebe and Danny Darling, eighteen and sixteen respectively, had been shot in the head in their beds while they slept.

'Yolanda Darling, too, had been shot. She was found beneath the rubble of the staircase, with forensic evidence revealing that she had been shot three times: in her leg, in her back, and finally, the fatal blow to her head. Three members of one family, wiped out in a single night.'

As the jury sits transfixed, waiting on tenterhooks during each of Niall's dramatic pauses, the room is eerily silent.

'This wasn't a spur of the moment attack, members of the jury. This was a carefully planned execution. The fuel used to ignite the fire was stored in an outhouse on the defendant's property. Every horse was shot dead in their stables before the structure was purposely set alight. The gates to enter the property had been bolted shut to prevent anyone coming to help. This wasn't just a case of arson, or a man covering his tracks – this was complete annihilation, with only one man's fingerprints on the murder weapon. It is these crimes that we are here to try before you, and it is Wade Darling – husband . . . father . . . provider – who is charged with their murders.'

Niall leaves a beat for effect, allowing time for the jurors to glance from the bench to the dock, disgust and curiosity flickering upon their faces as they look to Wade behind the glass.

'During this trial, you will hear from an array of witnesses. You will hear of Yolanda Darling's distress at her husband's mental health decline, of Mr Darling's sanity spiralling rapidly during the closure of his business, and the near-obsession he had with guns and hunting. You will hear from Yolanda Darling's mother, who was the last to see her alive, other than the accused. You will hear from the specialists who led the investigation and assessed every angle of the crime: the fire, the gunshots, the remains. And finally, you will hear from a criminal psychologist who specialises in domestic abuse cases that end in murder.'

He pauses at this. His insinuation is irrevocably clear.

'According to the law, a person is guilty of murder if they unlawfully kill another person with the intention to kill or cause grievous harm. We, the prosecution, must prove that, one: the defendant killed the three victims, and two: that the defendant intended to kill them while committing these violent crimes.

'It is the Crown's case that Mr Darling, after falling into a deep depression and losing everything he had built for himself and his family, murdered his wife and their two children to conceal the truth of his failures from them for eternity – that his pride was more sacred to him than those he was supposed to cherish most. And it is with our evidence during this case that we will prove this to you.'

Niall's eyes wander over the jury. The art of a good opening speech isn't just a matter of relaying the evidence of one's stance, it is a testament to the power of storytelling. Speeches in court are ways to grip the jury with your tale: pull at their heartstrings, deliver open questions the jury will be left to answer. It is our best chance to persuade the jurors to take our side. Niall has executed his well.

He sits down on the other side of the bench, straightening his robe as he sits, before throwing me a quick glance. He doesn't smile, but his eyes glint knowingly.

Now it is my turn. I stand on my side of the bench, my legs quivering beneath my robes. My mouth has dried with fear. I reach for my water glass, and spot the violent tremor running through my hand. Courtroom one is freezing, being in the older part of the Bailey, but I know I can't blame my trembling on that. The room is so quiet that the knock of my glass against the top of the bench echoes against the panelled walls. I clear my throat and begin.

'Members of the jury, I am Neve Harper, the advocate representing Wade Darling during this trial. My learned friend has just given you his terms for my client's charge, and the ways he intends to prove this to you. I will now break down the issues with the prosecution's statements, to ensure you have all of the facts.'

I peer down at my notes. The words swim on the page as my head goes light. I push my feet into the floor in attempt to ground myself, and take a deep breath before returning my gaze to the jury.

'Firstly, there is the matter of circumstantial evidence. In this case, we the defence will show you, the jury, that the evidence the prosecution is to provide for Mr Wade Darling's alleged guilt is inadequate to *categorically* prove he is responsible for the crime. For example, the evidence that will be provided to insinuate my client's guilt includes the discovery of his fingerprints on items that originated from his home – possessions that would already bear his fingerprints due to them belonging to him.

'Two, there is the matter of the prosecution using Mr Wade Darling's experience of depression in this case. We will explain that the defendant's depression was due to his circumstances – a combination of personal struggles and financial changes, two entirely relevant causes for depression. According to the Priory Group, a leading provider of mental health services, approximately two hundred and eighty million people in the world have depression. Demonising a person's mental health diagnoses to insinuate their role in a triple homicide leads us down a dangerous path, for which we will hold the prosecution to account.

'And finally, there is the matter of the police investigation. In our rebuttal of the prosecution's case against my client, we will provide evidence to prove the police actively pursued my client as the perpetrator of the crime, without exploring any other suspects.

'My role, as the advocate for the defence, is to ensure that the facts you receive from the prosecution can withstand interrogation and can be used to prove my client's guilt beyond a shadow of a doubt. Our evidence will prove to you that you cannot.'

I nod to the judge and take my seat. The room is ear-splittingly silent. I reach for my glass of water and clamp my hand upon it in a desperate attempt to keep it from quivering. Despite the numerous eyes that are set upon me, there is one pair I think of. One man who knows what the rest of the room do not. I glance towards the public gallery, and see the Messenger staring back at me. Next to him sits a man who appears taller than everyone else on the row, with tanned, wrinkled skin, and white tufts of receding hair. His eyes are an icy blue, and I know who he is as soon as I meet them. They are the same eyes as Yolanda's, staring out from the front pages.

Mr Viklund.

Judge McConnell bows his head towards Niall at the other end of the bench. It is time for the prosecution to call their first witness.

Niall stands.

'The prosecution calls Annika Viklund.'

27

As Annika Viklund is led to the witness box, she walks as all grieving mothers do: slow and lethargic, as though the life has been sucked out of her bones. Despite this, and her family's reputation for criminal undertakings, she appears glamorous and together. She glimmers with jewellery and her white hair is perfectly set. But her eyes are as hard as her husband's, staring at me from the gallery.

She reaches the box and stands before the court, giving her oath with a delicate tone and soft Swedish accent, with the threat of tears ever wavering behind her words.

Yolanda Darling had the same eyes as her father, but her face belonged to her mother. They shared the same button nose, the same high cheekbones and plump bottom lip. Annika is dressed formally in an all-black fitted suit as if in mourning. I wonder if she knows what her husband has orchestrated, if she too has a part to play in the corruption of the trial.

Niall stands at his end of the bench, and introduces himself, before asking her to confirm her name.

'Annika Viklund. Yolanda's mother.'

'I can only imagine how difficult this must be for you and your family, Mrs Viklund,' Niall says. 'So I will make this as brief as I can. When was the last time you saw your daughter, Yolanda?'

The room falls silent. It is so quiet that when Annika opens her mouth to speak, I hear her intake of breath.

'The day before she died,' she utters. 'At her home.'

'What was the reason for your visit?'

'Yolanda and I were close,' she says. 'We would talk every day on the phone, see each other once a week, sometimes more if we could. She was quite isolated in the countryside, so I liked to keep in touch as often as I could. But leading up to her death, we had spoken less and less, and I was worried.'

'What were you worried about?' Niall asks. His tone is soft. A noticeable charade, to anyone who knows him. But to the jury, he may seem sincere. The kinder he is, the crueller I will seem when it is time to cross-examine.

'She had become noticeably withdrawn,' Annika says. 'I know my daughter, and when she wants to hide something, she retreats into herself. She was never a very good liar, or at least, not a good enough liar to fool me. I only had to hear or look at her to know something was wrong.'

'So when you went to visit your daughter on Friday the sixteenth of November 2018, you thought something was amiss?'

'Yes. Our conversations had been getting shorter and further apart. She was worried about Wade.'

'What was worrying her about the defendant?'

Her eyes flicker, as if she is about to look up at the dock and meet Wade's eyes. She looks to the bottom of the witness box instead.

'He had become depressed.' She pauses. 'We know now that it was due to his business failing, but Yolanda was kept in the dark about that. All she knew was that her husband was going downhill, and she didn't know why or how to help. It affected them all, as a family. Yolanda and the children seemed to be walking on eggshells, waiting for him to snap.'

'Waiting for him to snap,' Niall repeats, glancing at the jury. He waits a few seconds, allowing the thought to sink into their minds.

'Was the defendant at the property during your visit?'

'No, he was out hunting, and the children were at college. It was just Yolanda and me. I was relieved, as I wanted to get to the bottom of what was happening.'

As Annika gives her evidence, I watch the jury for their reactions. Every one of them is transfixed by her story. They will have no reason not to trust her, the mother of the deceased.

'What did you think of the defendant's hunting?'

'My husband partakes in the sport, so I'm used to it. But over the years, Wade became almost obsessed with it. His collection of firearms grew, he spent thousands upon thousands on them. He would go on hunting retreats, was a member of several hunting clubs in the county. It got to a point where it would seem strange not to see him with a rifle of some kind. He would clean them, pull them apart to put them back together again, read books about them, talked about the guns he wanted next. There was a buck in the area that he obsessed over; he wanted to shoot it and mount its head above the mantel. I'm not sure he ever got it.'

A gunman waiting to snap. That's what Wade looks like, in the eyes of the jury.

'Tell us about your visit to see Yolanda on the sixteenth of November 2018.'

'I arrived at about noon, and I could tell she was in a bad way before I even saw her. Her voice over the intercom at the front gate was quiet and lacking her usual cheer. When I drove up to the house and she opened the door, I could have cried at the sight of her. She looked utterly drained. She was very pale, and had lost a lot of weight. Her eyes, her smile; the light inside of her had vanished.

'As soon as I asked her if she was all right, the tears came bursting out. Hers first, then mine. We went into the living room. I didn't even take off my coat or my shoes, I was so eager to hear from her. I got the sense she was finally going to open up to me.'

She stops briefly to compose herself, closing her eyes.

'What did she say?' Niall asks softly.

Annika opens her eyes again, blinking the water from them.

'She told me of Wade's depression. He was barely speaking to any of them by this point. Not in a callous way, she said – he would try to play the part. But he was utterly broken, and she was growing scared of what he might do.'

'Scared of what he might do?' Niall repeats.

'To himself,' she replies. 'That's what I thought she meant at the time. Now, I'm not so sure.'

I stand from my side of the bench.

'Your Honour, I'm not sure speculation of this nature is helpful.'

Judge McConnell nods to me in response, before turning to the witness.

'Stick to the facts of the matter please, Mrs Viklund.'

She nods dutifully, her cheeks pink, and looks to Niall at the other end of the bench, waiting for him to proceed.

'And was Wade hunting during all this?'

'Yes, he would go off for hours. She was a bag of nerves every time he left. She said that whenever she heard a gunshot, she feared it might have been one he bestowed upon himself. I think it was the first time she truly said aloud what it felt like to live in their household. She had been staying strong for Wade, for the children, keeping up airs and graces. But she was finally letting down her guard.' Her eyes flick upwards towards the dock, and her expression curdles with a grimace; venom seeping into her eyes. 'And then he came back.'

'The defendant?'

'Yes.'

'How did the defendant's return change things?'

Annika tears her eyes away from the dock. Her hands are held in fists at her sides, her knuckles white.

'It changed everything. Yolanda steeled up again, rushing to tidy her appearance, before inviting him to join us and making us all tea. I sat with them in the kitchen, watching them pretend that everything was fine, wanting to scream at them both to address what was going on, but they were so wrapped up in their lie. Lying to me, to each other . . . to themselves.'

'How did the defendant seem to you, during all this?'

'He was his usual upbeat self: attentive, making jokes. But beneath the surface I could tell something was wrong. They both looked like they had aged a decade. I wanted to try and get her alone again, but she made her excuses. I don't think she felt comfortable lowering her guard with him home. So I left.'

Tears come to her eyes. She tries to compose herself, her lip wavering.

'When I hugged her goodbye . . .' Her voice breaks. 'I hugged her as if it would be the last time. I just . . . *knew*. I don't know how. Perhaps it was a mother's instincts. But I felt as though I was about to lose her for good. I told her I loved her, got in my car, and drove home. I cried the whole way. I woke up that morning to the police at the door. They came to tell us of the fire at the house, and that Yolanda and the children hadn't been found. And I knew then that my premonition had been right. I think about the moment I left that house every minute of every day, wishing I had insisted upon her coming with me. We could have collected the children and I could have brought them home, where it was safe.'

'Safe from what, Mrs Viklund?'

The question hangs in the air. Her eyes flick towards the dock. 'From *him*.'

We all sit, watching as she stares at the man accused of killing her daughter and grandchildren. Tears slip down her cheeks until she finally bursts into a sob.

'Thank you, Mrs Viklund,' Niall says. 'I know that will have been extremely difficult for you.' He looks to the judge. 'Nothing more from me.'

It is a tricky business, cross-examining the mother of a victim. Come on too strong, and I will look bullish and callous, but tread too lightly, and I could allow the power of her testimony to sway the jury. It is even harder when the mother's husband is sat in the public gallery, with a figurative sniper pointed at my back.

I stand at my end of the bench.

'Mrs Viklund, I'm Neve Harper for the defence. I am so sorry for your loss; I will make this quick.'

She nods curtly. Her eyes are steely towards me, and I wonder if it is because I am defending Wade, or because like her husband, she knows she has control over me. The Viklunds, pulling my strings.

'I would like to highlight some of the areas of the testimony you just gave. You mentioned the defendant's enjoyment of hunting, and described his collection of weapons as "obsessive". You also told us that your husband also hunts, correct?'

'Yes,' she replies sharply.

'In fact, your husband went hunting *with* the defendant on numerous occasions, didn't he?'

'Yes . . .' she says, her stare deadly. 'They were family.'

'How many weapons does your husband own?'

She shrugs her shoulders.

'I'm not sure.'

'That many?' I reply with a cocked brow.

Annika gives me a look of warning.

'No, I was not implying that. I'm just not sure.'

'You must have some knowledge. An estimate is fine. Three guns? Four?'

'About ten.'

'Not much less than number owned by the defendant?'

She sharpens her glare.

'Less than half, I think you'll find.'

'But more than the average hunter would own, yes?'

'Perhaps.'

'So, in your opinion, would it be fair for someone to tar your husband with the same brush, because of his hobby? Suspect him of a crime due to this sport?'

'Without context, no.'

'Thank you. And lastly . . . you said your daughter changed when the defendant returned home during your visit. Said that you believed she "didn't feel comfortable lowering her guard around him". Correct?'

'Yes.'

'You were both talking about him at the time, isn't that right?'

'Yes.'

'About something very personal to him?'

'Yes.'

'With that in mind, isn't it possible that this is why your daughter's demeanour changed when he returned? So not to hurt his feelings?'

She purses her lips.

'Mrs Viklund?'

'Perhaps,' she says, her tone sharp.

'So would it be fair to say that it was your *perception* that Yolanda was uncomfortable around the defendant, rather than uncomfortable about discussing the *subject* in the defendant's presence?'

'Well, yes, it was my perception. But I do wish to remind you that I was actually *there*, Ms Harper. I felt the tension between them, I witnessed their dynamic with my own eyes. You weren't.'

'Thank you, Mrs Viklund.' I look to the judge. 'No further questions.'

I take to my seat, not daring to turn around to see Mr Viklund's expression, as he and his wife meet each other's eyes.

28

We break late for lunch, but I can't eat a thing. As I pace outside the Bailey, puffing on cigarette after cigarette, all I can think about are the rail works, of how much closer they are to finding Matthew with each breath I take.

How long does it take to uproot a tree? Or a dozen trees? I wonder where they will start, how much time I have to play with before they reach him. I wonder what his body will look like after three years. How much of him will still be flesh, and how much of him will be nothing but bone.

I open my text messages again. Still no response from Hannah. What if they've found him already, and she is with the police right now? Would she text me back if she thought I was the one who put him there?

Calm down. If she's truly sick, she's probably sleeping. Or maybe she's skiving and is out and about with friends. There will be an explanation. Even though I've never seen her without her phone in her hand.

I pace back and forth, faster this time, my mouth sapped dry from nerves.

I need to move him tonight. I cannot risk leaving it too long and returning home to a crime scene beyond the tracks, or the police officers meeting me at the doors to the Bailey. But how am I going to do this under Hannah's nose? And where on earth would I bury him?

I need to drive out of the city, as far as I can get.

Then of course, there is the matter of the trial.

Above my text to Hannah is the last text I sent. It was to Johnny, the errand boy we use at chambers. He is to meet me to collect the file on my client's past and deliver it directly to the prosecution. The first thing I did when the judge announced the break was run to the bank and withdraw the money to cover Johnny's fee, along with a large tip to keep him quiet. I can't have anyone knowing this evidence came from me.

Once I do this, there is no going back.

The body. The trial. The body. The trial. My thoughts spin in an endless, panic-inducing cycle. Each task is so overwhelming that tears of desperation sting at my eyes.

I drop my cigarette to the ground, toying with whether to light another despite the sickly taste in my mouth and tight, breathless chest, when I come face to face with the Messenger.

'Mr Viklund wishes to speak with you.'

⚖

I walk silently through the streets towards the meeting point, passing St Paul's Cathedral in a daze until I reach the Thames. Before me is the Millennium Bridge, where I am to meet Mr Viklund. I stare at its metal Jurassic spine jutting out from the walkway. Beyond it, on the other side of the river, the Tate Modern's brick mast towers up towards the overcast sky. I look to the right towards Blackfriars and think of Fredrick. We had stood just there, uttering the Viklund name. Now I am about to meet with the man himself and Fredrick is dead.

Mr Viklund is waiting for me in the centre of the bridge, staring out at the view of the city.

I slowly make my way across. The wind is strong today, and the bridge trembles beneath my feet as I walk. People pass me by, in their own little worlds. I wish I could trade places with one of them, steal their lives, wear their skin as my own, and disappear.

When I am mere feet away, Mr Viklund turns to me, his expression stoic. But his eyes seem to be forever vengeful. I had felt them burning into me from the public gallery during the trial proceedings, and I feel the heat of them again now. I force myself to hold his gaze.

'We don't have long,' I say, as I reach him and stand at his side. He looks out at the Thames snaking through the city, slipping beneath Southwark Bridge, then London Bridge, to Tower Bridge in the distance. 'And it's important we aren't seen together.'

'Then I'll make it quick.' His voice is deep and authoritative, with the same Swedish accent as his wife. When the wind blows, I catch the scent of his aftershave, potent and masculine.

'I'm sure you think what is happening to you is unfair,' he says. 'And that the predicament I have put you in is unjust. But I would like to offer you another take on the matter.

'My son-in-law – your client – took my most precious gift away from me. He murdered my child, and killed both my grandchildren. He lost his business, and as punishment, destroyed everything around him, and then had the audacity to save himself. This man you have been hired to defend deserves nothing more than to rot in a prison cell, to never breathe the scent of freedom again. Death is too good for him. Too merciful. I will not allow any other verdict but guilty.'

He tears his eyes from the water and looks at me. I can't help but squirm beneath his gaze.

'You are not the victim here, Ms Harper. You murdered your husband, as Wade killed my family. If you expect remorse from me for putting you in this situation, you will not get it. I don't care why you did what you did. Only that it can be used to get what my family deserve. And if you don't . . .'

He looks out to the Thames again, his eyes steeling, until they appear as grey as the water.

'The world will discover what you did, and you will go to prison for the rest of your life. But it won't end there. I will personally make sure that everyone you love will pay the price. You will lose loved ones, as I have lost mine, and you won't be able to do a thing about it, whiling away your last days behind bars and wire fences, as the guilt and the grief eat away at you, knowing that you could have saved the people you lost.'

He looks at me again, his eyes watery. I am not sure whether it is the chill of the wind, or the talk of his family. But as he talks of my demise, I can see the rage in them too.

'I have friends in all sorts of places, as I'm sure you know. And I can assure you, your time in prison would be unbearable. You'll be wishing the UK still orchestrated hangings, when I'm done with you. And when you're old and grey, and have had the life crushed out of you, you'll die alone, without dignity or redemption. I have many incarcerated friends who like to fashion knives out of toothbrushes and visit their victims in the showers. They won't stop until the water runs red and the life leaves your eyes.' His stare penetrates into me, until every one of my muscles twitches and squirms. 'Have I made myself clear, Ms Harper?'

I nod slowly.

'Yes, Mr Viklund.'

'Are you sure? Because you didn't seem to hold back when cross-examining my wife this morning.'

'I'm sure.'

The corners of his mouth rise slightly, followed by a brief nod of his head.

'Good.'

He looks back to the water and watches it for a while, the violence of the current, the algae on either side of the bank a glimmering emerald in the sun.

'I want you to know I'm serious about this task, Mr Viklund.'

I slip the file from my bag and pass it to him. He looks down at it suspiciously, before taking it slowly from my grasp.

'What is it?'

'The evidence I am sending to the prosecution to sabotage my client's case.'

His eyes flicker with something I can't pin down. It's not quite pride, or amusement. Perhaps he is impressed. He opens the file and begins to read, the pages fluttering in his grip from the breeze.

'This will ensure that whatever I say in defence of my client, we will lose the case. I will need to keep up appearances, looking to be doing my job while sabotaging it from afar. Just like I had been when I was cross-examining your wife. Do you understand?'

He is silent for a moment as he continues to read of his son-in-law's history. I see the corner of his mouth turn upwards with a smile, before he shuts the file and returns it to me.

'Perfectly,' he replies.

'Because I don't want you, or your . . . colleague, to be concerned if I appear to be going against what we've discussed.'

'Message received.' He drops his eyes to the file. 'When will you be delivering this evidence?'

My phone vibrates in my pocket. I long for it to be from Hannah, to put my mind at ease. I slip it out and peer at the screen. It's the errand boy. He has arrived at our meeting place, on the corner of Carter Lane, a small winding back street close to the Bailey.

'Now.' I clear my throat and look about me. 'I'm doing everything you're asking of me, Mr Viklund. I really hope you'll keep your word, about not harming me or those I love.'

'You'll remember the agreement, when all of this began,' he says. 'You were told it was a trade of sorts, correct?'

'Yes.'

'Well then. Fulfil your part of the agreement, and the trade is complete.' He takes his eyes off the view. 'We'll be watching to make sure you do.'

⚖️

The errand boy is perched on his bicycle, waiting for me on the corner of Carter Lane, occasionally looking about him for my arrival before returning to his phone screen.

I stop in the nearest doorway and slip the file in a large envelope, with Niall's name written on the front of it in large black capitals, which I had scrawled in the Bailey's de-robing room the moment I found myself alone.

I still have time to do the right thing. I could turn around now and be done with it. Face the consequences of my crimes. Sacrifice my freedom for my client's right to a fair trial. But Mr Viklund's words whisper in my mind, my heart rate climbing at the sound of his deep, crackling voice. *You will lose loved ones, as I have lost mine, and you won't be able to do a thing about it.*

A bout of panic ripples through me. This task Mr Viklund has laid at my feet goes against everything I have ever known as a barrister. It is everything that our society deems wrong. And yet, I have no other choice. If not for my sake, then for Hannah's. For Maggie's. I have put them through enough. But beneath the duty to protect them whispers my own selfish greed. If the truth of what I have done was exposed, I would lose the only family I have ever known. Clinging onto the family of the man I killed, to keep them as my own. The twisted nature of it makes my stomach lurch with shame.

I check the time, trying to concentrate on the ticking hands while my pulse drums loudly. The break is almost over. If I don't do this now, I will lose my chance. Any later and the judge may well refuse to admit the evidence out of principle.

It's now or never. Us or him.

I take a steeling breath and walk towards the boy. He looks up at me with a smile and the casual nod of his head.

'All right, miss?'

'Hi Johnny. Thanks for this.'

He gives me another of those boyish nods.

'It's going to the Old Bailey, right?'

'Yes. The recipient's name is on the front. You remember what I said?'

'It didn't come from you.'

'That's right. That part is really important.'

I pass him the envelope of cash first. A tip larger than his fee, paying handsomely for his discretion. He knows I've paid him more from the thickness of the envelope, and breaks into a beaming smile.

'Whatever you say, miss.' He shoves the envelope of cash inside his jacket before zipping it shut. 'You got the package?'

I hold the top of the envelope, just poking from my bag. I still have time to change my mind, to choose another path. But time is forever against me. I can practically hear the seconds ticking away, matching the beat of my heart.

It's now or never.

I lift the envelope free and pass it to him, my heart jolting as the paper parts from my fingers.

'Cheers miss. I'll drop you a text when it's delivered.'

He cycles off, standing on the pedals to build momentum, before zipping down the street.

It's done.

29

As the trial recommences and the judge enters the courtroom, I stand at my end of the bench feeling sick with anticipation. The prosecution will have had the new-found evidence for just fifteen minutes before we returned to courtroom one. Fifteen minutes to read through the file and gather their argument to add it into evidence for the case against my client. Johnny confirmed the package had arrived before I had even returned to the Bailey. I can see it in the way Niall stands restlessly at his side of the bench. When he peers down towards me, he smiles knowingly, no doubt anticipating his surprise reveal, with no notion that I was the stranger who planted the information. Antony catches his triumphant glare where he sits before me at the solicitors' row and turns to face me with a questioning expression. I shrug my shoulders to feign ignorance and look down at my files.

After welcoming everyone back to court, Judge McConnell looks to Niall to call back his witness to the box. Only the prosecution and I know what's to come next.

'Your Honour, before we begin, there is a matter I would like to address.'

I feel Antony's eyes as he turns back to me. I don't look back at him, but keep my focus on the judge, my face poker-straight.

'And what matter is this?'

'Fresh evidence has come to light, Your Honour, which we wish to have admitted so the jury have all the relevant facts.'

The judge raises his hand, silencing him instantly. 'I would like the jury dismissed before you go any further, Mr Richardson.'

'Yes, Your Honour.'

The jurors file out, an air of confusion and intrigue about them, as they glance to one another and head for the door. The public gallery seems to have woken up, talking to each other in hushed whispers. I look towards them, and find Mr Viklund staring back at me.

Once the jury has been dismissed, the judge returns his attention to Niall and me.

'You're aware you had the chance to submit your evidence prior to this trial, Mr Richardson? This is how proceedings are set for every trial. I can't think why this should be any different.'

The adrenaline must be surging through Niall at this moment. A piece of evidence that, if admitted, will land him the trial has just fallen into his lap without him lifting a finger. I can imagine he feels like the luckiest barrister in the world. And me, the unluckiest.

'Yes, Your Honour. Unfortunately, we were not made aware of this evidence until this afternoon. We cannot disclose evidence to the court in advance if said evidence isn't available.'

The judge sighs and slips his spectacles from the bridge of his nose, and begins to rub them clean with the sleeve of his robe.

'And what is this evidence you speak of?' he asks.

'It is to do with the defendant's medical history.'

'You were given this by the defence during the preliminary proceedings, were you not?'

'Not this evidence, Your Honour. This was not featured on his medical file; the health matter in question was dealt with privately, which one can only assume was to keep the evidence from his medical records—'

'You can save your assumptions, Mr Richardson. I am quite capable of forming my own judgement without your assistance.' He sighs again, before replacing his glasses upon his nose. 'I would like to see this evidence.'

'I would also like to see it, Your Honour,' I say from my side of the bench.

The judge nods dismissively, reaching out for the file as it is brought to him, and begins to read while another copy is brought to me. I look down, scanning it as if I wasn't the person to drop the file into the prosecution's lap, before passing it to Antony. I watch his shoulders tense up as he reads, and look with bated breath towards the judge. His eyes follow the words on the page, reading the history that will inevitably damn my client to a life in prison. All done by my hand.

The air in the room thickens, and the time creeps on, the faint ticking of a clock or a watch being the only backdrop to the judge's turning of the pages. He closes the file, exhaling deeply through his nostrils.

'Court will be adjourned for the day so I can consider this matter. I will have my decision on admission by the morning.'

The judge stands, and Niall and I follow suit, the creak of benches and squeak of chairs sounding through the room. Antony looks up at me, wide-eyed with confusion.

'Don't worry until we have to,' I say quietly. 'We will have a conference in the morning after I meet with the judge and go from there.'

I look towards my client in the dock, taking in the grey-pale skin of his face, and give him a deceptively supportive nod.

He doesn't know it, but I have just sacrificed his future for my own.

⚖

I return home to find myself alone, and yet I still feel that unfamiliar thrum in the air; there's a sense to the place now that I'm not the only one living in it, finding Hannah's presence wherever I look: her coat on the peg, a pair of shoes that aren't mine, a mug left on the coffee table, sticky at the rim with tinted lip gloss; the subtle, lingering scent of her girlish perfume in the air.

I need to see the train tracks.

I stride through the house without removing my shoes, and as I step into the kitchen, I spot a note on the breakfast table from Hannah: she is out with a friend and will be home for dinner.

So much for being ill.

I stand at the back door and stare through the glass past the garden, which is dark with the evening's shadows. Even from here, I can see the progress the workers have made. The trees at the bottom of my house are still standing, but by the long line of those felled before them, they will undoubtedly be the next to go.

I'm not sure how much time I have until Hannah returns. But I do know that if I want to retrieve the spade I used to bury Matthew without being seen, this is my window to do it.

When I was dealing with the aftermath, covering my blood-stained tracks, I knew that if I wanted a good chance at getting away with the murder, I needed to keep each damning item apart. The body at the bottom of the garden. The murder weapon hidden in storage. I wonder what Hannah would say if she knew that the spade I used to bury her father was hiding directly above our heads.

I head up the stairs and cross the landing, taking the long hook from the airing cupboard as I pass and using it to open the loft hatch, guiding the door open until it dangles on its hinges, its squeal echoing up through the hatch and into the darkness.

I drag down the ladder and climb up into the cold, dark loft, shivering as the draught greets me. I turn on the torch on my phone and clamber up.

The last task I had to cover my tracks was to hide the spade I used to bury him. I knew the police would search my premises. So, I found the next best thing.

I make my way towards the brick wall separating next door's property from mine and crouch down towards the right-hand side where I'd loosened the bricks. I begin lifting them free, stacking them beside me until my fingertips are gritty with orange dust. Lucinda's loft is filled to the rafters with boxes and bin bags of belongings heaped on top of one another; old files stacked bare and speckled with damp. She can't know half the things she has in there. Which works in my favour.

When the gap is big enough, I reach in, feeling blindly in the darkness, my fingertips collecting dust and cobwebs, until I feel the rustle of the black bin bag hidden behind a tower of boxes, and the cold metal of the spade within. I drag it forwards, edging it bit by bit so as not to send Lucinda's things toppling down upon me, and guide it through the gap. I sit with it in my lap, breathing heavily as dust tickles my throat.

Even through the bag, I can smell the earth that once coated the spade. It's impossible of course, after scrubbing it as thoroughly as I did, and the amount of bleach I used. But the weight of it in my hands instantly reminds me of all the gruesome details that haunt me to this day.

I am just putting the last few bricks back into place when I hear my name called from beyond the hatch.

Hannah.

I cock my head, and hear her footsteps on the stairs.

'What're you doing?' she asks from the foot of the ladder.

'Looking for something, I'll be down in a minute.' I blow a lock of hair from my face with a hot huff of air. 'Pre-heat the oven for me, would you?'

'Okay.'

I stay deathly still, listening as she heads back down, not daring to move again until I'm sure she's out of sight. When I hear the sound of the television downstairs, I crawl across the boards with the spade rustling in the black bin bag, dangle my legs over the open hatch, and slowly reach out for the first rung of the ladder. The metal creaks beneath my weight. I try to think of a place to hide it until nightfall, a place where Hannah won't find it. The longer she stays here, the more comfortable she seems about the place. It wouldn't surprise me if she spent her time alone in the house finding all of its nooks and crannies, looking for things her father left behind.

I've just reached the landing when I hear Hannah on the stairs again.

'Neve?' she asks.

I impulsively bolt into my bedroom, scanning furiously for a place to hide the spade, before dropping to my knees and thrusting it beneath the bed. Hannah appears in the doorway as I get back to my feet, and I pretend to collect something from the bedside drawer.

'What's up?' I ask. I find a Lipsol inside the drawer and play the part by running it across my lips.

She nods towards the ladder. 'Do you have anything of Dad's up there?'

She looks and sounds so childlike as she says this. It fascinates me how she can flit between a child and a young adult with just the flick of her lashes, the variable tone of her voice.

'What sort of stuff?'

She shrugs.

'I don't know. Photos, maybe? Of him as a kid, me as a baby, that sort of stuff?'

My heart sinks. I have been so caught up in my own dilemma that I hadn't considered how big of a deal this temporary move must be for Hannah. She stayed at weekends of course, and school holidays, but this was very much mine and Matthew's space that she came to visit, rather than a place to call her own.

'I'm sure I do. How about you make us dinner and I'll have a look up there.'

Her face softens, and a smile slowly curls the corners of her lips.

'Okay. What would you like for dinner?'

'Surprise me.'

She nods, the smile still firmly on her face, and turns back for the stairs.

'You're feeling better then?' I ask.

Right on time, she coughs.

'I had to meet a friend to collect homework, still feel rough. I feel worse at night.'

'Right,' I say, not buying it for a second. 'Well, we'll see how you feel in the morning then.'

She nods and heads for the stairs, and as I listen to the reassuring creaks of the floorboards, I sit down on the edge of the bed with a sigh and close my eyes, trying to calm my racing heart.

⚖

I sit in the armchair in my living room, watching the clock on the wall approach midnight. Once Hannah had gone up to bed, I snuck out of the house and moved the car to the church car park, closest to the wire fence separating the grounds from the tracks, ready to transfer the body to the boot. All I need to do is collect the spade from beneath my bed, and make my way towards the tracks.

I watch the seconds pass on the clock, my nerves jumping with each tick. If I'm going to do this without being caught, I need to do so in the dead of night, where there is less chance of being spotted. I have dressed in black from head to toe to blend into the shadows.

I have dreaded this day from the moment I buried him. Now I have no choice: it's time to dig up the past and face what I did.

The clock nears ten seconds, nine ... My chest grows tight. As the clock strikes midnight and the church bells sound, the memories hit me.

Gong.
Thwack.
Gong.
Thwack.
Gong.
Thwack.

They say you can't outrun trauma, that you must deal with it. But what might be a possibility for other people isn't an option for me; I cannot go to a therapist without confessing my crimes. In a strange way, I have accepted the notion that this will stay with me forever. That this eternal prison I have made for myself is the consequence of my actions. The punishment for my sin.

The clock ticks and ticks. Another minute has passed now, and the bells have stopped ringing.

It's now or never.

I force myself to get up and creep up the stairs, avoiding the areas I know creak underfoot. The higher I get, the faster my pulse climbs, echoing in my grip on the banister.

I reach the top and slowly tiptoe by Hannah's room, before stopping at a sudden sound.

The door opens slowly.

'Can't sleep either?' Hannah asks, child-like again in her soft, hopeful tone.

I pause at the door, torn. I can't do this while Hannah is awake. Her room faces the tracks; suppose she heard a sound as I was digging, and peered out from behind the curtains?

I steel myself on the landing, feeling the opportunity slipping from my grip.

'No,' I reply. 'I can't sleep either.'

Day Two

30

I wake to the sound of the rail works blaring on the other side of my bedroom window. The whine of the chainsaw ripping its teeth through the trunks of the trees.

I thought I would have more time. I would never have imagined that the workers would begin removing the trees on the first day of the project. When will they dig up the stumps, the roots? As soon as they do, they will bring Matthew's body with them. I think of the smell of decay hitting them, followed by their horrified faces as they spot a rotted hand creeping out from the earth.

There are many other trees they have to take down before they get to that stage. I can go back tonight, and continue with the plan.

But the doubt continues to chip away at me. *What if. What if.*

I shower and dress without thought or focus, methodically moving from task to task, all the while thinking of both the trial and Matthew's body. I stop before the bathroom mirror and stare at my paled complexion.

Today, I will find out if the judge has allowed the evidence I fed the prosecution to be added to the case. If he does, I will have to live with the fact that I sold a man down the river to save myself. But if he doesn't, I will have to find a whole new way to protect Hannah and my secret. The thought of going back to square one hits me with such a bout of fear that white blots fill my vision. I force myself to breathe.

Once I have met with the judge, I will need to meet with Antony and our client, and continue spinning my web of lies, before it's back to court where I will cross-examine Yolanda's mother, and question the detective leading the case.

As for tonight, I will meet Matthew again.

My stomach threatens to lurch; I run the tap urgently and gulp down water from my cupped hand.

I'm so sorry, Matthew.

I force the guilt down and leave the bathroom to continue with my tasks. Once I've blow-dried my hair and stepped out of my bedroom onto the landing, I hear a cough from behind Hannah's door. I knock briefly and peer inside. The curtains are drawn, the night still thriving inside her room.

'You still feeling rough?' I ask.

She coughs again for effect.

'Yeah,' she replies croakily. 'Can I stay at home one more day?'

Her presence in the house while I'm out makes me feel nervous, but it would help to have her here, to keep an eye on the rail works. If something happens, I can stay ahead of the curve. The works continue to clamour outside.

'All right, but keep your phone on you and text me back when I message you, okay?'

'Okay.' She eyes me through the gloom. 'How come you're so stressed about the train tracks stuff?'

I am immediately grateful for the gloom so she cannot see my face. I have been so panicked, and clearly I have been acting out of sorts, showing my cards.

'Not stressed,' I force. 'Just overwhelmed. This case is a lot;

coming home to mayhem is the last thing I need. Makes me feel better to think it'll be over soon.'

I venture in, tripping over a crumpled garment on the floor, and kiss her forehead, which to her defence does feel warm beneath my lips.

'I'll be back for dinner. Be good while I'm gone.'

I force a smile and shut the door, knowing that if I'm going to move the body with Hannah in the house, I will have to do something to make sure she isn't able to witness it.

I will have to do something bad.

⚖

The tension in conference room three is stifling and immediate. Antony, it seems, was up much of the night, no doubt analysing the evidence to try to conjure a strong rebuttal. By his faint smile in greeting, it doesn't appear he has found one.

Wade is sat on the other side of the table. The depression we had witnessed in earlier conferences is more evident than ever. He is dressed in the same suit as before, and a freshly ironed shirt, no doubt by the hand of Marianne. But his hair shimmers with grease, and his eyes appear utterly vacant, as if he doesn't know or recognise me, disassociating from the situation he has found himself in.

I did this.

I sit down with a held breath, trying to keep my composure.

'Good morning, Wade. How are you?'

A beat of silence takes over the room, the ring of it echoing off the windowless walls. Just when I think he isn't going to respond, his lips part.

'I wish people would stop asking me that.'

His voice croaks with despair. The man is becoming a mere shadow of who he once was.

'The new evidence from the prosecution has shocked us all, Wade,' I lie. 'I would be doing you an injustice if I said it wasn't pretty damning to our case. Your past ... it gives the prosecution a chance to paint what happened to your family as an escalation of previous acts.'

I wonder if he is even listening. He has disassociated again, staring into oblivion with his eyes set vacantly upon the surface of the desk.

'But we won't give up,' I continue. 'Antony and I have a strong argument for calling the police investigation into question. Even if the prosecution succeed in persuading the jury to see a link between your past and the crimes against your family, we can argue that other avenues went unexplored. This isn't over.'

'Isn't it?' he croaks. 'The prosecution team contacted my mother this morning. They've called for her to be a witness ... to talk about what happened.'

Antony sighs at the blow.

'Why didn't you tell us about all this, Wade?' he asks. 'We could have tried to prevent it from ever reaching court.'

'An innocent man doesn't think of the ways he may be seen as guilty,' he replies. 'I didn't think it was relevant to the truth.'

Wade rises from his chair suddenly, towering above us both.

'I want a minute alone.'

'We'll be right here, Wade,' Antony says, his words cut off by the shutting of the door. When the room falls quiet, Antony is the one to break it.

'When will they bring the evidence, do you think?'

'Their specialist witness Dr Heche is their last. I suspect they would plan to call Marianne just before Heche.'

'We're fucked, aren't we? I tried to find ways to counter-act the evidence, to keep it from being added. But it's killer, isn't it?' He leans back in his chair, his hands upon his head. 'Fuck.'

'We've got our angle to pursue too, Anthony. If we create enough doubt, their evidence might not stand as strong. Let's reconvene prior to their specialist witness, to think of a way around this.'

'Do you think the judge will agree to it? The new evidence?'

I hope so.

'I don't know.' I let the words sink in, hoping he will begin to accept the defeat, to allow me to send our client to the cells. 'But whatever happens, we have a strong argument too.'

Neither of us sounds convinced. Our client has given up, and our opposition's evidence casts a deep, dark shadow over our defence case. I've pulled the rug from under them both.

Now I just need to pray the judge makes the decision I need him to.

⚖

The judge enters, and everyone in the room stands. I try to distinguish his decision from his demeanour: the way his eyes stay downcast, the slow, tired way he walks. He looks to Niall first, then to me, and bids the court good morning, before we take to our seats. He turns towards the jurors' bench.

'Members of the jury, while you were called out of court yesterday afternoon, a matter of fresh evidence was brought to my attention. I called the day's proceedings to a close to consider this new evidence, and make my decision as to whether it should be admissible at such a late stage in the trial process. There is a manner in which we must conduct criminal trials, with numerous preliminary hearings long before you are called, to decide which evidence will make its way to court,

which witnesses will take to the box to give their statements.
It is unusual, but not impossible, for late evidence to be added
to a case.'

He looks down at his notes, before returning his attention
to the jury.

'Reasons for accepting late admissions of evidence are tied
to the importance of the evidence at hand – how important it
is for you, the jury, to know of what is enclosed, so you can
make your fair and honest verdict with all the facts to hand.'

He turns his attention to Niall, then me.

'That is why I have decided to accept this into evidence.'

Antony's head bows, and the press row shuffles excitedly,
as murmurs break from the public gallery. I turn to meet Mr
Viklund's eye, who is peering down at me. He gives me an
imperceptible nod, before I turn back towards the judge, but
not before glancing at Wade in the dock. He looks just as he
had when I first laid eyes on him: his shoulders concaved to
make himself smaller, his eyes towards the floor. He looks
utterly defeated. A defeat orchestrated by me, the one person
in the room he should be able to trust.

I stand before the judge, squirming with the rush of conflicting emotions; guilt and relief filling me up like oil and
water. I have betrayed my profession, my morals, my dignity.
Condemned a man to save my own hide. But it also means
Hannah and I will be safe.

'We will now continue with proceedings.'

Niall stands. 'Thank you, Your Honour. The prosecution
calls Rita Cummings.'

31

As the day's second witness takes her oath, Niall stands at the other end of the advocates' bench and asks for her to confirm her name for the court.

'Rita Cummings,' she replies.

Cummings stands straight but nervous, her hands knotted together before her and her eyes wide and alert, taking in the room and the people staring back at her.

'Thank you for coming here today, Ms Cummings. You're a paramedic, is that right?'

'That's correct. I've been a paramedic for close to nine years.'

Her years in service are painted all over her face. Her expression is warm yet tired, her eyes padded from sleepless nights.

'You were called to the Darlings' address during the early hours of Saturday, the seventeenth of November, is that right? Can you tell us how the evening unfolded?'

She takes a deep, resolute breath.

'I was on the night shift, my second in a row, with my colleague Sam. We had just finished escorting a patient to A&E when the Darling case was assigned. We were the closest to the scene.'

'What was your first instinct, when you were alerted to the incident?'

'It was called in as a house fire with four people known to

live at the address. By the sound of the description, the fire was severe. These aren't nice calls to receive. There isn't much we can do while the fire is still going, so we have to wait and hope that survivors are pulled from the blaze. The firefighters were en route when we arrived at the address just after half three in the morning. We were the first on the scene.'

Niall leaves a deliberate pause. *The scene.* I imagine the jury painting a picture of it in their minds. The fire burning wildly, curling up towards the night sky; the opulent gates of the country home lighting up blue from the ambulance's lights.

'And when you arrived, what did you find?'

'The fire could be seen from half a mile up the road. It had to have been about fifty feet in the sky. We could see the flames above the entry gates, and the shrubs and fences surrounding the property. It was clear to me that the fire would be fatal to anyone trapped inside, and I began to set my expectations.'

Niall allows a long, drawn silence to unfold in the court-room. The jurors shuffle awkwardly in their seats.

'When you and your colleague arrived, did you enter the grounds of the property straight away?'

'No.'

'Why not?'

'The entrance gates had been bolted and padlocked shut.'

Niall pauses for effect again, glancing at the jurors as he does so.

'Padlocked shut,' he repeats. 'From outside the property, or inside?'

'From the inside,' she replies. 'My colleague called it in to make the firefighters aware, who weren't too far behind. My colleague and I pulled the ambulance out of the drive to keep the gates clear. The fire team arrived with bolt cutters at the ready, and made their way into the property. We pulled in behind them.'

'What were your first thoughts about the entrance gates being locked from the inside of the property?'

The witness pauses, wringing her hands before her.

'In my mind, the only reason the gates would be locked from the inside was to keep us from gaining entry to help those trapped inside ... or to keep those within from escaping.'

The courtroom falls silent. A nervous cough sounds from the public gallery.

'What did you see when you got inside?'

'When we reached the end of the drive, the east side of the property had been completely engulfed. We parked up and got our equipment ready. It didn't seem possible that anyone would survive; our preparation was purely protocol. I was shocked when the firefighters said they had found someone alive.'

'And who had they found, Ms Cummings?'

'The defendant.'

Chairs creak as those in the room turn to glance at the dock.

'Could you describe the condition the defendant was in?'

'The patient was brought to us by the firefighters, and we immediately set him up with oxygen to combat the smoke inhalation. The patient was unconscious, and had second-degree burns to his left hand. He was dressed for sleep – a navy pyjama set, and his feet were bare and bloodied.'

'Was it his blood, on his feet?'

'No,' she replies. 'I inspected both soles for wounds to treat, but found none. The blood came from someone else.'

'Was there any other blood on his person?'

'Yes. His uninjured hand was also bloodied, but again, there were no wounds to signify the blood was his. His pyjamas were soiled with it, too. Neither my colleague nor I noticed at first, until I touched the fabric to attach the ECG pads to check his heart, and pulled my fingers away to find them wet and red.'

'The blood was still fresh?'

'It had dried on his hand and both feet, but his clothes were still damp with it, yes.'

'And was the defendant conscious during this?'

'No, but he was stable. My colleague treated the burns to his hand, and we set him up on oxygen and left the premises quickly, calling it in so we could be replaced, in case any further survivors were found.'

'Is it usual for only one ambulance to attend a scene of this magnitude?'

'We were particularly stretched that night.'

'Thank you, Ms Cummings. That will be all from me.'

Niall sits, and the attention of the room turns to me. The witness is stood in the box, waiting for me to pick her testimony apart, and now the nuclear evidence has been delivered, I can, but however efficiently I cross-examine the prosecution witnesses, the evidence Fredrick secured will blow it all out of the water. I stand on my side of the bench.

'Ms Cummings, my name is Neve Harper, acting for the defendant. In your nine years of service as a paramedic, have you come across patients bearing another person's blood in the past?'

'Yes. Plenty of times.'

'In what kind of scenarios did these instances occur?'

Ms Cummings looks away, thinking back. 'Usually, it's when one person has harmed another; the perpetrator is often covered in their victim's blood. Other instances might be during an emergency situation, in which one person may have attempted to help another who was injured.'

'Like a house fire, for example?'

'Yes, for example.'

I give her a forced, deceptively comforting smile.

'So, would it be fair to say that, in your opinion from nine years of service, it would be wrong to jump to the conclusion that a patient covered in another person's blood automatically means they caused harm to that person?'

She blushes in the box.

'It's not my job to judge a patient, but to treat them.'

'Thank you, Ms Cummings. And in your training to become a paramedic, were you taught about placements of blood on a person? Did you study forensic science?'

'Like a crime scene investigator might, you mean?'

'Yes.'

'Well, no. I'm not an investigator. I treat patients.'

'So, your professional opinion of this case, which you are here today to give, is simply that your patient – the defendant – was discovered with traces of blood on him that were not his own.'

'Yes.'

'And you have just acknowledged that it is not your role or expertise to assume where that blood might have come from, in terms of a motive? It's your job to look for wounds to treat, rather than to investigate the origin, or make assumptions of a person's involvement, correct?'

'Y-yes,' she replies nervously.

'Thank you.' I look to the judge. 'No further questions.'

32

After the lead firefighter was called to the box to give his statement on the deliberate nature of the fire and the time it took to
extinguish, the prosecution calls their last witness of the day,
Detective Inspector Markus Hall.

DI Hall is a tall, broad figure. The sort of man that com-
mands a room just by being in it. His heavy brow appears to be
constantly furrowed, and his buzz cut makes him appear more
like an army sergeant than a detective. He steps into the box
and gives his oath, before the prosecution guides him through
his history with the force. Twenty-two years since he joined the
police, nine years as an inspector. Building character, securing
credibility in the eyes of the jury.

'When I was assigned to the case, the home itself wasn't
safe to investigate; the fire was still going at this point, so it
was down to my team and me to interview those closest to
the Darlings to try and gauge the status of the relationships
between the victims, and if there was any reason to suspect
foul play.'

'And was there?' Niall asks.

'Yes. It was clear from the first responders' statements that
the fire had been started deliberately.'

'Deliberately,' Niall repeats. 'Which elements of the case drew you to this conclusion, in particular?'

'The gates to the property were locked shut with a chain and padlock. The gates were electronically powered and showed no sign of fault after inspection, so the only conclusion that could be drawn for the gates being chained shut were to keep the victims from escaping, and the first responders from intervening.'

'Was the padlock used to lock the gate fastened from outside or inside the property?'

'They were locked from the inside.'

DI Hall responds to each of the questions with calm confidence, stating the naked facts without emotional embellishments, which only seems to make the testimony all the more impactful. In the corner of my eye, I can see Antony, fidgeting nervously in his seat.

'Was there anything else to suggest foul play?'

'Yes. The fire appeared to have been ignited purposely in particular places to ensure destruction. There were puddles of gasoline found around the property. The canister was discovered on the forecourt.'

Niall instructs the jury to view their evidence packs. Inside is a series of photographs. If one looks closely at the picture of the main house and stables, the charred figures of the horses can be seen lying in the wreckage, their heads removed and taken to the pathologist's office to assess the bullet tracks through their skulls.

'Were there any suggestions at this point who the perpetrator might have been?'

'Yes,' he replies confidently. 'When we discovered Mr Wade Darling's fingerprints on the canister, he quickly became our first suspect. His fingerprints were also found on the murder weapon, which was found beside him by the firefighters when they discovered him.'

'Did the rifle exhibit anyone else's fingerprints or DNA, other than that belonging to Mr Wade Darling?'

'No. Just his.'

The courtroom falls quiet.

'Was that all the evidence you had to suspect the defendant?'

'No,' the inspector replies. 'There was more.'

'*More?*' Niall exclaims. It takes all of my strength not to roll my eyes at his faux dismay. 'What other evidence did you have?'

'The property had CCTV.'

The press bench creaks as each journalist leans in eagerly. The gallery is deathly silent.

'Members of the jury will now be shown a portion of this footage.'

The old, rickety trolley is pushed in, with the TV mounted on top. The tension builds as the room waits. There have been photographs, articles and third-party testimonies, but this is the most visceral glimpse the court has had into what happened on the night of the deaths. They will see the fire burning. The shadowy silhouette of the gun against the backdrop of fire.

The black screen bursts with colour as the footage plays.

The position of the camera shows the front of the property, with a view of the forecourt, and beyond it, the garages and horse stables. What appears to be a male figure enters the frame, dark with the night but with the unmistakable shadow of a rifle in one hand. As the minutes roll by, we watch him enter and exit the garage, returning with the bright red canister in his grip. He approaches the stables, rests the canister on the ground, and approaches the first door. A flash of white light bursts from the gun and reveals a glimpse of the scene:

the man stood with the rifle, pointed inside. He goes along the line of stables, the jury watching with ashen faces, as he sloshes the fuel from the canister inside, up the walls, the doors. The fire envelopes the stable in what seems like seconds, and the flames roar to life, lighting up the forecourt, as the man crosses towards the house and enters with the fire erupting behind him.

The footage stops and Niall clears his throat.

'Detective Inspector Hall, can you confirm the identity of the person in this footage?'

'We believe this is the defendant, Mr Wade Darling. As can be seen in the footage, this figure is familiar with the property: he knows where to retrieve the fuel canister, for example, and walks with purpose and conviction. We can also see the gunman holds the rifle with his right hand. The defendant is also right-handed. The figure in the footage also appears to be the same height, ethnicity and build as the defendant.'

'Is there any evidence to indicate a third party committed these crimes?'

'No. There is no sign of forced entry to the property, no CCTV or visual sightings of vehicles different to those owned by the Darling family. There was no other DNA evidence on the murder weapon, or the petrol canister, other than Mr Darling's.'

Niall appears to check his notes; an old advocate's trick to allow a witness statement to settle in the minds of the jury.

'And to clarify,' Niall asks. 'Who owned the murder weapon?'

'The rifle was bought and registered by the defendant.'

'Was this his only weapon?'

'No. Mr Darling owned a significant number of firearms. He had a gun room in the property to store his collection, which is worth over twenty thousand pounds.'

Niall allows the witness's last words to reverberate around
the quiet courtroom, as the onlookers do the maths. The sum
my client spent on firearms is likely to be more than some of the
jury could ever hope to spend in a lifetime on a mere hobby. A
good tactic, to reveal my client's alleged obsession and greed.

'Thank you, Detective Inspector Hall. No further questions.'

Niall takes to his seat.

'I'm afraid we've met our time limit for the day, Ms Harper,'
Judge McConnell says. 'We will reconvene tomorrow morning
for cross-examination.'

After the judge has left, Antony sighs heavily, his shoulders
sinking. I peer along the bench towards Niall, who undoubtedly has had a fantastic day in court. He gives me a playful
wink, and I look away.

'Don't worry, Antony,' I say in hushed tones. 'We'll skewer
him in the morning.'

'Yeah. Shame the judge had to give the jury the entire bloody
night to think over everything the detective said, though.'

He packs up his things quickly, looking towards the dock
as Wade is led out.

'I'll go and give him a pep talk. Let's meet later and plan our
attack on the new evidence.'

'I'm sorry, I can't tonight. Let's each work on it and reconvene tomorrow.'

'Neve, come on. We need to nail this. What could possibly
be more important?'

We stare at each other, unblinking.

I have to dig up my husband's body.

'I don't really think that's any of your business, is it?' He
flinches at my sharp tone. 'I'll see you in the morning.'

Antony sighs disappointedly. 'Fine. Tomorrow it is.'

As I watch him leave the court, I wonder how different I will be, come the morning. While the rest of the courtroom sleeps, I will be facing my biggest fear. Staring my worst sin right in the eyes.

Matthew.

33

The first thing I notice when I step out of the Bailey is how much the presence of the press and protesters has grown. Among the camera flashes and heckling photographers, they pace with their picket signs, chanting about Wade and his alleged crimes. I spot a blown-up photo of Yolanda Darling bobbing above the growing crowd, her eyes crossed out in red paint, a bloody handprint at her throat.

I forge on with my head down, my eyes blotted from the flashing lights, and stumble when a woman with a sign shoves through the photographers to reach me.

'Like cosying up to women-killers, do you? You make me *sick*!'

I feel the spray of saliva on my face, the heat of her words. A scuffle breaks out as the photographers shove her back, and I dart around the corner as fast as I can, but no matter how much distance I put between the crowd and me, I can still hear the shouts, their chants sing-songing in my head.

I dig around my bag for my phone, desperate for an update from Hannah. What if all of my worry was in vain? Perhaps they've found him by now, and this is already over. The lit screen shakes in my hand as I tap in the security code.

Hannah
Definitely made headway. Can't see any trees from
the window. What time will you be home? X

She sent that two hours ago, and I think of all the things that
might have happened between then and now. I imagine police
officers sat in my living room, awaiting my return to take
me in for questioning, with Maggie pacing the kitchen after
ordering Hannah to stay upstairs until I've been taken away in
cuffs. Maggie would make sure we never saw each other again.
Although, should Hannah discover what I did, all the lies I've
told, I'm sure she wouldn't need persuading. I feel that empty
twang in my chest, the same one my sleepwalking brings, and I
think back to being that little girl, wandering about strangers'
homes in the night, looking for her mother.

I fish my cigarettes and lighter from my pocket and light one
hungrily, as I think of my next steps. The nicotine seeps into my
bloodstream with the first hit and I exhale in a slow, relieved sigh.
I smoke the cigarette to the filter as I head for the tube station.

⚖

As I uncork the wine and bend down to check on the pizza in the
oven, not trusting myself with anything more mentally taxing,
I listen to Hannah padding around upstairs, the sound of life
within the house still foreign to me. She hadn't showered all day,
instead lying on the sofa tangled among blankets. I order her up
the stairs to get washed before dinner, and as soon as I hear the
water running, I bolt out into the garden towards the tracks.

The trees are gone. Every single one. All that remains are
the stumps in the earth, their roots still intact. No holes in the
dirt. He's still down there, waiting for me.

I return to the house and make my way upstairs. I slip the tablets from my bedroom drawer before returning to the kitchen, just as the shower turns off.

I couldn't sleep for weeks after the murder, replaying every swish of the club, every crack of my husband's skull. The warm splash of his blood spraying my face, the soft skin at my neck. Everyone around me thought it was grief that was eating away at me rather than guilt, and the doctor prescribed zopiclone sleeping tablets, which helped for a time, although she almost hadn't let me have them when I admitted to drinking heavily to get to sleep.

You mustn't mix this medication with alcohol, or it will intensify the effects. If I prescribe these, I need to know you won't drink.

I pour the crushed tablets into the wine glass and stir it in. The rioja appears to envelope the mixture whole.

'Smells good,' Hannah says.

I jump at the sound of her, picking up the wine glass as I turn.

'Here we go,' I say, and hold out the glass.

Her eyes gleam, reaching for it slowly, as if my offering is a trick to catch her out.

'Seriously?'

'You're old enough to have a drink with dinner. You like red wine?'

'Totally,' she replies quickly, her eyes fixed on the glass in her hands. I can tell she's never tried the stuff. But even if she doesn't like it, I know her teenage willpower will have her finish the lot.

I raise my own and eye her over the rim as I take a sip. She does the same, trying to hide a grimace.

'Gets easier to stomach the stuff the more you drink,' I say with a wink, before turning back to the stove. My smile drops instantly, and the guilt coils in my wine-filled gut.

It's the only way.

I listen as she takes a seat with a sigh and forces down another gulp.

'You feeling better?' I ask.

'I think so. I've slept a lot.'

'Ready to go back to school tomorrow?'

'Maybe.'

The oven timer goes off, and I remove the pizza and chips, both brown around the edges.

'Are you sure there's not anything else bothering you? Not making you want to go to school?'

She is silent as I cut the pizza into slices and place them on each plate.

'Han?'

I turn with both plates, placing one before her, and take to my own seat. She takes the ketchup bottle from the centre of the table.

'I'm fine.'

'That was convincing.'

She sighs, dipping a slice of pizza into the puddle of ketchup, moving it around rather than eating it.

'I don't really like this time of year.'

My heart drops. I take a piece of pizza and force myself to take a bite, despite losing my appetite too.

'Of course, you don't. It's tough.'

'Does it get easier? The whole grieving thing?'

I take a sip of wine to buy some time, and watch as she does the same. She had been sipping while my back was turned; nearly half the glass is gone now.

'I don't know. I hope so.'

We eat in silence, chewing and sipping at the wine. It usually takes thirty minutes to an hour for the tablets to take full effect, but when mixed with alcohol, it should take only half that time. She covers her mouth as she yawns.

'Have you heard from Nan?' I ask.

'She's not talking to me.'

'That can't be easy either.'

'You know what she's like.'

Her eyes look glassy now, and her words sound more drawn out than before, her lips and tongue growing lazy. What if mixing it with wine is too much for her system? Christ, what if she went to sleep and never woke up?

She takes one last sip, and I spot some of the undissolved tablets poking up from the dark pool at the bottom of her glass. I leap forward and snatch it from her hand.

'This was a bad idea,' I say as I head to the sink and throw the last dregs down the drain. 'You're not well, this won't help.'

'I'm fine,' she slurs, her eyes heavy.

A pang of guilt hits my chest. It's working much sooner than I thought.

Christ, what am I doing?

'Eat the pizza, it'll sober you up a bit.'

She yawns again, her mouth thrown wide, showing her wine-stained tongue.

'I'm not that hungry.'

'Eat it all, Han, or we won't have wine with dinner again.'

I watch anxiously as she chows down on the last of the pizza, ketchup on her chin and melted cheese on her fingers. Her eyes get hazier. The panic grows in me the drowsier she becomes.

You need her to stay asleep. You can't do what needs to be done without this.

She finishes the last mouthful, yawning widely.

'Why don't you have a lie-down, watch TV in bed?' I say. 'Perhaps you still aren't one hundred per cent.'

I expect her to fight me with it still being early in the evening, but she nods slowly.

'Yeah, okay.'

'I'll come and check on you.'

She rises from the table, swaying slightly, and heads for the stairs.

I sit with my guilt, waiting ten minutes, fifteen. When I don't hear any sign of her, I creep upstairs and pop my head into her room.

She is out for the count.

34

I decide to wait until midnight again to be sure that Hannah and most of the street are asleep, to limit the chances of me being seen, and spend the hours beforehand almost obsessively checking on Hannah: feeling her breaths on the back of my hand, making sure she's lying on her side. Now I sit in my armchair, waiting for the clock on the mantel to strike twelve. The arm turns around the dial, shuddering with age as it crawls towards twelve. The church bells ring out on the other side of the window.

It's time.

I head for the back door and step out into the night. The air is cold and thick, the sort of chill that clears the skies of clouds and reveals the stars. I stop in my tracks, my breath white on the air, and look up. I almost wish I was up there floating in the nothingness, where the guilt or repercussions couldn't reach me.

I continue my journey towards the end of the garden, shivering beneath my coat and gripping onto the handle of the spade. The trees have been sawn down, leaving nothing but a trail of stumps, their cream-coloured centres illuminated beneath the moon, as far as the eye can see. The train tracks reflect the night sky too, the moonlight glinting in the steel of the rails.

I hike myself over the fence, taking extra care not to knock the spade and alert anyone to my presence, and cross the track. I have already moved my car to the small car park wrapped around the church, right beside the fence that separates the grounds from the tracks. I look at the distance I will have to drag him, all the way along the tracks, following the length of the road from my house to the church. It's either that or drag him through the house.

When I reach what used to be the woodland edge, I close my eyes and think back to when there were trees, counting my way through the trunks, and open my eyes.

There is no going back now.

When I buried the body, I had been reeling from shock, moving on autopilot to get through the trauma of the night. I wasn't myself, but a raw, animal version of myself. But now, three years on, I must retrieve him with a sound mind. I will see and feel everything.

I stand before the stump and look around me. My heartbeat quickens. Without the trees, I am stood in plain sight. The row of terraced houses has a direct view of me. The majority of windows are dark with the night, but for the odd yellow glow emitting from hallway windows, the odd bedroom lit up behind the curtains. Hannah's, of course, is pitch black.

If I don't dig him up tonight, the rail workers will.

I poise the spade and stare down at the earth beneath my feet. How decomposed will he be now? He won't be a mere skeleton, not yet. But he would have begun to decay. His teeth and nails falling out, his skin waxy and slipping from his bones. I blink the fear back.

Just do what needs to be done.

I raise the spade and make the first crunch in the earth. The winter weather has made it almost rock solid. I raise the spade, and thrust with all my might. *Crunch.*

I push down on the handle, bringing up a pitiful amount of dirt, and close my eyes with a defeated sigh.

I am going to be here for hours.

⚖

An hour has passed. I have sweated so much beneath my coat that my clothes have stuck to my body, and locks of hair have plastered to my face. Every muscle throbs with pain. I'm so exhausted that I could cry for thinking about it if I dared to stop for too long, so I keep digging and digging.

The earth is practically frozen solid, but once I prepared a flask of boiled water from the kitchen and poured it over Matthew's grave, steam rose in white, whistling curls, and the water sank into the earth, softening it enough to break through. I have followed the shape of the grave as I remember it, thinking back to the way I laid him down: his head towards the tree, his feet facing east.

I thrust the spade down and stop when I hear a different sound. It isn't the earthy crunch, but a familiar rustle, and beneath it, a meatier thud.

Matthew.

I had buried him in the carrier my wedding dress came in. It was the only thing I had that was big enough to store him in; the closest thing I could find to a body bag. That night, as I dragged it out of storage in the loft and removed the dress, I'd found a small dried flower stuck in the netting of it that had fallen from my bouquet. I remember sitting among the rustling white fabric, my husband's body lying bloody in the hall as I twirled the dead flower between my fingers, tears running silently down my face.

I get down on my hands and knees, digging at the dirt with my gloved hands, and slowly reveal the dress carrier, its corner poking out from the earth. But I can barely see through my tears and the fog of my breath.

Even through the bag, I can smell him. The scent is rotten and musky, like that of a dung beetle, its tang so sharp that it catches at the back of my throat and lingers there, clinging to every drop of spit.

I look about me anxiously and towards the row of houses, looking for any silhouettes stood at the windows. But I see no one. As far as I'm aware, I am alone.

I have cleared most of the earth now. I can feel the shape of his body within the bag, as cold and hard as the earth. Will his eyes have rotted away? Those beautiful, captivating eyes that Hannah inherited? I clench mine shut at the thought of her, forcing myself to focus, and dash the last of my tears away.

I'm so sorry.

The roots have bound themselves around the bag, claiming him. I try to tug him free, but I can't dislodge him alone, and stagger to my feet. Loose earth slips from my knees. My head is spinning, but there are no trees to rest upon to catch my breath. I stand, swaying in the night, begging myself to focus.

You're almost done.

I lift the spade and try to wedge it beneath him to use as leverage. I lower the spade, watch the bag rise slightly, repeating the motions until I hear a dreadful sound.

A rip.

The smell hits me, suddenly and with force. It infiltrates my nose and throat, seeping through my airways. I lunge away from the grave as I cough and gag, landing on my hands and knees as strained, dying sounds retch up my throat. It is the most putrid scent I have ever known. It burns my eyes, coats my tongue and teeth. I spit against the mud in my desperation to clear it, but still it remains.

I rise up and sit on the ground, catching my breath, and see the scene before me. Piles of dirt, the abandoned spade gleaming beneath the moon, the shadowy grave. I look down the tracks, at the long distance I must drag him. I can't move him with the tear in the bag, the smell is strong enough to rouse even the deepest sleeper. The sort of scent that claims the air.

I'll duct tape it shut. Then all there is left to do is move him.

I check my watch. It is almost two in the morning. Just over five hours till sunrise, seven hours until I'm back at the Bailey.

I get to my feet, my entire body throbbing with stress, smoothing the piles of loose dirt over the bag to keep him hidden while I'm gone, and cross the tracks for home in search of duct tape for the bag, and wire clippers for the fence.

I had lied to myself before, when I said it was almost over with. For this is only the beginning of a long night ahead: once I have pulled the body free from the earth, I will have to bury him all over again.

⚖

I turn the corner sharply and hear the thump of Matthew's body hitting against the side of the boot.

I flinch at the sound, sending shivers of pain through me. My muscles are so tense that it hurts to move; every time I glance in the rear-view mirror, a splice of pain shoots up my neck.

It had been a nightmare moving the body. It was so heavy despite decomposition, and there had been no other way to move him but to drag him alongside the tracks, before finally having to tug him over them, hearing the thud of him falling from each rail. Next was the fence. I'd had to cut at the wire and drag him beneath, looking about me with every snip. A trail of mud and grass leads from the fence to where I had parked my car, and I lugged him into the boot with sweat dripping into my eyes and hair sticking to my lips with each heave for breath, before attempting to conceal the trail I left in my wake.

I drive out of the city towards the outskirts, forever looking behind me for the Messenger or one of his men following behind, while trying not to think of what I saw when duct-taping the bag shut. As my eyes watered from the stench, and I gritted my teeth to keep from breathing it in, I saw a flash of him. The yellowed, mummified flesh of his hand. His wedding ring mottled into him.

I will bury him in the woods at Low Valley Wood outside of East London. There are miles of trees, which will be completely empty but for the woodland creatures, and no witnesses to stumble across me. Matthew and I had taken Hannah there when she was younger. I continually force the memories of the visit out of my mind: holding his hand, Hannah running gaily before us, her auburn hair shining copper in the sun.

I take the next left and drive down a long, straight road. The further out of London I go, the thinner the range of buildings become. To my right is an open field, and to my left, a hedge grove. I check the time at the dash: it's gone three.

The steering wheel begins to shudder beneath my grip. Slow at first, before the vigour grows and the headlights begin to flicker. A beeping sounds from the dashboard: the battery light flashes at me in strobes.

'No ... *No, no, no!*'

The engine splutters as it slows, and the lights grow dimmer and dimmer, until the car falls silent and I am drifting to a stop

towards the roadside. I lift the handbrake and sit in the darkness, with no sounds to be heard other than my short, panicked
breaths and the violent thud of my heart.

My phone is at home to keep the Messenger from tracking
me. I am alone, in the middle of nowhere, with my husband's
body decaying in the boot, with less than four hours to go until
the sun rises.

I stare silently at the pitch-black road beyond the windscreen.

35

I have been stationed on the side of the road for over an hour, and not one other driver has passed me by. The night is impenetrably dark, and the inside of the car is as cold as the outside; even in here, I can see my breath on the air. The windows have fogged up, and my lungs crackle and wheeze as I breathe in the wet chill.

This is the only time it would have been beneficial to have the Messenger following me, for it wouldn't do him any good to have me caught either. But I seem to have evaded them, on the one night I need them. I go to check the time, remembering that I haven't got my phone on me, and the dashboard is as dark as the night.

What the hell am I going to do?

I get out of the car to get my blood moving, rubbing the arms of my coat, and light a cigarette, looking out across the fields at the miles of sprawling void. I had wished to float in nothingness, hadn't I? Although these weren't the circumstances I'd had in mind.

Something catches my eye, and I whip my head to the left.

Headlights appear in the distance.

I stare at the two taunting orbs, growing in size the closer they get, my heart rate climbing as the seconds tick by. What sort of character would be on the road at this sort of time? I know I should move for the car, but I am quite literally like a deer in headlights, watching as the vehicle gets closer. Should I flag them down for a jump-start, or hide and hope they pass without seeing me? A potential witness to my crimes.

There will be more passers-by when the sun rises.

Before I have time to act, the car begins to slow and pulls up before mine, our front bumpers facing one another on the side of the road. It's a beaten-up old Ford, with its trusty engine sputtering like a tractor. I can only see the silhouette of the person behind the wheel, and listen as the ignition is turned off, followed by the click of the driver's door. I drop the cigarette to the ground.

'You all right, lass?' The man asks. He's an older gentleman, his white hair crisp against the night, his tone warm and thoughtful.

'I-i-it's my battery,' I reply, my teeth chattering around the words.

'Poor mite, you must be freezing. Need a boost?'

I nod. 'Please.'

He steps closer with a kind, fatherly smile.

'You got the cables by any chance?'

I pause, unsure. My uncertainty must be all over my face, for he speaks again.

'You might have some tucked away in the spare tyre bed in the boot, with a car like that,' he says, pointing towards the rear. 'Let's have a look.'

'*No*,' I reply. The man stops in his tracks, his smile falling in an instant. 'I'll look. God knows what I've got back there.'

I feign a laugh and head for the rear of the car, shaking from the cold and the fear. Will he be able to smell the body from where he stands? What if the tape has been knocked loose from the bumps in the road? My mind is bombarded with questions as I take each step, the road crunching underfoot.

I have to appear as normal as I can.

'Thank you so much for stopping,' I say through chattering teeth. 'I thought I was going to be out here all night.'

I take the key from my pocket, jumbling in my shaking fingers, and crouch at the boot to try to slip it into the manual lock. It's so dark I can barely see my own hands.

'No problem, least I could do. You need some light?' he asks. He begins to approach, pawing for his phone.

'No, no,' I say, raising my hand. 'I'm good, thank you.'

I wrestle the key against the lock, listening to the metal scrape, all under the man's watchful eye as he appears to edge closer. I can't have him standing beside me as the door opens. The fear of being caught has me fumbling with haste; sweat breaks out beneath my coat.

'Are you sure you don't need—'

The key slips inside, and I turn it roughly, a relieved, white breath huffing from between my lips.

'Got it.'

I stand up and slowly lift the boot door.

The tape has remained intact, and yet the smell still hits me. I try to keep the disgusted expression from my face, but the potent scent makes my eyes water. My gut squirms beneath my coat.

'Corr,' the man says, sniffing the wind. 'You catch that? What's that God-awful smell?'

I blink the water from my eyes.

'Maybe it's field fertiliser,' I stutter.

'Bit early for that, pet.'

The body lies over the well where the spare tyre is stored.

I reach in and try to shift it, but with my strained arms shaking and useless, the weight of him seems immovable. I blow a lock of hair out of my face and heave against the bulk of him. The well's cover appears slowly with each shove.

Matthew's inside here, a voice whispers in my head. I imagine him twisted from each movement, his limbs bent, face frozen in an eternal, quizzical look.

'Christ love, what you got in there, a body?'

I bolt up and stare at him over the roof of the car. The smile drops from his face.

We stand in the dark, the arctic breeze howling between us.

'It . . . it was a joke, darlin'. No harm meant.'

I couldn't appear more suspicious if I tried. I cough to clear the panic from my throat and force a laugh. The sound is inauthentic and awkward.

'Sorry. The cold . . . I've lost my sense of humour.'

I give the body one last shove and lift the latch with a shaking hand, fighting against the weight of the body bag, shifting him enough to clear the way.

'Got it,' I say, as I reach in for the cables.

The man steps forward to retrieve them, so I yank them free and slam the boot shut just as he turns towards the rear of the car. I hold out the cables in my shaky grip.

'Thanks so much again for your help.'

He smiles, although it is smaller than before. Forced.

Christ love, what you got in there, a body?

'Course,' he says, heading towards the front of the car. 'Can't have you out here alone, can we? God knows who's about.'

I smile tightly. The irony is not lost on me.

I'm the most dangerous thing out here.

'I'll pop my bonnet and get them on. You should be able to pop yours from under the steering wheel somewhere; a small catch in the footwell.'

I silently resent him giving me instructions about my own car, but truth be told, I wouldn't have known had he not said. This was more Matthew's car than mine. He knew where everything was, was the one to change the oil and all the other tasks. As I head towards the driver's side, I fear I can still smell the body on the air.

I open the driver's door and use my lighter to search about in the dark, enjoying the faint warmth of the flame against my face, and pull the lever. When I close the door behind me, the man is already lifting the bonnet of my car and fitting the cables.

'Sorry love,' he says from beneath the bonnet. 'I never introduced myself. I'm Andy.'

'Nice to meet you.'

I hear a metal clang from beneath the bonnet.

'What's your name then?' he asks.

Why does he want to know that?

He could have jotted down the registration number plate when he pulled up. Will he think my behaviour odd, and look up the reg plate when he gets home? He could find out my address that way, couldn't he?

He steps out from under the bonnet and glances at me, awaiting my answer.

'Amy,' I lie.

'Nice name. Same as my niece.'

As the silence falls between us, I can't help but think of the testimony he would give at my trial.

I found her on the side of the road in the middle of the

night. She looked cold and scared, but it wasn't long before she started acting . . . oddly. She was reluctant to let me see inside the boot, and gave me a false name. I knew she'd lied because I'd seen her on the front page of The Times.

Andy blows hot air into his hands before rubbing them together for warmth.

'What brings you out here so late then, love?'

He's not doing anything wrong. He's just making light conversation. I'm being paranoid.

'I was staying with some family, but needed to head home for work tomorrow. How long does it take to recharge a car?'

He gives me a quizzical look. I force a smile, but I'm clearly on edge.

'We leave them like this for a few minutes, then I'll run my engine for another ten, then we'll turn off both cars and wait a minute before disconnecting. Hopefully your car should start after that, no problem.'

Ten whole minutes of talking to this man.

'Great.'

We fall into an uncomfortable silence. The treetops swish with the icy wind. My eyes stream from the chill of it. I'm sure I can smell the body from here.

'What do you do?' he asks.

I shouldn't have mentioned work; I practically asked for this question to be put to me. He stands rubbing his hands together, eyes on mine.

'An accountant,' I lie. 'What about you?'

He laughs. 'My niece Amy, she's an accountant too.'

I force one back. 'Small world.'

'Really is. You must currently be in hell with tax return season,' he says.

'Oh yes,' I force. 'So what is it you do?' I ask, trying to shift the conversation from me to him.

'Retired copper,' he replies.

My heart drops as I try not to let the shock show on my face. Of all the people who could have stopped to help.

'Been off the force a few years now. Haven't shaken the sense of duty yet though, as you can tell.'

No wonder he has been asking so many questions. He clearly senses something is amiss. Would he know what a body smells like, from his time on the force? Is that why he made that joke about the boot?

'Shall we turn your engine on now?' I ask.

'You really are keen to get home,' he says with a chuckle, and heads towards the driver's side door.

'Just cold and tired,' I reply.

The engine grumbles awake, and we stand in the cold, listening to it chug to life. Not a single other car has passed since he arrived.

'Your phone die, or something?' he asks.

'Sorry?'

'Your phone. Did it run out of battery? I'm surprised you didn't call anyone.'

'Oh. I planned to charge it from the cigarette lighter on the dash, but never got the chance. So, ten more minutes you said?'

My insistence only makes me seem more suspicious. I can see everything I say piquing his curiosity. His eyes are no longer kind, but inquisitive, looking me up and down, scanning the car as if to remember details later.

'Eight and a half by now,' he says. 'You'll be on your way in no time.'

The cold has seeped into my bones. No matter how much I pull my coat around my frame, or rub at my arms, the chill remains. The skin on my face is starting to burn from the ice-cold wind.

'You shouldn't be out this late at night without a phone, y'know,' he says. 'Never know who's about.'

The irritability bites back before I can stop it.

'Yes,' I snap. 'But we all make mistakes, don't we?'

His expression falls. I don't know the man, and despite his kind act of help, I dislike him. I hate his questions, his prying eyes.

'I wasn't telling you off,' he says. 'Just some advice from an old man.'

'Right.'

'Sorry, I've got a daughter about your age. It's the dad in me.'

And the copper, I bet.

I begin to pace back and forth, partly to keep myself warm, but also to keep him from studying me, in the hope that a moving target is harder to remember than a still one.

'So what have you got rattling around back there?'

I stop in my tracks.

'Excuse me?'

He nods towards the boot.

'You said you had to sift through stuff.'

'Is that really any of your business?'

He raises his eyebrows and shrugs.

'I just meant … I can give you a list of things that would be good to have in the car, should something like this happen again. Bottled water, blanket, battery-operated phone charger—'

'This won't happen again.'

I pace some more, faster this time. It mustn't be much longer now. Six minutes? Five?

'Christ, what *is* that smell?'

A copper would know what a corpse smelt like. If he hasn't pinpointed it yet, I have no doubt he will. If not here, then when I'm gone. The recognition clicking like a switch in his brain.

'Sewage, maybe,' I say.

'Nah, whatever it is, it's dead.'

'Roadkill then,' I reply smartly. 'How much longer?'

He gives me a look. The smiles have long gone. Now he is frowning at me.

'Are you sure you're all right?'

What do I do if he doesn't give up?

I think of him opening the car boot and seeing the body bag inside, the smell hitting him like it had me.

What would I do then?

He is still staring at me, awaiting my answer.

I hear the swish of the golf club. *Whoosh. Thwack.* Then an intrusive thought, a horrible one. I think of taking the spade from the back of the car, raising it through the night air, and cracking the back of the man's skull.

'Look, I'm really grateful you've stopped to help, but I'm cold and I'm tired, and in the nicest possible way, I don't know you. Being out here alone with a strange man is putting me on edge.'

A light sparks in his eyes. One of recognition and relief.

'Of course ... I'm sorry, I didn't think.' He runs his hand through his thin whisps of white hair. 'Why don't you sit in the car, warm up a bit?'

I get behind the wheel and shut the door behind me, but even here, behind metal and glass, I can sense him watching me, trying to figure me out. Why had he joked about there being a body in the car? The smell is in here too, drifting through the back seats. I cover my nose and mouth with my scarf, but it seeps through the fabric.

After a few more agonising minutes, he knocks on the glass and opens the car door.

'Right, start your engine for me. Let's see if she plays ball.'

I turn the key in the ignition, and the lights appear on the dash.

'It's working,' I say. 'Thanks for your help—'

'Hold your horses,' he says. 'Let's check the engine too.'

I turn the key further and listen to the engine spit and grumble, eventually coming to life.

'Let's give it a minute, then we should be done.'

'Look,' I say, desperately. 'Let's not. I should be getting home. But thanks for all of your help, it was really kind of you.'

'Want me to fit the cables back in the—'

'No ... I'll take them in here with me.'

We turn off our engines and he removes the cables. I rock with the car when he slams the bonnet shut, and gives me a nod.

'Thanks again for your help.'

'No problem,' he says, passing me the cables through the window, without the smile he had greeted me with. 'Get home safe, Amy.'

I start the engine again, praying it runs. When it grumbles to life, I lift the handbrake and speed off, spitting stones behind me, glancing in the rear-view mirror as I go.

The man is stood in the road, watching as I drive away.

⚖

It is early morning by the time I have dug the new grave, but the sky is still dark with the night. All I can see are the shadows of the trees, the odd bit of moonlight breaking through the treetops, and the white fog of my breath.

I reached the woods around five thirty in the morning, and dragged the body from the boot and down into the woodland verge with tears of pain and exhaustion blurring my eyes, my hands shaking and numb to the bone despite the gloves. I barely remember digging the grave. I dissociated from the act, thrusting the spade into the hard earth on autopilot. Had I thought about it, I would have wept from the work I had yet to do, and the pain screaming all over my body. My back has blown from dragging Matthew, twinging every time I raise the spade and bring it down again. Whenever I thought I was nearing the end, I quickly realised the grave was too shallow, and had to set about digging once more. As I dug, a fleeting thought crept into the forefront of my mind.

Give in. Give up. Call the police, and this is all over: the trial, the hiding. The guilt.

But it's not just my life at stake. I kept digging, and digging, muttering my motivation repeatedly beneath my white breath.

I'm doing this for Hannah.

When the grave is finally deep enough, I grab onto the edge of the body bag and tug with the last of my energy, lugging it into the grave until it lands with a lifeless thud. It's a snug pit, just big enough to have him lay down with each edge pressing against him: the top of his head, the flats of his feet, his arms pressed against his sides.

My husband.

My darling.

My victim.

I check the time: I have to be at the Bailey in under three hours. I won't get a single wink of sleep. I could cry for thinking of it, longing for my bed, but I deserve every wincing pain, every second of exhaustion.

I pile the loose earth onto him, listening to the rustle as it hits the bag, until soon enough he is out of sight. I pat the loose earth with the spade, then walk over it to pack it shut, before disturbing it with the shovel again to hide my footprints and dragging fallen branches and loose undergrowth across the grave. I stumble back and assess my work. Matthew's new resting place blends in with the terrain as though I were never here.

I claw myself up the dark verge, every muscle in my body spasming from excessive use, and my head is pounding from lack of sleep and water. When I reach the top, I check the road. No headlights. Not a sound. I stumble to my feet and turn around to look at the scene, trying to remember the exact spot where I buried him. Counting the trees, looking for landmarks. Something I never dreamt I would have to do again. But if I have done this right, I will never have to come back.

I let myself inside the car, quivering violently from exertion. I am covered in dirt: my black clothes now soiled brown, and when I catch my reflection in the mirror, I see how earth has stuck to the tear tracks on my face. My eyes are bloodshot and empty. The interior light slowly fades, plunging me into the darkness again.

I turn on the headlights, ignite my last cigarette in a shaking hand, and pull away.

Day Three

36

I am cleaning the earth from the spade when the phone rings.

I stand at the kitchen sink shaking violently from exhaustion, before summoning the energy to retrieve the phone.

'Hello?'

'What the *hell* do you think you're playing at?' Maggie barks down the phone. 'The school just called and told me Hannah hasn't been in for days, and there's been no word on her absence.'

The ferocity of her tone makes me jump; I'm nothing but a mass of nerve-endings, which shoot and fire at the slightest sound.

'Hannah didn't feel well—'

'Every teenager says that. Unless they're on their last legs, you send them in, for Christ's sake. And you didn't think to call the school to let them know?'

'I've been busy with the trial—'

'Right, well you insisted on coming between Hannah and me and playing the role of her guardian, so I expect you to bloody well act like one. Send her into school this morning – I don't care if her head is hanging from her neck by a thread. Understand?'

'Yes, Maggie.'

She hangs up the phone, and I stand listening to the endless tone. I don't know how long I stay like this, transfixed in a sleep-deprived trance. I am roused again by a car horn sounding outside and glance at the clock on the wall.

Hannah.

The memory of what I did to her the night before hits me. I had been so caught up with my task and the body, that drugging my stepdaughter, the most important person in my life, got lost among the many other sins I have committed.

I make my way upstairs, my heart beating wildly in my chest, and conceal the spade beneath my bed, before slowly opening the door to Hannah's bedroom.

Hannah is still fast asleep, her hair as wild as a nest, with spittle shining at the corner of her mouth.

'Hannah, you awake?' I creep through the gloom and open the curtains. 'You'll be late for school.'

She rouses languidly, the pull of the drug trying to drag her back down. Her eyes search the room for me, and when she speaks, her mouth and tongue are lazy around the words. My heart leaps with guilt.

I'm so sorry.

'I don't feel well—'

For once, she may well be telling the truth.

'You look fine, come on. You've had enough time away from school.'

'But—'

I turn at the door and give her a look.

'No buts. Your nan has just given me a bollocking down the phone after the school called her. I can't deal with this during the trial, Han. Please.'

She sits up in bed, staring up at me through a mess of hair

and eyes bleared by sleep. But when she takes in the sight of me, her gaze turns to a look of fear.

'Are you okay? You look ...'

As she stares at me in wonder, I glance at my reflection in the mirror on the wall. I look horrendous. My eyes are bloodshot and puffy. My hair is knotted, with a stray bit of dirt above my ear where I tucked my hair out of the way. I look like I've been dug up myself.

'I'll be fine once you're up and on the way to school.'

I stand before the Bailey, trying to muster the courage to step inside. I have showered the night away, but I can still smell the body on me. It's almost as if it's become a part of me, burrowing into my skin and rising from me with the slightest movement.

Today, the prosecution will bring more experts to the witness stand: there is the cross-examination of Detective Inspector Hall, the ballistics expert and the pathologist. Then there will be Wade's mother Marianne, before the prosecution will rest their case with the key and final witness, Dr Heche.

The press outside the Bailey seems even more excitable today, and the papers had been even more damning this morning. The protestors too have grown in number, pacing back and forth, their chants fogging before them in the cold air, their signs waving from side to side with each step, with uniformed police outside the Bailey keeping watch.

Among the crowd, I see a face looking at me, staring out from the others who are otherwise watching the front of the building: Melanie Eccleston. The smirk is undeniable. I try to steel myself as she approaches, to ready myself for whatever game she is set on playing.

'We need to talk,' she says, the smile still plastered to her face.

'Melanie, with the greatest respect, I don't have the time or the energy to deal with you.' She reaches into her bag as I talk, retrieving a high-end camera from inside. 'If you're after a lead, you're going to have to find it another way—'

'Oh, I have my lead,' she replies, and turns the camera screen towards me.

I peer down at the screen with a frown, trying to work out the photo she's showing me.

What I find hits me like a punch.

I cover my mouth with a shaking hand.

It is a photo of me, dragging the body bag from the tracks to the boot of my car in the church car park.

She presses a button and the screen shows the next image. It is of me hoisting my dead husband's body into the boot, struggling beneath the weight of him. Another, where I am looking up towards the bell tower as the clock struck and the sound boomed above my head; my face clearly identifiable as I stare up in the path of the full moon.

It was so dark last night. I thought I was alone, I didn't see any movement, hear any noise. But Melanie must have been there, staking out the house. Waiting for me to trip up.

I straighten and meet her gaze. She is stood so close to me that I can feel the warmth of her breath.

'I think we should have a chat, don't you?'

She heads down the street, away from the Bailey, not needing to glance behind her to check I will follow. She knows I will.

⚖

Melanie leads me to the coffee shop where I first met Wade Darling. The room is the same: near-empty and dimly lit from its position in the back street, shielded by the high buildings. The usual barista is making our drinks behind the counter. But despite the similarity, my life couldn't have changed more since the morning I met my client. Could that really have been only a week ago?

We sit down in the booth by the window. Melanie is practically jittering with excitement as she shrugs off her coat.

'You look shattered,' she says. 'Late night?'

Her face is straight, but she smiles with her eyes, a mischievous glint that tells me she's enjoying this.

The barista brings over our order, and I look down at the drink before me: a frothy latte that I'm not sure I can stomach. But the smell of coffee calls to me, the need for caffeine aching in my bones. I lift the mug to my lips and gulp.

'We don't have long,' I say. 'I need to meet with my client.'

'Yes, about that. What's your game plan, exactly? I mean, you're not exactly hitting it out of the park. That new evidence is said to be pretty damning.'

I give her a long, hard stare.

'If you think I'm going to give you anything – on or off the record – you're dumber than you look.'

She smiles.

'I can't say I blame your poor performance. You seem rather . . . distracted.'

'Cut the foreplay. What do you want?'

'An explanation, for a start.'

'I don't owe you anything.'

'Not me personally, no. But what about the public? After all these years of searching for your husband's whereabouts . . . don't you think they have the right to know?'

'That's quite the assumption.'

'What? That you were dragging your husband's body into the back of your car?'

The accusation sits between us like a held breath.

'Can you confirm there was a body in the bag, Melanie?'

She smiles wider and reaches for her camera again, sifting through what seems to be dozens of photos.

She holds it before me again. I lean closer, my heart beating wildly, and pause.

Melanie hadn't just taken photos of me in the church car park. She had staked outside my house all night and snapped photos of my return. In the photo, the sun is just beginning to rise. I look pale and exhausted, and I'm covered in mud: my clothes are soiled with it, with stray swipes on my face. I look like a feral animal with glassy, dilated eyes.

'How do you explain these, Neve? You didn't return with the body bag, and you were covered in mud. There's only one conclusion the police will come to . . . I'll be writing my story and backing up these photos as soon as I'm home, and will file it first thing in the morning, along with these.' She waves her camera from side to side, tauntingly. 'Hell, I'd have written it last night if I could have, but I've had just as much sleep as you.'

I feel myself grow dizzy, and grip the side of the table.

'That is, of course, unless you can give me something better . . . I doubt you can – breaking Matthew's missing persons case will be the best story of my career. But I'll give you the chance.'

I stare at her from across the table, a grimace of loathing set upon my face. She doesn't intend to give me a chance at all. She will be filing that story and those photos whatever I give her. She is hanging this over me, giving me a glimpse of hope, before snatching it away.

She checks her watch.

'Best get going if I want to get a good seat.' She slips the camera back into her bag. 'I'll wait to hear of your decision regarding my story. In the meantime, I'll be deciding which photo will look best on the front page. There are just so many good ones ...'

She stares at me from the other side of the table with an almost violent curiosity; a smirk creeps across her face. 'You and Wade make quite the murderous pair, don't you?'

⚖️

I hide in the furthest cubicle in the women's bathroom and sit on top of the seat with my knees held tight to my body.

I don't know what to do. Now Melanie has these photos, it won't be long until the whole world knows. I think of Hannah and Maggie's faces paling as they take in the sight of me on the cover of *The Times*, dragging Matthew's body to the boot of my car.

I need to tell the Messenger.

Melanie knowing this will lessen the Messenger's hold on me. She will be just as much of a threat to him and Mr Viklund as she is to Hannah and me. If the truth were exposed before the trial is over, they will never get what they want.

But telling the Messenger would be effectively killing her.

I toy with the thought silently. If there were any time to intercept, it would be now. She hasn't written her story yet; she hasn't backed up the photos. All we'd need to do is destroy the camera and all traces would be gone, as though this never happened.

But I can't shed any more blood. I have accumulated enough guilt to last me a lifetime.

I stare at the dirty grouting between the tiles on the floor, blinking away the tears of frustration that blur my vision.

But what if it's the only way to keep Hannah safe?

Despite my desire to hide away, I check my watch and leave the cubicle, fixing my messy appearance in the mirror before reaching down into my bag for my wig and placing it on my head. I remember the first time I tried it on, the pride I felt. All of my youthful hope for the future. The naivety and innocence that is lost to me now. My beliefs in right and wrong had been so concentrated, sacrosanct.

Now I stand here, breaking every vow.

Melanie is good at what she does, but by dangling her win in front of me, she has made one fatal mistake.

She has given me time to stop her.

37

'Christ,' Antony says when he meets me at the door of conference room three, and steps out into the corridor. 'Are you all
right? You look . . .'

His sentence trails off as he looks me up and down.

'Thanks.'

'Sorry, I just mean . . . I can't look much better.'

Thankfully, he doesn't. Despite his usually kempt appearance, his eyes look almost as bloodshot as mine. But he
certainly won't be as tired. My entire body thrums with pain:
every joint throbs, every muscle has been pulled taut.

'Were you up all night digging too, then?'

I flinch at his choice of words.

'Yeah. Not much luck.'

He sighs and shakes his head. 'I couldn't find much either.
Damn the judge for admitting this so late.'

'We still have a strong narrative with the skewed police
investigation. If we hammer this home as hard as we can, we
are still in with a chance. I'll do my very best, Antony.'

'I know you will,' he says, and pats my shoulder. The guilt
knots tighter in my chest.

'How is he?' I ask, nodding at the door to the conference room.

'No better than yesterday. Surely, we can't let him step into the box like this? He's in the grip of a depression and the prosecution's new evidence relates to just that. We'd be playing right into the prosecution's hands.'

'And say what: "The defendant can't give evidence because of the depression the prosecution has just lambasted him for?". No, we've got no choice but to stick this out and try to save face. He's expected to stand in the box tomorrow. We can't back out now.'

He runs his hands through his hair, the smell of fresh, nervous sweat creeping from his open blazer.

'I thought we had this in the bag. I really did.'

'It'll be close to the wire, but it's not over yet.' I give him a soft smile. 'Come on.'

Wade is sat at the desk in his own vacant world, staring in a trance at the surface of the table. I wonder if he is thinking of his family and the past, or the unknown nature of his future. Whether he will walk away a free man or live the rest of his life behind bars.

'Good morning, Wade,' I say, as we sit before him on the other side of the table.

'When will this be over?' he asks, his voice croaking as if they are the first words he has spoken since the day began.

'The prosecution's case will likely end today, if there aren't any delays. Then it will be time for us to deliver ours. As for today's proceedings, we will start with my cross-examination of Detective Inspector Hall. It's a crucial part of our case, in terms of causing doubt in the juror's minds.'

'Until the prosecution tell them about my past.'

'We still have time to get them on side, Wade—'

'Let's just get this over with.'

He stands up from the desk and heads for the door, which clicks shut before we have even risen from our seats.

Detective Inspector Hall seems as serious and composed as the day before, and unlike me, he appears to have slept well, with no worries gnawing away at him. No bodies to bury in the dead of night.

I rise at the other end of the bench, my back threatening to give. As I set my tired eyes upon the detective in the witness box, I am sure I can feel the Messenger's gaze on me from the gallery, lasering into the back of my head. Not twenty feet from him, Melanie sits, watching me with an amused smile.

I break out in a sweat beneath my garb and clear my throat to begin.

'Detective Hall, I am Neve Harper, for the defence. I have a few concerns about the statements you gave yesterday afternoon.'

I give him a long stare, building my authority in the minds of the jury. He meets my eyes confidently, having done this so many times before. I look down at my notes.

'I would like to start with the gates to the property. You said you believed they were locked from the inside. How were they operated?'

'The gates were controlled from the main house, via a control panel in the hallway of the property.'

'I see. So, if the defendant wanted to keep the first responders from entering, is there a way he could keep the gates locked using this control panel?'

DI Hall picks up the glass of water before him. 'Yes, I suppose,' he replies, before taking a sip.

'So, what need would the defendant have for a chain and padlock?'

'I don't quite understand the question.'

'*If the defendant wanted to keep the gates locked,*' I repeat sternly, 'why would he not control them from the main house? Why would he fit a padlock and chain, which could easily be cut through, when the gates' pre-existing security system would have easily kept anyone from entering? Arguably, it's their sole purpose, no?'

He glances briefly towards the jury, before returning his gaze to me.

'It is my belief that the chain was applied in case of any breach of the system by the police, and to keep the victims from getting to safety.'

'Your *belief*,' I repeat. 'The fire service cut through the chains relatively quickly, didn't they?'

'Yes.'

'So in retrospect, would it not be safe to say that getting hold of the supplier of the electrical gates at three in the morning to override the system would have taken far longer than using a pair of bolt cutters to sever the chain?'

'When put that way, yes.'

'What other way is there? It suggests that this would be the action of someone without such access, wouldn't it?'

'I don't follow.'

'A third party is far less likely to know the gate system to achieve this – which I believe is quite a complex array of numbered codes – and is therefore likely to employ other measures of locking the gates, such as a padlock and chain?'

'Perhaps. But as I said, the gates were locked from the inside.'

'Ah, yes, my next concern.' I look down at my pad for some

time, pretending to scour my notes to prolong the silence, as I wonder what the Messenger and Mr Viklund might be thinking in the gallery. Am I being too efficient for their liking, despite the trap I've set? 'You have stated the person responsible for fitting the chain could not exit through the front of the property. Is there any other way in or out of the grounds?'

'No.'

'No? A person couldn't climb any one of the perimeter fences or walls?'

'There were no signs of that occurring.'

'What signs would you expect?'

'Damage to shrubbery, scuff marks on walls. Footprints in the earth.'

'The weather was cold with it being winter, and the ground was rock solid. That would make it incredibly difficult for the perpetrator to leave footmarks behind them, surely?'

'Difficult, but not impossible.'

'What about the woodland at the rear of the property, could that not be used as a route to escape?'

'Again, it wouldn't be impossible.'

'I think the word you're looking for is "yes", Detective Inspector Hall.' I give him a pointed look, before continuing. 'So, when you mentioned there were no visuals of cars not belonging to the Darlings near the property on the night of the murders, could it be that the assailant made their way on foot?'

'That is not what we believe to be the case.'

'There's that word again.' I turn to the jury, meeting the gaze of the older woman with the pink rinse, the younger man with tattoos creeping from the collar and cuffs of his shirt. 'Detective Inspector Hall, can you categorically confirm the man in the CCTV footage is Mr Darling? Or is this just another one of your *beliefs*?'

DI Hall continues to stand tall and composed, but his cheeks appear more flushed than before. I'm rattling him.

'The man in the footage matches the defendant's description in height, ethnicity and stature,' he says. 'The rifle and the petrol canister the figure is holding only have the defendant's fingerprints on, with no DNA found at the scene not belonging to him.'

I look towards the clerk.

'Can we please see the footage once more, from' – I look down at my notes at the time stamp I jotted down – 'two minutes and twenty-three seconds?'

As the clerk rolls out the television set, the wheels on the trolley squeaking across the court, I wonder if this is a step too far. The move I am about to play is a strong one, one that Antony will expect me to play, but the Messenger might prefer I bury.

I have to keep up appearances.

For the first time, Hall appears uneasy. We all wait in deathly silence as the footage is rewound before stopping at the desired time, when the figure is firing the gun into the stables.

'I have two questions for you, Detective Inspector Hall. One: can you categorically confirm from this footage that the man we see here is my client?'

He stares at the screen, his eyes moving busily.

'It's a yes or no question, DI Hall.'

'No,' he replies gruffly.

'And why is that?'

He flashes me a look; his resentment for me is clear in his eyes, and I wonder if he ever has women holding him accountable, not least with an audience.

'The footage isn't clear enough.'

'Thank you. And now my second question.' I point towards the television screen. 'Do you see what the figure has on their hands?'

He squints to make out the footage from the witness box.

'I have a CCTV still printed, if that's easier for you to see, Inspector Hall.'

'I can see fine,' he replies, the deep crow's feet framing his straining eyes telling me otherwise.

'Then please, tell me – what does the figure have on their hands?'

He spots them and swallows. I watch his Adam's apple jump up his throat.

'Gloves.'

Over my shoulder, I hear muttering from the public gallery.

'You stated that both the rifle and the canister belonged to the defendant?'

'Yes.'

'So then we can rightly assume that his fingerprints would already be on each of those items?'

He clears his throat.

'Yes.'

'So is it fair to say that if a third party were to handle these items while wearing gloves, they wouldn't leave any finger-prints behind?'

The muscles of his jaw flex on either side. His chest deflates with a sigh.

'Yes, that's fair.'

I hear the scurry of pens from the jurors' bench.

'One last question, Inspector Hall: did you consider anyone else in your line of enquiry, other than the defendant?'

He looks far more nervous now than he had at the start of my questioning. I have taken his testimony, his whole investigation in fact, and shaken it until each thread he so carefully laid has come unravelled. I glance at the jury – their interest is well and truly piqued, hanging off my every word.

Perhaps I have gone too far.

No. All of this will change when they learn of the prosecution's new evidence.

I spot speckles of perspiration gleaming above his lip as he opens his mouth to speak.

'We were confident with the evidence collected that the defendant was responsible for the crime.'

'I'm glad to hear you're a man confident in your convictions, but that doesn't answer my question. Did you consider any other lines of inquiry when investigating the deaths?'

He closes his mouth, considers his answer for a moment.

'DI Hall . . .'

'No,' he replies reluctantly.

'Your focus was entirely on my client?'

'Yes.'

'Thank you. No further questions.'

The mood of the room has changed dramatically; the air buzzes with angst and trepidation. From the podium, Judge McConnell looks at me with a neutral expression, but his eyes gleam approvingly. And just to the side of me, sat in the front row of the press bench, Melanie watches with a smile.

The Messenger's smirk, however, has gone. I catch sight of him in the gallery, and his piercing eyes lock onto mine. Beside him, Mr Viklund rises from his seat and storms off towards the exit.

I return my gaze to the witness box, trying to ignore my

heart leaping wildly behind my ribs. With a single glance, I know I will pay for what I have just done. I told Mr Viklund I had to keep up appearances. But perhaps in my exhausted state, I forgot my true objective.

Niall rises once more.

'Quick question, Detective Hall. In terms of the defence's theory as to why the gates to the property were physically chained shut as opposed to being programmed to stay closed – is it fair to suggest that Yolanda and the children would have also known how to operate the gate system and make their escape, unless a chain was put in place?'

I stand to object to Niall's clear line of speculation, but Hall answers him before I can open my mouth.

'That is a fair suggestion, yes.'

Niall nods.

'Thank you. Nothing more.'

38

I lean against the wall outside of the Bailey and exhale a sigh of smoke.

After Inspector Hall, the prosecution called the forensic pathologist to break down the cause of death, followed by the ballistics expert who detailed how the shots were fired, confirming the weapon, the range, the trajectory of each shot, to back up the pathologist's claims. As each new witness was called, I felt the intensity of Melanie's attention from the press bench, her excitement practically radiating off her, as the time I have to intervene ticked away in my ears.

Ever since Matthew's disappearance, and my refusal to satiate her hunger for an exclusive interview, Melanie has had me firmly in her sights, waiting for her moment to take her shot. Last night, I gave her that opportunity. Hell, I might as well have been posing for her. Once the final witness has finished giving evidence and court has adjourned for the day, Melanie will leave the Bailey and my opportunity to intervene will be lost.

I rub my eyes, listening to the dry squeak of them beneath my curled fingers, and pop some painkillers I found in the bottom of my bag and swallow them dry, in the hope of easing my aching back. The only thing keeping me upright is the constant surge of adrenaline pumping through me.

I jolt at the sound of the Messenger's voice. He stands just a few inches from me. We meet each other's eyes, and I drag on the cigarette to buy myself some time.

'Care to explain what you're doing in there?'

I stare up at him, my heart racing.

'I explained to Mr Viklund that I had to keep up appearances—'

'Oh, is that what you call it? Because it looks like you were playing both sides of the fence. I'm sure I remember telling you what would happen if you didn't do what was asked of you. Do you need reminding?'

'No,' I stutter. 'Besides . . . we have a whole other problem.'

He scoffs. 'We?'

'Yes, we.'

His smile falters.

'What kind of problem?'

The words crowd in my throat. Once I say them, I cannot take them back.

This will kill her.

But if I don't tell the Messenger, she will destroy me and put Hannah in harm's way.

It's her or us. Just like Wade's case.

'Well?'

I stare up at him, take a drag on my cigarette, and sigh the smoke out of me, before crushing it underfoot.

'Someone knows what I did.'

Now it is the Messenger's time to pause. He looks at me closely, his gaze flicking between my eyes and mouth.

'Who?'

'A journalist.'

For the first time since knowing him, the Messenger looks nervous. His smirk falls into a grim line.

'And how did they find out?'

'Does it matter?'

He stares at me intently, his cool eyes burrowing into mine until a shiver runs down my back.

'She has incriminating photos of me on her camera. It's in her bag—'

'It sounds like your problem, not mine.'

'I think you'll find this is your problem too – she plans to file the photos along with her story with the newspaper in the morning. If I'm arrested before the end of the trial, this would have all been for nothing. Neither of us will get what we want.'

Despite his eyes twitching, busily thinking of his next move, his expression doesn't change. I listen to his incessant chewing of the gum rolling around in his mouth, the smell of peppermint so strong that my stomach churns.

'Name,' he says gruffly.

'If I tell you, what will you do—'

'I said give me a name.'

We stare at one another, knowing what will happen the moment I tell him. Men like the Messenger, they don't solve problems, they eradicate them. He steps closer, as if to force the name from my lips.

'Melanie Eccleston, from *The Times*,' I blurt out.

He nods once.

'I'll deal with it.'

He turns back for the building, leaving as quickly as he appeared. I stand frozen against the wall and consider running after him, telling him that I made a mistake, that I was wrong. That it wasn't Melanie I saw after all. But instead, I stay rooted to the spot, knowing that it won't make a difference.

I sealed her fate the moment I uttered her name.

39

'The prosecution calls Marianne Darling.'

The tension in the courtroom is palpable, as Marianne steps into the box. She is shaking from head to toe, and the first thing she does is glance to me for reassurance. I give her a soft smile, but it does nothing to stop her shaking. When she takes her oath and confirms her name, she is asked to speak up to be heard.

'Can you please tell the court how you know the defendant?' Niall asks.

She glances up towards the dock, her eyes glassy.

'I'm his mother.'

Heavy murmurs break out in the gallery. This is the killer evidence they have all been waiting for, the piece of my client's past that could potentially tip the scales. The judge asks for quiet.

'Mrs Darling,' Niall begins. 'I will keep this brief. I am particularly interested about your relationship with your son in the autumn of 1999, and the events that unfolded. Can you confirm how old your son was at the time?'

She swallows, her throat bobbing delicately above her necklace: a thin row of pearls.

'Twenty-four,' she replies, croakily.

'Thank you. And he lived with you at that time, is that right?'

'Yes. He had been to university, and then returned home for a while.'

'Why was that?'

She reaches down for her cup of water, which quivers violently as she brings it towards her lips.

'Mrs Darling, can you answer my question, please?' Niall asks this like he is lightly admonishing a child. She places down the cup again.

'He wasn't well.'

'In what capacity was your son not well?'

She glances up at her son, her expression pleading.

I'm sorry, her eyes say.

'He was experiencing depression.'

Niall allows for a pause, giving the jurors and the press time to connect the dots.

'Was this the first time your son had had a depressive episode?'

'No, but it was his most severe.'

He looks down and begins to recite from his notes.

'The symptoms of severe depression are described by the Mind organisation as the following: "down or tearful; agitated and restless; isolated; finding no pleasure in life; no self-confidence or self-esteem; hopeless and despairing; suicidal". Would you say your son's symptoms fitted this description of severe depression, as you described it?'

She nods solemnly. 'Yes.'

'Your son was suicidal?'

'Yes.' The word escapes from her lips in a clipped, pained fashion. Her eyes are glassy, reflecting the lights when she flicks her glare towards Wade in the dock.

'I see. And what treatment did he seek for this?'

She presses her lips firmly together, rolling them against one another to dissipate her nerves, but it almost looks as if she is desperate to keep the truth from coming out of her.

'Mrs Darling?'

'His father and I paid for him to stay at a psychiatric rehabilitation facility in Torquay in the autumn of 1999.'

'What was the name of this facility?'

'The Lodge.'

'Thank you.' Niall instructs the jury to turn to their evidence packs, where they find the admission sheet for The Lodge. The date and Wade's name are present at the top. 'And prior to the defendant's admission to the facility, how long had he been experiencing this depressive episode?'

'About six months.'

'I see. And what made you seek treatment for him at this point? Was there a deciding factor?'

Marianne looks to me, then the judge. She parts her lips and stutters.

'I-isn't there the matter of c-c-confidentiality here?'

'For his psychiatrist or doctor perhaps,' Niall replies. 'But not you. You have sworn under oath to tell the truth and nothing but the truth in court here today. So please, elaborate on what motivated you and your husband to have your son admitted to The Lodge in the autumn of 1999.'

She blinks back tears and bites down on her bottom lip. A clerk steps forward with a box of tissues. The courtroom waits in deafening silence as she dabs her eyes.

'My son's depression had been worsening for many months,' she says. 'And in October of '99 . . .'

She stops, pressing her lips together again.

'What happened in October '99, Mrs Darling?' Niall asks.

She sighs defeatedly, and closes her eyes.

'He tried to take his own life.'

Niall nods slowly, coaxing the damning information out of her.

'Can you please tell the jury *how* your son attempted suicide?'

Marianne sniffs back tears, dabbing the tissue in the corner of both eyes.

'He . . . tried to shoot himself.'

The gallery comes alive with whispers, and those on the press brench are practically salivating. I avert my eyes for a moment, racked with guilt at the sight of Marianne's pain.

'You and your husband found him as he was about to take his life, didn't you?'

I look back and spot a tear sliding down her cheek. She dabs at it furiously, leaving stray pieces of white tissue behind.

'Yes.'

'And you both stopped him from harming himself, isn't that right?'

She nods reluctantly. 'Yes.'

'Please explain to the jury how this unfolded.'

She looks to me for help, her bottom lip quivering. The judge peers down at her.

'Answer the question please, Mrs Darling.'

She nods up at him before looking down at the tissue in her hands, teasing it out of the scrunched-up ball she has made in her fist.

'We pleaded with him not to go through with it, but he was adamant. So my husband tried to wrestle the gun from him.'

'Did your husband succeed in getting the gun, Mrs Darling?'

She sniffs back tears again.

'No.'

'What happened?'

Silence. Her eyes are on the tissue in her hands. She reminds me of her son, the way he looks down rather than meeting me in the eye, when he must discuss a subject he doesn't like.

'You are under oath to tell the truth, Mrs Darling . . .'

She nods, her eyes remaining downward.

'To . . . to make my husband stop trying to keep him from going through with it . . . Wade grabbed me.'

'He grabbed you?'

'He wasn't going to hurt me,' she insists, looking up to meet his eyes; her voice is the loudest it has been since her evidence began. 'It was just a way to stop my husband from taking the gun.'

'How did Wade grab you?'

She pauses, her breathing loud and panicked. The tears are falling freely now, with the tissue tearing to pieces in her grip.

'He held me from behind. He had an arm across here.'

She moves her arm about her neck.

'Did Wade ever point the gun at you, Mrs Darling?'

She looks at Niall, her jaw trembling. Tears well in her eyes.

'Yes.' A gasp sounds from the gallery. 'But not because he wanted to hurt me, but because he was hurting so badly himself, and couldn't bear to be stopped. I-I-I . . .' She takes a breath to compose herself. 'Wade let me talk him round, and I was able to take the gun from him. He was crying out for help . . . my husband and I knew that.'

'You knew that when he pointed the gun at you, Mrs Darling?'

Marianne stares at him, dumbfounded at how to respond.

'No further questions.'

The courtroom comes alive with murmurings from the press bench and the gallery. I turn to look at Wade in the dock: he stares at his mother, tears streaming down his face. Before me, Antony's shoulders look as tense as rock.

Me. This is all because of me.

The evidence I planted is finally out there, on public record. I should feel relieved, but all I feel I guilt, barely able to draw air in my lungs from the weight of it.

The parallels between my client's past and the present-day case are scarily aligned. Both times, my client had a mental breakdown. Both times resulted in gun violence, only this time it ended with three homicide victims. Now, the prosecution can use Wade's history to insinuate his guilt in his family's deaths due to his past, and their star witness who specialises in familicide will be able to use this to show how my client's personal history with mental health and firearms would have followed the textbook route to gun violence in domestic violence disputes.

I gave them the evidence they needed to corroborate every one of their claims.

The judge calls for silence in the court and looks to me.

I stand up. 'Good afternoon, Mrs Darling. I understand this must be incredibly difficult for you. I only have a few questions, and then we will let you go, okay?'

I take a sip of water, trying to put the distance of time between Niall's questioning and mine. Marianne takes the opportunity to do the same, before taking a couple of deep, calming breaths.

'Why did you decide to seek private for treatment for Wade's depression in 1999?'

Marianne sniffles, dabbing her nose with the battered tissue.

'We didn't want this blip in his life to affect his future in any way.'

'How might experiencing depression or suicidal thoughts have affected his future?'

'Well, the stigma of course. The judgement around those who experience mental health problems is often so cruel and unnecessary. Most of us experience it at some time or another, don't we? I have. My husband did. Most of my friends. It's normal, but treated so abnormally. I didn't want anyone judging him for something he couldn't help. If we had gone through the usual route, his struggles and his stay at The Lodge would have been on his medical record.'

'I see. And could you explain to me your understanding of suicidal behaviour?'

She glances behind me, towards the dock, a fleeting look at her son. Her baby.

'Well . . . it's when a person thinks of taking, or attempts to take, their own life.'

'Does it mean a person wants to harm others?'

'*No.* They only want to harm themselves. It isn't about violence; it is about escaping the agony they feel. This is what I mean about stigma around mental health. My son would never hurt anybody. He just wanted to be free.'

'So, you don't think your son was capable of murdering his family?'

'Never. He loved Yolanda and the children more than anything in the world. He never so much as got in a fight on the school playground as a child, for Christ's sake. Violence isn't a part of him. He is sensitive, and caring, with a big heart. I think that's why he gets depression in the way he does. Sensitive people suffer the most in this dreadful world.'

I pause, allowing her heartfelt words to bleed into the jurors' minds, knowing full well that they won't mean a thing, with the prosecution evidence that has just landed in their laps.

'Thank you, Mrs Darling. No further questions.'

I sit down in my seat, exhausted, deflated, my body throbbing with pain, and sigh.

It's done.

40

In the courtroom, the air is thick with anticipation. It is time for the prosecution's key, and final, witness.

Criminal psychologist Dr Samantha Heche enters the witness box.

Heche stands, calm and collected, her dark hair pulled away from her face. She gives her oath, and Niall begins with questions about her education and professional expertise, spoon-feeding the jury with her supposed superiority on the subject, due to her speciality being that of familicide for the last twelve years. When she explains the term for the jury, the whole court falls still: *the act of killing one's own family.*

As Niall asks her more and more questions to build her integrity before the jury, my tired mind drifts towards the press bench. Melanie isn't anywhere to be seen. The Messenger, too, is missing from the gallery. I haven't seen either of them since the break in proceedings. My heart pounds beneath my robes.

'What led you to specialise in familicide, Dr Heche?' Niall asks, breaking me from my thoughts.

'It is one of those crimes that stops you in your tracks when you hear of it: an entire family gone, and usually by the person who is supposed to love them most. Beneath my horror and concern, I was immediately fascinated by how a person could do such a thing. I wanted to understand why it happened, in the hope of better preventing it.'

Niall speaks clearly and precisely, so every syllable projects about the room.

'From all you have learnt in the last twelve years, could you please explain to the court the nature of familicide?'

'Of course,' she replies with a smile, before turning her attention to the jury. 'In these kinds of cases, we so often know how familicide ends, but for a long time, no one knew how they started. Until about thirty years ago, familicide was grouped in with domestic violence, and not seen or studied in its own right. We now understand more about the complexity of these cases, and the theory of how they come to be.

'Most often in familicide cases, it is a family unit with a heterosexual couple at the centre. The perpetrator, whom we will call the annihilator, is usually the male in the equation, and often there are no outward signs to suggest anyone is in danger. Many annihilators are considered upstanding members of society, with successful employment and close relationships with family and friends. They aren't usually known to police nor have criminal records, with what could be deemed as good upbringings and backgrounds. This, it seems, adds to the shock factor of the crime, as this sort of character might not be what one expects.'

'How does one determine a risk of familicide before the fatal event?' Niall asks. 'How can, say, a person be seen to be at risk of annihilating their family?'

'To assess the risk of the crime occurring, we need to assess the environment that the perpetrator and victims are in, which could be deemed to motivate or trigger the annihilator. Over years of study, we have determined the different types of family annihilators, and the differences between them are down to what *motivated* them to commit the crime.

'For example, an annihilator may be motivated by a need for revenge, or experiencing an uncontrollable rage – say, during a divorce, or a child custody battle, or infidelity. These characters usually show possessiveness towards their spouse and children, and exert authority within the home. The victim putting an end to the relationship with the annihilator or leaving the family home can trigger the crime.

'Then there is what we call the "civil reputable" killer, studied and coined by author and specialist Neil Websdale. This type of killer annihilates their family out of a distorted sense of altruism. Their identity is highly dependent on their family unit and economic status, and should anything put them at risk – say, financial ruin – the annihilator murders their family in the belief that they are saving them from shame and hardship. This perpetrator often takes their own life after the killing spree. But whether deaths are caused because of possessiveness and control, or pseudo-altruism, it is clear that all offenders of this crime have a sense of ownership over their families, and a grandiose sense of self, believing the family will not survive without them.'

When Dr Heche has finished, I look about me, spotting the horror on the jurors' faces; the way the press remain transfixed on the specialist witness. There is no movement or sound from the gallery. If I closed my eyes right now, the silence might well convince me that I'm entirely alone in the court.

'You were asked to assess this case, is that right?' Niall asks.

'Yes,' Dr Heche replies.

'And with your twelve years of expertise in this area, what did you find?'

She pauses, seemingly choosing her next words with care.

'Although it is not for me to determine whether the defendant did or didn't commit the crime, I have assessed the factors surrounding the case, and assessed the relevant factors surrounding the defendant that could be seen to relate to a case of familicide.

'In my opinion, should the defendant be responsible for the crimes, Mr Darling would fit the criteria of the altruistic annihilator. Annihilators of this kind are typically highly educated, the provider for their family, and have underlying mental health issues and self-destructive tendencies. They will usually have a history of depression.

'From my analysis, Mr Darling was suffering from severe depression due to his financial status and the looming closure of his business. He kept this a secret from his wife, children, employees – from all who knew him, except for his business partner who shared in his troubles. He also collected firearms, and shooting and hunting were his main hobby. With the severity of his financial state, and his history of depression alongside his role of providing for his family, his ownership and frequent use of firearms – which is statistically the most-used weapon in familicide cases – these are potential triggers to cause a person in such a position to annihilate.'

Niall pauses, and looks at the jurors one by one.

'Thank you for your time, Dr Heche. That will be all from me.'

The witness stands tall, seemingly pleased with herself. I rise to cross-examine.

'Dr Heche, you said yourself that you cannot prove that Mr Darling did or did not kill commit the crimes he has been charged with, correct?'

'Yes, that's right.'

'So to be clear, the information you've given us today is nothing more than you sharing your opinion on a hypothetical scenario?'

She gives me a tight, almost patronising smile.

'I think my expertise can be considered a little more in-depth than that.'

'I'm sure you've worked very hard, but you didn't answer my question. You assessed this case on the hypothetical scenario that Mr Darling is guilty of the crimes, correct?'

'Correct.'

'So, if he is found to be not guilty, your analysis will be rendered obsolete? As an incorrect theory?'

Heche clears her throat.

'My analysis is based on many years of research in the field, and a multitude of familicide cases.'

'Which one might call a theory, Dr Heche.' I look down at my notes. 'You said that you look for indicators in a person's life or behaviour to assess whether they are likely to annihilate their families. You mentioned depression, financial insecurity, is that right?'

'Yes, those were a couple of the factors I mentioned.'

'Do you believe that every man who happens to suffer from depression due to the loss of his business and financial security is then automatically likely to kill his family?'

'No, of course not.'

'Is depression a likely outcome to one losing the business they have spent years creating?'

She pauses.

'I'd say it's quite a common response. Yes.'

'In fact, wouldn't one be *expected* to experience depression in these circumstances?'

'It would be a likely outcome I imagine, yes.'

'Thank you, Dr Heche. Nothing more from me.'

Once Dr Heche has been led down from the witness box, Niall turns to address the judge.

'The prosecution rests,' he says, before returning to his seat.

The weight of dread briefly lifts from my shoulders, allowing me to catch a rare deep breath. I sigh it away as discreetly as I can, closing my eyes for a stolen second. That is, until I remember what is still before me.

There is still the rest of the trial to go. Now, I must navigate the task of being seen to lead my client's defence, while sabotaging it behind his back. The prosecution may have concluded their case, but my task is only just beginning.

The dread returns, pummelling me in an instant.

I turn and glance towards the public gallery to see the Messenger has stepped back into the courtroom. When I catch his eye, he stares back at me, and gives me a nod.

I know in an instant he is referring to Melanie.

41

I arrive at my front door utterly exhausted, weighed down by my guilt. I don't have the luxury of lowering my guard when I return home. Not with Hannah watching my every move. If I were alone, I would crawl into bed and sleep until daybreak. Instead, I have to plaster on a smile and pretend my life isn't falling apart. That Melanie Eccleston wouldn't have died today, if it weren't for me. I imagine what might have happened to her as I slip the key in the lock.

I step inside and drop my bag in horror.

Hannah is in the middle of the living room. She has pushed the coffee table aside, pressed it against the back wall, creating a vast space to move in. I heard what she was doing before I saw it: the sound of a golf club hitting a ball, followed by a rattle as it enters the cup at the other side of the room.

She turns to me with a smile, which instantly falls when she sees my face.

'Stop.'

I march forward and snatch the club from her. The feel of the metal in my hands shocks my palms. *Whoosh. Thwack.* I smell his blood, feel the splatter against my face.

'I'm sorry, I—'

'Where did you get this?' I only realise I am shouting when she flinches from the spray of my words.

'I . . . I went in the loft. You said some of Dad's stuff was up there and—'

'So you went rifling around in places you don't belong? Taking things that don't belong to you?'

I can't hold the club anymore. It physically hurts to touch it, as if the metal is scorching hot. It isn't the murder weapon, of course, the Messenger took that. But it is from the same set that belonged to Matthew. I take it to the foot of the stairs and lean it against the wall, wiping my palm against my thigh as if it is dirty. On the counter by the stairs is a large stack of photo albums. She has clearly been going through them again today, when she said she would be at school. There is one loose photo to the side – it's one of Matthew, Hannah and me. Matthew stares at me from the photograph, smiling gaily. Tears creep from my eyes.

Whoosh. I hear the crack of his skull. *Thwack.* The pop of a tooth being knocked from his mouth.

'I didn't think you'd mind. I thought—'

I can't stop the tears now. They keep coming, and coming. I cover my face with both hands and sob silently into my palms.

'I'm sorry . . .' She's crying too. 'I didn't think you'd mind. He was my dad – it's my stuff too.'

She barges past me, and I hear the ruffle of her coat. I uncover my face as she is snatching up her bag.

'Where are you going?'

'Home.'

She grabs at the door latch, sniffing back tears of her own. I know I should stop her, to try and explain and apologise. But instead, I watch her go, jumping as the door slams shut.

⚖️

My home is a stranger to me now. Has been since I first raised the golf club above my head and swung. Whenever I dare to sit in the quiet without a case brief to distract me, the memories seep in: the incessant swing of the club, the thuds, the splatters, my screams lost among the noise of the church bells tolling on the other side of the window. Tonight, however, I do have a distraction.

Hannah is gone.

I sit in the armchair in the dark, the very place I have sat for hours, and think of the pain in her eyes as I shouted at her, the shock of my anger. She had every right to go through her father's things, and nor would it have been a problem had I not got so many secrets to hide.

I sit in the living room, listening to the silence ringing through the house, joining the tick of the clock in an ear-splitting chorus, and imagine Melanie Eccleston floating lifelessly at the bottom of the Thames beside Fredrick, chains about her body with her feet hooked to a concrete cinderblock, the camera loaded with incriminating photos waterlogged on the riverbed beneath their swaying feet.

No one foresees becoming a murderer, do they? When a person thinks of the future, they think of love, careers, hopes and dreams. I certainly didn't foresee I would be capable of killing a man. Even after murdering and burying Matthew, I didn't foresee I would be capable of doing anything like that again. And yet here I am, with Fredrick's blood on my hands, and Melanie's fate sealed by my lips. I haven't just killed one person now. In my attempt to save my own neck, I have killed three.

My body trembles beneath the blanket I have draped over

my legs. I can feel myself breaking; the grip I thought I had on the situation has unfurled, and with it has come all of the pain I had worked so hard to smother; the memories, the guilt. A violent split between who I was before, and who I have become, and an insurmountable sense of loss. I sit among the panicked thoughts, wondering how I got so lost. How I became a woman with so many people's blood on her hands.

I am a monster.

Sleep seems like a stranger to me now. Sleepwalking. Digging up bodies in the dead of night. I can't remember how long it has been since I've had an unbroken rest. My body aches for it, whining from each joint and knotted muscle.

I hobble upstairs to the bathroom and turn on the shower, slowly undressing as the room fills up with steam. As I grip the basin to steady myself, I look up at my reflection, watching the exhausted, broken woman in the pane as the glass slowly fogs up. My sins and lies have leeched the life from me, leaving my skin slack and grey, my eyes tinged pink and puffy, framed by deep, dark circles. I stare at the woman in the mirror, and fail to recognise the person staring back at me.

I step beneath the water and stand there until my skin blushes red from the heat, allowing tears of exhaustion to snake down my cheeks.

I need to sleep. My sins, my dilemma, the looming second part of the trial, Hannah; they will all have to wait until the morning.

⚖

For the first few seconds when I wake, I'm not sure where I am. I sway on my feet in the dark, dizzy and disorientated as my teeth chatter violently in my mouth from the cold.

Gong

Gong

Gong

The bells are so close, striking above my head in a deafening chorus.

The tower looms over me, obstructing the path of the moon. I am stood before the church steps, as if my sleeping mind has brought me here to confess my sins. My bare feet feel frozen against the ice-cold ground, glittering with frost, and my frantic, nervous breaths escape from me in short huffs of cloud.

I blink furiously to acclimatise myself to the darkness, and pull the clothes I have on closer to my body: a coat I don't remember putting on, pulled over a small slip nightgown, and nothing more.

Gong

Gong

Gong

The bells. They shouldn't be ringing out more than once. And yet they keep ringing and ringing to the count of three.

I turn and stagger towards my home. Do I have my keys? I rummage around in the pockets of the coat, but find nothing more than scrunched-up tissues. Thankfully, I can see the door was left ajar. I walk as fast as I can, as if trying to outrun the bells, and shut the door firmly behind me. I wrestle out of the coat and let it drop to the mat as I rest my head against the door, trying to calm my shivering teeth. That's when they start up again.

Gong

Gong

Gong

The sound can't be coming from the bell tower. The tolls only sound once to mark the hour. And yet, they are still as loud as if I were stood before them. Which means they can't be coming from the tower. The sounds are inside my head.

Am I going insane?

I try to take deep breaths, in through my nose, out through my mouth, as I lean against the door. It is just a bad dream, I tell myself.

I pinch myself and feel a stabbing pain in my flesh.

I'm awake.

I open my eyes and turn for the stairs – I just need to get back into bed and close my eyes – when I catch something in the corner of my eye: a figure of a man.

It's not real, I tell myself, as I begin to shake. *It isn't Matthew. He's dead.*

Before me, Matthew is in the living room, putting a golf ball into a cup. He looks up at me and smiles.

Gong

Gong

Gong

I cover my ears as tears fill my eyes. The memory is gone; the living room is dark and empty again. But the bells keep sounding. The deep, groaning tolls blaring against my eardrums.

'*Shut up!*'

I stagger up the stairs, each toll of the imaginary bells so loud and disorientating that they throw me off balance.

This isn't happening. I'm asleep. It's just a night terror. I'll wake up any minute.

I can smell bleach in the air, feel the aroma stinging at my eyes, and beneath it, the metallic tang of blood.

It's just a night terror. I'll wake up soon.

Please
Please
Please wake up

I reach the landing and freeze.

Matthew is lying in the hall in a pool of blood. His head is concaved, his beautiful face crushed. The walls are splattered with him. The golf club is lying by his side, gleaming wet and red in the path of the moon shining through the window.

Gong
Gong
Gong

Sobs heave out of me. I turn blindly for my bedroom door, dashing away the tears, only to find my hands slathered in hot blood. I stagger blindly into bed and hide beneath the white sheets. They are blood-soaked, just as I found them when I woke to find my whole world had changed, three years ago.

This isn't happening
This can't be happening

I roll up into a ball, my cries silenced by the ever-ringing bells. They grow louder and closer together until they become one long, deafening howl.

I cover my ears, begging for them to stop, and scream as loud as I can, when—

⚖️

I wake up with a jolt, sitting bolt upright in bed.

My chest is hammering with my heart and glistening with beads of sweat. My nightdress is completely soaked through. I can still hear the bells, but they are not tauntingly close, as if trapped in my head, but where they should be on the other side of the window. I check the time: it's 3 a.m.

It was 3 a.m. when I found Matthew dead.

I rip away the sheets and get out of bed, desperately trying to draw air into my lungs. I head for the window and throw it open to gasp in the nightly chill. The cold air pinches my cheeks, rousing me from my nightmare, and I stand heaving it in until my heart slowly begins to calm.

I'm safe. It was just a night terror.

Once I have caught my breath, I head back towards my side of the bed, and take the pack of diazepam I keep in my bedside drawer. I pop two tablets into my palm and drink them down with the water on top of the night stand.

I can't keep living like this. The secrets. The lies. They are finally catching up with me. So many people have been hurt by what I've done. Matthew. Fredrick. Melanie. Who else has to die for me to protect my secrets? Will it be Hannah next?

I think of all I have done to keep my past hidden, all of my lies, the deceit. Conning a client. Digging up a body. I watched a man drown right before my eyes, and destined Melanie to the same fate.

I can't keep doing this. Not for Hannah. Not for me. There has to be another way to keep her safe, so this can end.

I sit up and head towards the window again, inhaling the fresh night air into my lungs. My eyes fall on the earth before the tracks where Matthew's resting place used to be.

It's time that I stopped fighting the inevitable, and face all that I have done.

42

24 December 2016

I've always hated Christmas. As a child, I never really had
one. Each year would be spent with a different foster family. I
never celebrated with any of them more than once before I was
ferried off to the next.

So as an adult, I can't help but resent the obligatory enjoyment the season demands: the sickeningly enthusiastic songs
playing repeatedly on every radio station and in every shop,
the dry turkey and the paper hats from the crackers. Then
there is New Year, with its fireworks and obligatory kisses, or
lack thereof, at midnight. It's a time that demands joy, when
for some of us it is the most difficult time of year, inherently
reminding us of what we don't have, rather than what we do.
This is all topped off by the duty to improve oneself from the
first day of the new year. Drink less. Eat better. Quit smoking.
Try to last with the new depressing regime until at least the
end of the month.

I'm just tired, I tell myself, as the bitter thoughts form within
me. *Things always seem worse when I'm tired.*

I haven't slept much this week; the sleepwalking has been
relentless. I enjoy the festivities more when Hannah is here, but

what with her staying at her mother's parents for Christmas this year, and Maggie staying with my brother-in-law, the whole thing seems like a forced charade. I sit on the sofa with a glass of wine, watching a re-run of a sitcom Christmas special, as Matthew practises his putting, knocking the golf ball into the cup at the other side of the room, the faint smell of sweat from his evening run drifting off him with each movement. The sound of the club making contact with the ball makes my eye twitch and twitch.

The sleepwalking began again last month, triggered by work stress from all the cases continuing to pile up on my desk. Murder. Rape. Theft, after theft, after theft. It had been over a year since my last sleepwalking episode; I came down the next morning to that familiar pitying look on Matthew's face, and I knew it had started up again. It has struck almost every night since, whittling away my energy until I feel like a shadow of myself.

It could be genetic. Drink less caffeine, cut out alcohol. Try to form a good sleep routine. Work on managing stress and anxiety. That's what every so-called sleep specialist has told me. Hypnotherapy, CBT, I've tried it all. I sigh heavily and take a sip of wine; I'll be damned if I won't have a glass on Christmas Eve.

The house is in disarray from the redecorating project we have given ourselves over the Christmas break. Paint pots, a ladder and footstool, the floorboard sander; belongings hidden under old bedsheets.

I look at my husband, his brows knitted together with concentration as he looks from the ball to the cup, and putts. I love him, tremendously so. He is perhaps the most thoughtful man I've ever known. When he isn't putting that fucking ball, at least.

I flinch each time the metal club connects with the ball, brace myself for the irritating rattle as it enters the cup and makes my teeth chime. I love him with every part of me: I love his heart, his smile, his eyes. His soft, tender hands. But if he putts that ball one more time, I am going to fucking scream.

Matthew senses me watching him and looks to me, a smile growing on his face. How can he look at me like that, after all these years? So much love in his eyes despite all the burdens I carry, how difficult I can be.

'You're knackered, aren't you?'

I force a smile. 'Exhausted.'

'Why don't you go up to bed? The telly will be naff anyway. I'll call Hannah in a bit and then I'll come up and join you.'

'You sure?' I ask, my tone tinged with relief. 'That won't make me horrendously boring?'

He comes over and kisses my hair. 'You could never be boring.'

I tug his T-shirt as he goes to pull away, and bring him closer to me. Our lips meet. Soft, familiar, tasting of wine.

'You're an amazing man, you know that?'

'I try,' he replies with a wink, kissing me again before returning to his game.

As Matthew putts the ball with the same wince-inducing sounds, I head up the stairs for bed, silently praying that tonight is the night I sleep straight through. But even as I lie in bed, I can hear each tap of the ball echoing up from the floor below, chipping away at my hold on myself; a chisel working its way into a crack until I finally burst open.

Please, for the love of God. I just want to go to sleep.

⚖

I release a hot, ragged scream.

I am holding a golf club above my head and straddling a man in the dark.

I don't know where I am. I don't know what I'm doing. Only that I'm terrified. A church bell is sounding from somewhere; a deep, sombre song that makes me flinch with each note.

A swirling shriek of noise screams from behind me, terrifying me in the dark, followed by an explosion of colour on the other side of the window. The man kicks out beneath me, tugging violently at the clothes covering my chest. He shouts something through the noise, and I feel his hand lunge for my neck. I swing the club back and bring it down with a scream as the church bell rings out.

Gong.

Thwack.

Gong.

Thwack.

Gong.

Thwack.

The church bells stop ringing after twelve tolls to ring in midnight, and I pant for breath, my face and body splattered with blood, the metallic taste of him in my mouth. Fireworks light up the sky on the other side of the window, bathing us in red, blue, white. With each flash, I see more of my surroundings. I'm on the landing. The walls are painted with violent swipes of blood, sprayed along the ceilings. My clothes are covered in it. Below me is a man. His face is mangled; wet, fleshy pulp flashing with each explosion. The hand that had been tugging at me releases its grip, and falls to the floor with a lifeless thud, as a ragged breath bubbles out of his mouth, and I spot the wedding ring on his finger.

I recognise that wedding ring.
And then everything goes dark.

I wake up in bed, my eyes flickering open to the distant sound of the bell tower.

The nightmare I had comes back to me all at once. The blood. The violence. The terrifying confusion I'd felt, totally at a loss as to what was happening, and the horror I'd felt as I recognised Matthew's wedding ring, just before I woke.

My heart is pattering fast in my chest at the thought. I've never had a dream so visceral in my life. I instinctively reach for Matthew on his side of the bed so that I can pull in close to him, feel his warmth and kiss the nape of his neck in sweet apologies for thinking such a vile thing, even if it was against my will. I paw his side of the bed blindly.

Matthew isn't there.

I frown in the dark, and perch on my elbow to peer at the clock on the nightstand.

It's just turned three.

Where the hell is he?

And then I feel it. The wet, sticky substance on the sheets.

I reach for the lamp on the side, flick the switch, and freeze.

Blood. So much blood. It is splattered across the white bedding in violent splashes. There are lashes of it up my arms; my hands are smothered in it.

The headboard begins to shiver against the wall from my violent shaking.

'Matthew?'

My voice echoes through the open doorway, followed by

nothing but silence and the incessant racing of my pulse pounding in my ears.

I peel back the sheet, feeling where it has stuck to me with blood. I am completely covered in it: frenzied splashes dashed across me in all different directions. The skin on my face feels dry, and I reach up to inspect it with my fingertips and find more there, dried on me in flecks.

I stumble out of bed, flattening myself against the wardrobe doors, unable to shake the fear throttling the air out of me to make sense of the scene.

'Matthew?' I call, and look to the open doorway, longing to hear his reply. He had a nose bleed in the night, that's what he'll say. He has just gone downstairs for supplies to clean up the mess.

A minute passes with no response. Then another.

I force myself away from the wardrobe door and walk shakily into the hall, heading for the stairs to call down to him, when I step in a wet spot on the carpet.

I look down and see dark blood soaked into the carpet.

This isn't happening This isn't happening I'm still dreaming

I reach a quivering hand towards the light switch on the wall, and flick on the light.

That's when I see Matthew, lying in the same spot he had in my dream. His face is crushed as it had been. The blood is splashed up the walls in the same frenzied pattern. The golf club I'd held is beside him, smothered red with blood, the end tufted with skin and hair.

My knees buckle and I hit the floor with a thud, as a scream works up my throat. I clamp my hands over my mouth and bellow.

I stare at his body; the animalistic groans claw out of from my chest and the tears leak from my eyes, as the truth slowly sinks in.

It wasn't a dream.

PART III

The Defence

Day Four

43

Imagine going to sleep and dreaming up the most terrifying moment of your life. A dream where you're in the dark, fighting against an unknown assailant, struck by the instinctual need to protect yourself. To fight and hit and scream, pummelling the man to death to the call of the church bells ringing out Midnight Mass. You wake up with a pounding heart, relieved to escape such a dark, imaginary place. Then you realise it wasn't a dream at all. You wake with no recollection of what led you to such violence, and no control over your own autonomy. No clarity. No answers. All you have is the bloody aftermath and your husband's body ground to a pulp on the hallway floor.

The aftermath is almost as much of a blur as the violence. I wasn't thinking logically, but instinctively. People often imagine how they would act in a desperate situation such as this. I can see them now, watching a crime drama on the television of an evening, shouting profanities at the protagonist as they take the wrong turn. If they were me, they would do everything right. They would call the police. They would contact a lawyer. They would act rationally. Perhaps that sort of response might be expected of me because of my work. My entire role is to be concise, controlled, level-headed. But the truth is, there is nothing rational about waking up to find you have murdered your husband. You cannot think clearly as you wash your loved one's blood from your face, with little memory of how it came to get there but for flashes in a dream.

There was a brief moment in which logic prevailed: as I knelt beside Matthew's body, I began to type out the number for emergency services. The first nine, then the second. Then I thought of Hannah. She would hate me for what I had done. How could she not? I would not only lose the love of my life, but the only family I have ever known, the same family I had craved ever since I can remember. I would be thrown in prison for something I would never do while awake, punished for an act I never wanted to commit, with no one missing me on the other side of the prison walls.

So, I acted irrationally.

I buried the body. I bleached every wall and surface, ripped up the carpet and bleached the stained boards below, before sanding them down, and laying the new roll of carpet myself, after painting the walls and ceiling. I hid the club, the spade. I tried to hide the memories within me too. As the whole street celebrated Christmas, I spent three days working to cover my tracks, redecorating the hall as we had planned, making sure nothing looked out of place, all the time concocting my lies while I worked. If I had done the right thing and called the police, I wouldn't be in this position now.

Matthew and I had an argument, that's what I would tell the police. I packed a duffel bag of his clothes, toiletries and medication, and placed them in the boot of his car. I told the police I thought he had left to stay at his mother's the night of our argument, which was vacant while she was away with family, and it was only when I finally picked up the phone three days later and Maggie asked to speak to him that I realised he hadn't been seen for all that time, and I discovered his bag in the car. The three days he was supposedly missing gave me time to cover my tracks, to work on my alibi as closely as possible, digging myself a deeper hole the more I plotted, until I saw no way out but to continue on with my lies. I worked to conceal my husband's murder while those around me were distracted with Christmas celebrations; holding their loved ones close as I buried mine.

And the rest, as they say, is history.

Now I am here, finally paying for what I have done; all of the mayhem I have caused thereafter. Fredrick, Melanie: more blood, which would never have been shed had I faced the consequences of what I had done. I would never have met Melanie – her obsession with the missing person's case wouldn't have been born. I wouldn't have met Fredrick at Blackfriars Station on that cold winter's day. I would have never met Wade Darling, or been sucked into the Messenger's game.

My mind spins as I think of all the lies I have told. Lies, upon lies, upon lies. It's easy for a person to lose who they are among them after so long; fact and fiction bleeding together as one. Because once made, the lies can never stop being told. That is, unless I finally tell the truth.

Before I make any plans, I need to make sure Hannah is safe from the Messenger, should he retaliate. I reach for my phone and call Maggie.

'Yes?' she asks pointedly.

'Is Hannah okay?' I ask.

'She left your house in tears. What do you think?'

I bite down on my lip. Now is not the time to argue with her.

'Maggie, I need you and Hannah to get away for a bit.'

'I'm sorry?'

'You both need to leave London. Just until the trial is over.'

She scoffs. 'And why on earth would we do that?'

'Because those close to me are a security risk right now.'

She pauses.

'At risk from who?'

'People are very invested in this trial, and they won't like it if my client succeeds. They may want to retaliate. If you won't do this for me, please – do it for Hannah.'

As my words sink in, I cradle the phone to me, silently willing her to shed her usual stubbornness and to listen.

'This all sounds a little dramatic . . .' she says.

'It isn't.'

She falls quiet again. I stand listening to my pulse racing in my ears.

'Perhaps you could stay with your sister,' I say.

'I'll decide where we go, thank you,' she snaps. But my racing chest eases with relief; she is considering it.

'So you'll do it?'

I listen to her breathing on the other end of the line.

'For Hannah, yes.'

She hangs up the phone and I close my eyes, rub my temples. *Hannah will be safe.*

I look at the clock on the wall. I haven't long before it's time to lay out the defence's case. Before Wade himself steps into the box. Hannah will be safe now, at least for a while, until I plan my next steps. But first, I must focus on the matter at hand.

It's time I set the record straight and give my client the fair trial he deserves.

It's time I stop running from my past, and pay for the consequences of my crimes.

44

Wade enters the witness box, pale and visibly shaken as he gives his oath. Every pair of eyes will be on him: judging him, condemning him. They have heard of his alleged crimes in gruesome detail; many will have decided on his guilt before he has even opened his mouth.

I stand in the courtroom feeling surprisingly calm, despite the course I am about to take. The Messenger sits behind me in the public gallery, expecting me to condemn my client. I wonder how much time will pass before he realises I have changed tack. How long it will take for him to set the wheels in motion to expose my crimes.

Wade raises the plastic cup of water to his lips, the liquid jumping about until it drips from the rim.

'I understand that this is going to be very difficult for you, Mr Darling, so I will go through this as quickly as I can. It is not easy to stand where you are today. Do you need more water?'

I want him to appear almost child-like in the eyes of the jury. He is someone who needs attention and care; the polar opposite of the man they will have imagined he'd be after hearing of his alleged crimes.

He shakes his head. 'No, thank you.'

I look down at my notes, allowing this idea to take hold: he is not the monster they imagined. The tension drags out until it is unbearable. What I am about to do will change everything. For my client's case. For me, and the objective I have been given by the men staring into the back of me from the public gallery. Once I do this, there is no going back.

I brace myself and look up towards the witness box.

'When did you learn of your wife's affair with your business partner, Mr Darling?'

Several gasps break from the public gallery, muttered conversations breaking out until the judge has to call for quiet. During the commotion, I glance towards Niall at the other end of the bench. The smirk has been wiped from his face. I daren't look behind me towards the Messenger.

Wade clears his throat, and the room falls silent.

'About six months before the fire,' he says. 'An employee raised concerns about two mobile phones on the work plan that didn't appear to be assigned to any particular employees. She had accessed the call logs as the representative of the company who had organised the phone plan, and discovered ... unprofessional messages.'

'What constitutes unprofessional messages, Mr Darling?'

He looks down at his hands, his cheeks blushing pink.

'They were of a sexual nature.'

A nervous cough from the gallery. It never surprises me, the reactions the mention of sex in court will bring. We talk about blood, murder, a ream of injustices, and yet sex is what makes the British public the most uncomfortable.

'And who did these phones – these messages – belong to?'

'My wife, Yolanda, and my business partner, Alex Finch.'

I turn to my attention to the jury and ask them to open their evidence packs. As they turn the pages, I pick up my copy of the call log and read the text messages aloud.

'"I want to fuck you on top of his desk" Alex wrote on the fifteenth of September, 2015. Yolanda replied three minutes later with, "There is glass, people will see." To which Alex replied immediately, "I want them to see." Whose desk are they referring to in these messages, Mr Darling?'

'Mine.'

The room is hanging off our every word.

'How did this make you feel?' I ask softly.

'I was devastated.'

'Were you angry?'

'Yes. I think anyone would be.'

'Did you ever think of hurting Yolanda, for betraying you?'

'*No*,' he replies sternly. 'I was angry for the children's sake, and I was deeply hurt, but I'm not that kind of man.'

'What did you do then, when you discovered their affair?'

He pauses, emotion welling in his eyes.

'I just . . . let it happen.'

'You didn't say anything to your wife or Mr Finch?'

'No. I had to protect my children and my business. I couldn't let their affair destroy everything we had. They were being reckless; one of us needed to hold the fort.'

'That's very admirable of you, Mr Darling.'

I take a moment to collect myself as I flush hot beneath my robes. Whenever I ask a question, I think of Mr Viklund in the public gallery, planning on how he will make me pay for this. I fight the urge to dab at the sweat gathering beneath the rim of my wig.

'How did keeping this secret impact you? Knowing the affair was going on right under your nose?'

'I fell into a deep depression. However hard I tried to hold things together, I could feel myself losing my wife, and the business was failing under our broken leadership. Through it all, I hoped and prayed that Yolanda would see sense. That whatever phase she was going through would pass. That she would come back to me.'

'And did she?'

He smiles softly.

'Yes, she did.'

Another pause. A juror shuffles noisily in their seat, the wood creaking beneath them. I can see Wade's testimony is getting under their skin; many of their faces have softened towards him.

'When did this reconciliation happen?' I ask.

His smile falls.

'The night of the fire.'

You could hear a pin drop in this room. The pluck of a hair, popping in the silence.

'You reconciled the night Yolanda and your children died?'

'Yes. The business was going under, and our marriage seemed to be hanging by a tether. I had been trying to hold down the fort, hoping things would work out in time, but things were too far gone. I had planned to confront her, but I didn't need to. She came to me and confessed to the affair, and that it was over. She wanted to try and make our marriage work.'

'And you took her back?'

'Without question.'

I look to the jury, make eye contact with the front row, before returning my attention to Wade.

'You didn't hold anything against her? You didn't at least give her a hard time?'

'Things were already hard enough. I was just relieved to have her back. I felt so alone with the failing business, and having my wife back made me feel stronger; I felt I could face what was to come with her by my side. However, I needed time. I had agreed to reconcile, but I needed to take it slow.'

'Did their affair end amicably?'

'It was clear to me that Alex Finch was angry at her for breaking it off.'

'What made you think that?'

'He sent her threatening text messages.'

I ask the jury to turn to the evidence packs to see the messages for themselves, sent the week of the murders. I pick up my copy and read aloud.

'"You will have nothing, Yolanda. Wade will leave you. You'll be broke. Your kids will know you're a whore who fucks her husband's mates. You'll die of shame when I'm finished with you." Can you confirm this is a text message you found on the phone archives, sent to your wife by Mr Finch?'

'Yes.'

I leave a purposeful pause, allowing the tension in the courtroom to rise before my next question.

'What happened on the night of the murders, Mr Darling?'

He takes a moment to compose himself, closing his eyes as he takes a deep breath.

'Yolanda and I had reconciled after dinner, when the children had gone up to their rooms. It was relatively late. She asked if I was coming to bed with her, and I explained I needed time. She looked hurt but understood. However, I did go upstairs to check on the children. Danny was asleep, so I pulled their door to, but Phoebe was awake on the phone. I kissed her goodnight. She asked if I was okay.'

And what did you say to her?'

'I said . . .' His eyes sheen over. 'I said everything was going to be better from now on. In fact, I *promised* things were going to get better . . . and then . . .'

His voice breaks with the encroaching tears.

'Take your time,' I say, almost at a whisper. The courtroom is hushed now, each sniffle and whimper echoing about the room.

'I planned to sleep in one of the spare rooms, but decided to watch TV for a while, as I was too distracted to sleep, after everything Yolanda and I had discussed. I had a couple of drinks to take to the edge off, and ended up falling asleep on the sofa in the living room.'

'And what happened next?' I ask, my words echoing against the walls of the deathly silent courtroom. 'What happened when you woke up?'

A single tear slips from his right eye. He dashes it away.

'I saw the flames.'

I stare at the jury, noticing how many of the men have cast their eyes downward; two of the women are teary-eyed. The press bench watches him hungrily.

I turn back to my client and smile softly.

It's time to ask the questions Antony first put to him, during our conferences in Marianne's home. To have him guide us through the night he found his wife dead on the stairs, his children eternally sleeping in their beds. The open door to the gun room, passing out only to wake up with his hand on fire. But before I begin, there is a question burning to be asked, one I know will have Niall bolting from his pew to object to Wade's inevitable answer.

'Mr Darling: what do you believe happened that night?'

By the quick flash in his eyes, I know he has spotted the

opportunity I have given him. He utters his next words as quickly as he can.

'I believe Alex Finch murdered my family.'

Niall shoots up from his seat. 'Your Honour—'

'Strike that from the record,' the judge demands among the noise of the court, stating that the jury are to forgo the comment when assessing the case.

But as I give my apologies to the judge, we all know it's too late. Words can be struck from the record, but not from the heart.

I turn slowly, stealing a look towards the gallery, and see the Messenger staring back at me. His usual smirk is nowhere to be seen, and a hateful stare is in its place. Beside him, Mr Viklund glares at me, his skin boiled red with anger.

They know whose side I'm on, and they know it isn't theirs.

I turn back towards the judge, trying to calm my racing heart.

Whatever happens, Hannah will be safe.

45

'How long have you participated in hunting, Mr Darling?'

Niall's first question comes hard and fast, making Wade visibly brace.

'My father hunted. It was something I grew up doing.'

'What do you like about it?'

Niall asks this as if inspired by curiosity. His tone is soft and upbeat. But I know that all will change when he decides to go in for the kill. Wade seems to sense it too.

'I like the calm. The quiet. I have to focus on the task at hand. It helps to clear my mind.'

'That's a nice sentiment, Mr Darling. But I think you're missing one crucial element. You like the control it gives you, don't you? The power.'

'There is an element of power, but no, that's not what draws me to it. There is the calm, followed by the exhilaration of hitting a target.'

'Exhilaration after a kill, you mean?'

'It could be clay shooting,' he says, flustered. 'It doesn't have to be a live target.'

'You predominantly hunt live prey, correct?'

'When we moved to our last address, I used to hunt in the woodland. The wildlife there. Pheasants and deer. It made sense.'

'And what would you say gives you the biggest thrill? A clay pigeon or a live target?'

I stand to object.

'Your Honour, is this line of questioning entirely necessary?'

The judge peers down his nose at me, then Niall.

'It's relevant, Your Honour,' Niall says from the other side of the bench.

'I'll allow it.'

Niall smiles as I return to my seat. 'Thank you, Your Honour.'

Wade thinks of his answer. If he says the latter, he will be painted in the light Niall wishes him to be seen in: a blood-hungry killer. But if he says the former, the jury will assume he is lying.

'The latter.'

'Taking a life?' Niall asks.

'Hunting live targets, yes.'

Niall makes sure to glance at the jury before returning his attention to my client.

'And you find that exhilarating?'

'Your Honour,' I say, standing again. 'I'm failing to gauge the point of this line of questioning other than to antagonise my client.'

'There is a point to make, Your Honour,' Niall says in rebuttal.

'Then please,' Judge McConnell replies, 'make it.'

He clears his throat. 'Yes, Your Honour.' Niall checks his notes, seemingly rattled, his cheeks flushed. 'I'll move on to my next question – Mr Darling, could you tell the court how many guns you owned, at the time of the murders?'

'Twenty or so. Perhaps more.'

'You don't know how many you owned?' he asks incredulously.

'I had participated in the sport for many years,' Wade replies. 'I bought more guns as my skill progressed. Money wasn't an object at that time.'

'I'm sure even you'd agree that that's rather excessive. Does one man really need over twenty firearms?'

'Some people collect cars. Others buy watches. I liked guns for my sport.'

Surprisingly, Wade seems calmer than before. Although he is still shaking, he holds himself well in the box, and is speaking clearly. He knows the importance of this. He's doing much better than I had anticipated.

'Did you have a favourite weapon in particular?'

The room falls quiet. It seems everyone knows where Niall is taking this line of questioning. The tension pulses in the air, like a heartbeat.

'Yes, it was the Tikka T3x Compact Tactical Rifle.'

'This was the weapon used to murder your wife and children, correct?'

Wade swallows. 'Yes.'

Niall calls for the jury to turn to their evidence packs. I reach the page in question at the same time as the jurors: it's a photo of the murder weapon covered in the victims' blood.

'This is the rifle in question, yes?'

Wade is looking intently at the image, seemingly transfixed.

'Mr Darling?'

'Yes,' he replies.

'You had a secured gun room in the property, didn't you? The place where you kept' – he makes a show of checking his notes – '*roughly* twenty weapons?'

'Yes.'

'Who else knew the code to this room?'

'I was the only person with the code. But I didn't make a habit of hiding it around people I trusted. Someone could have seen me enter the code.'

'That's convenient, isn't it? You were the only person who knew of the code, but someone just *might* have made a note of it?'

'It's the truth,' he replies. 'However convenient.'

Niall leaves a pause. I know from watching him work before that he is preparing to begin his onslaught. Until now, he has been working to paint Wade into a corner. Soon my client won't have anywhere else to turn.

'Did you ever leave the gun room unlocked?'

'No. It's important to keep them secure for licensing purposes.'

'And was it locked the night of the murders?'

'Yes.'

'Were the front gates to the property also locked?'

'Yes.'

'And the front door?'

'Yes.'

'Were all doors to the property locked?'

'I don't remember checking the back door. As I said, I passed out on the sofa. I usually check that before going up to bed.'

'So, let me get this straight,' Niall says. 'The entrance gates were locked, the front door was locked, and the gun room was locked, but you expect the jury to believe that an unknown stranger managed to waltz in, pick up your favourite rifle out of the twenty others you own, and murder your entire family in cold blood?'

I sit, tapping my leg silently, fighting the urge to object.
There is a balance to be had with objections, and advocates
must choose their windows wisely. Object too little, and the
prosecution may walk away with the win. Object too much,
and I could frustrate and alienate the jury, who want to hear
the story. If I continuously halt my client from speaking freely,
they may wonder what we are trying to hide.

The room is unbearably quiet, and the air is stifling. Sweat
is speckling across Wade's face. A drop slips down his temples.

'Like I said, the back door might have been unlocked. It's
perfectly possible for someone to have scaled the exterior walls
to enter the grounds.'

'Someone could *possibly* have scaled the walls . . . the back
door *might* have been unlocked . . . other people *might* have
witnessed you keying in the code to your gun room . . . an
unknown gunman was allegedly in the property at the time of
the murders, *despite* no concrete evidence of this other than
your testimony . . . Do you see my concern here, Mr Darling?
A lot of your story rests on convenient possibilities and uncer-
tainties. Where are the hard facts in all of this?'

Wade finally gives in and wipes his brow on his blazer sleeve,
which comes away dark with sweat.

'The fact is,' Wade replies, 'the police didn't pursue any
other suspects for this crime. They fixated on me, despite my
insistence of a third party inside my home, holding my gun.
They failed to interview or suspect anyone else other than me.
There isn't more evidence because the police failed to investigate any other possibility other than their desired outcome.'

'There *are* hard facts in this case, Mr Darling,' Niall continues. 'Only, they don't back up your claims. The property was
locked up, according to your own testimony. Only you knew

the code to your gun room. Your fingerprints were the only prints found on the gun – your favourite gun, by your own admission. You were found covered in your family's blood. You say that you and your wife reconciled on the night of the murders, but other than your testimony, do you have any proof of this? Is there anyone else who can corroborate *any* of your claims?'

Wade stands silently in the box, chewing on his bottom lip.

'No,' he says finally.

'So, for all we know, your wife might not have wanted to reconcile at all; she might well have suggested you separate. Is that fair to say?'

'No. The text messages between my wife and Alex Finch prove she didn't want to stay with him.'

'But that doesn't automatically mean she wanted to stay with you either, does it?'

Wade stares, open-mouthed. He is starting to crack under the pressure. The sweat continues to slip down his face. I would object if I could, but I don't have the grounds. It's a question he will have to answer on his own.

'You were hoping, praying – in your own words – that your wife would end the affair,' Niall continues. 'What you didn't expect was for her to leave you too, right?'

'That's not true.'

'Yolanda wanted a fresh start. To get away from the toxic men who had been pulling her every which way. But you wouldn't let that happen, would you?'

'You've completely twisted this, sir.'

'You were severely depressed, in mountains of debt. The world you had built for your family, and the role of provider you had so proudly taken on, had crumbled. You had failed them and yourself. You had nothing but your wife and children, and then they decided to leave you too, didn't they?'

'That's not what happened—'

'Isn't it? Then why did your wife have three tickets booked for a flight to Sweden the following day?'

A gasp from somewhere in the room. Antony whips around to face me, his bewilderment mirroring mine. I flick furiously through the brief for the agreed evidence list.

'S-s-she and the children had planned that weeks before,' Wade says. 'To visit family. I couldn't go because of the state of the business; I had to stay to try and fix it.'

'But can you prove any of this?'

'It's what happened!'

'I'm sorry, Mr Darling, but all we have is your word. Because it seems to me that your wife was finally planning to leave you, and take the children with her. And that's what finally made you snap, isn't it?

'You had lost your money. Your business. Your status. Your mental health. Your best friend. All you had left was your wife and your children. And they were leaving you too, weren't they?'

'No.'

Niall begins to instruct the jury to turn to their evidence packs for the plane tickets when I stand, my finger pressed to the list. The tickets aren't there.

'Your Honour. This evidence was not agreed upon prior to trial.'

Judge McConnell looks towards the other end of the bench.

'It was, Your Honour,' Niall injects. 'I have it confirmed right here—'

The judge raises his hand. 'We will dismiss the jury before going any further.'

Niall and I stand in tense silence as the jury files out. I can tell he is furious at my stopping him, just as he was hammering home his point.

'Continue, Mr Richardson,' McConnell says.

'It was agreed upon and submitted into evidence before Ms Harper joined the case, Your Honour. My learned friend then agreed to this list in our last hearing before this very trial.'

'The list I agreed to does not contain any evidence regarding plane tickets, Your Honour—'

The judge shakes his hands dismissively to silence us both.

'Let me see what you have,' he says, reaching out for both forms, as the judge's clerk begins to search his notes on the case. She places it open on the correct page before him. He looks back and forth among each list. 'You're right, Ms Harper – the evidence in question is missing from your list. But it's not missing from Mr Richardson's or mine, which was agreed upon by you in the hearing before commencement, you'll recall.'

'Respectfully, Your Honour, I can't have agreed upon evidence I didn't know existed until this afternoon.'

The judge contemplates the files, his frown knitted deeply between his brows.

'Under the circumstances, Mr Richardson, we will have to strike this from the record. This is clearly an oversight that was missed during the changing of hands between the previous counsel and Ms Harper.'

I see Niall go to protest, before remembering his place, nodding in agreement while his cheeks flush.

The judge instructs his clerk to deliver to me a copy of the correct list, and calls the jury back into the courtroom. Antony grins at me before returning to face the witness box.

'The evidence you have just heard has been struck from the record,' the judge tells them. 'You must not consider this when you gather to deliberate.' He turns to Niall. 'Did you have further questions for the witness?'

'No, Your Honour,' he replies, jaw tensed. 'No further questions.'

46

I try to shake Niall's words from circling my mind while Wade steps down from the witness box.

Why did your wife have three tickets booked for a flight to Sweden the following day?

That is a question I would like answered, too.

Judge McConnell had put the missing evidence down to a clerical oversight, but there is much more to it than that. I received the brief that very day of the administrative hearing before the trial, after the list of evidence had been agreed upon months before. Which means someone had to have purposely led me astray like this; omitting the tickets from my list of evidence before I had a chance to lay eyes on it. I had thought Adrian Whittaker hadn't planned for the trial ahead of him, but perhaps he did after all. Maybe this omission was his last act of betrayal against our client before being thrust in front of the oncoming train.

It seems to me that your wife was finally planning to leave you, and take the children with her. And that's what finally made you snap, isn't it?

My heart is racing, and racing.

Antony and I certainly could have created a defence for this, had we been given the chance. If our theory is correct, and a third party like Alex Finch wanted to harm Wade's family, this would also be their last chance to act; the trigger that could have caused them to snap. As for Wade's testimony, he did well. Much better than I initially feared. He came across as genuinely pained, forthright and, ultimately, human. He will be so much more relatable to the jury now than he had before. But as I stand from my bench and call Alex Finch as our next witness, one question continues to linger in the forefront of my thoughts.

Why didn't Wade mention the plane tickets to us?

Finch steps into the witness box and takes his oath.

He is dressed in what appears to be an expensive pin-striped grey suit, a crisp white shirt, and navy tie. I imagine his shoes and belt are made of expensive Italian leather, and that his cologne costs a small fortune; I can smell it all the way from the advocates' bench. He looks like the sort of man whose ego depends on wearing expensive things.

This is my chance to give my client the fair trial he deserves. No holding back, no second-guessing. If I am to show the jury the skewed nature of the police investigation against my client, it's now. I won't stop until Finch has dug himself a hole he can't climb out of.

As he gives his oath and I ask him the preliminary questions, he speaks clearly, without nerves.

'How long have you known Mr Darling?'

'We met in the first year of university,' he replies.

'I see. And whose idea was it to go into business together?'

He frowns as he appears to think back.

'I can't remember, it was too long ago. I think we had always toyed with the idea, but we decided to take it seriously about fifteen years ago.'

I nod along as he talks, allowing silence to build between us before asking my next question.

'How long had you known Mr Darling's wife?'

A twitch under his eye. The first sign of distress I have spotted since he entered the box.

'Pretty much as long as Wade. I was there when they met, back in 2007.'

'I see. And when did you first have *sex* with Mr Darling's wife?'

His jaw drops. The court is deathly silent.

'Was that around the same time, too, Mr Finch? Or did the sexual element to your relationship with your best friend's wife come later?'

He stops. Swallows. He glances nervously at the dock where Wade stands, before throwing a quick glimpse at the jury. He can't have known that the affair had been brought to light before his turn in the box. He will have been kept away from the public gallery until it was his turn to speak.

Finch looks around, meeting the stares of the room.

'Why are you asking me that?'

'Because Yolanda Darling is dead, Mr Finch, and we are here to discover why.'

I ask the jury to turn to the text messages in their evidence packs, and pick up my copy of the page for the witness. The clerk steps forward and hands it to Mr Finch.

'Can you confirm these are messages between you and the deceased, Yolanda Darling, dated thirteenth of August 2017?'

He reads through them, the worry growing on his face the more he reads. I take it upon myself to read them aloud.

'"I'm going to fuck you in his bed. Make you come where he sleeps." These are your words, correct?'

He looks up from the paper, which shakes in his hand. His whole face is flushed now, whether with anger or embarrassment, I can't quite tell.

'Answer the question please, Mr Finch,' Judge McConnell says from his podium.

'Yes,' he forces.

'And when you refer to wanting to "fuck" the victim where "he sleeps" and in "his bed" ... Who are you referring to?'

He swallows, his Adam's apple bobbing against the collar of his shirt. His tie suddenly looks too tight, like a noose.

'Wade,' he replies hoarsely.

'You wanted to "fuck" the deceased in Wade's bed? Make the deceased "come" where Wade sleeps?'

'Yes,' he bites. 'I've confirmed that already.'

'I see. Had your relationship with Mr Darling changed by this point? In your statement, you spoke of being inseparable since your first year of university, but in your messages, you appear to hold him in contempt.'

'We were still close.'

'And yet you chose to pursue a sexual relationship with his wife?'

I hear a creak from the other end of the advocates' bench.

'Your Honour ...' Niall says, as he stands.

Finch isn't Niall's client, but he might as well be; if I successfully highlight the police's poor investigation, Niall's case comes apart at the seams.

The judge gives me a look of warning for badgering the witness.

'Apologies, Your Honour, I'll rephrase the question.' I return my gaze to the box. 'When did the affair with Yolanda Darling begin, Mr Finch?'

He swallows, eyeing me suspiciously.

'The summer of 2015, I believe. I can't remember the month. June or July.'

'And when did it end?'

He falls quiet. The silence becomes deafening.

'Mr Finch,' I say, sharply. 'When did your relationship with Yolanda Darling end?'

'The week before.'

'Before what, Mr Finch?'

He looks at me, shaking with what appears to be loathing. 'Before she died.'

The tension stretches, swells.

'Who ended it?' I ask.

He pauses, chewing on his bottom lip, as if trying to keep back his reply.

'Mr Finch . . .'

'Yolanda did.'

I glance at the jury. Their faces are awash with hostility towards the witness, and a sense of exhilaration bolts through me. It feels so good to be doing what I'm best at, despite the threat of harm that awaits me. Throughout this trial, the power I am so used to having has been within another's control. To have it back, even if only for a short while, brings an over-whelming sense of relief.

'How did you take her decision to end things?'

'I wasn't thrilled about it, obviously.'

'For the sake of doubt, Mr Finch, let's assume that nothing is to be deemed obvious during your testimony.'

His eyes, set firmly upon on mine, glitter with hatred. I wonder if it's because of my questioning, or because I'm a woman.

'Your wife left you upon discovering the affair, correct?'

'Yes.'

'And what date was this, exactly?'

'The fourteenth of November.'

'Three days before the murders?'

'Yes. Although I don't see how that's relevant to—'

'I'll decide what's relevant and what isn't, Mr Finch,' I reply, before allowing the room to fall quiet again. Stretching out the silence as long as I can before the blow. 'Where were you the night of the murders?'

Niall jumps up from his seat.

'Your Honour, the witness has not been charged with a crime, nor is he on trial—'

'I'm merely establishing where he was on the night the crimes took place, Your Honour.'

McConnell contemplates this from his pew, staring at me over his half-moon spectacles.

'I'll allow it,' he replies finally.

Niall reluctantly sits back down.

'Thank you, Your Honour.' I turn to the witness box. 'Where were you the night of the murders, Mr Finch?'

'I was at home, in bed,' he replies.

'Was your wife in bed with you?'

'No. I was in the spare room. But she and the children were home.'

'Could they corroborate that you were at home all night?'

'Yes.'

'You can prove this?'

'How would you expect me to prove that?' he asks sharply.

'I believe that means you can't prove it, Mr Finch,' I reply. 'And to confirm, these are the only witnesses who can attest to you being at home the entire night? Your family members who were asleep in different rooms to you?'

He stares at me, practically shaking with rage, his cheeks bright red, as Niall shoots to his feet.

'Your Honour, my learned friend is clearly making insinuations here.'

The judge nods and turns to me.

'I think you have established where the witness was, Ms Harper.'

'Yes, Your Honour.'

I turn to Mr Finch. He looks far less confident than he had when he stepped into the box. Perhaps one of my most treasured moments in a trial is looking into a witness's eyes and seeing the fear of the unknown staring back at me. The fear that, at any moment, I could change the course of our conversation, and their lives, to the point of no return.

I take a deep breath, treasuring the adrenaline pulsing through me.

'Here is my concern, Mr Finch. My client has been accused of killing his family due to a breakdown after the collapse of your joint business. But from where I stand, you've lost an awful lot too, haven't you? You *also* lost your business, your livelihood. Your marriage broke down, just like Mr Darling's. Your mistress left you. You destroyed your relationship with your longest, oldest friend. It seems you too lost everything you held dear ... Were you angry that Yolanda ended the affair with you and returned to Wade?'

'I was ... disappointed.'

I ask the jury to turn to their evidence packs, and give them time to reach the right page.

'Were you expressing your disappointment when you sent

the following to the victim: "Your kids will know you're a whore who fucks her husband's mates"?'

'I was upset, and sent messages that I regret.'

'"You'll die of shame when I'm finished with you". Is this one of the messages you regret?'

He clears his throat, his eyes flicking towards the jury before returning to me. 'Yes.'

'I see. And were you ever interviewed by the police about your whereabouts during the early hours of the seventeenth of November, 2018?'

'No.'

I give him a look of contempt, before turning my attention to the jury, making sure my last question sinks in.

'No further questions.'

I sit down on my pew, my heart racing, as Antony turns to me with an exhilarated smile, which I can't help but match. But as I treasure the sense of approval from Antony, knowing I've achieved exactly what we needed to, the dread slowly creeps in. I have met the objective I set out to achieve by exposing the affair and painting Finch as a suspect the police missed. Now, I must pay the consequences. I stare ahead, unable to bring myself to turn towards the gallery and meet Mr Viklund's eyes.

47

I hide away in the chambers at the Bailey, preparing for the last few witnesses for the defence. With Wade and Finch complete, following Niall's cross-examination of him before the break, we only have three more witnesses to go before the trial is wound down: Wade's former executive assistant, the pathologist to confirm the blood found on his person, and the nurse who told him of his family's deaths. Then all there is left to do is give our closing speeches before the jurors go off to deliberate. If all continues to run smoothly, we could even arrive at the jury's deliberation by tomorrow.

I wonder if I will make it till then.

Mr Viklund and the Messenger must have gauged that I am working against their wishes by now. Defending my client's case to create a sense of credibility in the eyes of the court is one thing, but essentially suggesting the witness may be responsible for the crime rather than my client is something else entirely; it is clear from my tactics today that I am working on behalf of Wade's best interest instead of theirs.

I push the fears for myself aside momentarily and focus on my client. The case we have laid before the jury for his innocence is strong: we have dismissed a key piece of evidence with the plane tickets, which would have been a killer move for the prosecution. We have humanised Wade in the witness box, making it so that his giving evidence actually worked in our favour, rather than against us. And then of course, there was the decimation of Alex Finch's character, creating doubt around the police investigation and their charge against my client. It was virtually impossible for Niall to deliver a cross-examination to match. After my interrogation of Finch, Niall was stuck as to where to go. He couldn't paint my client as an abuser by asking Finch questions about their marriage without a heavy dose of hearsay, which I shut down each and every time. He couldn't have the jury see Wade as a bad businessman, without dragging the witness into that very same category, what with him being the financial director and heavily responsible for the funds that got their business into trouble. After twenty minutes of attempting to refute our argument, Niall sat down, defeated.

I think back to the close call we had with those plane tickets, and stare at both of the evidence lists: the most recent copy, and the original from the brief I was given. The tickets are clearly on the approved list of evidence, but they're missing from mine; the only difference between each of the forms. Could I have really had an older copy? Or did someone make sure I didn't know of it ahead of time, hoping to trip me up?

I raise half a sandwich to my lips before placing it back down again, unable to stomach it. I am running purely on coffee and adrenaline.

'Ms Harper?'

I look up and find a clerk from the Bailey's chambers stood in the doorway.

'There's someone asking after you.'

The possibilities run through my mind, none of them good.

'Who is it?'

'Tinsley Adams. She's the personal assistant for a gentleman named Fredrick Hurst.'

My heart jumps at the name. I immediately think of him tied up in chains, staring up at me.

'She's here?' I ask.

'Not in the building, miss, she's on the phone and waiting outside. What shall I tell her?'

I close my laptop and begin to tidy away my things.

'Tell her to meet me at St Bride's Church.'

I have no idea why she might want to meet me. Perhaps she knew that Fredrick and I had been working together and wants answers. But it's the possibility that she has some information for me that makes me hurry. Fredrick had said he had found something that day. Whatever Tinsley has to say, I need to hear it.

⚖

St Bride's is a small church set back from the road, not far from the Bailey. It's a hidden gem among the bustle of the city, accessible through a set of black iron gates, and a courtyard overshadowed by trees. I'm not a religious person, but I have escaped here in the past between trial adjournments, when the buzz of the court became too much and I needed quiet. That is, until Matthew's death. I haven't set foot in a church since.

I make my way inside, admiring the tall, arched ceilings, the gold detailing and panelled pews. My footsteps echo across the black and white tiled floor to where Tinsley is sat waiting for me.

Tinsley is younger than I imagined. Although in hindsight, perhaps I should have guessed; her name seems youthful, modern. She has long blonde hair, straightened to death with visible split ends. She doesn't smile as I sit down beside her.

'Tinsley?'

She nods. 'Thanks for meeting me.'

Despite her age – twenty-four, twenty-five – she has the confidence of someone older, instantly taking control of the conversation.

'Fredrick is missing,' she says bluntly. She pauses as if to gauge my reaction. Perhaps I'm being paranoid.

'I'm sorry to hear that.'

She gives me a long look, as if she is trying to figure me out. After what feels like a long time, she reaches into her bag and removes a file.

'I found this on his desk when I was looking through his office. He'd left a note, asking for it to be passed on to you. Good thing he did, with him going missing and all.'

Almost as if he knew what might happen, I think to myself.

Her tone makes me wonder again if she is suspicious of me, wondering if I know more than I'm letting on, or whether it's just her blunt, monotone delivery.

'What is it?' I ask, with a nervous wavering to my voice.

'I'm not entirely sure,' she replies. 'But . . . I wouldn't broadcast that you have it, if I were you.'

I nod and take the file, noticing how it shakes in my grip, where it had been still in hers.

'Thank you for bringing this to me.'

She nods once and rises from her pew.

'Good luck.'

I watch her as she leaves, her heels clacking against the cold tiled floor, the sound echoing up to the eaves.

Once I am alone, I open the file and read.

⚖

It's the list.

I stand on the tube station platform, thinking of the names printed in the file Tinsley gave me. Fredrick had found the list of names the Viklunds have collected to call upon should they need them.

High-up police officials, members of parliament, lords, judges. It could be mistaken for a list of who's who in London.

Then I reached a name I never would have imagined I'd find. It was one of those moments you can't quite believe, doubting yourself despite the truth staring up at you in black and white.

Artie Mills, Senior Clerk of Whitehall Legal Chambers.

I then had to go through the remainder of the day in court with his name rolling around in my mind, questioning Wade's former personal assistant to confirm her discovery of the work phones used between Yolanda and Finch during their affair.

Does Artie know what the Messenger is doing to me? Or worse, did he have something to do with it? He was the one who got the case for me, after all. He had shown no guilt as he handed it over. He had been his usual, chipper self. Maybe that doesn't change the fact that he's implicated in this. But I've known him for practically my whole career; he was a mentor of sorts. The anchor to keep me from drifting. The colleague I could always count on.

You'll be the most hated clerk in the city this morning. Who'd you have to kill to get your hands on this?

He'd said nothing, just tapped his nose playfully.

Perhaps I don't know him at all.

Once the trial ended for the day, I returned to the court chambers immediately, the lamps on the desks around me shutting off one by one as the other barristers left, until it was just me and the brief bit of light beneath my desk lamp. If I were to leave the premises at the end of day, I was far more likely to bump into the Messenger or Mr Viklund. It was better to wait until dark.

The station is practically deserted. I stand back from the edge, swaying on my feet from exhaustion, battling my anxiety at the thought of being alone on the platform, open and exposed.

I need to sleep; I am practically drifting off where I stand. But I know my memories of the night before will continue to haunt me. I glance up at the tube timetable rolling across the screen. My train is only a minute away.

That's when he appears, snatching me roughly from behind.

'Did you really think you'd get away with it?'

I stand, frozen in the Messenger's tight grip, his large hands clamping down on both my arms. I hadn't seen or heard him approach; perhaps Adrian Whittaker didn't either. I should have left for home when there was a crowd, instead of waiting until now when I have no one to help me, and no witnesses.

The train is approaching, clangs of metal echoing through the tunnel. A strangled sound creeps up my throat. His grip tightens.

'You can't say I didn't warn you,' he says close to my ear. 'You remember how Adrian Whittaker died, don't you? You remember who pushed him?'

The train appears around the bend.

'I wonder what your husband will say, when you see him again?'

I feel his grip tighten, and his body shift. I try to scream but no sound comes out, even as I am forced forward, my feet skidding across the tiles, air stuck in my throat. My feet teeter over the yellow line running along the platform edge. The sound of the train clangs in my ears. The rush of air. The grind of metal. Just as the train approaches, he thrusts me forward.

The train passes an inch from my nose, my hair whipping against my face in a frenzy, dizzy as the passing carriages blurs before my eyes. I feel his breath against my ear again.

'One last chance, Harper. Or it'll be Hannah on the tracks.'

His hands release me, and then he is gone. The tube pulls to a stop and passengers pour out, the crowd moving about me like a rock in a river, as I stand frozen to the spot.

Day Five

48

I wake up with a lurch.

For a brief moment, I'm not sure where I am. I had expected to find myself in my bed, legs tangled in the sheets and my alarm blaring on the bedside table. But instead, I am curled up in my chair in my chambers. The morning light beams through the window, hot on my face, dust floating in its path, as the memory of how I ended up here slowly returns.

After the Messenger's trick at the tube station, I had been too afraid to go home. I had boarded the tube in a trance and sat down, watching platform after platform pass me by, realising how close I had been to death. I had felt it as the train brushed so close to me, sensed the heavy mass of metal. I tasted it in the polluted air, smelt it on the Messenger's breath. I'd stared death straight in its face and managed to walk away. When I arrived at the stop for chambers, I got off instinctively, too deeply in shock to think beyond putting one foot in front of the other.

Today is the day. The last day I have to defend Wade Darling's case before the jury goes off to deliberate. There are only two more witnesses to enter the box, and then it is time for closing speeches from Niall and me. After that, it is down to the jury. The case will be out of my hands.

I think back to what the Messenger said during our first meeting: it is my client or me. The choice has always been there, dangling over me like a blade, but despite all I have done, I have silently hoped that I could save us both. I had initially chosen what I thought was the right path for Hannah and me – to keep her safe, and hide my sins – by putting my client in jeopardy. But the thought of Hannah being somewhere far from the Messenger's reach, and my truth finally being out in the open, makes me feel a strange sense of calm despite the fear. This laborious secret will be lifted from my shoulders, and the truth will be out there: I will pay for what I have done. And even though I am likely to be sentenced to prison for a very long time, in an odd way, I'll be freer than I am now, wandering in the open. But there is one last thing I must do. Hannah will have to come back to London after the trial, and I want to ensure it is safe for her when she does.

My eyes fall on the file Tinsley gave me, poking out of my bag. The list of names. I slip it from my bag and place it on the desk.

As a defence barrister, it is my job to pinpoint my opposition's power, and use it against them. Anticipate their every move, and remain one step ahead. This list is Mr Viklund's power. I just have to find a way to use it to my advantage.

A knock sounds at the door.

'Yes?' I ask, frantically smoothing down my hair and wiping my eyes.

The door opens, and Artie appears.

'You're in early,' he says, the same usual smirk on his face. 'I thought you'd want to hear the good news.'

He chucks a print-out from *The Times*' website, an online

article posted this morning about Melanie Eccleston's disappearance. My stomach turns.

'Won't have to worry about those front page stories now, will you?'

Rage seeps into me like venom. It must show on my face, because his smile falls.

'Sit down,' I say.

'Everything all right, miss?' he asks tentatively.

'You tell me.' I nod towards the file Tinsley gave me. 'Open it.'

He looks down at the file on the desk. I watch closely as he opens the cover, and his expression changes.

'I think it's about time you told me the truth, Artie.'

He swallows. His eyes flick from the file to me, his gaze awash with pity.

'I'm sorry,' he says gravely.

'I don't care if you're sorry. I want to know what you've done, and more importantly, why.'

He looks like a different man. His usual chipper bravado has gone; the man who sits before me looks smaller, older. I wonder, after all these years, if I am seeing the real Artie Mills for the first time. The man behind the bravado. He closes the file and returns it to the desk. He looks at me for a moment before releasing a heavy sigh.

'When I started my career, I did so with a bullseye on my back. Only I didn't know it. My boss was under Viklund's thumb. His name was on this list, and as his most promising clerk, he added mine too.

'That's how the Viklunds work. They get those under their control to recruit the next generation. Once they receive a name, they look into you – into your past, your family, your lovers. Every aspect of your life. If they don't find anything to exploit, they watch and wait until you slip up.'

'How did my name end up on this list?'

I know the answer, but I need to hear him say the words. He looks at me across the desk; there isn't any way he can back out of this now. The only thing left to do is confess.

'When it was my turn, I had to give the names of my most promising barristers. You were my best.'

He watches me, waiting for my reaction. Perhaps he is expecting me to cry, or scream in rage. Fling the files from the desk. But I just sit, watching him.

'So, for all these years, you have known this would happen?'

'I didn't have a choice.'

'We all have choices to make. You *chose* to make this happen to me, so you could protect yourself.'

'So were you, at the beginning of the trial.' He stares at me, a glimmer of resentment flickering in his eyes. 'That killer piece of evidence didn't just magic itself out of thin air, did it?'

My cheeks blaze with shame.

'Question is,' he says. 'What are you going to do now? Don't think they won't follow through with their threats, because they will.'

'Yes, I know all about what happened to Adrian Whittaker.'

'And yet, you're still planning to play the hero. You'd sacrifice yourself for a man who killed his family?'

'You don't know that he did it – none of us do. I won't be like you; I won't sacrifice someone else's freedom to save my own.'

'Let's see where that moral compass gets you. A prison cell, if you're lucky. Death if you're not.'

'At least I'd be able to sleep at night. You're looking pretty tired over there, Artie.'

He looks down at his lap, a quiet sigh unfurling from between his lips. I wonder how long they have been threatening him, and what secret they might be using against him. By the look of him, they've been in his ear a lot longer than they have mine.

The truth dawns on me.

'The evidence list,' I say. 'You tampered with it, didn't you? You made sure I wouldn't know about the plane tickets until it was too late.'

Artie averts his eyes.

'You'd fired Eddie Chester, who was employed to help you lose the case. I was aiding you in his place.'

'By stitching me up?'

'By taking some of the burden,' he replies.

I hone my eyes on him, taking in his glum, self-pitying face.

'Do you know what they have against me?' I ask.

'No,' he replies. 'Nor will I ask. I hope you pay me the same mercy.'

I scoff at the word. 'Mercy.'

He gets up without a word and heads for the door, slowly, painstakingly, as if he is desperately trying to muster a way to fix the mess he has made.

'I'm sorry, Neve,' he says.

I stare back at him, watch as a shiver runs down his spine from the coolness of my glare.

'Goodbye, Arthur.'

I watch him until he clicks the door shut behind him, before returning my attention to the list.

This is his power. Now I just have to make it mine.

49

I stand in the courtroom, convinced I can hear the chants of the crowd waiting outside. The police presence outside the Bailey is unprecedented compared to the cases I've worked on in the past, as if the public can sense the end of the trial looming and each wants a piece of it.

Wade, Antony and I had our final conference first thing, before the last few beats of the trial. It was clear that Wade hadn't had a wink of sleep. No one can truly know how exhausting it is to have one's fate hang in the balance like this; to have strangers decide your fate. But I know. My fate has been dangling right beside his, and worse, I've been made to decide which one will fall.

The jury looks drained. They have absorbed so much information in such a short space of time. So many conflicting testimonies pulling them in opposite directions. One can almost see the burden thrust upon their shoulders, dragging them down until they slump.

I break from my thoughts to a silent courtroom, and find Judge McConnell looking at me from his podium – it is time for me to call in my next witness.

'The defence calls Dr Allison Fadden.'

Forensic scientist Dr Fadden stands in the witness box.

'You were tasked with analysing the blood found upon Mr Darling, is that correct?'

'That's right. The evidence was collected from Mr Darling's person and his clothes, a pyjama set.'

I instruct the jurors to turn to their evidence packs, listening as pages flip in the otherwise silent court, until they reach the photographs of the blood-soiled pyjamas Wade had been wearing. Their eyes come alive at the sight of the blood. His clothing was soaked in it. What originally had been a set of navy pyjamas appear deep burgundy. There are grazing strokes on the fabric by his clavicles from Yolanda's hair as he held her, but from the chest down, the clothes are completely soaked through, pooling at the front of the pyjama bottoms where he had positioned himself beneath her and held her body to his.

'Dr Fadden, from your analysis, can you determine whose blood this was?'

'Yes. The majority was found to belong to Yolanda Darling, but there were also traces from both of the children, Phoebe and Danny.'

'Thank you. And have you determined how the blood was deposited onto Mr Darling's clothes and person?'

'Yes. The smaller deposits to the defendant's face, and the fabric of his night shirt by his shoulders, indicate close contact with the victim. An embrace, for example. As for the blood found on the defendant's soles, this implies the defendant walked through an area where the blood was present, with fibres that match that of the carpet that had been present in the hallway and on the stairs.'

All of this matches Wade's testimony of finding and embracing Yolanda on the stairs.

'And what of his clothing? What do the blood deposits indicate?'

'This indicates that the blood was allowed to settle for a time, rather than a quick transference.'

'Can you elaborate on that?'

'Well,' Dr Fadden says. 'The blood could have been transferred to the clothing if, say, the body had been resting against him for some time.'

'Like an embrace?'

'Yes.'

'Thank you. And from your analysis, does the evidence indicate the wearer of these clothes inflicted violence on the victims?'

'There were no patterns to indicate the person wearing this clothing was responsible for the violence inflicted, no.'

'Thank you. No further questions.'

I take to my seat. Niall stands abruptly for cross-examination.

'Dr Fadden, I'm Niall Richardson, the prosecutor in this case. Using your scientific analysis, is it possible for a person to commit a crime in one outfit, and then change into another?'

His patronising tone hangs in the air. Dr Fadden straightens her posture, her chin rising.

'Well, yes. But I don't work with hypothetical scenarios, Mr Richardson. I analyse evidence, not the lack of.'

'Then perhaps we can discuss the evidence of gunpowder residue on the defendant's hands. From your analysis, can you tell when this was deposited?'

She nods. 'The gunpowder residue found on the defendant's hands would indicate the traces were left that same day.'

'And the residue matches the ammunition used to kill victims Yolanda, Phoebe and Danny Darling?'

'Yes.'

'Thank you. Nothing more from me.'

Niall takes to his seat as I shoot up from mine.

'One last question from me, Dr Fadden: can you determine the gunpowder residue was left during the hours that the victims were shot? Or is it possible that the deposits were made earlier in the day, when Mr Darling was out hunting, using the same gun and same ammunition?'

'I cannot determine that the deposits were left during the time frame of the murders, no.'

'Thank you. No further questions.'

I take to my seat, and glance along the bench where Niall sits at the other end, nervously tapping his foot beneath the desk.

50

When the last witness is called to the box, I am overcome with both relief and dread in equal measure. The end is in sight. But in this story, there is more than one ending. Whether the completion of the trial brings an end to my freedom or my life, I'm not quite sure. I can't bring myself to fathom the outcome; only that this must, and will, end.

I rise from my seat and call the last witness.

One can always tell a trial is coming to a close by the air in the courtroom. It buzzes with anticipation. The last witness is Christine Vinson, a nurse at Queen Elizabeth Hospital where Wade was treated after the murders. It is to be a short exchange, with only a few key facts to confirm for the jury. It often feels anticlimactic to end a case like this, after such a long, drawn-out trial. One expects it to finish with a bang. Niall and I will save that for our closing speeches.

Christine Vinson takes her oath and answers my preliminary questions with nervous assertion. Her voice is as mousey as the colour of her hair; sweet, tender. Traits that I hope will inspire the jury to plead not guilty – a woman as timid as this wouldn't defend a killer.

'You treated Mr Darling during his stay in hospital, is that right?'

'Yes,' she replies, an anxious rattle to her voice. 'The patient was in a coma for the first two days. I spent my time checking his stats, bathing his wounds, helping with sanitary care. That sort of thing.'

'Were you there when Mr Darling woke up?'

'I was,' she replies. Her face softens with the memory. 'I was re-dressing his burns, and when I looked up he was staring right at me.'

'And how did he appear to you?'

She swallows, and glances up at the dock.

'Terrified.'

'Did he say anything when he woke up?'

'Yes. The first thing he asked was where his family was. If his wife and children were okay. He just kept saying his wife's name. *Yolanda. Yolanda.*'

I pause, letting the name linger.

'What did you say in return?'

She rubs the back of her hand nervously, her gold rings catching the light. 'I said I would get the doctor, but he took my hand as I turned to leave. That will have caused him great discomfort from the burns, but he still didn't take his eyes off me. He said he needed to know immediately.'

The silence in the courtroom thrums like one, collective heartbeat. Ms Vinson takes on a grave expression.

'I told him there had been a fire, and his family hadn't yet been found.'

'And how did Mr Darling take this news?'

'He ... bellowed. That's the only word I can think to describe the sound. It wasn't a scream, or a shout ... just pure pain. I've never heard a sound quite like it before.'

'If you had to describe your patient in that moment with a single word, what would it be?'

She considers this for a while, wringing her hands before her, her teeth chewing on her bottom lip.

'Heartbroken.'

'Thank you, Ms Vinson. That will be all from me.'

She nods, a small triumphant smile curling at the corners of her lips at surviving her testimony, which quickly falls when Niall stands for cross-examination.

'Nothing from me,' he says, and returns to his seat.

A sound from the back of the courtroom sends heads turning towards the dock.

Wade is sat behind the glass with his face in his hands, wracked with sobs he is trying to smother. When he lowers his hands, and sees the room staring back at him, his tear-streaked face blushes red.

I stand silently and address the court.

'The defence rests.'

I lower myself to my seat, lightheaded with exhaustion. All the witnesses have been called. The cross-examinations have been completed. We only have the closing speeches left, before the jury deliberates. The task I had thought impossible is almost over with. My heart flutters angrily in my chest.

And then what? I think to myself, as I feel the hot, searing gazes of Mr Viklund and the Messenger from the gallery.

Hannah will be safe, I remind myself, as I keep my head down, refusing to look.

⚖️

The break goes by in the blink of an eye. I smoke two cigarettes in quick succession, before hiding away in the loos, pacing back and forth until someone enters, which sends me scurrying back towards the courtroom doors.

The day passes as though I am in some sort of trance. Scenes unfold before me, but I have no memory of them. Hours tick off the clock in what feels like fleeting seconds. The closer we get to the end of the trial, the more my fear grows. I both crave the end, to finally be free of it, and dread it in equal measure, for the consequences of my actions await me.

All that matters right now is that Hannah is somewhere safe, and I do right by my client.

The judge begins the proceedings quickly, the exhaustion just as evident on his face as those of the jury. Niall gives his closing speech first, speaking of his case as though it were black and white, as though he holds the answers to the week-long question of my client's guilt.

The court has taken his views, digested them. I watched every juror as their thoughts glinted in their eyes, disgust and confusion etched in their expressions. Niall might be arrogant and self-assured, but he is also a good lawyer. His closing speeches rarely fail to potentially sway a jury.

And now it is my turn. The last hurdle, before my client's case is out of my hands, and both our fates are sealed.

I think of all the events that have brought me here to this moment, and all that I have done. My life changed within a single tube ride. My bones ache with the memory of thrusting the spade into the earth, the weight of my husband's body pulling at my muscles as I dragged him through the woods, the smell of him getting caught in my nostrils. I think of all the lies I've told. The sleepless nights I've had. The danger I have put people in. The deaths I have caused. The list of my sins seems endless. But now I am finally doing the right thing, whatever the consequences may be for me. There is only so much guilt one person can live with before they reach their limit, and as I stand at my bench with the jury's eyes upon me, I know I have reached mine.

Whatever lies ahead for me, I will accept it.

I clear my throat. The sound echoes about the silent room.

'Members of the jury, in the late hours of the sixteenth of November, 2018, Wade Darling fell asleep on his sofa after reconciling with his wife, who'd had an extramarital affair with Mr Darling's business partner. Despite his business failing, his money running out, and while experiencing a deep, debilitating depression, Wade had reason to hope that things would get better. Instead, he woke up to his house burning to the ground around him.

'Coughing and terrified, Wade's first thought was of his family, and he made his way from the living room to the hall. That is when he came face to face with a masked intruder holding Mr Darling's gun in gloved hands. After the intruder escaped, Wade put his own safety aside to search for his family. He found the love of his life, dead on the stairs, shot in the leg, back, and finally her head. He sobbed and cradled her, inadvertently covering himself in her blood, as the world they had built together smouldered around him. Then he found his children, dead in their beds, shot as they slept. Wade Darling fell asleep on the sofa with hope, and woke to find his entire world had been ripped out from under him.

'Members of the jury, I want you to imagine waking up in the middle of the night, disorientated and dazed, to your home burning to cinders all around you. I want you to imagine that, upon searching for your family, you find an armed intruder coming down the stairs from where your loved ones sleep. Then, I would like you to imagine finding your spouse and your children, shot dead. The entrance gates have been chained shut. Every way out is blocked by flames. And despite falling unconscious and suffering severe burns, you survive. You survive against all odds. Only, upon investigation, your version of events is not believed. The police accuse you of the murders, despite all the other unexplored avenues the investigation could have – and should have – taken. I want you to imagine being made to sit in court and listen to twisted versions of events, as an untrue picture of you is painted before a jury. What would you do? What *could* you do?'

I pause, looking at the jurors one by one.

'The Crown must build their case on evidence, but as this trial has shown, the evidence is lacking or easily discredited. The Crown's main points of evidence are thus: Wade Darling suffers from depression. This is not grounds for a murder conviction. This depression was due to his wife's affair with his long-time friend and business partner, and the closure of his business. Is this such an outlandish outcome? Does a person experiencing depression automatically mean they are to be suspected of murder?

'Then there's the fact that Mr Darling's fingerprints were the only prints present on the murder weapon. But we have seen the CCTV footage, and know the figure holding the gun was wearing gloves, thereby removing any possibility of a third party's fingerprints being left behind. Mr Darling's fingerprints would be on the rifle regardless of a crime taking place.

'As for the gunpowder residue on the defendant's hands, the Crown wish for you to believe this is proof that Mr Darling murdered his family. What they omitted to tell you is that Mr Darling had used the weapon earlier that day, which would easily explain the presence of such residue.

'Members of the jury, the Crown want you to believe that

because the weapon belonged to the defendant, and because he was the main bearer of the code to his gun room, that he must have committed these crimes. But someone close to him could have learnt of the code to gain access for themselves. The same person who would know which weapon was most frequently used by the defendant. The same person who would know that there was fuel on the property, and knew where each of the family members slept.

'It is up to the Crown to prove to you – beyond a shadow of a doubt – that the defendant committed these crimes. But instead, the Crown has submitted to you an imperfect, incomplete argument, born from a spectacularly problematic investigation, in which the police failed to consider if anyone else could have been responsible for the crime. What you must decide now is whether the Crown's case is enough to submit a guilty verdict. Your decision will ultimately decide whether the defendant is allowed to grieve his family in peace, and for the case to return to the police for a thorough investigation, or whether Mr Darling will go to prison for crimes he did not commit, and the unknown, undiscovered intruder will be allowed to walk free.

'You are not here to decide upon a verdict based on your emotions, but upon the evidence that has been presented to you. And it is up to you to ensure that the Crown's case has convinced you of the defendant's guilt without a *shadow of a doubt*. So I ask you, when the evidence is assessed on the basis of hard, cold facts: can you honestly submit a verdict of guilty?'

I stand in the silence, analysing the jury one by one, before returning to my seat.

As the judge begins his speech to the jury before sending them away to deliberate, I sit with the realisation that my part in the trial is over. What will happen to me now, I can't say.

Only that in some way or another, it will be deserved. It's time I stopped running and paid the price for my past.

Once the jurors have filed out to begin their deliberations, the air in the courtroom shifts. The press bench busies with anticipation, journalists eager to type up the stories burning at their fingertips. From the back of the court, a clerk hurries from the judge's doorway, his robe swishing at his feet with his hurried steps. He whispers in the judge's clerk's ear, and I watch as her face changes. Her eyes flick towards me, before returning to the clerk, and nodding.

My stomach drops – I know they bear bad news before I have even heard a word of it – and shoot my eyes towards the gallery. When I look to the Messenger, that familiar smirk creeps across his face, and my heart contracts.

'Ms Harper,' the judge's clerk says, having approached the bench. 'We have a message for you. I'm afraid it's of an urgent nature.'

'What is it?' I ask.

The clerk swallows nervously.

'There appears to have been an accident, miss,' she says.

By the look in her eyes, and the pity in her tone, I know.

I know she's talking about Hannah.

51

It takes me over an hour to get to the hospital. Throughout the journey, I replay the scene in my mind, trying to divulge more information. But the clerk only knew so much.

What kind of accident?

A car accident, miss.

The accident didn't just involve Hannah. Maggie was behind the wheel. I wonder if they had been heading out of town when it happened, as I had suggested. When I was stupid enough to think I could go against the Messenger, and still keep them safe. The clerk knew nothing of their condition, just that the accident had happened, and that it was urgent enough to call me. Mr Viklund's words have haunted me ever since.

I will personally make sure that everyone you love will pay the price. You will lose loved ones, as I have lost mine, and you won't be able to do a thing about it.

I rush through the entrance doors, and look about me wildly for the reception, approaching the desk out of breath and sheened with sweat.

'I need to find someone,' I blurt out.

The receptionist holds her finger up at me, signalling me to wait, a phone cradled between her ear and her shoulder. I

reach over the desk and press the button at the base to discon-
nect the call.

'Hey! You can't just—'

'This is *urgent*. I need to find Hannah and Margaret Harper.
They were in an accident.'

The receptionist stares at me, anger darkening her eyes,
before slowly admitting defeat. It must be clear by my demeanour that I won't give up until I get the answer I need. She types
the names into her computer.

'Miss Hannah Harper is in the children's ward,' she says,
and then her expression softens. 'Mrs Margaret Harper is
currently in surgery.'

In surgery. Oh God, oh God.

'Thank you.'

I rush off down the corridor, eyeing the signs for the children's ward. The receptionist hadn't said Hannah was in the
children's ICU. That must mean she's okay, mustn't it? At least
relatively. I rush towards the ward, my heart racing so fast that
I feel dizzy. I try to enter the ward, but the doors are secured
shut, so I bang wildly on the pane of glass until a disgruntled
nurse appears in view and heads towards me. She presses a
button on the wall.

'I need to see Hannah Harper.'

'Visiting hours—'

'I am going to see Hannah right now,' I interject. 'You can
either take me to her, or call security to try and stop me. But
regardless of what happens, I'm not leaving until I've seen her.'

She seems to weigh up her options, clearly taking my conviction into consideration, and how much hell I might kick up
if she tries to turn me away.

'She's just been in a car accident and she's all alone,' I plead.

The nurse's expression softens.

'This way.'

I follow behind her anxiously, wishing she would walk faster. Every step she takes is too slow, too small. We pass sickly children and exhausted guardians, who are nothing but a blur to me. My mind only focuses when Hannah comes into view, lying in a bed by the window, tears shimmering on her bruised face.

I rush to her bedside, looking her over for plaster casts, bandages, stitches. Her face is swollen and bruised, and she has two black eyes. The more I look at her, the more damage I see. Her nose is cut and swollen; her lips indented with scabs where her teeth must have sunk into the flesh upon impact. Her face crumples with approaching tears.

I sit down on the seat the nurse brings to the bedside, and take her hand. It's cold and shaking. 'What happened?'

She cries for a while, too tearful to get out the words. As her face contorts with her tears, the graze on her cheekbone begins to ooze.

'We were driving to Auntie May's. Nanny said we needed to take a break from the city . . .'

She stops to try and catch her breath.

'Take your time, sweetheart.' I stroke the back of her hand, feel the rush of her pulse beating beneath the skin.

'We didn't get far from home before it happened. We were heading down the hill from King's Street. Towards the lights.'

I picture it. A steep hill, the kind that makes your stomach turn as you cross the hump before the drop. The lights are positioned at the bottom before the crossroads. I close my eyes with dread, knowing what will come next.

'The brakes weren't working. Nanny kept pushing but . . .'

She heaves for breath between sobs. 'But we kept going faster. And faster. The lights were red, and . . .'

The speed would have been increasing rapidly with the gradient of the hill. Forty miles an hour. Fifty. I imagine the car careening through the traffic at the crossing. The pile-up that followed. Smashed glass and crushed metal. Blood. Screams.

'I looked over to Nanny, but . . . she wasn't there anymore.'

. . . everyone you love will pay the price. You will lose loved ones, as I have lost mine, and you won't be able to do a thing about it.

This is all my fault.

I wipe away my tears. 'I'm so sorry this happened to you.'

'Is Nanny all right?' she asks, her eyes wide with hope. 'I keep asking, but—'

Maggie will be on the operating table right now. There will be a tube down her throat. A scalpel cutting into her.

'I'm not sure. But I will find out, okay?'

We sit in silence for a while, unsure what to do, what to say. As I hold on to her hand, feeling her pulse calm, I am struck with the overwhelming need to hold her and never let go. Most of the pain Hannah has experienced in her short life has been because of me.

'I'm sorry about what happened between us,' I utter quietly. 'I wasn't angry with you, I was overwhelmed with work, and trying to juggle everything. Your father's belongings . . . they bring emotions up, and I have to try and keep them down.'

'I know,' she says, with a sniffle. 'I take things too personally. It's so easy to feel like I'm not wanted. I don't have Mum, or Dad, the two people who should be there. I know I can be a bit much sometimes.'

She's too young to be saying these things, feeling these things. I reach out and kiss her hand.

'*I* need you – I really hope you know that. And so does Nanny. You are so deeply loved by us. What happened between us, it was just a bad moment. It doesn't mean we don't love or need each other.'

A smile tugs at the corner of her lips.

'A bad moment. Yeah.'

I reach up and stroke her hair. She closes her eyes, and lets me lightly dab at her tears.

'I'm not going anywhere.'

The sound of my phone ringing makes us both jolt. The nurse approaches the bed before I've even got it out of my pocket.

'No phones—'

'Yeah, okay. One second.'

I wait until she leaves before looking down at the screen. It's Antony.

'I have to answer this really quickly,' I say, and give her hand a gentle squeeze. 'But I'll be right back.'

As I make my way out of the ward, I know what Antony is going to say before I even take the call. I feel sick with dread as I press the green button to answer.

'Antony?'

'Neve.' He sounds excited, anxious. My heart begins to race. 'We need you back here.'

I hold my breath as my heart races.

No. It's too soon. It's not even been two hours.

Antony breaks my train of thought.

'It's time.'

52

I rush from the tube station to the Bailey, adrenaline coursing through me, my heart in my mouth. It had started to rain while I was underground; the pavement is dark and slippery, and I have to squint to protect my eyes, as my hair grows heavy and drips down the nape of my neck.

I shouldn't be doing this. I should be with Hannah, holding her hand, waiting for news of Maggie's surgery. My heart tugs at the thought of Hannah in bed alone, while my head begins to wonder what lies ahead of me.

The jury must have a question about the case. They can't have reached a verdict so soon.

Don't think of it. Just get there.

But it's all I can think about. Maggie in hospital, Hannah in tears. All because of this trial. Now it is about to come to a close. So many fates hanging in the balance.

I turn from the road towards the Bailey, slipping momentarily on the wet surface as I move too fast, and stop at the corner.

The crowd outside is the biggest I've seen for one of my trials. The road has been cordoned off, and protesters outnumber the police officers at least ten-to-one. A maze of bobbing signs and contorted, angry faces. The red paint on some of the signs has run from the rain, flowing like blood. The press is stationed before them: camera crews, photographers, camped out under anoraks and umbrellas that amplify the rainfall as it ricochets against them.

An officer sees me stationed at the corner and ushers me over. I follow his lead, allow him to escort me to the door. It only takes a second for someone to clock me. The shouts start, the chants begin, questions bellowed from the press as their cameras flash, and flash, and flash.

The courtroom thrums with expectation. Nervous mutterings from the public gallery, fidgeting from the press bench. In the dock, Wade stares out, pale with fear. His fate will be determined with the simple uttering of one word or two. But he's not alone. My fate hangs on the same, dwindling thread. I anticipate the deafening snapping sound in my ears. Wait for the inevitable fall.

The jurors file in with their heads down. None of them glance towards the defendant, nor Niall and me at the advocates' bench. In these few, passing seconds, it's sometimes possible to gauge a jury's verdict: a kind glance towards the defendant, a knowing smile to the winning barrister. But none of them look up or make eye contact. We will find out with the rest of the room.

The usher speaks to the judge's clerk with bowed heads and hushed tones. I watch them, trying to read their lips. Niall and I share a look from each end of the bench, our only act of solidarity, before returning our gaze to the usher. Then the clerk nods to the usher's words. The clerk signals to us in turn.

We have a verdict.

It's almost over. The hell of the trial, the sleepless nights, the panic, the violence. All of the lies. But I can't settle, and I daren't allow myself to feel relief. Once this is over, a new challenge awaits Hannah and me. One that I cannot see myself getting through unscathed.

I don't care what happens to me, as long as she is safe.

The judge enters the room, and we all rise, taking to our seats again once he is in place. McConnell address the court, but I can't hear a word. I can only hear the sound of my heart pounding in my ears. I take a deep breath to compose myself as the jury is read the indictment, and the jury foreman stands.

'Has the jury reached its verdict?' the clerk asks.

The foreman is a man in his late fifties, too tanned with sun spots on his balding head and deep-set wrinkles around his eyes. He parts his lips to speak, revealing crooked smoker's teeth.

'Yes.'

A palpitation knocks against my ribs. I grit my teeth together until I'm sure I'll hear a crack from inside my mouth. I have tried to do the wrong thing, then the right thing. But neither will serve me. Not completely. I finally realise that now. Whatever the verdict, I was never going to win.

The room is perfectly still, with not a single sound nor movement. Those on the press bench are sat forward in their seats, practically dragging the words from the foreman's mouth. Family members hold hands in the public gallery for support. Outside the Bailey, the crowd waits. Poised to cheer in celebration or chant with rage.

'And do you, the jury, find the defendant guilty or not guilty of count one on the indictment?'

The room is absolutely silent. The air itches with impatience, with dread. But beneath it all, fear thrums. Lives are about to change irrevocably. We all hold one, collective breath.

'Not guilty.'

My jaw drops as the two words hit the room all at once.

Did he really just say—

A scream from the gallery rips through the room, making everyone jump. My heart leaps in my chest. It's Wade's mother, sobbing with relief. Behind her, Mrs Viklund is crying, but for the very opposite reason: Wade Darling has been found not guilty of murdering her daughter.

The clerk goes through the indictment, asking the foreman for the jury's verdict on each count. Each time, the answer is the same.

Not guilty.

Not guilty.

Not guilty.

A mess of conflicting emotions thrash within me, as the room continues to explode with noise and the judge has to shout to be heard. Tears of both relief and fear bite at my eyes, as my breaths grow shallower each time I inhale.

I just gave my client the fair trial he deserves, and helped him walk away a free man. Even if it meant risking everything I myself hold dear.

I blink back the tears and turn to Wade in the dock, who looks fit to faint. His eyes and mouth hang wide, water pooling in his eyes. He looks to me, as if he can't quite believe his ears.

I turn my attention to the public gallery.

Mr Viklund and the Messenger are forcing their way out. I can see by the flushed, red skin on Mr Viklund's neck that anger has consumed him.

Wade Darling may be free, but my verdict has yet to be cast.

All I can do now is wait.

53

Wade, Antony and I make our way into the nearest conference room. Even from here, the heckles can be heard from outside the court. The news of Wade's acquittal has reached the baying crowd. I imagine them pacing, their picket signs bobbing above their heads, spit flying from their mouths as they chant.

Usually, a client would rush into the arms of their loved ones after a not-guilty verdict has been called, but Wade had exited the dock in a trance, visibly overwhelmed with shock. When he met my eyes, I found them pleading.

Get me out of here. I can't face them. Not yet.

I understand the feeling. I cannot bear the thought of what comes next: head in the guillotine, waiting for the blade to drop. I shuffle into the conference room behind the men, silently grateful for the respite. Antony, however, sits with a confused expression on his face. He had expected to cheer and celebrate. Instead, we settle at the table in silence, while Wade sits with his eyes closed, trying to breathe through the panic visibly throttling him from the inside. Then his tears start to fall. This isn't the behaviour of a free man.

'Why don't you give us a moment, Antony?' I ask.

He looks to me, the confusion deepening on his face, before nodding and exiting the room. As soon as the door clicks shut behind him, Wade opens his eyes. I wince as I stare into them. I have never seen so much pain. Without even a word, I know. I realise where the pain manifests. I recognise it in myself. It's not the realisation that his family are still gone despite the ordeal being over, or the fear of the media circus awaiting him at the bottom of the court steps.

It's guilt.

My heart sinks.

Wade Darling killed his family.

He sees the click in my mind, the awareness seeping into my face. His expression crumples.

'I'm sorry,' he whispers. Tears flow silently down his cheeks.

'Why?' I ask, as if there is a simple answer to the question. 'Why did you do it?'

He covers his face and cries a while, as I sit imagining the scene. Wade, holding the gun. Wade, carrying the canister. I imagine his children asleep in their beds, as the man who brought them into this world stands above them, cocking his gun to take them away again. Yolanda would have known it was him. Seen him raise the rifle in her direction. Feel the burn of the gunshots to her leg, her back. The last, merciful gunshot wound to her head to end the pain.

Wade lowers his hands. He looks like a broken man, drowning in self-pity.

'I don't know,' he replies finally.

'Yes, you do,' I reply curtly. 'This is your only chance to unburden yourself. As soon as I'm out of those doors, you're going to have to live with this for the rest of your life. I suggest you seize the opportunity.'

He notices my difference in tone. How much colder it sounds.

'My world had crumbled,' he says. 'I couldn't ... I just couldn't take it anymore.'

He looks down at his lap.

'I wrote notes to each of them. Saying goodbye, that I was sorry. I was going to go into the woods and shoot myself. But I couldn't stop thinking about how selfish it was of me to leave them in the mess I had made.'

'So you decided to kill them?'

'I don't know who that man was that night, the man who did those things ... I wasn't in my right mind. It was like someone else took over. I looked down at the gun in my hands, and I ... just started shooting.' Tears fall again; his bottom lip quivers like a boy's. 'I didn't see red ... I didn't see anything. I was numb. I was blind. I was ... a monster.'

He sobs into his hands again, and I can't help but feel repulsed at how weak he is. How selfish. But I have no right to judge him, not after what I've done. There are two monsters sat at this table. And yet, I cannot stop hating him. Perhaps I hate the killer part of him with such ferocity because I loathe the killer within me.

'Why not confess?' I ask. 'Why hide it?'

I ask from my own guilt of doing the same. Of trying to move on after my horrendous deed. For claiming my victim's family as my own. For not wanting to be alone.

'I couldn't ... I couldn't do that to my mother.'

But deep down, I know he's lying. He did it for the same reason I did. Survival. Self-preservation.

'Come on,' I say, sitting up in my seat. 'The crowd won't go away, however long we hide. It's time to face them. It's time to face what you've done.'

He looks up at me like a scorned child. He knows that once

we part ways, we will never see each other again, and that he has lost the ally he once had in me. That after this is over, he is on his own.

He wipes his face and takes a deep breath as I lead him towards the door.

It is time for us both to face the repercussions of our crimes.

⚖

The crowd erupts as we approach the steps outside the Bailey. Cameras flash. Journalists immediately begin shouting questions, their microphones thrust towards us with a series of logos printed on them. *BBC. ITV. Channel 4. Sky News.* Behind the journalists, the protestors push against police, who have formed a line between them and us, their red faces screaming in our direction. The police have a canine unit with them today, too. German Shepherds whining with excitement on their leashes.

I lead the way down the steps towards the waiting journalists and clasp my shaking hands before me. Wade stands in the centre, with Antony and I flanking either side of him. I clear my throat, and the crowd hushes, the microphones edging closer.

'We are delighted with today's verdict,' I say. 'This was an incomplete, imperfect case against an innocent man, held together by circumstantial evidence and fantastical theories that could not withstand interrogation.'

The protestors bellow at the words; the angered faces I can see are practically foaming at the mouth. I continue to speak, but I can barely be heard over their taunts.

'Today, Mr Darling gets to—'

'*MURDERER!*'

'—return to his life, and the police must now look into who truly—'

'*GUILTY! GUILTY! GUILTY!*'

'—killed the Darlings. In the meantime, we hope this result will allow Mr Darling time to grieve, and for the public to—'

It all happens in a brief, dizzying second. The protestors break free from their cordon like water from a dam. The police shout with their batons raised, pushing back but failing to make ground, as the dogs are freed of their restraints and run towards the protestors. I hear a bark, a scream.

The police are too preoccupied with the protestors to see him. The man rushing forward, rage painted on his face. Mr Viklund looks at me, hatred boiling within him. He has something in his hand. Black, metal. I only compute it's a gun when he aims it towards us. The Messenger is chasing after him, but Mr Viklund is too fast. I barely have time to draw breath before the gun fires.

The sound explodes in my ears, as something hot splatters against my face. Blood. Wade Darling's blood. I look to him, blinking furiously as it drips down into my vision. The bullet hit him straight in the eye and tore through the other side of his head. He twitches, bubbles of blood forming on his lips, before falling to his knees, flailing slightly, and lands on his back on the steps with a deafening crack.

Another shot. Another. I instinctively drop to the floor. There is more blood down here. It is pooling out of Wade's eye socket and the back of his head, painting the steps red and seeping beneath me and into my clothes. Something is cutting into my palm. I raise my hand and inspect my wet, glistening skin. My brain tries to tell me it is a rock, or stone, rather than a piece of my client's skull. I look to him and see his other eye is staring lifelessly into mine, the pain I had seen in the conference room blown away.

Antony crouches on the other side of him, eyes wide with terror. The crowd is screaming. The police scrum in a high-vis knot around Viklund where one of the dogs is attacking his ankle, ripping the flesh to ribbons as he screams. Among the rushing crowd I see the Messenger, choking on his own blood on the ground where a stray bullet must have clipped the side of his neck. I just catch sight of his hand falling limp from where he'd held the wound, when I feel hands upon me. It's Antony, pulling me up and dragging me inside. We stumble to our feet and run, dripping with our client's blood, leaving a warm, red trail along the foyer's tiled floor.

54

Four months later

'Do you think he did it?'

Hannah's voice tears me from my thoughts. She is sat on the other side of the garden table, her hair lit bronze from the beaming sun. The weather seems miraculous after the torrential rain last night that threatened to wash half the city away. It had been the worst storm the south of the country had had in four years, blowing down trees and flooding residential streets further out of the city. Now we're sat in the sun, as if it never occurred at all.

In the distance, I can hear Maggie preparing tea, the high-pitched ding of the teaspoon whirling around china mugs. Hannah flicks a stray piece of lettuce onto the lawn that had fallen from her lunch plate before the table was cleared.

'Wade Darling,' she says. 'Do you think he did it? Killed his family?'

She has asked me this question a lot since the shooting; I think she is trying to work out if he deserved to die. She had seen the video footage plastered all over the internet, along with the rest of the country. Saw Wade's blood hit my face before he fell lifelessly to the ground. I wonder if her knowing me makes it all the more real somehow; these weren't just characters in a trial – she watched her stepmother narrowly miss a bullet to her head.

'The jury determined he wasn't,' I reply.

'But what do *you* think?'

When I lie in bed at night, I often think about the fact that I am the only living person who knows of Wade Darling's guilt. Bound by client confidentiality, his confession added another skeleton to my closet.

'I don't think,' I reply. 'It's not my job to decide who's guilty and who's not. My only task is to defend their case and ensure they get a fair trial.'

'But what if he didn't *deserve* a fair trial?'

'That's not how it works, Han. People convicted of crimes are innocent until proven guilty. Imagine you or Nanny were charged with a terrible crime, and the one person who has been hired to defend you thought you didn't deserve to have your case heard? Wade was deemed innocent in the eyes of the law.'

Hannah rolls her eyes. 'But you must have a *theory* about his potential guilt, at least—'

'Hannah, that's enough,' Maggie snaps as she steps through the back door with a tea tray. 'You'd give a parrakeet a headache with all that chatter.'

Maggie hobbles towards the table, her weight shifted to her good leg. She broke her hip in the car accident, and has yet to fully bounce back. She is still as grouchy as ever, but with a difference: it seems she has finally let me in. It only took a decade.

I had moved in with them for almost a month to help Maggie around the house after the crash. It was harder for her to dislike me when I was the one who cooked her meals, helped her to the loo in the middle of the night. By the end, she was almost fond of me, and her biting digs had turned into playful jabs. Hannah, of course, had loved me being there, and Maggie had reluctantly agreed that she could stay with me every other weekend. At least something good came out of all this.

It was good to have time away from home too. When I returned, the rail works had been completed. The trees were a distant memory, the trains were running again, and Matthew was gone. At least his body was. His spirit, his essence, it seems to have worked its way into walls, whispering at me whenever it's quiet. Nor will I ever escape the church bells. Even when I have finally found the courage to pack up the house and move on, I know the sound of them will follow me, calling to me in my dreams.

Maggie places a mug of tea before me. I'd been about to make my move, but turning down small acts of kindness like this from Maggie seems impossible. I'm forever waiting for her to retract her openness, to shut me out again. Not that I wouldn't deserve it, after everything I've done.

'You've got to work today, you said?' Maggie asks.

'On a Sunday?' Hannah interjects.

'Just a meeting,' I reply, refusing to let my dread show. 'Nothing exciting.'

'I'm surprised you continued with the job after all that business to be honest with you,' Maggie says, waving her hand in the air, as if the shooting were nothing more than an inconvenience.

I had thought of quitting after the trial. Not because of Wade's death, although perhaps that would have been wise, but because of the damage I had caused trying to save my own neck. For a brief while, I had decided to take justice into my own hands, sway a trial at the expense of my client for my own

benefit. There should be no grey area when it comes to justice –
only black and white. Guilty and not guilty. For a time, the lines
had blurred, and boundaries were crossed. I'd taken a break
after the trial to look after Maggie, and when I finally returned
to chambers, under a new head of chambers after Artie made his
departure, I sat at my desk and opened my emails. I would look
at a case brief, and know if I was up to the task. That was my
plan. It had taken me less than a minute to be sucked in again.

Being a defence barrister is all I know.

'It's complicated,' I reply with a smile. 'Besides, what else
would I do?'

'You could teach,' Hannah says.

'She hasn't the patience for that,' Maggie quips. 'She'd need
a job where you're paid to argue, be stubborn.'

I smirk, knowing this is as close to a compliment as I'll get
from Maggie.

'A traffic warden then,' Hannah says, and bursts into laughter.

'No, no. I couldn't bear to wear that uniform. I'll stick to
my wig and robes, thanks.'

I glance down at my watch and sigh. I can't put it off
much longer.

'I'd best get going.'

Hannah accompanies me to the door, with Maggie trailing
close behind. I give Hannah a squeeze, inhaling her sweet
scent. Maggie and I haven't got used to hugging yet, but to my
surprise, she gives me a brief embrace with a sharp pat on the
back before pulling away.

I've finally earned her love.

If only I deserved it.

'Don't work too hard.'

'I'll try, thanks.'

'Who are you meeting anyway?' Hannah asks. 'Is it a new client? Anyone exciting?'

'No, no one exciting,' I reply, as my heart begins to race at the thought of him.

I had secretly hoped that I would never have to lay eyes on Mr Viklund again.

⚖

I wasn't sure what emotions or reactions Viklund might claw out of me when I saw him again. The last time we looked into one another's eyes, he'd had me at gunpoint. Would seeing him bring it all up again? I stand in the queue for the visiting area of the prison, my mouth sapped dry with nerves.

Mr Viklund was deemed too dangerous to be released upon being charged and was refused bail. He is to wait in prison until his trial. The barrister in charge of his case had pushed for a manslaughter charge rather than murder, citing loss of control, but the plea bargain was denied. Viklund is to plead not guilty to murder, and have the manslaughter charges added to the indictment. It is up to the jury to decide which charge fits his crime. I don't pity his barrister, and wonder if it's someone with a secret like mine. I didn't notice the barrister's name in the list Tinsley gave me, which I had checked over repeatedly after learning of the appointment in *The Times*.

The visitors are filed in one by one, directed to tables by a sour-faced guard.

I had almost ignored the visitor request. I could have ripped it up, burnt it. But I knew that if I didn't see him now, he would send someone to make me reconsider. Despite the invitation giving off the appearance of a choice, I know I have none, that I never truly did, from the moment I met the Messenger.

I reach the front of the line and am instructed to head to table seven by the gruff guard.

Despite being in prison, Mr Viklund hasn't changed one bit. He doesn't look to have lost a wink of sleep over the ordeal. But then, with all the power he has, I am sure he has many friends here. In fact, he probably rules the place, telling the inmates to jump and how high. At least, that's what he must think.

My angst heightens as I approach the table, my heart racing as his cold blue eyes take me in. I drag the seat out from under the table, the metal legs scraping against the lino floor, and sit before him.

'You came,' he says.

'I assumed you would have sent someone to convince me if I hadn't.'

His smile seems to agree with me.

'How's freedom?' he asks, a touch of resentment in his tone.

'Fine. How's prison?'

He smirks at my slight, but I know his smile isn't one of amusement; he would reach over the table and knock me down if he could get away with it.

'Just fine, thanks.' He stares at me, his glare piercing and unrelenting. 'Although I don't plan on staying long.'

'You're being represented by Nathan Lane, I hear.'

'Know him?' he asks.

'Afraid not. But I hear he's good.'

'Shame. I don't want good – I want the best.'

'If you want legal advice, it's best to ask your lawyer.'

'It's not advice I'm after.' The smile returns. 'Tell me, when no one came for you after the shooting, did you think you'd got away with it?'

My cheeks flush, but I keep my composure, swallowing down my nerves.

'You didn't strike me as the sort of man to let go of a grudge too easily,' I muster.

'That's wise,' he replies. 'I haven't forgotten what you did, in the trial. How you changed sides. Got him off. Hell, I wouldn't be here if you hadn't, would I?'

'I didn't pull the trigger, Mr Viklund. You did that on your own.'

On the outside, I appear confident, together. But beneath the table, I dig my nails into my legs until I'm sure I've drawn blood. I try to tell myself he's just a man, no more special than anyone else in the room. But that is difficult to believe, after he spent so long with my life held in his palm. All while I waited anxiously for him to clench it shut and grind my entire world to dust.

'Ah,' he says. 'High and mighty, eh? And there was me thinking I was among friends, in that regard.' He leans closer. 'I heard you got a look at that list of mine. Did you think I'd let someone wander around free with information like that rolling around in their skulls?'

I stare into his eyes, and he mine. We sit in the uncomfortable silence, with only the quietened chatter of the other tables around us.

'What do you want from this meeting, Mr Viklund? If it's to taunt me, you've accomplished your goal. If there's nothing more—'

I go to stand, and his smile vanishes.

'You know there's more. Sit down.'

I return slowly to my seat.

'My trial is coming up,' he says. 'I need the jury to decide I'm guilty of the lesser charge to reduce my sentence.'

'I'm sure Mr Lane will do a fine job.'

He looks at me with a vindictive glint in his eyes.

'Mr Lane won't be representing me during the trial, Ms Harper. You will. That's the thing about the list … Once you're on it, you never get off.'

I'd been anticipating this was the reason for the visit request. In fact, I'd been banking on it. A smile crawls across my face. I see his confidence quiver like a flame behind his eyes.

'Yes, the list,' I reply, as he stares at me, seemingly perplexed by my smile. 'I knew you wouldn't give up, Mr Viklund. It's not in your nature. But it's not in mine, either. Unfortunately, I think you've forgotten that it's my job to anticipate my opponent's next move. Counteract every possible attack. To do that, I need to find their point of power and use it against them. Yours, as we know, is the list. That's why I decided to form a list of my own.'

I pause like I would in the courtroom, letting the tension mount. His brow knits together with confusion.

'I didn't use blackmail, obviously. Not like you. There wasn't any need for that. Everyone on my list has something in common: they were all wronged by you.'

He huffs a laugh, albeit nervously.

'You got a death wish, have you, girl? I could have you shot before you've even reached your car.'

'I've worked in courtrooms for almost fifteen years, Mr Viklund. I know a bluff when I see one. Wasn't it you who shot your right-hand man in the neck? As for the rest of them, word on the street is your business has gone deep underground without you at the helm. Laying low until the fanfare around you settles. If you wanted to hurt me – if you had the *power* to hurt me – you would have done it by now. But they've thrown you to the wolves, haven't they?'

'I didn't have you killed because I have a use for you, remember? No point killing an asset.'

'I'm afraid I won't be defending you in your trial, Mr Viklund. Because there isn't going to be one.'

His face pales. As I lay in bed at night imagining this moment, I had expected him to flush with anger, to mutter threats under his breath. But he's not angry. He's scared.

'My list is comprised from yours. Remember when you threatened me, on the Millennium Bridge? About your friends in prison, waiting for their right moment to strike, as soon as you gave the word? Well, I have friends you've wronged in these settings too. In this very room, in fact. They want you off their backs just as much as I want you off mine.'

He peers around, scanning the other prisoners sat before their visitors.

'Bullshit,' he spits.

'I guess we'll have to wait and see, won't we?'

I watch as his expression changes, until he almost looks like a scared little boy. I lean in and keep my voice low so only he can hear.

'I'd sleep with one eye open from now on, Mr Viklund.'

I rise from my seat, only this time he doesn't try to stop me. He has shrunk in his chair, his shoulders concaved, making him look smaller, frailer. A man who is only powerful when he has a group of violent men behind him. A group of men who turned on him on a dime.

I head for the exit without looking back, a small, triumphant smile pulling at the corners of my mouth.

⚖

The smile continues to tug at me until I am back in the car park, and slip a cigarette between my lips. I've cut down, close to quitting, in fact. And now I've dealt with the hold Mr Viklund once had on me, the weight that has been resting on my shoulders inevitably feels lighter; now, the need for my vice feels almost trivial.

I head to the car and sit behind the wheel, turning the key in the ignition to lower down the window, and blow clouds of smoke towards the stark blue sky as the radio hums quietly in the background.

I should feel free at this moment. Vindicated, even. I have finally dealt with the man who threatened to hurt me and those I love the most. But perhaps that's because vindication is for the innocent, and when an injustice has been righted. I can't possibly feel that. Not after I have gotten away with murder.

Matthew. Fredrick. Melanie. They are all dead because of me. I could still turn myself in – do the right thing – but still, I push the deed back, and back, and back, too terrified to lose Hannah and Maggie; to lose my career, and step into the dock myself, staring out at the courtroom from the other side of the glass. I would never be allowed try a case again. I would never smell Hannah's sweet, youthful scent. If I told the truth of what I have done, what or who would I have left? My conscience would be clear, and yes, a wrong would be righted. But then what? A good person can make mistakes, make bad decisions – I didn't mean to kill Matthew; I adored him with every bone in my body – but can a good person continue making that same bad decision? Or does that make them bad?

I take one last drag on the cigarette and flick the end under the neighbouring car.

Maybe I am a bad person after all.

I turn the key in the ignition and the engine grumbles to life. The radio comes on again and I turn it up as a song comes to an end, and the news segment begins. I am just pulling out of the space when I hear the broadcaster reading a news bulletin. The engine stalls and I brake sharply.

> The body of a man was discovered in Low Valley Wood earlier today, said to have been unearthed by a flash flood in the area after the storm that wreaked havoc across the South East for much of the night.

As the broadcaster continues with the news headlines, I sit in stunned silence, white-knuckling the wheel and only managing to muster one, desperate thought.

They found him.

Acknowledgements

It's true what they say: writing a book really does take a village, and I have many people to thank for bringing this book to life.

Firstly, my agent, Madeleine Milburn, for being the best champion an author could ask for, as well as the amazing team at the Madeleine Milburn Literary, TV & Film agency: Rachel Yeoh, Liv Maidment, Esmé Carter, Valentina Paulmichl, Georgina Simmonds, Liane-Louise Smith, Hannah Ladds, and many more. Thank you for all you do for your authors.

At my publisher, Simon & Schuster, my first thanks must go to editor Bethan Jones, who signed me back in 2020 and launched *Do No Harm* with unrivalled passion and vision, and worked on *Conviction* with me before flying the nest. Thank you for your invaluable feedback, which made this book the best it could possibly be. It was a dream come true working with you, and although I was and am so sad to have lost you as an editor, I am equally happy to be able to call you a friend.

My next thanks go to Katherine Armstrong, who has taken over the role of editor seamlessly. Your long list of editor-author friendships gained during your time in publishing is a testament to your talent and character, and I am so excited to work with you and join this list.

The Dream Team thanked at the front of this book not

only includes my agent and editors above, but also the truly phenomenal marketing and publicity teams I'm so lucky to work with.

First, I want to thank Richard Vlietstra and Sarah Jeffcoate. I am beyond lucky and spoilt to have both of your brilliant minds as part of Team Jordan. Your enthusiasm, passion and dedication are utterly infectious. To my publicist, Harriett Collins: thank you for being truly amazing at what you do. You make the intense role of publicist look utterly effortless.

I also owe additional thanks to the following people at Simon & Schuster: Craig Fraser, Clare Hey, Suzanne Baboneau, Ian Chapman, and everyone who played a part in launching *Do No Harm* and *Conviction*. I also wish to thank my copy-editor, Sally Partington, for catching the pesky errors that slipped by me and helping to make the prose that bit tighter.

As always, I wish to thank Waterstones Colchester for their phenomenal support and commitment to making sure my books reach their readers, and to whom I owe much of my success due to their professional and personal support. To the team past and present: Jon 'The Bitch with the Pitch' Clark, Helen Wood, Violet Daniels, Liv Quinn, Joe Oliver Eason, Karl and Chloe Hollinshead, and Mark Vickery. And also to Karl Nurse of Waterstones Chelmsford, who we sadly lost in 2022. He was the kindest man, who dedicated 25 years to Waterstones. Rest in peace, my friend. I also owe special thanks to Gaby Lee and Bea Carvalho for their amazing support and kindness, and to booksellers around the country supporting my books – you are amazing.

To my main support system, my family and friends: thank you for your continued support through the good times and the bad and for never letting me give up. I wouldn't be the writer

I am today without the following: Sandra and Carl Jarrad, Pamela and Tony Jordan, Martin Chester, Jess Savory, Abbi Houghton, Anna Burtt and Bibi Lynch.

To authors, bloggers, bookstagrammers and early readers for your support, quotes and reviews of this book (with special shoutouts to Stu Cummins and Lex Brookman) – I cannot tell you how much your support means to authors like me.

I would also like to thank Christine Vinson for bidding on having their name featured in this book, as part of the auction in support of Ukraine, founded by Sally over at @whatsallyreadnext on Instagram. Thank you both for creating and supporting such an amazing cause.

Lastly, I would like to thank *you*, the reader: thank you for picking up this book, and for making my dreams come true – I hope you loved it, and that you enjoy my other books, as well as the books yet to come.

DO NO HARM

'Chilling and perfectly paced' **Sarah Pearse**

My child has been taken
And I've been given a choice . . .
Kill a patient on the operating table
Or lose my son forever.

The man lies on the table in front of me.
As a surgeon, it's my job to save him.
As a mother, I know I must kill him.
You might think that I'm a monster.
But there really is only one choice.
I must get away with murder.
Or I will never see my son again.
I've saved many lives.
Would you trust me with yours?

'A belter of a thriller with proper breathtaking,
pulse-racing levels of tension' **Louise Candlish**

'Had me on the edge of my seat' **Nadine Matheson**

'An absolute rollercoaster, you won't be
able to put it down' **Holly Seddon**

'Brilliant. Relentlessly tense' **Lesley Kara**

AVAILABLE NOW IN PAPERBACK, EBOOK AND EAUDIO

SIMON &
SCHUSTER